# CLOUDED ISSUES

## 16 Days | 7 Lives | 1 Act of fate

MARGARET CUNNINGHAM

ISBN: 9798511559681

www.margaretcunninghambooks.com

Margaret Cunningham

# CLOUDED ISSUES

16 Days | 7 Lives | 1 Act of fate

# Icelandic volcanic ash grounds UK & Irish flights

AN ASH CLOUD from an Icelandic volcano brought all but emergency flights above the United Kingdom and Ireland to a halt today, with thousands of planes grounded and passengers stranded.

Volcanic ash movement is tracked by nine advisory centres worldwide. The London centre monitors ash over the UK, Iceland and the northern Atlantic Ocean.

"Although this is a relatively small area it covers some of the busiest airways in the world," says the centre, adding that an Icelandic eruption is capable of affecting a large section of airspace in a short time.

The Irish Aviation Authority, following advice from the centre, will start to close sections of Irish airspace from 12:00 today.

With a flight ban in place from noon today, airports will effectively shut down and passengers were warned to expect more disruption tomorrow.

With thousands of flights and tens of thousands of passengers affected, a spokesperson for Nats (the UK's air traffic control service) said "This is certainly one of the most significant instances of flight restrictions in living memory."

The ash, from the Icelandic mountain Eyjaffjalljokull, also caused airport and aircraft movement shutdowns across all of Europe.

In many main airports, confused passengers sought reassurances that airport staff were unable to give in this unprecedented turn of events.

Confusion turned to anger, with many passengers claiming the decision to shut down air travel was an over-reaction.

However, the Nats spokesperson vehemently disagreed, saying: "We certainly do not think we have over-reacted. Safety is our main priority and volcanic ash is a serious threat to aircraft."

It was also suggested that the situation was unlikely to improve in the immediate future. Passengers were advised to check with their airlines before travel.

We will bring you updates as soon as they are available.

CHAPTER ONE

# Thursday 15th April

*Hollie*

The Mediterranean sun forced its way through the slatted shutters of Hollie Kavanagh's hotel room, resting warmly in stripes along her naked, sleeping body. She stirred groggily and blinked as she took in her surroundings. A feeling of disorientation descended on her as she struggled to remember how on earth she had got back here. She remembered nothing of the night before, but a deep sense of foreboding told her that all was not well with the world.

Slowly she raised her head, but the pain in it was overwhelming and she collapsed back on to the pillow. The room was warm and stuffy which enhanced the feelings of nausea that assailed her as she once more tried to lift her head. She had to open the windows and let some air in, she could barely breathe in this acrid atmosphere, but her body seemed unable to perform even this simple task. Trying a different approach, she attempted to ease herself on to her side but screamed aloud at the pain that shot through her ribs. Looking down the length of her body, she saw the massive bruises that ran from her armpit down to just below her hip. She gasped in horror, causing another blast of pain to overcome her, forcing her back down flat on the mattress.

"Think! Think!" she told herself earnestly. "What the hell happened last night?" But, it was useless — she could remember nothing that could have left her in this condition. And Eoin. Where was Eoin? Painfully she reached across to his side of the bed and her suspicions were confirmed — it was empty. Had they both been attacked? Was he lying alone in some hospital bed? Jesus! She had to remember what had happened.

She remembered getting ready for the night and meeting him in the hotel bar, she remembered arriving at the restaurant down by the sea front with Eoin, she remembered telling him that she saw no future for them and that he had reacted quite angrily, but after that…., after that — nothing. What a complete eejit she had been to come away with him like that in the first place. She barely knew him.

She knew enough to know that he was involved in a relationship and that money seemed to be no object. She knew that he oozed charm and she had found his suggestion to fly to Majorca for a couple of nights too exciting and tempting to turn down. It had just seemed so adventurous, so glamorous, so different from her humdrum, boyfriendless, existence. For once, she had wanted to do something impetuous, something crazy — it had certainly turned out to be that.

It was just after the plane had taken off from Dublin airport the previous day that Eoin had confessed to the fact that he had a live-in girlfriend. Herself a victim of a philandering ex-boyfriend, she never wanted to inflict that pain on another living soul and despite his protestations that the relationship was all but over, she knew that she could not possibly start seeing someone who was still embroiled with someone else. She would never have had him as the cheating type, but then again, what did she know? It wasn't until she had walked in on Martin in their bed with some red-headed bimbo that she found out that he was one. And she had known him for almost four years, whereas Eoin she had met for the first time less than a week ago when he had come in for a doctor's appointment in the clinic in which she worked as a receptionist.

Struck by his easy manner and large, dark-lashed, blue eyes that seemed to dance with amusement, as he casually flirted with her and the other receptionist, Niamh, before his appointment. When he had gone, she and Niamh had joked about the fact that neither of them would 'throw him out of the bed for eating crisps'!

Later that night, sitting in the pub with her friends, she was surprised to receive a large margarita from a waitress, who, in answer to Hollie's quizzical look, had pointed to the bar, where a smiling Eoin nodded back at her and raised his glass in salute. Confidently, he had joined her and her friends and, succumbing to his charms, she had barely noticed when one by one, her three closest girlfriends had taken their leave, until it was just her and Eoin left alone.

She had sensed their disapproval at her staying on her own with a stranger, but dismissed it as jealousy over the fact that she had managed to pull the best looking bloke in the place. She knew that that had been a bitchy way of looking at things but in truth they were getting on her nerves with their unadventurous approach to life. Christ knows, you're a long time dead, she had told herself as she had accepted his spur of the moment invitation to join him on a business trip to Majorca.

But, where the hell was he now? And what on earth had happened to her? Thinking that a shower might help to clear her fogged brain, she eased herself carefully from the bed, unable to ascertain which part of her aching body hurt the most. It was only when she had managed to stand erect beside the tousled bed that she saw the blood-stains that marked the sheet on which she had been sleeping. A pungent smell, one she instantly recognised, hit her nostrils as she simultaneously felt large globules of semen slide down her inner thighs. Retching violently, she dashed to the bathroom, only just making it in time to heave the contents of her stomach down the toilet bowl.

When she had finished vomiting, she shakily turned on the cold tap in the basin and splashed cold water on her face and neck, catching sight of herself in the mirror as she did so. She looked a mess. Her face was all streaked with mascara and her eyes were red and swollen as if she had spent the night crying, her dark hair, that normally framed her elfin face with feathery strands, stood in spiky tufts all over her head giving her the appearance of someone who had slept rough for several nights.

The mirror showed her the extent of the bruising over her petite frame. Her torso was covered in welts and bruises, but she heaved a bizarre sigh of relief to note that her face and arms were bruise free. At least when she was dressed she wouldn't look like a car crash survivor, which of course she wasn't — she was a rape survivor.

The powerful jet of lukewarm water sprayed down on her whilst she vigorously scrubbed herself from head to foot in the shower cubicle, tearing at her skin trying to erase all traces of whoever had done this to her. She knew enough from working in the clinic to know that this was the last thing she should be doing in the aftermath of a rape, but she couldn't help herself. Scrubbing away the evidence of her violation was somehow therapeutic, as if in doing so she could eradicate the crime. Who could she report it to anyway? She barely knew where she was and she didn't speak a word of Spanish. She couldn't remember anything about the attack, or her attacker, the Spanish police would just put her down as another pissed up tourist who had gone out asking for trouble and found it.

Her thoughts were racing round and round as she tried her utmost to recall even one sliver of detail from the night before. But, it was futile. It was as if her memory had been obliterated. She thought of Eoin and how angry he had been and an ugly notion entered her mind. Was it him who had done this to her? Surely not. But, then again, the argument with him was her last conscious memory. Could he have put something into her drink? Drugged her, then, taken her back to the hotel and carried out the vicious attack that she had so obviously been subjected to? She found that difficult to believe. But…where was he? Was his absence a sign of guilt? Or was he a victim too? Was he lying in the street somewhere injured? She simply had to find out what had happened. Turning off the water, she stepped from the shower and began drying herself off.

As she sorted through her clothes, trying to select something to wear, it dawned on her that Eoin had come here on business, he had told her that his meeting was scheduled for Friday morning, but perhaps there were things he had to attend to today. Yes, that would be it — that would explain his absence. Crossing the room to the wardrobe, she told herself that if his briefcase was gone, then, she would have her answer. She gasped in disbelief as she slid the large sliding door that covered his half of the wardrobe and discovered it contained nothing but a couple of wire coat hangers. Gripped by panic, she dived at the drawer of the bedside locker where they had deposited their passports and airline tickets and yanked it open — empty!

## Rachel

"Rise and shine!" enthused Rachel, throwing open the balcony doors, flooding the room with bright sunshine and a warm sea breeze that carried the sounds of children playing and splashing in the large swimming pool, three levels down from their luxury hotel room. "Wanna coffee?" she asked, thrusting a large steaming mug in his direction, as Jack sleepily stretched and yawned, nodding at her whilst he did so.

"Mmmm," he mumbled, a broad smile breaking across his face as he took the mug from her hand. "Jesus, Rach — where did you learn tricks like that?" he asked, referring to the sexual marathon that had kept them up 'til dawn. "That was fucking incredible!"

With a salacious grin, she wagged her finger at him in response and said. "My dear, Mr. O'Brien — I never reveal my sources!"

Clearly amused by her response, he laughed and leaning back against the propped up pillows, he said, "That's probably for the best. It's just that never in a million years could I imagine Liz….,"

But, she broke him off there, saying "Ah ah! Liz is out of bounds — remember? This week is about us. Us and the four 'S's!"

"Yes, I know! Sorry."

With her eyes fixed on his, and her finger placed over her lips in a shushing gesture, she climbed astride him on the bed and gently pulled back the sheet that covered his chest, before licking her lips and planting a wet kiss along the side of his neck. "Sea," she said, before kissing the other side. "Sun," she added, gently biting one of his nipples. "Sand," she continued, allowing the silky robe she wore to slide down from her shoulders exposing her large breasts with their erect pink nipples, then staring straight into his eyes, she finished, "And sex!"

Rachel Wallace had learnt at an early age just how powerful a tool sex was, and from the time of that discovery she had used this tool shamelessly to her own advantage. In her opinion, there was precious little that the world could offer that couldn't be secured by the sexual manipulation of the right man. Christ, they were such fools, she had often thought to herself as she watched them turn to putty in her hands at the sight of a bare breast or the flash of a bit of thigh and the promise it offered. She scorned the feminists who militantly demanded equality to men — men and women would never be equal — women would always be the controlling force.

And, Jack O'Brien was no different to the rest. When Rachel had the urge for a week's sunshine, she had little trouble persuading her latest conquest to fulfil her desire. A longstanding booking for a golfing holiday in Portugal was hastily replaced with a week in Majorca, where the lure of uncomplicated, no strings attached sex, with someone who stood to lose as much as him if they were ever to be discovered, was too much to turn down. Rachel smiled as she released herself from the satiated Jack's arms and thought to herself that no, Jack was no different to the others, apart from the fact that he was her 'best friend's' husband.

### Annette

"Yes, Maureen, I'm fine," replied Annette to her mother-in-law's ninety-fifth enquiry of the morning as to her well being. Maureen was a pet really, but far from the ideal pool companion when it came to lazing around, soaking up the sun and indulgently dipping in and out of a good book between naps, which all happened to be essential ingredients to Annette's ideal week in the sun. Her mother-in-law, on the other hand, spent her entire life in servitude to others, constantly looking after her husband, until he had passed away some months previously, her five grown-up children and now, in turn, their off-spring, and she had never spent an idle day in her life.

Sensing Maureen's restlessness, Annette abandoned all hope of grabbing one more peaceful hour and sitting upright on the sun lounger, she asked if Maureen fancied a coffee at the little bar situated at the far end of the pool. Maureen's eyes lit up at the suggestion, but delight turned quickly to anxiety when she thought of her two granddaughters who had not yet returned from the market.

"But, what about the girls?"

Annette laughed. "Honestly, Maureen — you are a worrier! The girls will be fine. They are big and bold enough to find us if they need us, otherwise we'll see them back here later. Now, come on, I could murder a nice cappuccino."

"Yes, that does sound good," smiled Maureen, gathering up her bag and cardigan from where she sat, she dutifully followed her daughter-in-law to the bar.

Still only mid-morning, the pool bar was quiet and scanning the area, Annette selected a table that offered them shelter from the sun. Paddy should be here in a few hours, she thought happily, realising just how much she was looking forward to her big, softie of a husband joining them. She smiled to herself as she remembered the hard time she had given him when an urgent meeting had been scheduled, by the Directors of the leisure club he managed, for the day after they were due to fly out on holiday.

"I'm sorry, love," he had offered, shrugging his shoulders in a helpless gesture. "Last month was just woeful on the sales front and with the year end looming for the end of April, the Directors are insisting that all club managers are in attendance. At least, it's to be in Dublin, so, I promise I'll be on the first available flight out to join you and the girls after the meeting."

"And, your mother!" she added grumpily.

"And my mother," he had smiled sheepishly at her.

A soft touch, Paddy had invited his recently widowed mother to join them, and, although Annette hadn't minded all that much, she didn't really relish the prospect of doing it without Paddy. But, it hadn't been so bad and another couple of hours and Paddy would be with them.

"What d'ya fancy, Maureen?" she asked, perusing the limited menu that 'Cheerful Denis', the ultra-camp, bar attendant, had passed to her.

"Oh, just a coffee for me, thanks," replied Maureen, unused to self-indulgence.

"Ah, c'mon Maureen, you're on your holidays — what about a nice Danish?"

"Yeah, maybe — what are you having?" she asked, unsurely.

At times, Maureen's self-deprecating ways grated on Annette's nerves, but refusing to allow herself be irritated, she smiled sweetly and said. "I'm having the biggest Danish that they have on offer and a large cappuccino."

"Me too," grinned Maureen, relaxing.

Catching Denis's eye, Annette called him over and laughed at the overt way he minced his way up to their table, with his notepad held effeminately in one raised hand, the other sitting firmly on his hip.

"G'morning ladies," he greeted them. "What delightful treat can I tempt you with this morning?"

Annette gave him their order and glancing towards the newspaper stand by the bar, she went to fetch a couple of the morning papers that were on display. Grabbing a couple of papers she made her way back to the table.

"Nothing terribly exciting," she said to Maureen as she glanced through the headlines. "Same ole, same ole!"

"What time is Paddy due in?" asked Maureen, lighting up at the thoughts of her beloved youngest son.

"Late afternoon, I think," replied Annette, reaching into her bag to retrieve her mobile phone. "He texted me his flight details last night, I'll just check them." Surprised to see several messages and missed calls from Paddy, she hurriedly opened up the messages, offering up a silent prayer that work wasn't going to prevent him joining them. "Oh my God!" she exclaimed, a look of disbelief on her face as she read the first one.

"What? What's wrong?"

"Paddy says 'Dublin Airport closed — phone me asap'. He's bound to be winding me up," she muttered, more to herself than to Maureen. "I'll give him a call, see what the story is."

Strolling off in the direction of the pool whilst the call connected, she wondered what on earth was happening. It took several rings before he answered, sounding harassed.

"Annette? Hi. I've been trying to get you," he began. "Have you seen the news? There are no flights from Dublin at all today."

"Well, I've seen the papers," she said. "But there's no mention of anything in them. What's happened? Is it a terrorist threat, or what?"

"No. It's a volcanic ash cloud that's disrupting flights all over Europe. All Irish airports are closed and several in the UK. There's not a hope in hell of getting a flight today."

"You're kidding me!" she exclaimed, still unconvinced that he wasn't winding her up.

"Honestly, love. There must be a TV there — turn on Sky News — it's all over it. Give me a call back in a few minutes."

Hurrying back to the bar, she let a screech at Denis to turn on the telly. True enough, report after report featured airport closures throughout Europe, with Ireland and England being the worst hit. It was chaotic. Scenes of outrage and disbelief reigned amongst stranded passengers. Even those airports that were open were filled with discontented travellers, as the closure of European airports plunged the entire globe into utter chaos. Reporters were predicting greater mayhem than the aftermath of the 9/11 terrorist attacks with some suggesting that if the closures lasted up to twenty-four hours, which now appeared likely, it could take days to clear the congestion created by such universal disruption.

### Donal

Donal Kavanagh was now utterly convinced that there had to be a conspiracy against him for this latest bit of bad luck to land on his lap. Blinking, disbelievingly, at the TV screen he took in the reports of the global shutdown of air traffic and firmly believed this had come about just to punish him. What had he done that was so bad? He was basically a decent bloke and all he had ever wanted was the simple life - not for him the heady expectations of fame or riches.

The son of an alcoholic mother and an inept father, his and his younger sister's childhood had been spent in a string of foster homes where he had learnt the value of the simpler things in life. A loving home with a secure, steady income was all he had yearned for through his teenage years, whilst his contemporaries dreamt of bigger things, but they hadn't known the misery of coming home from school to a cold, dark house with little or no food in it, a father who rarely bothered to show up when arranged and a mother passed out in an alcohol induced coma on the couch.

At least, in the majority of the foster homes he had been dispatched to when his mother needed 'respite', he had experienced snatches of what normal family life had to offer — the physical and emotional warmth these other kids took for granted was something he vowed to provide for his own children one day, when he met the right woman.

He thought that he had done just that when he had met and married Susan. But now, five years later, he knew he was wrong. The one time vivacious, pretty, party girl had morphed into a bitter, materialistic lush who drank herself into oblivion on a nightly basis whilst chastising him and his lack of ambition for creating the monster she had now become. He knew it wasn't his fault, but that didn't help.

Her descent into the person she now was had begun with the monthly disappointment of discovering, yet again, that she wasn't pregnant. Desperate for a child and without the financial means to pursue the artificial insemination route, she turned all her negativity towards him, blaming him for everything. Once her alcoholism had taken a hold of her, she reminded him of his mother and this made him reluctant to even consider having a child with her. And so, the situation perpetuated itself, until now, he was no longer sure if he still loved her, but knew that despite the animosity she harboured towards him, she would go to pieces if he left her and he felt trapped — horribly trapped.

His new business venture had proved a great distraction over the past couple of months, offering him an outlet into which he could channel all his energies. He had a 'make or break' meeting lined up for Monday next in London and perhaps a successful outcome could turn everything around for them. Maybe if they had the money, and Susan underwent a proper 'rehab' plan for her drinking, bringing back the girl he had married, they could then consider IVF and then, who knew what could happen? A lot of 'what ifs' he knew, but he wanted to exhaust all routes to saving his marriage before he threw his hat at it.

But now, looking at the news on TV, there was no guarantee that he would be able to even get his flight on Monday morning. What were the odds against that happening?

## *Jack*

Standing beneath the powerful jet spray of the shower, watching through the open doorway to the bedroom, where Rachel moisturised her toned body, her long blonde hair falling silkily over her face, Jack O'Brien pondered about what a charmed life he led. He hummed happily to himself as he shampooed his hair, relishing his good fortune.

In these days of economic strife, he was in the fortunate position of having a secure, well-paid and pensionable job in the Civil Service — a job, that in truth, he could do in his sleep, not that it wasn't mentally challenging from time to time, but overall it posed no major stress in his life. His wife of eighteen years was an amazing woman — an accomplished home-maker; wonderful mother, superb entertainer and all round good egg. So? Their sex life wasn't all it used to be, but he supposed that that was to be expected after all these years — so the media led you to believe anyway. His eighteen-year old son, Joshua, was in his final year of school and captain of the school rugby team. Jane, who was sixteen this coming summer, was a terrific kid. Full of fun, yet accomplishing great things in school — oh yes, she had a great future ahead of her, not to mention the fact that she was turning into a real heartbreaker.

He really had it all — and now, he had Rachel. Beautiful, sexy, unpredictable, Rachel. She was like no other woman he had ever met. Quite apart from her physical attractiveness, which was undeniable and which she went to great lengths to preserve, regularly attending the gym and sparing no expense on any beauty treatments available, she was incredibly intelligent and independent and he found both of these traits mind-blowingly sexy. Of course, she was a bitch — through and through. But, hey, he wanted to screw her, not marry her.

In truth, he found her lack of emotional warmth a real turn on. It gave him the freedom to carry on the affair without fear of her becoming attached or needy. This suited him down to the ground as he had no intention whatsoever of leaving Liz. He had had several dalliances in the past, nothing too serious, but one or two of them had exhibited signs of expecting something long

19

term and he had dropped them like hot cakes as soon as he recognised the danger signals. But Rachel, all she wanted was some fun, despite displaying no remorse for carrying on with her best friend's husband, he knew she didn't want Liz to ever find out and that suited him just fine.

She and Liz had first become friends a couple of years previously, when she had been the doctor administering vaccinations to Liz in a private clinic before he and Liz had flown to Thailand on holiday. Amused by Liz's phobic reaction to needles, the two women had struck up a conversation with Rachel good humouredly teasing her about being a big baby. It turned out that Rachel had recently moved back to Dublin after living in London for several years and was still finding her feet. With not many friends, she eagerly accepted Liz's invitation to attend a make-up party that she was hosting the following evening, with Liz encouraging her that, if nothing else, it should be a bit of a laugh and a good way to meet some new people. She did attend and, over the course of the subsequent months, an unlikely friendship was forged — Rachel, the career driven, independent, girl-about-town and Liz, the busy full-time mum of two teenagers.

Jack found it difficult to remember the first time that Rachel had come on to him. At first, he thought he had imagined it. That first flirtatious brush of the hand — that lasted a moment too long; the odd suggestive comment - loaded with innuendo. But, then, last Christmas, when he and Liz had hosted a drinks party and, not much of a drinker, Liz had over im-bibed and gone to bed as soon as the bulk of the guests had left, Rachel had followed him out to the kitchen, sidling up behind him as he rinsed some glasses at the sink and slipped her arms around his waist - he knew this was more than imagination.

He had kissed her that night, there, in his own kitchen with his wife and children asleep upstairs and a couple of remaining guests still in the sitting room and the thrill he experienced in the face of all that danger had excited him beyond belief. From then on, he couldn't get enough of her. He took advantage of every opportunity afforded him to see her and her appetite for sex left him reeling, but she insisted that that was all she wanted.

She both appalled and excited him with her handling of Liz. He could easily come in at night from work and find her sitting in the kitchen, companionably sharing a bottle of wine with his wife and there would be no hint of awkwardness at his arrival. In fact, once she had even gone so far as to leave him in no doubt as to the absence of underwear beneath her dress, as she parted her legs when he bent to retrieve her dropped keys from the floor, whilst Liz fetched another bottle of wine from the wine rack, then, casually sat and shared the bottle with the two of them before heading home in a taxi. He found her thrilling and the danger posed by her was the greatest aphrodisiac imaginable.

Hearing her call to him to hurry up, he turned off the shower and wrapping a towel around his waist, he went into the bedroom and turned on the TV.

"Ah, c'mon, Jack," she pouted, "let's get down to the pool. It's our second last day and I want to get some sun."

"Relax!" he laughed. "I just want to catch the sports news while I'm getting dressed. It's not going to delay me. Besides," he grinned, "you look like a Grecian goddess as it is — look at the colour of you!"

Proud of her developing tan, she allowed herself to be placated by his compliment and busied herself with gathering up all the pool-side accoutrements.

"What the hell's this?" asked Jack, as flicking through the channels for Sky Sports, he happened upon the news, where a reporter, with a sombre expression stood outside Heathrow Airport.

"Probably a terrorist threat," muttered Rachel after glancing at the screen, far more interested in getting a move on down to the pool, than another security alert in an English airport.

"No. There are no police or anything — must be some kind of a strike," he said, looking around for the remote control to turn up the volume. "It looks like there are several airports affected."

"Don't even think about it!" she snapped, grabbing a hold of the remote before he could get to it. "Whatever it is, it doesn't affect us, now, are you coming or what?"

Shrugging off his interest in the news article, he smiled indulgently at

21

her. "Okay! Okay! So what if the whole world is falling apart, so long as you don't miss some essential rays!"

"Now, you're talking!" she grinned back at him, taking a hold of his hand and pulling him towards the door.

### Denise

Denise Richardson could not believe her own eyes. For the third consecutive time her eyes flicked between the slip of paper that she held in her hand and the computer screen in front of her that displayed the winning lotto numbers from the previous night's draw. Things like this didn't happen to people like her, she thought to herself, as once again the numbers on the screen matched those on her lotto slip.

"Jesus Christ!" she exclaimed aloud. "It's a winner — it's definitely a fucking winner!"

Her hands shook as she fought to think of any reasonable way in which she could have this wrong. But no, she knew these numbers by heart — she had been playing the same ones religiously for the past twenty years, never really believing that they could come up. Could someone be playing a trick on her? But, who? Had John not done one of his regular disappearing acts the week before, she might have suspected him. After all, he was a wizard with computers. He could have got her numbers, fed them into the computer, knowing that she routinely checked them, before he did his moonlight flit. He certainly hated her enough at the moment to do that, but, then again, this would be too cruel — even for him.

Paranoid now, and fearful of starting to believe that she could conceivably have won the lotto, she wracked her brain for some other way to verify the result. "Aha!" she thought, searching around the living room for the remote control, "It'll be on teletext."

Switching on the TV, she fumbled her way through the teletext menu until she found what she was looking for and pulled up last night's results. Her knees turned to jelly and she felt her stomach somersault as the very same numbers presented themselves to her once again, confirming the fact that she had won almost six million Euro. Her legs gave way beneath her and she sank heavily on to the couch as the enormity of what was happening hit her.

"Jesus Christ!" she exclaimed for the second time that morning. This was it. This was her ticket to freedom. She would finally be safe. With this kind of money, she could go anywhere, do anything — start again. Fear gripped her, John must never find out. He would never let her go, especially now, if he knew about the money. She must tell no-one. She simply couldn't risk him tracking her down.

But then again, she half laughed to herself, who was there left to tell? Both of her parents had been killed in a car crash not long after her twenty-first birthday and as she had been an only child, relatives were thin on the ground. She had inherited her parent's house along with a substantial sum of money after their death, but lonely and grieving, that had been of little interest to her and she fell into a depression that rendered her a hermit for most of her twenties.

Devoid of self-confidence and uncertain of her social skills, she had been more than a little wary when a very handsome John Kelly had approached her in the coffee shop in which she worked and asked her out for a meal. At first, she doggedly refused his invitation, but when he showed up daily for the next week and persistently repeated his invitation, she eventually capitulated, reasoning that the surest way to get shut of him was for him to spend an evening with her. Then, he could see for himself just how dull she was.

But, John seemed to really like her and they started seeing each other on a regular basis. For the first time in years, she felt she had something to offer. He was interested in everything that she had to say and when his landlord gave him notice on his apartment, it seemed like a natural progression for him to move in with her.

Initially, he paid his way, but when he lost his job six months into the relationship, she funded everything. He seemed to be in no rush to find another job and began taking charge of all things domestic, slowly morphing into a 'house-husband'. For the main part, she liked it. It was lovely to come in from work after a long day on her feet in the coffee shop and find the house clean, the clothes washed and a hot meal on the table.

It was her who had suggested that they open a joint bank account one night, when John, overcome with embarrassment, told her that he hated always having to ask her for money. He told her that he would be back working soon and when he was that he would have his wages paid directly into their joint account and that as far as he was concerned, he was in this relationship for the long haul. and his temporary unemployed status would soon be forgotten once he was riding high again. He promised her that they had a great future ahead of them and she believed him.

It was a subtle transformation from John entering her life to John controlling her life, but by the time it had taken place, she had nowhere to turn. It began with small criticisms of the way she dressed, and she changed her style to suit him. Then, one by one he took a turn against the few friends that she had and, eager to please him, she cut them off. Soon, he took charge of their finances, assuring her that he was much better with money than she was. It wasn't until the violence started that she realised what a big mistake she had made and by then, it was too late.

He was always contrite after he hit her, and for several days he would revert to the charming John that she had first met, lavishing gifts and attention on her, but inevitably it would happen again. What scared her now was the fact that his bouts of violence were becoming more and more frequent and last week, after a particularly brutal beating, which had been easier to take than the verbal vitriol he had spat at her, he had disappeared.

This wasn't uncommon — often, he would run away afterwards and return when he figured that she would have calmed down and promise her profusely that it would never happen again. What worried her this time, was that after he had left, she had taken the pregnancy testing kit from her handbag and had been horrified when a thin blue line appeared in the window.

### Liz

Liz O'Brien was ecstatic. She had a guilty secret and she was loving it. For a brief moment, she wondered what Jack would make of her news but, deciding that today belonged to her, she dismissed his reaction as inconsequential and allowed herself bask in the glory of her own achievements.

In eighteen years of marriage she had never kept anything from him, well nothing major anyway, and she did feel a flicker of guilt in doing so now. But, the time had come in her life when she had to do something purely for her or abandon the notion forever. And, she had. This morning, Liz had completed the requisite number of hours necessary to obtain her 'Life Coaching Certificate' and whether Jack liked it or not, she was now officially a fully trained Life Coach.

She hadn't told him about her course initially, because she had been uncertain of her own ability to go back to studying after a break of more than twenty years. In truth, she had never been much of a studier in school and although she was undoubtedly an intelligent, capable person, the enormity of seeking a qualification in her early forties had been a daunting prospect. But now, she had done just that.

The fact that Jack was away in Portugal on a golfing trip when she earned her certificate, was no coincidence. From the moment he had announced several months earlier that he would be away that week, she had set herself the goal of completing her training whilst he was gone. This was something she had done for herself and she wasn't ready to share it with him just yet, she wanted a couple of days to savour her success first.

Her only regret was that his week away also coincided with her sister, Annette's family holiday and her friend Rachel had decided on a last minute week in the sun as well. Rachel had invited her along, but Liz had the distinct impression that Rachel hadn't really wanted her to go and was relieved when she had declined. Oh well, she would have to celebrate alone for now, but perhaps when they were all back in the country she would organise a dinner party and celebrate in style.

Jack must have thought she was mad with the enthusiastic way she had seen him off on his golf trip, blatantly eager to be shut of him. He would understand why now, when she told him and she really hoped that he would be happy for her once he got over the shock.

When they had made the decision to have children, Jack had made it clear that he would prefer if she stopped work and was a stay-at-home mum. He, himself, had been brought up as a 'latch key' kid and remembered envying his mates whose mothers drove up to collect them after school.

Liz had no objection to leaving the mundane secretarial job she had been working in and enjoyed the luxury of staying with the kids. She would have hated to drop them off at a crèche on a cold, winter's morning, as she saw so many of her peers having to do, and not get to collect them until the day had turned dark once again.

No, it suited her fine to stay at home and bring up the kids, but now, with Josh seventeen, and Jane coming up sixteen, she wanted to do something for herself. It was Rachel who had introduced her to the notion of life coaching, when she spoke about how busy the Life Coach who was attached to her clinic was.

"D'ya know Liz, you'd be good at that," she had said casually one night over a bottle of wine. "You've such a positive outlook on everything and you are a really good listener. You should think about it."

At first, Liz hadn't given it much thought. The prospect of going back and spending several years in college simply didn't appeal to her. But, when she googled some information on the internet and discovered that it was possible to procure an accreditation through a correspondence course in the UK, she decided to give it a blast. She had resisted telling Rachel about it, because Rachel's self-assured manner intimidated her at times and she didn't need the pressure of Rachel breathing down her neck, asking her how the course was going. She knew that Rachel would be very happy for her when she heard the news and she was really looking forward to telling her.

CHAPTER TWO

# Friday 16th April

*Denise*

Bleary eyed from tiredness, Denise abandoned the notebook and pen she had been using to plan her future, since giving up all hope of sleep at around five o'clock that morning. Rolling her tension-locked shoulders, she pushed back the chair from the kitchen table and went to put on the kettle. A nice mug of coffee was required to stimulate her brain back to action and give her some clarity of thought. History told her that she had two, maybe three more days before John reappeared and she had a lot of decisions to make in the interim.

Glancing at the wall clock, she saw that it was nearly seven thirty — almost twenty-four hours since she had discovered her gargantuan win and, as yet, she hadn't got one solid plan in place. She knew that she had to be careful to cover her tracks, or, if John discovered her win, her life would be planned out for her. She thought about the inheritance from her parents that he now controlled exclusively, only depositing what she needed to live on into their joint account and keeping track on what she did with that, constantly requesting receipts for things and berating her for her carelessness if she purchased what he deemed to be unnecessary items.

On the rare occasion that she questioned his tight hold of the purse strings, there had been uproar. Initially, his tone had been reasonable, as he pointed out that he was merely trying to secure their future for them and offered her the choice to take the reins if she felt that she could do a better job than him — she knew better than to agree. And then, he had become a little more menacing, telling her how ungrateful she was for all he did for her by taking on all the responsibility. No matter how justified she felt at first, by the end of each argument, she had found herself abjectly apologising for upsetting him, in an attempt to ward off a violent outcome — not always successfully.

Smiling to herself, as she stirred her mug of steaming coffee, she thought how, as far as she was concerned, he was welcome to her inheritance. She knew now that it had been a tip off from a temping secretary in her parent's solicitor's office that had led John to her. He had unwittingly confessed as much to her one drunken night, when, out of his mind with anger, he had beaten her black and blue, and sneeringly asked her did she think for one minute that he would have been interested in her if he hadn't known about the money. Her damaged self-esteem took a greater battering that night than her broken body, as she realised what a fool she had been to believe that anyone, even a monster like John, could be with her because they loved her.

No, he could keep that money, and the house for all she cared, he had tainted both for her over recent years, and she no longer felt any connection between these material possessions and her beloved parents. In any case, she now had more money than she would ever need - what he was left with was a mere drop in the ocean by comparison.

And now, he had tainted her. Now, her body played host to his spawn, she couldn't bring herself to think of it as a baby. All she knew was that this thing that was growing inside of her would tie her inextricably to him forever and she couldn't allow that to happen. The one certainty in her decision making process was the need to rid herself of this shackle and that must be her first priority. Reluctant to seek abortion information on the home computer, lest he get to know about it, she decided to go to the internet café in the village and listed that down as the first task on her to-do-list.

Alert now from the caffeine, she felt her senses sharpen and she quickly drew up a plan of action to carry her through the next week or so. Her need for anonymity worried her in relation to collecting her lotto cheque, but she figured that she had spent so much of her life paling into the background, that she should be able to pull that off without attracting attention.

She needed to open a new bank account and remembering a friend of her father's who was the manager in a branch in Ranelagh, she phoned him and was hugely relieved when he told her that he had a meeting cancelled for that afternoon and could see her then, if that suited her.

Next, she booked herself in to the luxurious Ritz-Carlton Hotel, set in the grounds of the exquisite Powerscourt Estate on the outskirts of Enniskerry - a picturesque village in Wicklow, where, not in a million years would John think of looking for her. Unsure how long she would be staying, she made an initial two-week reservation.

Her long-term plans would have to wait until she was in a position to give them proper consideration. Satisfied, she went upstairs to shower.

## *Annette*

The news from Dublin was still the same. The airport was closed and there were no flights in or out of the Country. An unprecedented situation, it was impossible to establish when normal service was likely to be resumed. In any case, it certainly wouldn't be today and resigning herself to that fact, Annette pulled closed the hotel room door and went in search of her daughters and their grandmother.

Megan spotted her as soon as she entered the pool area and, standing up, waved furiously at her from the table that they occupied in the pool bar. Annette laughed at her eagerness, knowing full well that it was based on the fact that her granny was doing her head in. Both sixteen year old Megan and her fourteen year old sister, Hannah, adored their grandmother but, she had tested everyone's patience the night before when, at regular fifteen minute intervals, she had proclaimed "Ah, you'll see — the airport will be back open again by now and your Daddy will be on his way."

A collective sigh of relief had been released when claiming the onset of 'one of her headaches', Maureen had excused herself and retired early to bed. Judging by the truculent expressions on both of the girl's faces, she was back in full swing this morning.

"Good morning! Good morning!" sang a cheerful Denis waltzing past her, precariously balancing a tray of debris from another table as he did so. "I'll just pop these up at the bar and I'll come take your order."

"Cheers, Denis. That would be great," she said in answer, pointedly ignoring the seething glares thrown at her by her daughters. Pulling back a seat, she joined them. "Have you lot ordered yet?"

"Oh, yes," beamed Maureen. "I had some really delicious crustaceans."

"You mean 'croissants', Nan," scoffed Hannah with barely disguised teenage contempt. "Crustaceans are crabs."

"Oh yes, croissants," repeated Maureen, rolling the word over her tongue as she blushed furiously.

"Oi! Don't be so rude to your grandmother," admonished Annette, sternly.

Instantly remorseful, Hannah said. "I'm sorry Nan, it's just that I want Dad to get here. Did you speak to him yet Mum?"

"Yes, I did. And to be perfectly honest, he is as clueless as we are. He's still planning to be on the next available flight, but there's no sign of the airport re-opening, all they are saying is that they will give an update at about six o'clock this evening. So, all we can do is wait until then. Hopefully, they'll get it re-opened and he can come tomorrow, but we'll have to wait and see."

"Oh wow! That sucks!" moaned Megan, "poor Dad. At least we're the lucky ones, if you have to be stuck somewhere, it's got to be better to be stuck here than in Dublin."

Smiling at her older daughter's positive take on a bad situation, Annette agreed. "Yep, being stranded by a beautiful pool, whilst basking in the warm Spanish sunshine is a hardship I can endure."

"Talking of which," said Hannah, with a mischievous glint in her eye, "you don't mind if me and Megan go for a swim? We've finished eating and I'm sure you and Nan can cope without us for a while."

"Go on, off with you," laughed Annette, signalling to Denis that she was ready to order.

After Denis had skipped off to the kitchen to order her a mushroom omelette, Annette couldn't help but notice how quiet Maureen had become, as she sat staring into the middle distance with a somewhat troubled look on her face.

"Are you okay, Maureen?" she asked gently, assuming that her timid mother-in-law was feeling anxious or ill at ease in her son's absence. "I'm sure everything will be alright and Paddy will be here by this time tomorrow."

"Oh yes, love, I'm fine," she replied, nodding in the direction in which she had been staring. "It's just that I've been watching that young woman since we came in here and she seems to me to be very upset about something. Do you think I should go over to her?"

Following Maureen's stare, Annette quickly identified whom she was talking about, as a lone, forlorn figure sat staring blankly into her coffee cup. Seeing her pick up the cup, there was a noticeable tremor in her hand, but the dark glasses that she wore made it difficult to read her face.

"She's probably just hungover or something," said Annette, "she's only a young one, I'm sure her friends or boyfriend or whoever will be down to join her shortly. I wouldn't worry too much."

Not looking convinced, Maureen shook her head. "No, I've been watching her for a while now and she seems pretty distressed to me. I think I'll go see if she's okay."

Not wanting her well-intentioned, but not always diplomatic, mother-in-law to make a nuisance of herself, Annette held up her hand and said. "No, leave it. I'll be bringing my plate back up to the bar in a minute and I'll have a quick word with her."

"Oh would you?" asked a relieved Maureen. "I don't want to interfere, but I'd like to think that if one of my daughters was alone and in a state that someone would care enough just to check if all was well."

Smiling kindly at her, Annette said, "You are a good soul, Maureen."

### Jack

Jack hung up his mobile phone with a worried expression on his face, just as Rachel arrived back at the poolside with two exotic looking cocktails. She ignored his troubled face and handed him a glass. Taking the proferred drink from her hand, he sipped on it contemplatively before speaking, not wishing to rattle her cage.

"Look Rach," he began, tentatively. "I really think we've got to come up with a 'Plan B' if we are to get out of this undiscovered."

"You worry too much," she responded, dismissively. "It's Dublin Airport that's closed, not Palma. If you keep your head, there is no reason why we are any more at risk than before."

"But, Rachel, I just spoke to Liz and it sounds like this mess could go on for days. What then?"

"Well in fairness, if you were where you said you were, then you would be in exactly the same boat — so why the big fuss?"

"'Cos if I was away on the golfing holiday, with Jimmy and Peter and all that crew, there is no way that they would be able to just sit it out. They would have to find an alternative way of getting home. The majority of them work for themselves and there is no way that they could afford to neglect their businesses for any length of time. Liz will know this, even on the phone that time, she was joking about there being a prize on offer for the most imaginative route home."

"Oh, relax will you, for chrissake. It'll probably all have blown over by tomorrow and we'll be able to get our flight as planned. This time tomorrow you'll be sitting at home with your pipe and slippers, playing 'Mr. Wonderful'. Now, I for one, am not going to start worrying about something that we have no control whatsoever over and ruin the final day of my holiday. So, just shut up and enjoy yourself."

More than a little peeved at her dismissive attitude, Jack drank the rest of his drink down in one gulp and pulling his T-shirt out from under the sun-lounger, he stood up and pulled it over his head. "I'm going for a walk," he said petulantly. "See you later."

"Yeah, see you later," muttered Rachel, studiously applying more sun protection and looking around to see where she had left her book, refusing to be drawn into any further conversation.

Jack's head was filled with dark thoughts as he made his way down the short wooden staircase that led to the private beach, which was attached to the luxurious hotel in which they were staying. "Liz would love it here," he thought absentmindedly to himself, then, guiltily chased the thought from his head.

There was a warm sea breeze blowing, capping the waves with white froth and pushing the smell of the ocean inland, clearing his head as it did so, invigorating him. Reaching the water's edge, he perused the entire beach. It was one of those secluded coves that offered privacy to the privileged residents of the five star hotel, and looking down the length of it, he saw mainly couples stretched out on its golden sands. Not many families, he noted, feeling alienated for the first time since his arrival on the island. At heart, that was what he was — a family man, and this charade of coupledom now seemed a dangerous game when faced with the possibility of discovery.

Still, he reasoned, setting off at a brisk pace to walk the length of the beach, he mustn't turn alarmist just yet. Clearly, the aviation authorities would be doing their utmost to get things back up and running as soon as possible, minimising the financial fall-out in an already tumultuous economic time, and the knock on effect of any such expeditious resolution could be to avert the dire repercussions in his personal life should his lies and deceptions be discovered.

By the time he reached the end of the beach, he was feeling calmer. Turning to walk back, he felt the therapeutic effect of the warm sun on his back, releasing the tension in his muscles as he walked in its warm embrace, and a feeling of optimism swept over him, enabling him to believe that he could survive this unscathed. He promised himself that if that was the case, he would end this dangerous liaison with Rachel and be a better husband and father in the future.

He hoped that Rachel wouldn't be churlish about his little moody earlier. After all, if this was to be their last night together, they might as well make the most of it. Instantly, he felt himself become aroused and with a spring in his step, he scaled the steps back up to the pool area, two at a time, his sexual urges taking precedence over his good intentions.

### Donal

The minute that Donal put his key in the lock and tried to open the front door, he knew that there was something wrong. There appeared to be something wedged up against the interior, preventing it from opening. With an exasperated sigh, he pressed the doorbell and called through the sliver of an opening to Susan. But, there was no answer. Turning his body sideways, he put all his weight behind his upper right arm and tried to force the obstruction out of the way, but to no avail. Whatever was blocking the door was immovable from this angle.

It was raining heavily and dressed, as he was, in a business suit, the prospect of scaling the side entrance gate and letting himself in through the back door didn't appeal to him. Annoyed now, he rang the doorbell again, keeping his finger pressed on it for several seconds this time. But still, no answer. Resigning himself to go around the back, he was just about to pull closed the door, when he heard a low moan, one he recognised immediately, coming from behind the door.

"Ah, for fuck sake, Susan," he seethed, realising that it was his drunken wife, slumped in a heap on the floor that was blocking his entrance. "It's only four o'clock in the after-fucking-noon, for Chirssake. Get up and open the door, will ya?"

When she didn't respond, he angrily abandoned his brief case and shimmied over the side gate, getting himself soaked in the process. Letting himself in by the back door, he wiped his feet on the mat, then taking in the untidy state of the kitchen, he shook his head incredulously. This was getting completely out of hand. Not only, were the remnants of the previous evening's meal still cluttering up the sink and the worktops, but, the bin was overflowing, mainly with empty beer cans and the place stank like a brewery.

Susan must have attempted to make herself some scrambled eggs at some point, and the charred remains were congealed to the bottom of a blackened saucepan where, she had obviously got side-tracked and forgotten that she was cooking. On the table sat an empty vodka bottle and an overturned carton of orange juice, the contents of which had spilled right across the table and dripped down to form a puddle of orange on the already grubby looking floor. Jesus, this was no way to live, he thought, and certainly not an environment to consider introducing a baby to.

Looking out into the hallway, he saw her curled up on the floor and avoiding the temptation to leave her there, whilst he cleaned up the rancid kitchen, he walked purposefully to where she lay and, determined not to be drawn into an unpleasant confrontation until she sobered up, he planned to coax her in to the living room where she could sleep it off on the couch.

It wasn't until he bent down to shake her awake that he noticed the pool of blood beneath her head. Turning her leaden head as gently as he could, he saw a big gash in her forehead, just above her right eyebrow. She must have been lying there for some time as the blood had dried, sticking strands of hair across the gaping wound. Getting no response from his repeated efforts to rouse her, he took her wrist and, as he had seen done so many times in movies, he checked for her pulse, hoping that he was doing it right. He could definitely feel a light pumping sensation coming through his flattened fingers, and relief swept over him. The cut on her face required stitches and realising that he would never manage getting her unconscious body into the car by himself, he reached into his pocket for his mobile phone and called an ambulance.

It was shortly after the ambulance crew had wheeled Susan into the Accident and Emergency department in St. Vincent's Hospital that she regained consciousness. Donal watched her as she took in her surroundings and his earlier anger dissipated when he saw the real fear in her eyes as she did so. She was lying on a gurney in a curtained cubicle and the frenetic activities of the busy casualty ward were audible, but she still wore a confused expression as she spotted Donal sitting in a chair next to her.

"Where am I?" she asked, her voice little more than a croak. "What happened, Donal?"

His heart softened as he caught a glimpse of the girl he married, gone was all the anger and resentment that she harboured towards him and in its place was a vulnerability that made him want to protect her.

"You had a fall, love," he answered, gently. "You got a bad bang on the head and you were unconscious. We came in by ambulance, the doctor will be back to you soon — you're gonna need some stitches."

"Where?" she gasped, her hands flying to her face automatically.

"Easy!" exclaimed Donal. "There, on your forehead, just above your eye."

"Oh my God! Will it scar?" she asked pitifully, her eyes welling up with tears.

Taking a hold of her hand and squeezing it, he said. "Probably — a bit. But, mostly it should be covered by your fringe — you were lucky, Sue."

"No, Donal. I wasn't lucky — I was pissed — again!" she said, turning her ahead away from him, her self-loathing palpable. "I have to get myself sorted out — I can't go on like this. I need help, Donal — WE need help. Look at us, both of us are miserable — maybe…., maybe….," she hesitated, "maybe we are just no good together Donal."

"Ahh, Sue, you don't mean that," he said, despite having had those self same thoughts himself earlier. But, as he watched the large tear drops slide unchecked down her cheeks, he wanted to protect her from the pain and torment she was suffering as the full extent of her drink problem seemed to register with her. She would need him now, more than ever, if, as he suspected, she was finally going to tackle her alcoholism. And, Donal liked to be needed.

## Liz

Liz knew how fortunate she was not to be dependant on generating an income from her life coaching straightaway. Ultimately, she hoped that she would make a living out of it, but for now she was happy to follow the advice given to her by her mentor and try out her newly acquired skills in a small way, with the long term goal of establishing a potentially lucrative practice over the course of the next couple of years.

Diana, her mentor, had informed her that henceforth, she would be on their accredited list of practitioners, and as such, her name would be given out, along with other accredited members, to potential clients on demand. This should, she assured her, provide her with a foothold on which to build a client base. In time, Diana promised her, these initial clients would be the source of newer ones, as her name would be passed to interested friends and relatives, and the ripple effect of such word of mouth recommendations could well fill her books in their own right. However, Diana did strongly recommend that she set herself up with a website and to this end, she gave her the name of an excellent web designer who happened to be Dublin based.

Grateful, Liz thanked her and jotted down his name and contact details.

Googling the name of the designer, she was very impressed by his own website and throwing caution to the wind, she decided to call him and set the ball in motion. Out of the workplace for so many years, and wishing to sound every inch the professional, she forced an officious tone to her voice, which, even to her own ears, sounded affected and was somewhat disarmed to discover that it was Peter McClafferty himself who answered the phone, not affording her the opportunity to tone down the voice. Feeling a little foolish, she persisted with a forced poshness, until suddenly, feeling too ridiculous, she started to giggle.

"Eh, what's so funny?" asked a perplexed Peter, mid sales spiel, assuming incorrectly that she was making fun of him. "If our services don't interest you, that's okay, but I want you to know that we look after numerous life coaches and I have a very good handle on ….."

"Oh, no, I'm so sorry," she said, trying desperately to regain her composure. "It's just that I couldn't keep up that preposterous voice, I was trying to sound uber professional and it just came out all wrong."

"Well, I did think you were sucking on something very bitter," he said, a smile audible in his voice. "You sound much nicer now. New to this, are you?"

"Yes, I only completed my training yesterday and I'm trying to get cracking with things as soon as possible. Anyway, apologies for my stupidity. I'm not normally like that," she added unnecessarily, relieved that it was a phone call and not a face to face meeting that had her make such a fool of herself.

"Ah, don't worry about it. I suppose I should be flattered that you were trying to impress me."

"I'm not doing a very good job of that though, am I?"

"Don't be so hard on yourself. You made a mistake, but you were big enough to recognise it and laugh at yourself in the process. No harm done."

"Hey, ever thought of life coaching?" she quipped.

"Oh, God no! Awful people! Terrible bunch of pretentious gits, all completely up their own asses. I mean, you should hear the accents on some of them."

Both of them were laughing now and with the ice well and truly broken between them, they got down to the nitty gritty of designing a website for her. Peter clearly knew his stuff and put forward several suggestions that she liked the sound of. They arranged to meet the following Friday at his office when he hoped to have the basics of the site ready for her to look at.

Jack was really in for a big surprise when he got home, she thought, feeling empowered at the prospect of telling him that not only had she secured a qualification, but had a website under construction and could even, according to Diana, conceivably have one or two client bookings. That was a lot of ground to cover during one short golfing week. Talking of which, she wondered if there was any news on the airport reopening and went online to check.

It didn't look good. There would be a further review of the situation at six o'clock that evening, but in the meantime, the airport would remain closed. A second day of flight disruption was bound to have a negative impact on scheduling and, too early to make a definitive assessment, she had increasing doubts that he would be on his flight as planned the next evening. Thinking it best to prepare him for this eventuality, she picked up the phone.

"Ah, good, I caught you," she said when he answered the phone on the second ring. "I wasn't sure if you would be out on the course yet or not."

"No. No," he said. "We're not teeing off until after lunch today. Bit of a big night last night and all that."

"Yeah, you sound a bit rough," she giggled, unsympathetically. "Dear, dear! And you so enjoy being hungover!"

"Very funny!" he replied. "Guess I'll just have to go for a quick swim in the pool, or maybe stretch out in the sun for an hour or two, you know, just 'til I'm feeling a bit better!"

"Okay! You win! But, seriously, have you seen that the airport here is still closed."

"You're joking," he said with an unexpected element of alarm in his voice. "When do they reckon it'll reopen?"

"No idea. They are hoping to give an update at about six o'clock, so I'll give you a shout if I hear anything. Anyway, I suppose from your point of view it's not the end of the world if you're stuck in sunny Portugal for another couple of days."

"No, I guess not," he said, sounding a little unsure. "But, I'm certain Peter and Jimmy wouldn't be too happy about it."

"Oh, of course not. They'll want to get back to their businesses. Anyway," she said, trying to introduce a note of optimism into the situation. "They are such an inventive pair, that I'm quite sure if you told them that there is a prize for the most inventive route home, that they would come up with something."

"Yeah. Yeah, I guess you're right," he added, distractedly. "Hey, look I'd best be going. I'll talk to you later."

### Hollie

Hollie sat staring into her empty coffee cup, feeling more alone and isolated than at any other stage in her life. All she wanted was to get home and put this whole sorry mess behind her, but she didn't even know how she was going to manage that. As if it hadn't been bad enough having Eoin disappear, she now had to contend with a missing passport and flight cancellations due to a fucking volcano, in fucking Iceland, for Chrissake.

Eoin's continued absence had her convinced of his guilt. But, ridiculous as it seemed, the fact that he had raped her was the least of her immediate pressing problems. She had somehow managed to consign that matter to something that would have to be dealt with at a later date. Right now, she had to concern herself with how the fuck she was going to get home.

The midday sun was beating down on top of her and she shuffled her seat to get beneath the protection of the large parasol in the centre of the table. The effort made her yelp with pain and glancing around to ensure that no-one had heard her cry out, she saw the older woman at the far end of the bar staring over at her. That wasn't the first time that she had caught her looking this direction. Hollie was grateful for the privacy that her large dark glasses afforded her, she really didn't think that she was up to small talk with strangers right now and direct eye contact could be tantamount to an invitation to chat.

Hastily, she signalled to the waiter to bring her another coffee, more out of the need for something to do than the desire for more caffeine. Right, she thought, as he delivered a large frothy mug of cappuccino to her, I need a plan of action. First of all she needed to find out where the Irish Consulate was and go and speak to them about her missing passport. Then, she needed an update on the air travel situation.

She had some money, though not a lot, and if she was going to be stuck here for a few extra days, she would definitely need some more. Her only option there was her brother, Donal, but that could wait as she really only wanted to ask him as a last resort. Then, there was work — what the hell was she going to do about that? With complete reckless abandon, she had phoned in sick to work and would undoubtedly lose her job if her lie was discovered. Never before had her actions come with such dire consequences.

Filled with shame, she let her head fall into her hands and made no attempt to curb the stream of tears that erupted from her as she sunk into despair at the awfulness of her situation. Startled, she let out a muffled shriek of pain when she jumped in response to somebody placing a hand on her shoulder.

"I'm so sorry, I didn't mean to scare you," said a gentle voice, "but, are you okay?"

Too upset to answer, she nodded her head emphatically as she tried to brush away the cascading tears with the back of her hand, before finding her voice.

"Yeeess. Yeeess," she answered weakly, not sounding convincing even to herself.

"Are you sure?" asked the woman, pulling out a chair and sitting down beside her. "Look, I'm not trying to pry, but you really look like you could do with some help."

As Hollie looked into the face of the kindly stranger, she felt all her resolve go and shaking her head slowly, she sobbed. "Not really. I'm in a bit of a mess."

"Hey, messes are what I specialise in," quipped the woman gently, in, what Hollie was glad to note was, a Dublin accent. "You'd never know maybe I could help."

"I doubt that. I've actually got a list of messes as long as my arm," said Hollie, reluctant to confess her stupidity to this well meaning, self-composed woman who was bound to be horrified at what Hollie had to say.

"Hey, try me," persisted the woman. "My name is Annette. Annette Forbes."

"I'm Hollie. Hollie Kavanagh."

Succumbing to Annette's kindness, Hollie gave her a very abridged version of events, leaving out the rape and the fact that she had only known Eoin for little more than a week, she made out that he had been her boyfriend, had turned aggressive with drink on him and had done a bunk from the hotel, taking her passport with him. Annette absorbed all that she was told calmly, not interrupting Hollie as she spoke, allowing her to finish before asking.

"And, did you check if he left the passport with reception?"

Hollie shook her head. Such a simple solution hadn't even occurred to her. But, then again, she had hardly been thinking straight at all since yesterday morning.

"Ok. You wait here. I'll go check," said Annette, pushing back her chair and heading for reception, before Hollie could stop her. Two minutes later she emerged, grinning victoriously at Hollie, who felt her first surge of relief in days.

## Rachel

It was when she was eighteen years of age, and a young medical student, that Rachel had had her first affair with a married man. A forty-something lecturer in the Royal College of Surgeons, he had been completely smitten by the vivacious blonde with a confidence that belied her young age and a firm, supple body that his flabby, middle-aged wife could not compete with. He made no secret of the power that she wielded over him, treating her like a precious jewel for the six-month duration of their affair. She remembered how broken hearted he had been, when, a bored Rachel left him for her next target.

She smiled now at the memory, recalling her first experience of the excitement such illicit liaisons brought to her. As she watched her friends, none of whom she had been particularly close to, endure relationships with lads their own age, who never had enough money to bring them to nice restaurants or buy them expensive gifts, she knew that life wasn't for her. The thing with older, married men was that they were always so damn grateful that someone like her was interested in them, that they flashed their cash around, bringing her to all the best places in town, giving her a taste for the high life that she possessed to this day.

She was now pushing forty, but her love of material things had always far outweighed her love for any of the many men who had passed through her life. She valued her independence and loved her own space, so short term flings worked for her, providing her with the heady thrill of a perpetual fresh romance and an added element of danger that kept her adrenalin levels high. It was all a game to her, and she loved it.

Every now and again, and it generally signalled the beginning of the end in her experience, her latest amour behaved in a manner that necessitated her to give him a reminder that he was a willing participant in the game they shared. It angered her that these foolish men could try to twist the rules if their 'precious' lives were in any way put at risk, relegating her, in the process, to a mere tool of the game as opposed to the star player.

Jack had crossed that line this morning, as far as she was concerned. Where were his concerns for Liz when he had enthusiastically embraced the notion of a week's holiday with Rachel? In his trousers — that's where, she fumed. His concerns weren't for Liz, they were for himself. Jack O'Brien needed taking down a peg and she knew just how to accomplish this.

Keeping a watchful eye on him as he walked down the beach, she waited until she saw him heading towards the stairs up to the pool area, before flipping open her mobile phone and keying in a number. With perfect timing, the call connected just as he appeared by the pool and, sitting with her back to him, she spoke into the handset in a voice loud enough for him to hear, before turning in his direction.

"Liz, hi! How's it going?"

She watched him blanch visibly at her words, lowering himself unsteadily on to the adjacent sun lounger, unable to do anything to stop her. As she had known he would, he sat and listened to her call, and she enjoyed the feelings of empowerment that watching his discomfort gave her.

"Yes. Yes. Furteventura is fantastic. The weather is fab and the talent —

well, what can I say? Young, single, greased-up, tanned men with the bodies of an Adonis — you'd hate it! And, looks like I could be stuck her for a few extra days too — where's the justice in that?"

Jack's face was thunderous as Rachel held the phone away from her ear, allowing him to hear his wife's laughter ringing down the line.

"And poor ole Jack too. He must be stranded in Portugal, is he?"

Unable to hear Liz's response, Jack just sat there, throwing her dirty looks as, with a wry smile, she said.

"Of course he's behaving himself, Lizzie. Don't be daft! Anyway hon, I've got to go, so many young men, so little time," she finished with a giggle, ending the call.

"What the fuck was that about?" spat Jack, looking like he was going to murder her.

"That, Mr. O'Brien, was called 'saving your ass'! Liz's mind is now full of images of her 'cougar' friend, behaving in a predatory fashion in the Canary Islands, hundreds if not thousands of miles away from where her 'model' husband is enjoying a week's golf with the lads. No! No! There's no need to thank me," she threw casually over her shoulder as she walked to the bar to get herself another cocktail.

CHAPTER THREE

# Saturday AM 17th April

*Donal*

Donal went into the sitting room to check on Susan. He found her lying on the couch in the same almost catatonic state in which she had been ever since their return from the hospital the previous evening. She seemed oblivious to her environs and to his presence as she sat staring into space, her eyes averting his every attempt to catch her attention. Her shoulder length, normally silky brown hair, remained pinned back from her forehead where the nurse had secured it in order to allow the plastic surgeon to stitch her wound, which was now covered by a blood stained dressing that needed changing.

Bending down on his hunkers, he brought his face level with hers and, gently brushing back the loose matted strands of hair that fell across her face, he tried to speak to her.

"Hey, Sue," he said. "How's about I run you a nice hot bath and I'll get some tea and toast ready for you afterwards?"

But, her only response was to close her eyes, clearly willing him to go away, which, after several more minutes, he did, not wanting to agitate her. In all their years together, he had never seen her like this before and he didn't know how to handle it. Even sober, she had always been volatile, quick to temper, but equally quick to make up and it had been these passionate extremes that had sustained their relationship so well in the early years, before she had started drinking heavily. With the drinking came more temper and less remorse, but never this, never silence. This wasn't like her and it had him worried.

## Jack

Wide awake, Jack reached for his mobile phone to check what time it was. Still only, six-thirty in the morning, he lay back on the pillow listening to Rachel's rhythmic breathing as she slept soundly beside him. Turning to look at her, he wondered, for the first time, exactly what it was that made her tick. Up to now, he had just assumed that it was sex. He had even gone so far as to flatter himself that it was sex with him that she found irresistible, but yesterday, watching her on the phone to Liz, he realised that there was a lot more to it than that.

After fetching herself a cocktail, she had returned to the poolside as if nothing had happened, making no further reference to the conversation with Liz. She had blithely chatted to him about how much she liked the hotel and suggested that they try out a seafood restaurant that the waiter had recommended to her at breakfast. Non-plussed by her callousness, but keen to avoid a scene, he had eventually played her at her own game, resolutely vowing to himself to end their affair when they got back to Dublin.

He knew that her continuing friendship with Liz could well make this difficult as she would still be a frequent visitor to his home, but he would cross that bridge when he came to it. For now, he wanted to pursue the damage limitation route and having seen what she was capable of the previous day, he knew that he had to manipulate the situation such that their inevitable break-up appeared to be a mutual decision and turned his thoughts to how this could be achieved.

As he wracked his brain for some trigger that would make her want out as much as he did, he realised just how little he actually knew about her. She never spoke of family, and other than Liz, he couldn't recall her talk about any close friends. Sure, she had people that she went out with, these seemed to be mainly work colleagues, but no-one in particular, no-one close. He wondered why he had never noticed this before. But then, there were lots of things he hadn't noticed before. He had never noticed just how controlling she was. How everything had to be her way — how they only met on nights that suited her, even though she was the single one. How they only went to places that she wanted to go to. And, of course, how his golfing holiday plans had changed because SHE decided that they should go away together instead.

An irrational fear suddenly gripped him as he realised that this situation might not be as easy to extricate himself from as he had hoped. He now knew that someone as accustomed to having things her own way, as Rachel undoubtedly was, wasn't going to accept being dumped and the prospect of her assuming the role of a 'woman scorned' was too frightening to contemplate. He doubted very much that she held Liz in sufficient esteem to weather such a putdown, otherwise she wouldn't be having an affair with her husband — would she?

### Hollie

Since unleashing her tears at the pool bar on Friday afternoon, Hollie hadn't been able to stop crying. The relief she experienced when Annette located her passport, was transient and faced with the kindness of a complete stranger, the full horror of her circumstances seemed to hit her and she had cried her heart out, alone in the hotel room for the entire night. Fearful of falling asleep, in case Eoin made an unwelcome reappearance, she had spent the night curled up on a wicker chair at the foot of the bed, reliving the nightmare that she had woken up to the previous morning.

Fraught with nerves, she had bristled with fear every time she heard the elevator activate, holding her breath as she listened to hear if it was stopping on her floor, then, heaving a sigh of relief each time an unfamiliar voice or laugh signalled that its occupants were strangers. In truth, she very much doubted that Eoin would come back to the hotel, but she still had the awful prospect of encountering him on the flight home and was unsure how she would be able to handle that. Perhaps the resultant chaos from the flight disruptions would spare her this ordeal and she clung to this hope with fervour.

As the dawn began to break, her tears finally subsided, leaving her with a thumping headache. Searching through her handbag, she found some paracetamol and a half drunk bottle of water. She unscrewed the cap of the water and swallowed down two tablets, then, feeling like she could do with some fresh air, she moved the wicker chair over to the balcony doors and opened them wide. The dawn air, though not exactly cold, had a chill to it and pulling a large blanket around her, she once more curled up, resting her head against the back of the chair and looked out across the beach.

Up to that point, the beauty of the place had been lost on her, but sitting there now, she took it all in. The early morning sky, with its colourful promise of another glorious day ahead, the soft sea breeze that left a fine residue of salt on her lips as she licked them, the uniquely Spanish look of the buildings and pathways that populated this delightful seaside paradise were all things that she was aware of for the first time.

A remarkable shift took place within her as she allowed herself be drawn into the splendour of the moment. Gone, were the feelings of abject misery that she had been experiencing since discovering the rape and in their place she felt a sense of confidence grow. She had been wronged; she had been violated; she had been raped. She knew now with certainty that no matter how foolish she had been to come away with this man, she did not deserve what had happened to her. He had committed a crime against her and she couldn't simply let him get away with it.

Her restored confidence brought with it an appetite that she had not had for the past couple of days, and hearing the first stirrings of life from the restaurant below her balcony, she went to shower and resolved to sketch out a plan of action over an early breakfast.

Twenty minutes later, showered and refreshed, she walked confidently out on to the terrace with a breakfast tray filled with a selection of cooked meats, crusty bread and a large bowl of fresh fruit. Still early, she had her choice of tables. Selecting one with a view of the pool, she had just started unloading her tray when she spotted Annette coming outside with a large mug of coffee in her hand. With a surge of determination, she waved over to her asking her if she would like to join her. Annette smiled in response and made her way over.

Feeling so much calmer than she had the day before, Hollie felt indebted to this stranger whose kindness had enabled her to purge herself of so much misery. Barely giving her time to sit herself down, Hollie got up from her seat and making her way around to Annette's side of the table, she embraced her warmly.

"I'd like to thank you so much for yesterday," Hollie began, uncertain how far she was going to go with this conversation.

"Ah, don't be daft! Sure, wouldn't anyone have liked to help you? You looked so sad and sometimes, it just takes a different perspective to find a solution to a problem. You look much better today — I'm glad."

"I am, and that's thanks to you. You see, I just had so much bottled up inside of me and you helped me bring it to the surface. To be honest, I cried my eyes out after I left you, but today, I feel the better for it."

"Yes, a good cry can do that for you. Any word from that scoundrel boyfriend of yours?"

Annette's genuine concern for her emboldened Hollie, weighing up the situation she decided that if the truth were to out, who better to begin with than this benevolent woman sitting opposite her. Looking straight into Annette's warm brown eyes, she took a deep breath and said.

"Look, I wasn't entirely truthful with you yesterday. You see, my head was all over the place and I genuinely didn't know what I was going to do. But, I've been up all night thinking about it and now, I know, what I have to do."

Intrigued, Annette remained silent, but raised an eyebrow in encouragement.

"Eoin isn't my boyfriend. In fact, I barely know the bloke. He came into the clinic where I work last week and to cut a long story short, he charmed the pants of me and despite the disapproval of all my friends, I took him up on his invitation to join him here for a few days. It just seemed so glamorous and these kind of things don't happen to people like me and…, and… I stupidly took him up on his invitation, without knowing him or anything about him."

Her lip started to tremble at this point, but not wanting to interrupt her, Annette simply reached across the table and held her hand. Then, in a gentle whisper, she said. "Go on."

"Well, on the plane, he told me that he was in a relationship and that night when we went for dinner, I told him that I wasn't interested. He got very angry and after that, I don't remember anything. All I know, is that I woke up the next morning and he was gone, and I was left in this condition." Looking a little uncertain, she raised the corner of her loose fitting T shirt, displaying the horrendous bruising to her ribs.

Annette gasped, clamping her hand to her mouth to suppress the shock that registered in her eyes. "Oh my God! You poor thing. He did that to you?"

Hollie shrugged, shifting uncomfortably in her seat to alter her position so she could show Annette the bruising on the other side of her torso. "There are more on my back," she whispered, barely audibly. "But, that's not all…. he…, he…,"

"He what?" asked Annette, fearful that she knew the answer.

"He raped me."

"Jesus Christ — the fucker!" Annette's eyes blazed with anger as she took in the state of this slip of a girl, sitting there bruised and battered. "Did you go to the police?"

"No. I didn't see the point. I figured that they would just mark me down as another drunken young one who went out asking for trouble. But, I wasn't drunk, Annette," she said in a pleading tone. "I barely had anything to drink. I think he must have spiked my drink when we were in the restaurant, be-cause everything is blank after that. I was stupid too — I just felt so dirty. I showered the next morning, scrubbing and scrubbing myself, and me, who works in a clinic — I should have known better. But, I had to get rid of him somehow and that felt like the best way. Now, I've removed all the evidence and I don't think the police will be interested."

"Christ! Of course they'll be interested. You need to go to the hospital, get a medical report done up. Even if there's no seminal fluid there or anything, there could be other signs of rape. There's all that bruising for starters — Jesus, you obviously didn't do that to yourself. You should get that photographed. I have a camera, I'll do that for you if you like. And, if you want, I'll go to the hospital with you, my mother-in-law is here with me, she can stay with the girls. You'll need someone with you."

"Are you sure?" asked Hollie incredulously, the tears returning. "I could really do with someone, but I don't want to intrude on your holiday."

"Nonsense," responded Annette emphatically. "I'll just go tell Maureen and I'll see you back here in ten minutes."

## Annette

Letting herself into the hotel suite, Annette knocked gently on Maureen's bedroom door, and opening it, she peeked her head around to find Maureen sitting up in bed, sipping a cup of tea.

"Oh, g'morning, love," said Maureen, cheerfully. "I hope I didn't wake you, but I was dying for a cuppa. I'm sorry, I did try to be as quiet as possible, but….,"

Annette shook her head, mildly irritated at the way Maureen had to apologise for everything, then, quickly dismissed the notion as inconsequential in the overall scheme of what she was about to deal with this morning. "No, Maureen, don't worry. I woke up really early, went for a bit of a stroll and had a coffee downstairs."

"Oh, dear. Everything okay, love? You worried about Paddy? Don't be. It'll be fine……"

Again, Annette stopped her in her tracks. "No. It's not Paddy. But, I do need your help with something."

Concerned now, Maureen placed her tea mug on the locker beside the bed, then pulling back the sheet, she got out of the bed with a speed that belied her age. "What is it? What's wrong? Is it the girls? Did they not come home or something?"

Struck, once again, by her mother-in-law's instinctive concern for everyone but herself, Annette, smiled fondly at her and slipping her arm around the older woman's shoulders in a reassuring gesture, she said. "No, Maureen. The girls are fine. But, you were right about that young girl at the pool bar yesterday. She does have problems. Big ones. And, I promised that I'd try to help her sort a few things out, if you don't mind being here for the girls until I get back."

CLOUDED ISSUES

"Not at all. But, what happened?"

Annette filled her in on bumping into Hollie again this morning and her revelations about what had actually happened to her. A look of true compassion rested on Maureen's features as she listened to the woeful tale. When Annette had finished, Maureen bundled her out the door, assuring her that the girls were in safe hands and there was no rush on getting back. Gratefully, Annette hugged her and went to meet Hollie, stopping at reception to get the address of the nearest public hospital en route.

Hospital Son Llatzer was a large, modern hospital situated in Palma de Mallorca, and the taxi driver brought them to its A&E department, dropping them straight outside the doors. One glance in Hollie's direction and Annette could tell by the look of abject terror on her face that there was no way she would have been able to see this through alone. Taking full control of the situation, she paid the driver and in a kind, but firm, manner, urged Hollie out of the car. Once out, Annette could see how much the young woman was trembling, furtively watching the departing taxi whilst fervently wishing that she was still in it.

Gently, she linked Hollie's arm and steered her around in the direction of the entrance doors, slowly ushering her towards them, uttering words of encouragement as she did so.

"C'mon, Hollie," she murmured, "Let's get inside and get this over and done with. I'm with you and I'm not going anywhere. But, you've got to do this. You know you do."

"I know," whimpered Hollie. "But, Christ, I don't want to."

"I know, I know," soothed Annette. "But, think how much better you will feel when you have."

Not looking at all convinced, Hollie nodded meekly and did as she was bid.

With each step, Annette could sense the mounting trepidation in Hollie, and deciding that it would probably be easier to initiate proceedings on her own, she settled her down on one of the plastic seats in the waiting area and, reassuring her that she would be right back, she went to the desk to speak to the triage nurse.

To her enormous relief, the friendly-faced young nurse spoke perfect

English and Annette quickly outlined the purpose of their visit, keeping a close eye on Hollie as she did so. Instant sympathy registered on the nurse's face and picking up a clipboard and pen, she followed Annette over to the trembling Hollie.

"Buenos dias, Hollie," she said, lowering herself to her hunkers and placing a hand on Hollie's shaking knee. "I am Maria Alvarez," she added, pointing to the name tag clipped to her pristine uniform. "I will be looking after you today. There is nothing for you to worry about."

Hollie nodded mutely as Maria shifted herself into the seat beside her. Annette took the seat on the other side and reached across, taking hold of Hollie's hand.

"Your friend has told me what happened to you and I will arrange for you to see a doctor in a few minutes. But, first, there are some things that I must explain to you. Because of the nature of your visit, we must telephone la policia and have someone interview you."

Annette felt Hollie's grip tighten as a look of panic shot across her face.

"Sshhh," soothed Annette. "You'll be fine."

"Yes, you will be fine," reassured Maria. "I will request a female officer and it will be a female doctor who will examine you. Your friend must wait here while we examine you, but she can sit with you for the police interview."

Hollie started to protest, but Maria held up her hand in a calming gesture. "Please, don't worry. I will stay with you for the examination, but the rules of the hospital say that your friend must wait here."

"I'll be right here," appeased Annette. "I promise, and the minute you are finished, I'll be with you."

A reluctant Hollie nodded her assent, resigned to her lack of choice. Annette watched helplessly as Maria escorted Hollie into the examination room, and her heart filled with sympathy for the young woman whom a mere twenty-four hours ago she had not known, and now she was privy to her deepest darkest secret.

"What a difference a day makes," thought Annette, ruefully to herself.

## *Liz*

Despite promising herself a lie-in, Liz woke early on Saturday morning. Josh's rugby match had been cancelled and Jane had stayed the night in her friend, Clare's house, for once leaving Liz with a clear day. Normally, she would have taken advantage of such a rare occurrence and spent the day with her sister, having a girlie shopping day, but Annette was in Majorca, still hoping that poor Paddy would make it over to them, something that was looking increasingly unlikely, as the airport remained closed in Dublin.

Wondering how her less than tolerant older sister was coping with being stranded with her irksome mother-in-law brought a smile to Liz's face and reaching across to her bedside locker, she picked up the house phone to give her a call. Knowing Annette, she would be firmly ensconced by the pool even at this early hour, for fear of murdering Maureen if the two were confined to a hotel room for any longer than necessary. Surprised by the speed with which the call was answered and instantly aware of the strained tones in her sister's voice, she knew that something was wrong.

With no preamble, she cut straight to the chase. "Hey, Annette? What is it? What's wrong? Are you okay? Are the girls okay?"

"Yes. Yes, we're fine," replied Annette in a hushed whisper. "Just give me a minute and I'll go outside."

Liz's imagination ran away with her as she envisaged all kinds of disasters in the interminable couple of minutes it took Annette to come back on the line.

"Hi, sorry. I was in the hospital and there were signs plastered everywhere saying 'no mobiles'. I had it in my hand, just about to turn it off when you phoned."

"In the hospital?" interjected Liz. "Why? What's happened? Did something happen to Maureen?"

"No. As I say, we are all fine. It's a bit of a long story really."

She proceeded to fill Liz in on all that had happened to Hollie and how she was waiting for Hollie's medical examination to finish before accompanying her for the police interview.

"Jesus!" exclaimed Liz when she had concluded. "This sure is turning into the holiday from hell for you — isn't it?"

"Not as bad as poor Hollie's," said Annette. "Honestly, Liz, you'd want to see the poor girl. She is in absolute flitters. It's just so awful for her. I mean, she has no-one. She's clinging to me like I'm her saviour or something. She doesn't even know me, for Chrissake, I only met her yesterday, but she's just so alone. I'm really glad that Maureen insisted on me approaching her, I can't bear to think how much worse it would be for her doing this on her own."

Liz could hear the tears in Annette's voice and tried to comfort her. "But, at least she does have you sis, and personally I could think of no better person to have with me if I was in that situation. You are so strong and pragmatic. Look, only for you convincing her to come to the hospital, she wouldn't even have done that."

"I know. It's just, I keep thinking what if it had been Hannah or Megan?" A plaintive sob erupted from her at this point. "It could so easily have been. I mean, that bastard spiked her drink. He could easily still be hanging around the clubs and bars, waiting for some other poor unfortunate girl. What would Paddy say if he knew that I've been letting them go off on their own? What kind of a fucking terrible mother am I?"

"Now, you listen to me, Annette Forbes. You are anything but a terrible mother and you know it. It wouldn't have made any difference whether Paddy was there or not, it would have been your decision — it always is. Paddy trusts your judgement with the girls, and with good reason. I bet those clubs are full of teenagers. You chose the resort because it was family friendly, and as such, it was reasonable to assume that your girls would be safe. Knowing you, I bet that they had to be home by midnight — right?"

"Yes! Yes! I insisted on that, and, I insist on strolling down to meet them. But, I didn't know there was a fucking madman on the loose, or I would never have let them go in the first place. I knew Maureen was doing their heads in and, in part, it was selfish of me letting them go, I only did it so I wouldn't have to listen to them moaning. Now, that was just plain irresponsible."

"Don't be so hard on yourself, Annette. You only did what all mothers of teenagers do on holiday. You extended the boundaries. That's normal, now stop beating yourself up over it. Obviously you have to talk to the girls, point out the dangers. But, they are a sensible pair — Hannah and Megan. You know that they are. You can't punish them for what happened to Hollie. But, you can make sure that they are being extra careful. You can make your allowing them go conditional on certain rules. They must stick together; absolutely no alcohol; that they keep whatever drinks they have in their hands. You can even insist that you collect them from the club, but what you can't do is stop them from going after already allowing them — that isn't fair. Is it?"

"I suppose you're right," responded Annette, hesitantly, then, in a lighter tone, she added, "When did you become so wise?"

Smiling at her weak joke, Liz said, "Ah Sis, 'font of all wisdom' me — ya know! Incidentally, do you know if Hollie has let anyone at home know what has happened to her? A family member, or a friend?"

"I doubt it. I get the impression that I'm the only one she had told."

"Well, it might be a good idea to get her to do that. She's going to need support."

"I'll talk to her," said Annette. "And Liz, thanks."

"No worries! I won't even charge!" quipped Liz. "Any news on Paddy? Doesn't look good for him getting out there — does it?"

"No. To be honest I doubt he'll make it. We're due back on Wednesday. Unless he can get out tomorrow at the latest, it's hardly going to be worth his while coming."

"How's Maureen behaving herself?"

Annette laughed at the question and the two sisters chatted away for several more minutes before Liz, satisfied that she'd raised Annette's spirits sufficiently, rang off and went to fix herself some breakfast.

CHAPTER FOUR

# Saturday PM 17th April

*Rachel*

There was a flurry of discontent rippling through the crowd gathered in the reception area of the luxurious Port Adriano Hotel, where the nervous looking holiday rep was imparting the devastating blow that there would be no flights to either the U.K. or Ireland that day. Rachel was amused by the pompous egos who seemed to genuinely fear that the world of business would grind to a halt if they didn't manage to get their egocentric arses into their oversized desk chairs by first thing Monday morning.

Possibly for the first time in their self-important little lives, the money that they had thrown around so freely during their ostentatious Spring break could buy them no favours. The airports were closed and there was nothing they could do about that fact. There were murmurings of alternative modes of transport, but with air travel off the agenda, even the most affluent were faced with a couple of day's travel. For some reason, their temporary paralysis tickled her.

Looking about her now, she wondered how many 'Jack O'Briens' were amongst those gathered — men who now ran the risk of having their philanderous ways exposed and, judging by the expressions on some of the faces, there were quite a few. She knew her feelings to be somewhat perverse on this subject, but she had always found this fear of discovery to be a major turn on during the course of her many illicit liaisons, as it put control firmly in her hands and she got off on the power that it gave her. Scanning the crowd, she recognised a similar reaction from some of the more mature, glamorous women present. The secret society of 'habitual mistresses' understood this power and found their position enviable — a position that they would never in a million years swap for the poor deluded, misled, lied to wives who stopped at home, generally raising a tribe of kids, whilst the mistresses soaked up the benefits of their errant husbands wealth.

A supercilious smile touched her lips as she went in search of Jack to share the bad news.

*Denise*

Denise was astounded to discover that it was past midday when she opened her eyes in the unfamiliar surroundings of the plush hotel room in the Ritz Carlton. She couldn't remember when she had last slept so late, or so soundly. Her thoughts drifted back to all that she had accomplished the previous day and a sense of satisfaction descended on her. She had well and truly set the ball in motion for her new life.

She idly wondered if John had resurfaced back at the house yet, and if so, what had been his reaction to finding her gone? Knowing him as she did, she guessed that he would have been irritated at first, but that the irritation would soon give way to fury and he would probably plan on teaching her an forgettable lesson. She cringed as she thought of this, but reminded herself that he had harmed her for the last time. It struck her as funny that at no point did she speculate that he could be worried about her disappearance — she knew that worry simply wouldn't enter the equation.

Pushing thoughts of him from her mind, she threw back the covers, got out of bed and headed for the bathroom. A wave of nausea washed over her as she did so, and the pattern of the last few mornings was repeated, whereby she clasped her arms around the rim of the toilet bowl and dry-retched vigorously. This unwelcome reminder of her pregnancy almost succeeded in dampening her mood, but she fought against it, and pushing herself upright, she turned on the taps in the sink, and, cupping water in her hands, she splashed her face, breathing deeply as she did so, until the sickness passed.

Finally feeling better, she reached for the soft hand-towel and gently patted her face dry, simultaneously studying her reflection in the mirror. Even in the flattering light of the hotel bathroom, she could see that she looked terrible. The face staring back at her looked years older than her thirty-four years. Her gaunt features bore the stresses and strains of the last decade. The insurmountable grief she had experienced at the loss of her beloved parents had etched itself into every part of her face, leaving 'worry' lines on her forehead, which seemed to be fixed into a frown, and fine wrinkles surrounding her mouth.

Shocked at first, as if seeing herself for the first time in years, she blinked hard and looked again. It was then that she realised what it was that disturbed her most about what she was seeing. Her eyes. Not just the crows' feet, that were prominent on either side of her face, but the eyes themselves — they were so lifeless. She vaguely remembered a time, before she had descended into the awful depression that had left her vulnerable to John's predatory ways, when those eyes of vivid blue had sparkled and danced back at her when she had looked in the mirror. Now, they just looked muted. So too, her hair - the formerly vibrant, glossy, copper sheen of her once regularly cut and styled wavy locks was gone and instead dull, lank, ropey-looking tendrils hung unflatteringly from the top of her head, seeming to drag her once pretty face downwards so that now she habitually looked to the floor in a subconscious effort to keep the world at bay.

As she studied her reflection, she experienced a feeling that had eluded her for years — hope. Her new life started here. It was almost as if a switch inside her had been flicked and the momentous plans she had made over the last forty-eight hours were now within her grasp. How often had she heard tell of people needing to hit rock bottom before beginning the transformation that turned their lives around? She now knew with certainty that that was where she had hit and smiling at herself as she saw the first flicker of life come back into her eyes, she went to get the laptop she had bought the afternoon before.

She had been correct in her assumption that the greyness which enveloped her in recent years, had indeed protected her anonymity when she had slipped in and out, unnoticed, of the lottery headquarters, pocketing her cheque for 5.8 million Euro. So as not to arouse suspicion, she had walked a short distance from the lottery building before flagging down a taxi and getting the driver to take her directly to meet Mr. Horgan, the bank manager, in Ranelagh.

Although several years since he had last laid eyes on her, and despite his attempts to conceal it, his shock at the change in her was almost as evident as his surprise when she passed the cheque across his large office desk to him.

"Jesus Christ!" he said, his eyes out on stalks, before scrambling to his feet and hurrying around the desk to congratulate her. She spent a couple of hours with him, during which, he gave her the names of a couple of reputable financial advisors who would be better placed than him to recommend how best to manage her vast fortune. When their business was concluded, in deference to his much-valued friendship with her father, he voiced concerns about her general well-being, but she laughed them off assuring him that she had everything under control.

Her new accounts would take several days to be operational and with no means of accessing any funds elsewhere, she had requested five thousand euro in cash in the interim and he had happily accommodated her. Her state of the art laptop had been her first purchase and she had stayed up virtually the entire night, thrashing around some ideas before finally concluding a master-plan that had afforded her the level of untroubled sleep she had experienced.

With an abortion booked in a London clinic for Monday, she had tried to check out flights, but air traffic was at a standstill, and she opted to travel on Sunday by ferry and train instead. It wasn't ideal, especially as Sunday rail travel could be subject to lengthy delays in England when essential track maintenance was frequently carried out, but she wanted the termination over as soon as possible.

She had kept herself to herself in the hotel, making use of the magnificent leisure centre with its crystal lit swimming pool, whilst studiously avoiding any attempts at conversation from her fellow guests. Choosing to order room service for dinner, she selected the feel good movie, Mamma Mia, to watch whilst she ate, not wanting anything too mentally challenging. It was half way through her juicy fillet steak, as she took in the spectacular setting of the idyllic Greek island, that the notion came to her — she was going to move to Greece.

## Donal

With his mind in overdrive, Donal paced the length and breadth of the kitchen, thinking, thinking, thinking — what to do. It was mid afternoon and Susan remained ensconced in her own impenetrable world, refusing all attempts at communication. Time was running out and there were decisions to be made. It had literally taken him months to secure Monday's meeting with a high-ranking executive from Britain's leading travel company and his failure to attend this meeting would substantially set back, if not, obliterate his chances of success. He simply had to attend.

As if the air travel situation hadn't been enough of a complication in itself, he now had the very real problem of Susan — he couldn't leave her alone in this condition. If he had been able to fly, he could have got over and back in the one day and that could possibly have been manageable, but now, his only means of getting there was to take the ferry and drive down, necessitating at least one, if not two nights away. There was no way that he could leave her alone for that long. But with their future hinging on a successful meeting, there was no alternative but to go.

There had to be a solution, but what that was eluded him. His tormented pacing continued, until with a flash of inspiration, he thought of Hollie and her enthusiastic response to his invention, picturing her face as he had told her all about it and her absolute certainty that it would make him a fortune. He would call his sister and ask her to baby-sit Susan for a couple of days. Her and Susan's relationship was somewhat fraught at the best of times, but Hollie adored him and he knew that if she could at all, she would help him out.

With the first stirrings of hope, he pulled his mobile from his pocket and called up her number. To his dismay, a foreign ring tone greeted him. Where the hell was she? She hadn't mentioned anything about going away. Maybe he had got a crossed-line, hanging up, he tried again. But no, it was definitely a foreign ring tone and she didn't answer.

Feeling deflated, he threw his mobile on to the table and in a fit of pique, grabbed the kettle to fill it. As he turned off the tap, Susan opened the kitchen door and stepped into the room. She looked like shit and casting his own frustrations to one side, he went to give her a hug, but she shrugged him off. Refusing to look him in the eyes, she kept her head low and spoke in a quiet voice.

"Donal, I don't want you to argue with me, 'cos the subject isn't open to discussion. I've decided to go and stay with my mother for a week or two."

He started to object, but emphatically she held up her hand. "Please don't do this, Donal. I need some space. I need to sort some things out and I can't do that here — with you. I just can't. My mind's made up. Mum will be here in about an hour to collect me. If I mean anything to you at all, Donal, then, you won't stand in my way."

Donal exploded. "What do you mean 'if you mean anything to me'? You know bloody well what you mean to me!"

"At the moment Donal, I don't know anything. That's why I have to get away."

Leaving him speechless, she turned away and headed up the stairs to pack. His confusion was tinged with relief as it dawned on him that her unexpected departure solved his London dilemma.

## *Hollie*

It was almost six thirty when, turning off her hairdryer, Hollie picked up her mobile phone to check the time and groaned in dismay to see two missed calls from Donal.

"Shit! Shit! Shit!" she exclaimed, annoyed with herself for not turning off her mobile as she had intended. More of a texter than a caller, she hadn't expected her brother to be looking for her and knew that he would be cross with her for going away and not letting him know.

Her self-assigned protector, Donal was the quintessential older brother. It was him that had sheltered her from the worst aspects of growing up with an alcoholic mother and an indifferent father. She remembered still the separation anxiety she had experienced when, on occasion, they were forced to stay in different foster homes whilst their mother dried out, and the intense joy she felt when they were eventually reunited. The unpleasantness of her home life was always preferable to the comfort of foster care because of him. She adored him and the prospect of him worrying about her was unthinkable. She was going to have to call him and hoped she could keep the trauma of the past couple of days from her voice whilst she spoke to him. Inhaling deeply, she punched his number into her phone.

"Hols! Where the hell are you?" he asked on answering. The concern in his voice making her feel guilty.

"Hey, nice to talk to you too, brother dear," she laughed with a forced casualness.

Mollified by her light tone, he said, "Aw, sorry sis, just got a bit of a shock to hear a foreign ring tone. You never said you were going away — did you?"

"No, sorry about that. It was just a last minute thing. One of the girls in work invited me away for a long weekend, all expenses paid and it was too good an opportunity to miss. I meant to give you a call, but it all happened so quickly. Anyway — what's up? It's not like you to ring on a Saturday evening."

Donal talked her through the purpose of his call, telling her that the situation had resolved itself with Susan's decision to go stay with her mother. Relieved to find him so preoccupied with his own problems that he hadn't picked up on anything out of the ordinary with her, she kept the conversation brief and told him that she would be in touch when she knew what the story was with her return flight and wishing him the best of luck for Monday, she rang off.

His dedication to Susan, whom Hollie considered to be nothing more than a spoilt lush, irked her, but with more than her share of problems to contend with, she dismissed these thoughts and continued preparing for dinner. Annette had kindly invited her to join them and she didn't want to be late.

## *Annette*

It was late afternoon before Annette and Hollie got back to the hotel. Brooking no argument from Hollie, Annette insisted that she join them for the evening and wanting to make up to the girls and Maureen for her prolonged absence, the first thing she did on her return was buy five tickets for a cabaret show, promising Megan and Hannah that they could go across to the clubs later as usual. The girls were delighted and she didn't bother to disclose her ulterior motive of being in close proximity to them — she needed that tonight, not wanting to let them go at all, but hearing Liz's wise words ringing in her ears.

To her relief, the girls had made friends at the pool with two English teenagers, Jody and Debs, cousins from Manchester, whose parents echoed her own concerns regarding the level of freedom to afford the youngsters. Without wishing to appear alarmist and, being careful to protect Hollie's privacy, Annette told them that she was aware of an incident involving drink spiking and irrefutable guidelines were established governing the boundaries of their clubbing. Grateful for the solidarity provided by the other parents, she volunteered to collect all four girls from the club when returning home at around twelve thirty.

"Go on, Nan, have a Harvey Wall Banger!" giggled Megan good-humouredly. "Live dangerously! I bet Mum'll have one — won't you?"

"Too right!" grinned Annette, "I've been looking forward to it all day. What about it, Maureen?"

"Do you know? I think I will," beamed Maureen, looking more relaxed than Annette could ever remember seeing her. "I think I could get used to these 'girlie' holidays. Tom didn't really like me drinking, never really said anything, but would kind of shuffle about in his seat and mutter something like 'an orange juice for you, Dear', until it got to the point that I never even thought of ordering anything else."

Taken aback by her mother-in-law's, albeit mild, criticism of her much revered husband, Annette wondered if 'big Tom Forbes' had clipped his wife's wings in other ways. She had always been very fond of her father-in-law, but he was a product of his generation and, without a doubt, 'Master of the House'. She had often teased Paddy about him, warning him that no such title would ever be bestowed on him, to which Paddy would invariably reply 'yes, Boss,' whilst bowing and doffing an imaginary cap.

Perhaps all these years, she had done Maureen an injustice, underestimating her strength of character and accepting a lack of personality that she was now seeing for the first time. She had been so compassionate and caring about Hollie, and was far more in tune with the girls and their sometimes wicked sense of humour than Annette would have ever given her credit for, even coming back with the odd witty riposte of her own. Certainly the girls were far more relaxed with her than a couple of days ago and it was with affection that Megan goaded her into ordering a cocktail. Sipping on her over-sized Harvey Wall Banger, Annette felt a rush of affection for the older woman.

Hollie looked nervous as she approached the table, and keen to put her at her ease, Annette jumped up and quickly introducing her to everyone, signalled to Denis that she wished to order a round of drinks. By the time they left the pool bar thirty minutes later, she was pleased to note that Hollie was chatting away happily with everyone. Conscious that money was probably an issue for Hollie, she insisted that the night was her treat and was glad when Hollie didn't make a big deal out of it.

After an enjoyable and inexpensive meal in a busy little sea-front steak house, they hurried along to the cabaret venue where the show was due to kick off at eight thirty. Annette's fears of not getting a good table proved unfounded, as the place was less than half full when they arrived. The girls slagged her for being a fuss-pot and not allowing them to digest their food properly, but Annette ignored them, victoriously claiming a prime table straight in front of the stage.

The combination of early cocktails and subsequent wine with dinner had left Maureen quite tipsy, and her overt excitement was infectious, as their peals of laughter drew curious looks from more sedate members of the audience. The MC, quick to spot the more outgoing personalities in the room, homed in on their table, flirting outrageously with Maureen, who lapped it up, oblivious to the fact that it was the entire bar who could hear her droll retorts and not just him. Unbeknownst to herself, she quickly assumed celebrity status amongst the audience, who fervently shushed each other each time she spoke, for fear of missing what she said.

"Oh no, dear, it would play havoc with my lumbago," she said in response to his request to join him on stage where a limbo dancing bar had been erected in preparation for the next act. "Though I do do a bit of salsa at my 'over sixties' club on a Thursday morning."

A wave of laughter seemed to suddenly alert to her audience, and blushing furiously, she turned to Annette for reassurance that she hadn't said anything wrong. Dabbing the tears from the corner of her eye, Annette grinned warmly back at her, "You are a ticket, Maureen," she said.

## Liz

A message on her voicemail from Jack confirmed what she already suspected, he was going to be stuck in Portugal until at least Monday. He told her that he would give her a call later, but not wanting him to call in the middle of the takeaway she had just ordered for herself and the kids, she decided to call him back straight away. She rarely was the one to call him when he was away with his friends, as she didn't want to appear the clinging wife, but her plan was to curl up on the sofa with her curry, a nice bottle of Merlot and watch a DVD — preferably, without any interruptions.

He answered almost immediately and she smiled to hear the over-enunciation of his words that signalled that, despite the early hour, he was well on his way to being drunk.

"Ya big lush!" she laughed, "Just as well I rang you back, another hour or so and you would be incoherent!"

"What are you talking about Liz?" he asked in an indignant fashion. "I have merely partaken in a small aperitif!"

"Yeah! Yeah! Whatever!" she said. "Anyway, I'll talk to you tomorrow. No offence, but if it comes to chit-chatting with my drunken husband or drooling over Javier Bardem — there's simply no competition! Love ya! Talk to you tommorow."

"Whoa! Whoa! Just a minute. Which movie?"

For reasons completely different to hers, he was a big fan of Bardem, and when she told him that it was 'No Country For Old Men', a particular favourite of his, he even managed to sound deprived at missing the movie.

"I'll just have to console myself with the 'Company of his Country men'," he retorted, laughing heartily at his own weak pun.

"Jesus, Jack! You must be drunker than I thought."

"Eh?" he asked, perplexed.

"Javier Bardem is Spanish, love — not Portuguese!"

"Do you always have to be such a fucking smart arse?"

Taken aback by his decidedly unpleasant tone, and not wanting to get embroiled in an argument with him half-pissed, she took a deep breath, then said. "Hey, look, why don't you give me a call in the morning? Have a nice night — talk to you then." And with the hackles on the back of her neck standing on end, she hung up the phone.

## Jack

"Fuck! Fuck! And, double fuck!" exclaimed Jack, staring incredulously at the phone in his hand. How had he been so stupid? A small slip like that and he could have blown this whole thing. And why on earth had he snapped the head off her like that? That could only make matters worse. Too agitated to think clearly, he headed back into the bar where he had left Rachel to take the call from his wife.

"Jesus, I've really fucked up big time," he said, flopping down into the seat beside her, grapping hold of a serviette and mopping the beads of sweat that had formed on his brow. "I nearly blew the whole fucking thing."

Remaining calm, Rachel reached across and filled the glass in front of him, before raising a questioning eyebrow, waiting for him to elaborate. He told her what had been said on the phone, and felt his fury grow at the nonchalant shrug she gave in response.

"Jesus, Rachel — I almost gave the game away. How can you be so calm?"

A derisory look crossed her face before she answered him. "You really are a bloody drama-queen — aren't you?"

"What do you mean 'drama-queen'? I as good as told her that I'm in

Spain not Portugal."

"No, you made a drunken slip up and that's all she saw it as. She said as much herself. You simply text her — apologise, tell her you're off to bed to sleep it off and that you'll call her in the morning. Drama averted!"

"You are one hard bitch. Do you know that?" but, even as he asked the question, the simplicity of the solution she had proffered struck him. "But perhaps you are right," he grinned, visibly relaxing and hurriedly texting Liz. "What would I do without you?"

"Play a lot of golf and fantasise about the kind of sex you will experience tonight."

CHAPTER FIVE

# Sunday AM 18th April

*Jack*

True to character, Liz accepted his contrite apology when he called her early on Sunday morning.

"I'm so, so sorry, love," he began when she picked up his call. "I don't know why I was such a prick last night. I know I was drunk, but that doesn't excuse it. You've got to believe me though, Babe, I am really, really sorry."

"Yep! You were a 'Class A' prick alright," she said, though he could detect a half smile in her voice as she spoke.

"I know, and again, I'm sorry. What can I say? The result of a testoster-one-filled week. I was really looking forward to getting home last night. I miss you and the kids like crazy and God alone knows when I'll be able to get back. I wish I'd never come on this stupid holiday."

"Oh stop your whingeing," she had laughed. "There's far worse things than being stuck in a golfer's paradise with all your golfing buddies. As for me, and the kids, you'll be back ten minutes and you'll be sick looking at us. Now, back to this apology of yours, I feel the need to hear a bit more grovelling."

Jack laughed, relief flooding him as his wife's usual good humour was restored. "I'm so, so, very, deeply and abjectly sorry for being a total asinine gobshite on the phone last night. Will that do it?"

"For the moment, but if I need a top-up, I'll give you a call — okay?"

"Okay, Babe. Talk to you later. Love you."

"Love you too." And, she was gone.

Leaving Rachel still asleep, he had slipped from their room and come down to the terrace café to ring Liz, not wanting to do it in front of her. He expected her to sleep for another couple of hours as it had been daylight before her sexual proclivities had finally given way to exhaustion. His mind wouldn't rest until he had smoothed things over with Liz, and now that he had, he felt relaxed and at ease. Ordering himself a coffee, he grabbed a couple of newspapers and found a table.

Without exception all the papers were full of stories surrounding the volcanic ash cloud. Countless pictures of stranded passengers and irate air line personnel filled page after page, accompanied by numerous reports, none of which seemed to hold out much hope of normal service being resumed any time soon.

His earlier anxieties regarding a flight home were replaced with a resignation that this was an international problem and not his uniquely. Rachel had been right when she had told him that if he managed to keep his head, then, there really was no reason why the truth should ever out. Keeping his head meant avoiding any stupid faux pas like the previous night and he determined to do just that.

## Denise

The switch that flicked in Denise's head when she had studied her reflection in the bathroom mirror continued to illuminate more and more facets of her character, shedding light in areas that had lurked in the dark for so many years.

With a sense of purpose, she tried on several new outfits that she had bought herself the afternoon before on a shopping spree to the large shopping mall in Dundrum. Gone were the grey muted tones that her dull and uninspiring wardrobe of the past decade had consisted of and in their place, were sleek, sophisticated garments with splashes of colour that caused her confidence to soar as she viewed her well groomed reflection in the full length mirror.

A three-hour visit to a hair salon had restored her hair to its former glory and its natural coppery gloss was enhanced by a selection of complimentary tones, leaving it looking healthy and lustrous as its soft curls framed her face. Unable to believe the transformation, she kept tossing her head to one side, relishing in the silky swish as her hair fell easily back into place. An hour with a make-up and beauty consultant in House of Fraser had yielded a more than adequate starter kit of make-up essentials. She laughed as she opened the beauty case and perused the many lotions and potions contained therein, hoping fervently that she would remember the purpose for which each one was designed.

Carefully removing everything, she laid them out on the marble work surface in the bathroom. Following the guidance offered by the consultant, she worked her way through the array of products, finishing thirty-five minutes later with the application of a rich copper-coloured lipstick that worked flatteringly with her hair. Stepping back from the mirror, she was undeniably pleased with the results achieved. It was an entirely different person who looked back at her and she was surprised to feel herself attractive for the first time in years.

A quick time check told her that she better get a move on if she was to have breakfast downstairs before the arrival of the taxi she had booked to take her to the ferry. For the hundredth time, she cursed the airport closures as the prospect of not arriving at her hotel in London until some time close to midnight filled her with dismay. The train journey would be an arduous ordeal, but she had been reluctant to hire a car as she was unsure how she would be feeling on the return journey. Emotionally, she had no fears, but physically, she had been advised that she could experience some residual cramping and thought it foolish to inflict a long drive on herself just in case. She could have stayed in London for an extra night, but felt certain that she would want to get away from the place as soon as possible after the termination.

## Donal

Aware that he had a long couple of days ahead of him, Donal had indulged himself by setting the alarm for nine thirty on Sunday morning. He planned to be on the road by ten-thirty and an hour would give him plenty of time for a shower and to load up the car. But, he needn't have bothered with the alarm, because whether it was nerves about his impending meeting or anxiety regarding his wife, he was wide-awake with little hope of further sleep by seven o'clock. Try as he might, he couldn't seem to calm his racing mind as he lay in the semi-darkness of the bedroom. The silence created by Susan's absence was deafening and he turned his back to her empty side of the bed, refusing to speculate on what the future held for their marriage.

With a rising sense of panic, he got out of bed at 7.20 and stepped straight into the shower. As the therapeutic effect of the powerful hot water spray pummelling his back took hold, he felt himself begin to relax. He knew that for the time being he had to keep all his focus on his business and to this end, he halted all thoughts on other subjects in their tracks as soon as they tried to inveigle their way into his head.

The potential for the product that he had developed himself was enormous. He had been very selective regarding whom he told about his idea, but those that he had were completely blown away by it. He was constantly being told that it would make him a wealthy man — wealthy beyond his wildest dreams according to some people who would be in a position to know such things. In Donal's mind, such speculation was all well and good, but to date, he hadn't earned a cent from it and had invested whatever he had been able to get his hands on into the venture. Failure at this point would not only leave him in the unemployment line, but substantially in debt. He couldn't let that happen. Tomorrow was to be his first proper crack at securing the kind of order that it would take to get his product out there in any real way and until the dotted line was signed on, his idea would remain just that — an idea, a bloody good one granted, but nothing more than 'an idea' all the same.

Although still not yet even nine o'clock, Donal was anxious to get out of the house and on the way. He had carefully secured his demonstration working sample and associated literature in the boot of the car and hung his suit holder in the back seat. There was an eerie feel to the empty house and he had spent the best part of the last half hour pacing around the downstairs, killing time. Too highly charged with adrenalin to sit and watch TV, he decided that the best plan of action would be to leave and stop off for breakfast en route to the ferry.

Stopping only to put in a quick call to Susan before he left, he cursed under his breath when her mobile went straight to messages. Sadly, he realised that it was more out of a sense of duty than a desire to talk to her that he was calling, and he felt guilty as he dialled her mother's landline that the purpose of this early call was to be able to dispense with his duty and not have it impinge on him throughout his journey.

He knew that he was fortunate to enjoy a good relationship with Kay, his mother-in-law, and she had proved herself to be a strong ally in respect of Susan's drinking, but Susan was her daughter after all and she would probably disapprove of him going ahead with his planned trip to London. Not wanting to be drawn into a major discussion on the subject, he braced himself to keep the conversation short and sweet.

"Good morning, Kay, it's me," he said.

"Hi Donal, love, how are you?"

"Not bad, all things considered. What about Sue? How's she doing?"

"Not great, to be honest, Donal."

He felt his heart sink as the pain in her voice was audible and he knew that he wouldn't be capable of cutting her short, but to his surprise it was her who seemed anxious to keep the conversation brief.

"Look love, I'm not going to stop and talk now if you don't mind, it's just we had a bit of a night of it and I'm feeling really shattered. She's hit rock bottom, Donal, but I did always warn you that that would happen — had to happen. It's the only way that she can start climbing back up. She spent the night just talking and talking to me and she's very unhappy."

"I know that," he said mournfully. "But, I don't know what to do. At least she spoke to you, I couldn't get a word out of her."

"No, I know. And, she doesn't want to talk to you just yet. You've got to give her some space, she has a lot of thinking and a lot of recovering to do and the very best thing you could do for her at the moment, love, is give her that space. Now, you go off to London, knock 'em dead, as I'm sure you will. Leave Susan to me and remember, Donal, whatever happens — you're a good man."

"Thanks, Kay," he said, and replacing the phone, he picked up his keys and wallet and headed out to the car with a heavy heart.

## Liz

"Uh, what's the story with Dad?" muttered Josh, incoherently as he plodded barefoot across the kitchen floor, pulling open the fridge door and removing a carton of orange juice, which he promptly put straight to his lips.

"Oi! Use a glass!" said Liz, looking up from the kitchen table where she sat reading the Sunday papers.

"It's empty, Mum," he growled at her, shaking the carton to prove his point. Then, peering over her shoulder at the papers, he added. "No sign of the airports reopening then?"

"None yet," she said, shaking her head. "I spoke to your Dad earlier and he said they're not expecting any news until tomorrow."

"Ah, poor Dad," said Jane hearing the conversation as she walked into the kitchen.

"'Poor Dad', my backside!" sneered Josh, throwing his sister a contemptuous look. "What's poor about being stuck on holiday? I wish I was stuck in sunny Portugal instead of this dump."

"Oh, that's reeaalll mature, Josh," she countered. "I'm sure that's just what Dad wants — to have to come back from his holiday and work loads of flexi-time to make up for being stranded with a load of disgruntled people in a crowded foreign airport. They only had the hotel booked until yesterday so, he probably doesn't even have anywhere to stay now. So, yeah — I reckon he's having a ball!"

"Ok, Miss Smarty-Arse! If you're so clever, then tell me how if Dad and everyone else can't get out of the country — how are the new arrivals meant to get in? Heh? Didn't think of that — did you, thicko!"

"Knock if off, you two — will ya?" Said Liz, getting up from the table and turning on the grill. "Cooked breakfast?"

"Yes, please, Mum," said Josh, whose humour was greatly improved thanks to his little victory over his sister. "Can I have two eggs?"

"Yeah, well, it'll probably cost him a fortune and I don't reckon Dad'll be happy at all about it — do you, Mum?" asked Jane, petulantly.

"Enough! I said. Now, do you want one or two eggs?"

"Just one, please," she said, pleased with herself for at least managing to have the last word. "Did you tell him about your Life Coaching yet, Mum?"

"No. Not yet. I'm still planning on waiting until he gets back. I kinda want to see his face when he hears. Mind you, it's difficult not to say anything."

"It must be. You should be really proud of yourself, Mum," said Jane. "I think you're going to make a brilliant Life Coach."

"Oh wow! The twerp says something I agree with," scoffed Josh - throwing up his hands in a placatory manner when he found himself on the receiving end of one of his mother's withering looks. "Only joking, Mum," he said, giving her cheeky wink.

"Please let your father get home soon," offered Liz up, as if in prayer. "Otherwise, the only Life Coaching that I'll be doing will be in a high security women's prison where I'll be locked up for murdering you pair. Josh! Set the table. Jane! Empty the dishwasher. Now, move — move — the pair of ya!"

## Hollie

It was close to midday when Hollie resigned herself to the fact that there was no chance of any concrete news regarding flights and, with no real alternative, decided to spend the afternoon by the pool. She had passed the morning, with many of the other guests, sitting around reception waiting for some glimmer of hope that all the airports would re-open and that airlines could begin the arduous task of rescheduling flights to get the back log of passengers home. However, no such news was forthcoming.

The hotel management had assuaged her fear of being without accommodation when they made an announcement that they would retain guests in their current rooms for as long as possible. This, at least, offered relief, although she was still unsure how she was going to be able to pay for the extra nights. From what she could gather when talking to some other residents, it was likely that their holiday insurance would cover any costs incurred, but that still left her with the problem of paying for it and waiting to be reimbursed. It looked increasingly likely that she would need to ask Donal to put it on his credit card as hers was virtually up to the limit and she would need whatever was available on that to live in the meantime. She hated having to ask him, especially now that she knew of his problems with Susan, but if push came to shove — she would.

Walking out into the bright sunshine from the darkness of the reception area temporarily blinded her, causing her to stop in her tracks and blink until her eyes adjusted. The pool area was surprisingly quiet which suited her just fine, as her intention was to read and snooze for the afternoon. She had once again slept fitfully the night before, waking with a jump at the slightest sound, leaving her feeling thoroughly exhausted. She felt safer out here in the open and relished the prospect of a couple of hour's sleep.

The pool looked inviting, but her torso, with its multitude of bruises that seemed to change shape and colour on an hourly basis, prevented her from venturing in for a swim. Instead, she had covered her swimsuit with a beach dress that effectively concealed all her injuries. Selecting a sun lounger in a quiet corner, she adjusted the parasol to keep her sheltered from the sun and settled down with her book. After only a couple of pages, she was fast asleep.

She was woken a short while later by her mobile phone going off and fumbling beneath the towel she was using as a pillow, she pulled it out and looked to see who was calling. Seeing a Spanish number, she started to tremble, automatically assuming it had to be Eoin. Who else would be calling her from a Spanish phone? She didn't want to answer just in case it was him, though surely he would have to have a real brass neck to contact her now. She considered ignoring it, letting it just go to voicemail, but then, angry at the notion of being afraid to answer her own mobile, she pressed the answer button so hard, she accidentally knocked the phone out of her hands. She was busy deliberating whether or not to call the number back, when her phone went again.

"Hello," she said cautiously, waiting to see who was at the other end.

"Hola, is this Hollie?" asked a voice she found vaguely familiar.

"Yes, this is she. Who is this?"

"Ahh, Hollie — this is Maria. Maria Alvarez from the hospital."

"Oh, hello," said Hollie, surprised to be hearing from the friendly young nurse who had helped her through her medical examination. "Is everything okay?"

"Yes. Yes. Fine. I just wanted to see how you were doing."

"I'm fine thanks. Still here, but apart from that, I'm fine."

"Oh, good. Look, Hollie — there is something else. There was a young woman brought in here this morning who had suffered an attack very similar to yours."

"Oh Jesus!" exclaimed Hollie, feeling her blood run cold. She started shaking uncontrollably and her eyes stung with tears. "Is… is… is she alright?"

"Not really, Hollie. She's in a bad way."

"Oh my God," she sobbed. "Is she a local? Is she Spanish?"

"No. She's a young English girl. She's only twenty. A seasonal worker, she does promotions work for one of the local bars. This guy has been hanging around the bar the past couple of nights and she got talking to him. He seemed really nice and she agreed to go on to a club with him last night and woke up black and blue this morning. Like you, she can't remember a thing after the club. She has no idea how she got to be in his hotel and again, like with you, when she woke up — he was gone."

"Oh Jesus! Jesus!" cried Hollie, horrified to think of someone else going through what she had, the terror of that first morning flooding back to her. Through her upset, there was something niggling at her and she struggled to identify what it was. Then, it occurred to her. "But, what makes you think it was Eoin? Did they catch him?"

"No, they didn't," answered Maria. "But, according to her, and this is what leads me to think that it might be him, the guy that she was with last night was Irish. But his name wasn't Eoin, it was, let me see…" Hollie could hear her shuffling through some papers, before she said. "Sean. That was it — Sean."

"Oh," gulped Hollie, disappointed. "But, he could have easily just called himself that. It doesn't mean it wasn't him."

"That's exactly it," said Maria excitedly, "and the thing is, that this time we managed to get a DNA sample. So, if the police do find him, then, they can charge him with this attack and, even if they can't prove that he did that to you, at least now there is a chance he will go to jail. I know it's not much consolation, but I thought it might offer you some."

"It does, Maria — thanks," said Hollie, before adding despondently, "but the thing is, they still have to catch him first."

## Rachel

Rachel's spirits were up. She had woken to find herself alone in the hotel room and anticipating that it was Jack's, now familiar, angst that had caused him to slip out of the room without waking her, she braced herself to put him firmly in his box if he started fretting about Liz. This was her holiday and she had taken just about as much shit as she was prepared to take.

Oozing self-confidence, she went downstairs and striding purposefully out to the terrace restaurant, she scanned the crowd looking for his worry-ridden face, but to her immense relief, it was a very calm and relaxed looking Jack that sat browsing through the Sunday papers in a sun-drenched corner.

"G'morning gorgeous," he offered as she approached, his self-composure seemingly restored to that of the lover with whom she had come away.

"Good morning, Jack," she said, stooping to kiss him on the lips. She felt a bolt of electricity shoot through him, as her lips touched his. She knew for certain that his thoughts were filled with the untold pleasures her lips had given him through the night and not with thoughts of his wife, as she had feared. She pulled back her chair and settled herself down at the table opposite him, smiling seductively as she did so.

He really was quite an attractive man, she thought, eyeing him critically as he endeavoured to get the attention of the waitress who was busily flirting with a table full of 'hooray henrys' at the far end of the terrace. His fair hair, bleached from a week in the sun, was thick and full, with no signs of greying. Despite the presence of some fine lines around his eyes, their vivid blue stood out against his sun-tanned face, giving a youthful appearance. He had kept himself in shape too, with broad shoulders giving way to toned, muscular arms, providing just the body type that attracted her.

And, in fairness, he was pretty good in bed too — almost as good as her, she mused, with a smirk forming on her face.

"What are you grinning at?" he asked.

"Oh, nothing. Just remembering," she said, moistening her lips in a manner designed to turn him on.

"I've done a bit of that myself," he laughed in response, holding her gaze intimately. "Hey, sorry I've been such a wimp these past few days. And I know that you're right, if we keep our wits about us then, there is no reason why Liz would ever find out, it's just that if she did, the double whammy of me and you would destroy her."

"That was always going to be the case, Jack. You knew that and I knew that when we got into this whole thing."

"I know, I know. But who in the hell could have predicted this fucking ash cloud? I mean, why this week of all weeks?"

"I dunno. 'Thems the breaks' — that's all," she said, finding that the direction of the conversation was irritating her. "So, what'll we do today?"

"Whatever you like."

"Well, I was thinking, why don't we take a drive up the coast?"

"Anywhere in particular?"

"Yeah. I was reading about a fabulous sounding hotel, it's a five star, but it's meant to have these amazing landscaped gardens and the restaurant is supposedly to die for. I thought if we took a drive out to there, had some lunch, it would make a nice change to lounging by the pool, what d'ya reckon?"

With a shrug of his shoulders, he said, "Whatever you like. I'm easy."

Driving up the long driveway to the majestic Montanas de Tramuntana Hotel, set at the foot of the mountains that gave rise to its name, Jack let out a low whistle at the sheer opulence of the place. Rachel soaked it all up, she thrived on immersing herself in such luxury and with a 'cat who's got the cream' expression on her face, she stepped from the car, then with only a cursory glance in Jack's direction, she made her way up the entrance steps alone, not bothering to wait for him.

By the time he caught up with her, she had already gone into the restaurant, the review of which had enticed her to visit in the first place, and her face reflected her satisfaction in what lay before her. Sweeping the beautiful 16th century room with her eyes, she took in the magnificence of the two stone arches that rose to a height of at least ten metres where they met in the centre of the dining area. The frescoes that covered the walls were even more striking and vibrant than their photographs depicted. The place oozed sumptuousness as she had hoped that it would.

"Isn't it incredible?" she asked Jack, over her shoulder, without averting her eyes. "It's just so beautiful." Turning around, so as to better gauge his reaction, she let out an involuntary whoop of delight when she spotted the tall, distinguished looking man, standing in line behind Jack waiting to be seated.

"Jeremy! Jeremy Whitticase!" she exclaimed.

CHAPTER SIX

# Sunday PM 18th April

*Denise*

With growing impatience, Denise glanced at the wall clock in the ferry waiting room and wished for the umpteenth time that she was allowed to board the ferry. If she had stopped to think, commonsense would have told her that there was every likelihood the place would be this busy, but she hadn't, and the noisy crowds were grating on her nerves.

Maybe she should have just waited. Another few days and this ash cloud situation would have been resolved and she could have hopped a flight to London, which would have got her there in under an hour. But, when she had weighed it all up, waiting hadn't been an option that appealed to her. She needed to terminate this pregnancy as soon as possible and if that necessitated being transported in a manner more befitting a herd of cattle, then, so be it.

Taking solace from the fact that she was first in line for when boarding began, she determined to find a secluded corner of the ferry, settle in quietly and immerse herself in the promising looking novel she had bought for the journey. The reality proved considerably different however, when on boarding as a foot passenger, she realised the crowd of people who had surrounded her in the waiting room only represented a small proportion of the overall passengers, as hoards more of them teemed up the staircases from the car decks, filling the ship to capacity.

Ahead of the posse, she managed to secure a corner table in the main lounge, which due to the position of a tall cylindrical pillar afforded her just about as much privacy as she was likely to attain. The pillar restricted access from one side and to the other, sat a businessman, studiously poring over a document and looking unlikely to try and engage her in unwelcome conversation. Settling down, she pulled out her book and started to read.

Her heart dropped, when just after the ferry left the dock, a motley looking crew of young fellas, clearly still inebriated from their weekend's revelries, attempted to plonk themselves at a table to the other side of the pillar, but to her immense relief a loud mouthed Cockney accent roared over to them to "Come on over 'ere, mate. There's loadsa room 'ere and we're roight by the bar 'ere — c'mon, 'urry up!"

Her relief must have been palpable, because when she looked up, the businessman was smiling over at her and with a nod in her direction, he said. "Thank Christ for that!" She smiled in response and they both resumed their reading.

Despite admonishments from the cabin crew, the Cockney gang became increasingly raucous throughout the crossing, downing copious pints of lager and belting out tuneless football songs. Her years with John had instilled a deep fear of drunks in her, as she knew, all to well, the unpredictable behaviour that alcohol could produce and although she would have welcomed a mug of coffee, she was reluctant to approach the bar and order one. She flinched nervously when the businessman reached across and tapped her on the arm.

"Oh, I'm sorry. I didn't mean to startle you," he smiled warmly at her. "I'm just heading up to the bar and wondered if I could get you anything."

Unsure at first, she glanced over at the bar where one of the revellers caught her eye and winked at her in a bawdy fashion. Quickly averting her eyes, relief flooded her and she said. "A coffee would be lovely, thanks." Then, reached for her purse.

"No. No, my treat," said the kindly stranger and before she had time to protest he was gone.

On his return, he took the seat opposite her and put two large coffees on the table between them.

"Thank-you," she said.

"No worries," he replied, "I thought the prospect of heading up there would be a daunting one. I'm Donal, by the way, Donal Kavanagh."

"Denise Richardson," she said in response.

"Bloody ash cloud! Who would have thought?"

"I know. It's unbelievable. London always seems so near, but when you have to go this way, it's something else. I think it's about five or six hours on the train as well, which should be fun," she grimaced nodding towards the lads. "I doubt they are driving somehow. I just hope I don't end up in the same carriage as that lot."

"Now, that's not a pleasant thought," said Donal. "I've got my car with me, thank God."

"I was going to take mine, but I'm only in London for a couple of nights and it just seemed like an awful lot of driving for such a short visit. Mind you, I'm beginning to regret it now."

"You'd be more than welcome to take a lift with me," offered Donal, and then sensing her discomfort at the prospect of getting in a car with a total stranger, he added. "Oh, I'm sorry, you don't even know me. Of course, that's the kind of thing my kid sister does all the time and I kill her for it. She can be very reckless and I keep telling her 'Hollie, if you're going to take chances, then, at least, put some safeguards in place. Let someone know who you are with and where you are going.' But, it falls on deaf ears, I mean only yesterday, I called her to find she's in Majorca with God knows who and now, with this ash cloud, for God knows how long."

Denise smiled at the concern that was etched on his face, "Still, it must be nice to have a brother like you to worry about her."

"I'm sure your family would be the same," said Donal and the faraway look in his eye told her that his thoughts were once more with his sister.

"Mmmm," she nodded, not wanting to disclose the fact that there basically was no one to worry about her. Something about this stranger instilled confidence in her and prompted her to make a decision that was completely out of character. "If that offer of a lift still stands, then, I'd be happy to take it. However, if you don't mind, I will take your advice and let someone know what I'm doing."

"Absolutely," agreed Donal and without hesitation he showed her his passport, his hotel booking confirmation and even gave her the registration number of his car. She looked embarrassed, but he insisted that these were the kind of things he was constantly telling Hollie to do. With no one else to call, she took out her iPhone and sent an e-mail to the hotel in which she would be staying.

## Annette

The stallholders were beginning to pack up and the Sunday morning market seemed to be coming to an end. Annette was pleased by this fact as the new sandals she had bought for her holiday had been rubbing incessantly since they'd arrived at the market a couple of hours earlier. A large blister had formed and she was desperate to find a seat and slip the offending sandal off as soon as possible. The girls however showed little sign of slowing down; their frenzied quest was to ensure that no potential bargain went undiscovered and they traipsed tirelessly from one stall to another.

A look in Maureen's direction told her that the older woman had had enough of the market for one day as well, and she jumped at Annette's suggestion that they wait at a little coffee bar across the road for the girls to finish up. All too glad to be rid of their impatient mother and grandmother, the girls bid them farewell and continued foraging through the endless racks of clothes and tons of locally produced handmade jewellery.

The day had turned hot and the sun blazed down on top of the two women as they took a seat outside the coffee bar. Annette gratefully slipped off her sandal and enjoyed the relief of liberating her foot. A smiling young waitress appeared instantly at their table asking them if they would like a parasol to offer them some shade. Unused to the hot sun, Maureen nodded eagerly and the girl slotted the large umbrella into the hole in the centre of the table. Annette adjusted it so that it covered Maureen adequately, but left herself soaking up the sun's rays.

"I've never been much of a sun-worshipper," said Maureen, fanning herself with the plastic menu that the waitress had given them. Then, chuckling to herself, she added, "My memories of family holidays when they were kids, was them all huddled up on the beach in Tramore, shivering like little monkeys with their skin all blue and orange from the cold, refusing to get dressed into their dry clothes 'cos they were too cold to move."

Annette smiled. "Sounds a lot like our holidays too. Except ours were over the west of Ireland, both my parents came from Mayo, so we would always go over there each summer. I remember the first time we came abroad, I was about 17, so Liz would have been 14 and I couldn't believe it. People actually went into the sea for a swim to cool down — not just to prove that they could do it."

"I know. Mine used to challenge each other. 'Last one in is a rotten egg' and off they'd run." She laughed. "Then, Tom would give them each fifty pence to go and spend on the amusements."

"Ah, the simple life," said Annette. "I could just imagine my two spoilt little madams, if that was what was on offer."

"Yes! Indeed!" enthused Maureen, then, blushing she hurriedly added. "Not that I think they are spoilt, it's just…."

"It's just that they are," laughed Annette. "Don't worry Maureen, I'm not offended. Paddy and I have it a lot easier than you and Tom did. For starters, we only have two — you had five — that's a big difference. And besides, foreign holidays just weren't the thing when you guys were bringing up your family."

"They certainly weren't. And, to be honest, even if they were, I can't see Tom wanting to go. He was very set in his ways you know, Annette. Didn't like anything out of the routine. For him, two weeks in Tramore with familiar food and familiar faces was his ideal holiday, bless him."

"And what about you, Maureen? Didn't you ever fancy pastures new?"

A wistful look crossed Maureen's face fleetingly, and then vanished. "Well, yes, there were times that I did, but Tom was the breadwinner and his say was final. I know you probably find that hard to understand, love, but they were different times. We weren't like you and Paddy. Everything seems so… so…, I dunno… equal between you two. For us, Tom was the boss and what he said went."

"I just can't imagine that," said Annette, thinking of her easy going husband and trying to imagine him laying down the law. "Although, I suppose it is a little like that in my sister, Liz's marriage. You know, Jack didn't want her to work, so she didn't. Everything seems to centre around what Jack wants and sometimes I feel that Jack's life just swallows up Liz. I would hate if Paddy were like that, but then again, he never would be."

"No. You're one of the lucky ones," said Maureen. "I know he's my son, but he's a good one. You're a good team, Annette. You and my Paddy."

### Rachel

With a flash of recognition, Jeremy Whitticase's face broke into a broad grin in response to Rachel's enthusiastic greeting.

"Good lord!" he exclaimed. "Rachel Wallace. Whatever are you doing here?"

His English accent held an aristocratic tone that spoke of a private education and a privileged upbringing. He bent down to embrace her, planting a kiss on each of her cheeks. Then, holding her at arm's length, he proclaimed, "You look marvellous, bloody marvellous."

"You're not looking so bad yourself," she replied, with a slightly flirtatious edge to her voice. "It's good to see you, Jeremy. It's been a long time."

"Yes indeed. It must be what, four, maybe five years?"

"Closer to six, I'd say," she said, screwing up her face as she tried to work it out. "I've been back in Dublin almost four years now and you left London a good two years before me."

"Has it really been that long?" he asked, his eyes filling with memories of when they had last met. "You don't look any different."

"I wish," she laughed. "A few more lines and wrinkles, I'm afraid."

"Well, you carry them well, my dear."

Jack cleared his throat behind her, suddenly reminding her of his presence. Apologetically, she turned to him, and placing a hand on his arm, she said, "I'm sorry, Jack. It was just a surprise to see Jeremy here like this. Jeremy Whitticase, this is Jack O'Brien, my partner. Jack this is Jeremy, an old friend of mine from London."

They shook hands and whilst they did so, Rachel felt a sexual thrill rush through her, as their outward affability belied the fact that both men knew that Rachel and Jeremy had been more than just friends. Once again, the illicit nature of her relationships, past and present, excited her.

Jack looked anxious to get away from Jeremy, but before he got a chance to extricate himself, the door of the dining room swung open. A young, overly made-up girl, teetering on heels that were at least six inches high and sporting a mini dress that left little to the imagination, breezed through it. Catching sight of Jeremy, she strutted over and putting her arm proprietarily around his waist, she smiled an orthodontic smile at Rachel and Jack.

"There you are babes," she proclaimed in a strong Essex accent, taking in the others in a glance. "What's the story?"

"Rachel, Jack, this is uh, Wendy."

Rachel had to choke back the laughter at Jeremy's obvious discomfort. He hadn't expected to bump into anyone he knew and the discrepancies between him and Wendy were far too huge to pass off as any manner of real relationship. Clearly they were in Majorca for one reason and one reason only — sex.

Unable to resist the temptation to wreak a bit of havoc, Rachel jumped straight in and asked, "Jeremy — why don't you and Wendy join us for some lunch? It would be such fun."

Despite both men visibly cringing, their fate was sealed, when the gormless Wendy enthusiastically responded. "Oh yes, babes, why don't we?"

## Jack

Unable to believe that Rachel had roped him in to having lunch with this awful couple and not trusting himself to speak, Jack sat glowering at the menu after they were seated. He found Jeremy to be nothing more than a pompous asshole and as for the bimbo he was with, well… Rachel, on the other hand, appeared to be in her element, lapping up the attention from her ex-lover and wallowing in the sexual tension she was creating between the two men.

Her not so subtle innuendos were lost on Wendy who was too busy scanning the room for potential celebrities, clearly awestruck by her opulent surroundings. Just as Jack was contemplating feigning a migraine and suggesting that they return to their hotel, she turned her attention to him, sidling closer to him on the pretext of seeing what he was going to order. Keeping her eyes on the menu, she slid her hand beneath the crisp, white linen tablecloth and eased it slowly onto his crotch, causing him to throw a surreptitious glance at the others to make sure that they couldn't see what she was up to.

With her inimitable expertise, she gently massaged his balls whilst running a carefully manicured index finger down through the menu, keeping her eyes fixed on its contents and asking him what did he fancy. Jack emitted a low groan, which he quickly tried to camouflage with a cough, as he felt himself grow hard. Beads of perspiration formed on his upper lip and he reached for a glass of water.

"I think I'll have the steak," she announced, withdrawing her hand and folding over the menu, giving him a salacious look. "What about you, love?"

"Yeah, yeah. Sounds good to me," he answered, desperately trying to regain his composure, having lost all interest in what he was going to eat. "I'll have whatever you are having."

Somehow or other, he made it through the meal, enduring pompous Jeremy's endless stories that seemed to serve no other purpose, other than to highlight just how important and rich the arrogant sod was. Even Wendy proved more entertaining than him — like something straight off the set of 'Footballers' Wives', she, at least, managed to make Jack laugh on several occasions, although not necessarily intentionally.

At the earliest opportunity, Jack made moves to hit the road and was relieved when Rachel put up no objection. Jeremy's 'big man ego' kicked in and he insisted on paying the bill. Jack was quite happy to let him do so, even though it was nothing more than a blatant attempt at impressing Rachel, whom he was obviously still attracted to.

Once back in the car and finally on their own again, Jack turned to Rachel and despite his earlier annoyance, he grinned at her.

"Well, Miss Wallace? What was all that about?"

"Ah, now, Mr. O'Brien," she smirked sexily back at him. "That was called 'living dangerously'! And don't tell me that you weren't turned on by that, because I held the proof in the palm of my hand."

"You are truly incorrigible, but where on earth did you dig up that obnoxious pratt, Jeremy Whitticase, never mind the glorious Wendy? Do you reckon that she has finished school yet?"

"Ooohh! Nasty!" she laughed.

"I think he's still got the hots for you big time," said Jack, with an attempt at nonchalance as he pulled out on to the main coast road.

"Jealous — are we?" asked Rachel, licking her lips in a provocative manner. "There really is no need to be," she added, once again sliding her hand towards his groin.

"Behave yourself, Miss Wallace!"

"I think you should pull into that lay-by up there," said Rachel, in a husky voice, thick with desire, unfastening his trouser belt and letting her silky blond hair cover his lap as she lowered her head.

### Hollie

The afternoon sun was beginning to lose some of its warmth, but Hollie remained on the sun lounger keeping a watchful eye out for Annette's return. She didn't want to make a nuisance of herself, yet she knew that she had to share the news of this other rape with someone and Annette was all she had.

Eventually, she spotted four figures in the distance crossing the busy main street and heading in the direction of the hotel. Craning her neck around the tall bushes that surrounded the pool area, she satisfied herself that it was Annette, Maureen and the girls. She then quickly gathered up her stuff and made her way to the café area where they would have to pass on their way back into the hotel. Buying herself a Coke, she sat at a table by the low level wooden fence, managing to throw them a casual wave as they walked up the pathway.

"Hey, Hollie," beamed Annette, who walked barefoot, dangling her sandals by the straps. "Room for four little ones?"

Laughing Hollie cast her eye theatrically around at the collection of empty tables surrounding her and said, "I think you could squeeze in here — if you're quick!"

"Oh, thank God for that," said Annette in a tired voice, working her way in through the gap in the fence and plonking down in a chair next to Hollie. "We've just spent the day at the market and I don't think my feet could go two more steps! These bloody sandals are killing me. Look! Look what they've done to my feet."

Hollie made a sucking noise as she took in the multiple blisters and red weals covering Annette's feet.

"Oh, you poor thing," she clucked, sympathetically. "Was it good though? I wouldn't have minded going myself, but I wanted to hang around here to find out what the story was with my room and that."

"And did you?" asked Maureen, taking a seat alongside them, a look of concern registering on her face. "Will you be okay here?"

"Yes. Yes. They were very nice about it and said that for the foreseeable future, they will try to keep all guests accommodated in their current room."

"I bet that's a relief."

"You could sing that," smiled Hollie wanly. "I could really do without being homeless right now."

"Mum, I thing me and Hannah are going to go for a swim — ok?" said Megan, peeking her head through the gap in the fence. "We're all sweaty and horrible from the market."

"It's 'Hannah and I,'" corrected her Mum in an exasperated voice. "And yes, it's grand. We're going to stop here and have a cold drink with Hollie. But, we might be gone up to the room for a shower before you're finished — if so, we'll see you up there. Don't be too long though, 'cos we'll be going for dinner in about an hour or so."

"Cool," she sang over her shoulder as she ran off.

"Honestly, I don't ever remember having as much energy as those two!" laughed Annette, sinking lower into her chair and tilting her face up, with eyes closed, in the direction of the sun.

"I know, they make me tired just looking at them," said Maureen. "In fact, I think I'm going to go up and have a bit of a lie down."

"No problem. I'll see you up there shortly. I'll give you a call when I've had my shower."

"Oh that would be great, love. Thanks."

Hollie felt more comfortable now that she was alone with Annette. Inhaling deeply, she tried to keep the tremor that was rattling inside of her from her voice as she said. "You'll never guess what happened today?"

"Go on," muttered Annette, looking very relaxed.

"I got a call from Maria - the nurse in the hospital. There's been another rape."

Annette's eyes shot open and she sat bolt upright, staring directly at Hollie, willing her to go on.

"Looks like Eoin has struck again."

"Are you serious?" gasped Annette. "When?"

Hollie filled her in on all that Maria had told her, including the fact that this guy went by a different name. Annette listened intently, dismissing as inconsequential the name issue, proclaiming, as Maria had, that DNA was irrefutable.

"Yeah, but they still have to catch him," reiterated Hollie. "And, if they don't have his actual name, that's going to make the process more difficult."

"Yes, I know that. But, you've got to remember that this ash cloud has him trapped on the island, same as everyone else. There's every chance that the police will pick him up on the streets. You can be sure that they will be going around with some kind of a picture, looking for him. Someone, somewhere will finger him and then, he'll be in custody. Tourism is a major part of the economy here, they don't want a rapist, especially 'some foreign guy' on the loose threatening their livelihood."

"You really think they'll catch him?"

"Bloody sure. Think about it this way. If all else fails, he's got to try and leave the island at some stage. The police will have informed the airport security, so, if he evades capture on the street, they will definitely nab him at the airport."

Hollie blanched visibly and her big blue eyes grew even larger when, for the first time, she contemplated encountering Eoin in the airport, or worse still, on the flight.

"Oh Jesus!" she exclaimed, "What if he made it through and ended up on the same flight as me?"

"You're worrying unnecessarily," soothed Annette. "Besides, we'll take a trip to the airport tomorrow and see if the airline can organise it that you are on the same flight back as me, Maureen and the girls. Would that make you feel better?"

"Oh definitely. Who did you fly with? I came with Ryanair."

"So did we," said Annette. "So, I'm quite certain there will be no problem. Now, you must stop worrying."

Not completely convinced that she would be spared another encounter with Eoin, Hollie tried to calm herself down, but fear and unease were still etched on her face and she wished for the hundredth time that she was back home safe in Dublin.

## Donal

With a sigh of relief, Donal finally inched his way off the ferry and slotting in to the long line of traffic, he checked the time.

"Right," he said to Denise. "Ten past three. All things going well, we should be in London about eight or nine o'clock."

"That sounds good. I had resigned myself to not getting there until close on midnight."

"Yeah, it's a bit of a marathon on the train alright. You okay?"

"I'm fine, thanks. Honestly, when we were going down to the car deck and I passed those yobs at the bar and thought about what it would have been like stuck on a train with them for six or seven hours, I could have been sick. Thanks, Donal. I really do appreciate this."

"No worries," he grinned. "I wouldn't have fancied it myself. So, if we're going to be stuck in a car together for several hours — tell me a little about yourself?"

He could feel her tense at his innocuous enquiry and unwilling to cause her any discomfort, he quickly added. "Hey, I didn't mean to be nosy. Don't feel under any pressure. Susan, my wife, always tells me off for sticking my nose into other people's business. I don't do it deliberately, I just like people and am always curious to hear their stories."

"Mine's not that interesting," she replied, for some reason relieved when he mentioned his wife. "I'm single, work in a coffee shop and live a pretty dull life all in all."

"I'm sure that's a bit of an exaggeration," he laughed, but sensing her reluctance to discuss her personal life, he lightly changed the subject. "So, what brings you to London?"

Again, her shoulders tensed and intuitively, Donal realised he had once more ventured into uncomfortable territory for her. "Whoa! I'm sorry. There I go again. Of course, it's none of my business and I didn't mean to pry."

"It's no big deal," she shrugged, his awkwardness strangely putting her at ease, "I'm not very good at talking about myself. When I say that I'm single… well…., that's a recent development and I have some loose ends to tie up in that regard and hence, my trip to London."

"Okay. Fair enough." Then, with a dramatic change of subject, he asked, "So, who do you fancy to win the World Cup then?"

To his surprise, this question amused her intensely, causing her to giggle and rendering her unable to respond.

"What?" he laughed. "What's so funny?"

"Just your change of subject technique," she said. "If you thought I didn't have much to say about my life, I'm afraid I would have even less on the subject of the World Cup. I know sod all about football. And I'm sorry. I didn't mean to appear standoffish; there just truly isn't a lot to tell. But, what about you? What are you up to in London?"

Relieved that the tension had dissipated, Donal chatted away easily about his planned business meeting. He told her how he had come up with an idea a couple of years previously and had spent the intervening time developing it. He explained how he had had to protect his idea by registering a patent for it and the cost and time involved in safeguarding it had meant that he was unable to start selling it until this point. Now he needed either a massive order or an investor to get the project off the ground and he was hopeful that tomorrow's meeting might provide him with the former.

Intrigued, she asked, "Do you mind if I ask what the idea is?"

Months of keeping the whole thing under wraps caused him to hesitate, but then realising that it would soon have to be in the public domain in any case, he shrugged and taking a deep breath, he told her.

"You know when you are on holiday and you go to the beach?"

She nodded. "Well, what's the first thing that you do?"

"Lay out my towel, put on sun screen and…."

He cut across her, "Exactly," he said. "And invariably there are parts that you struggle to reach or sand blows into the cream and the whole process turns messy."

"Guaranteed!" she grinned. "I hate the whole thing, but it's a necessary evil if you want to avoid sun damage."

"Well," he said, his confidence growing. "I've developed a walk through booth, a bit like the one you walk through in airport security. But, as you enter it, you insert a little capsule of sun screen, depending on what factor you want, and you stop for a minute and the sun screen is sprayed evenly all over you, leaving you fully protected."

"That's incredible!" she enthused. "How on earth did you think of that?"

"I dunno. We were in Italy a couple of years ago and it was really windy on the beach and I just got thinking."

"Well, it sounds like a winner to me," she said, obviously impressed. "I think you'll make a lot of money out of this. This guy tomorrow would have to be a fool not to go for it."

Thrilled by her positive reaction, he said, "Let's hope so."

93

CHAPTER SEVEN

# Monday AM 19th April

*Liz*

Swinging the car back into the drive on her return from the school run, Liz determined to make today a day of action. She had spent the entire weekend contemplating the potential for her life coaching and had reached the conclusion that if she was going to go for it, then, she would go for it hammer and tongs. Her meeting with Peter McClafferty wasn't until Friday morning, but that wasn't to say that there weren't plenty of things for her to do in the meantime.

In fact, she was going to start the day by calling him to check on the progress with the website and to pick his brains on other ways to promote herself. Technologically challenged as she was, she knew enough to know that the Internet with all its social networking facilities was the key to making her presence known to a limitless number of potential clients. Familiar with terms such as 'Facebook' and 'Twitter', she was unsure as to how to use them to her best advantage and felt certain that someone like Peter would be far more in the know than her. Of course, the kids could help her familiarise herself with the workings of these forums, but their use of them was purely social, and she needed some guidance as to their commercial value.

Walking through the kitchen, she studiously ignored the breakfast debris that was scattered across the kitchen table and worktops. Her mentor had cautioned her often enough about the potential pitfalls involved in working from home and she was now well versed in the fact that it was imperative to divide one's time into working hours and home hours. She could deal with any household chores at her 'break' times, but otherwise she would avoid the kitchen area other than to make herself a coffee. This she did, then, carried her mug to the computer room where she sat herself down at the uncharacteristically clear desk which she had spent the weekend de-cluttering. "Right," she thought, "time to get cracking!"

The next couple of hours proved very fruitful as, on contacting Peter, she was thrilled to discover that he had already done up a proof of a home page which he e-mailed to her and she was genuinely chuffed with what he had come up with. He had managed to portray her in a professional, yet approachable, manner, instilling a confidence in potential clients that, not only could availing of her services enhance their lives, but to by-pass such a golden opportunity for self-development would be foolhardy in the extreme. They talked through a few minor tweaks to the text, but overall, she loved his ideas and knew for certain that they were singing off the same hymn sheet.

As she had hoped, he was a mine of information regarding social networking and how to use it to her advantage, promising to put together 'an idiot's guide' which would take her through the rudiments of the various platforms and this, he would email to her later on the new email address he had registered for her — info@lobrien.lifecoaching.com.

The conversation with Peter left her feeling upbeat. The whole thing was now definitely in motion and within the next few weeks she would be actively making a living from her coaching. A frisson of excitement shot through her and, as if to validate her progress, she decided to check out her new email address. She loved the professional ring to the new address, so different from the lizluvsya@hotmail.com that Jack so relentlessly teased her about. But this was different; this was professional. Now, her email was the gateway to her practice and there was an undeniable pleasure attached to keying in the address and a moment later her 'in-box' appearing on the screen showing two unread messages awaiting her.

The first was merely a 'welcome' message form Hotmail, and the second a quick note from Peter confirming that he would forward the social networking information to her as soon as he had it compiled. Signing out of her account, she smiled to see the silly names that the kids had applied to their own email accounts. Jack's was the only sober sounding name and she knew that it was his Civil Service background that prevented him from using anything zanier than jackobrien57@hotmail.com. Amused by his conservatism, she scrolled down through the addresses displayed by the various users, mainly friends of Josh and Jane, who accessed their email from the computer — none were as formal as his.

She was just about to cancel out of the directory, when an address caught her eye that unwittingly caused her to smile, bringing back memories of her early dating days with Jack — gr8ass992@hotmail.com. Following an encounter in a night club, Jack had earned himself the nickname 'Great Ass' when a somewhat inebriated, but very attractive, young woman had groped his backside as he passed her and loudly exclaimed, "You've one great ass!". The name had stuck through his twenties and she giggled to herself as she recalled how desperately he had tried to lose it, getting mad as hell with his friends who refused to let it go. The madder he got, the more they persisted and it was only when he learnt not to react that it finally petered out.

Visualising his amusement to learn that one of Josh's cocky friends had assumed the dreaded nickname, caused her to laugh aloud. Momentarily, she felt guilty for assuming that it had to be one of Josh's friends, but she found it difficult to envisage any of Jane's angst-ridden teenage girlfriends giving themselves such a title. She supposed she could be wrong, but the likelihood was that it was one of the lads.

### Denise

The plush surroundings of the private medical centre on Harley Street, failed to disguise the distinctive hospital smells that served as a constant reminder to Denise as to the purpose of her visit. Although not yet 9 o'clock, she had been in the clinic for over an hour already and despite her sublime confidence that she was doing absolutely the right thing in terminating this pregnancy, the waiting for the procedure to begin was making her nervous.

In reality she had only been alone for about fifteen minutes, having been brought to her room directly on arrival. There, an empathetic nurse in her mid-forties had sat with her, explaining in great detail exactly how the medical termination would work, completing the necessary paperwork once she was satisfied that Denise knew what to expect. The nurse had since gone to fetch the Mifepristone, the drug she would be administered with that morning.

Nurse Williams, as her nametag identified her, had explained that this first drug would serve to block the hormone, progesterone, which was essential to maintain the pregnancy. Once this hormone was blocked, the lining of her uterus would start to shed and a return visit on Wednesday morning would be necessary to receive a second medication, Misoprostol, which would cause the uterus to contract, expelling the contents of her womb, cutting her free from John for ever.

She had hoped to head back to Dublin on Wednesday, but Nurse Williams strongly advised that she remain in London for an additional night, as the residual cramping could frequently be quite severe, rendering travel an unpleasant prospect, and one that should be avoided if at all possible. Reluctantly, she had agreed, seeing the sense in the advice offered. In the overall scheme of things, one more night wasn't going to make a huge difference.

To her relief, Nurse Williams returned before her nervousness had a chance to escalate, exuding calm as she walked into the room bearing a small tray with Denise's medication and a glass of water. She sat on the bed beside Denise and in a firm but gentle manner proffered the contents of the tray.

"There you go, love," she said, "Drink this and the whole thing will be over soon."

The nurse's quiet confidence relaxed Denise. Distractedly, she found herself thinking that nursing was definitely more of a vocation than a career, as she obediently popped the tablets in her mouth, washing them down with the water, barely aware of what she was doing, all due to this woman's calm professionalism.

"Thanks, Nurse," she said. "And I don't just mean for the medication. Thanks for your kindness and support."

Blushing, Nurse Williams responded. "All part of the service. Are you all right now, lovie? You looked very nervous."

"No, I'm fine, thanks. Just want to get this whole thing over and done with and get on with my life."

"And you will. But please, do take my advice and be kind to yourself for the next couple of days. Remember, avoid alcohol and smoking. Take the opportunity to rest up in your hotel and if you have any problems at all, or are worried about anything, give me a call. If for any reason, I'm not here, then, speak to Nurse Bennett on this same number. I'll fill her in on your details and she'll look after you."

She handed Denise a card with the clinic's phone number on it. Denise stared at the card before slipping it into her purse. Nurse Williams stood up and smiling at Denise in a reassuring manner, she said. "We'll see you back here on Wednesday morning."

"Yep," nodded Denise, "See you then."

### Donal

In a deep sleep, the alarm on Donal's mobile phone had reached maximum volume before he finally woke up enough to realise what it was. Sleepily, he reached his arm across the bed, patting around until he found the offending item and hit the snooze button. Ten minutes, he promised himself before burying his head back into the pillow. Then, as if hit by a bolt of electricity, he suddenly remembered where he was and what he was doing there. Instantly alert now, he hopped out of the bed and, stopping only to have a pee, was standing beneath the powerful torrent of satisfyingly hot water within seconds.

With the prospect of today's big meeting ahead of him, combined with the anxieties of the last few days with Susan, he hadn't anticipated sleeping as well as he had, but was relieved that he had done so. He needed to be top of his game today and fatigue would have taken some of the sharpness required to give it his all. Today's meeting was the culmination of months of hard work and his one true shot at a better and brighter future for him and Susan. The second she crossed his mind, he felt saddened. Drawing on the 'mindfulness' techniques he had read so much about lately, he forced her from his thoughts, focusing only on the meeting ahead. There would be time enough for Susan later.

It was one of the lads on his five aside soccer team, whom he played with twice a week, that had introduced him to the mindfulness concept which enabled him to push away anxious thoughts about the past or fears for the future and concentrate on the here and now. It was a remarkably calming process and one that he used with increasing regularity.

With a white hotel towel tied around his waist, he towel dried his sandy, short-cropped hair with another, before slathering shaving foam on his face. Having set his alarm in good time, he worked at an unhurried pace, hungrily anticipating the leisurely breakfast that awaited him in the hotel dining room.

Forty minutes later, Donal pushed back the empty plate from his full English breakfast, letting out an inadvertent burp as he did so. Glancing around to make sure that he hadn't been heard, he reached for his coffee mug and gratefully accepted the refill that the waiter offered him. A look at his watch told him that he had the best part of ten minutes to drink it before he needed to be getting on his way.

Recalling the long journey of the day before, he found himself thinking about Denise. Something about her had intrigued him. Perhaps it was just his nosy nature, but he couldn't help feeling curious as to the reason for her trip. She had mentioned loose ends that needed tying up and he wondered what they were. There had been an air of fragility about her that had made him want to reach out and help her, but the shutters on her personal life had been firmly pulled, leaving her privacy impenetrable. Her eyes, which he clearly remembered, and not for their striking blueness, but for their deep sadness, were indicative of traumatic experiences. They reminded him of the numerous pairs of eyes he had seen in the many care homes of his youth — empty, soulless eyes, fearful of the future.

He had been deeply touched when, on dropping her off at her hotel, she had given him her mobile number and asked him to text her and let her know how his meeting went. Even though she clearly had things on her mind, she had seemed genuinely interested in him and his venture. He liked that about her.

Downing the last of his coffee, he made his way to the lift to get to his car in the underground car park. Alone in the confined space, he looked at himself in the mirror and in a self-affirming manner, winked at his reflection, proclaiming aloud, "Showtime!"

## Hollie

With the time difference of an hour between Majorca and Dublin, it was still too early for Hollie to phone work. She had stayed up half the night deciding what was going to be the best way to handle the situation. Still uncertain as to when she could get a flight home, she had decided that she was going to feign a chest infection in the hope that she could buy herself sufficient time to preserve her job. In her favour, she had never missed a day in her two years working there.

Lying didn't come easy to her and if nothing else, this trip had shown her how one single lie could lead to an unimaginable web of deceit that was going to take forever to put behind her. She had felt so bad lying to Niamh in work last Wednesday when she had phoned in sick. They had become good friends over the past eighteen months and Hollie hadn't wanted to compromise her by telling her the truth. One little lie, she had told herself, planning on telling her the truth on her return. But now, she was about to tell her another one and God knew how many more she could have to tell before this nightmare ended.

Of course, this also meant that she could never tell her about the rape. That was a big secret to keep from a close friend, but what choice did she have? Yet another consequence resulting from her foolish actions. Feeling herself being sucked in to the downward spiral of guilt and despair that had kept her awake, she forced herself back to the task in hand. A quick time check told her that Niamh would, in all probability, be at her desk by now and taking her courage in her hand, she keyed in the clinic's number to her mobile.

"Good morning Greendale Medical Centre," sang Niamh's familiar voice down the line after only a couple of rings. "Niamh speaking. How can I help you?"

Having answered the phone to enough sick patients over the years, Hollie spoke in what she hoped was a credible manner for someone suffering with a chest infection.

"Hey, Niamh," she began, closing over the back of her throat to give her voice a nasal quality. "It's me, Hollie."

"Jesus Hols! You sound rough."

A series of coughs and splutters followed before Hollie spoke again. "I am. I've got a terrible chest infection and I'm not going to be in for a few days."

"Ah, you poor thing!" said Niamh. "I bet it was that awful auld fella who was in here last week — remember? He never once put his hand over his mouth, just coughed his guts up all over the reception desk."

In spite of the circumstances, Hollie laughed, then quickly coughed for effect, as she remembered Niamh's annoyance at the elderly gentleman whom she had slapped a box of tissues and a hand sanitizer in front of in an unceremonious fashion.

"Anyway, Hols," she continued. "Sounds like you need to get yourself back to bed."

"I think you're right," coughed Hollie, in a suitably pathetic voice. "I'll give you a shout later in the week. Tell them I'm sorry about this."

"To be perfectly honest, I don't think they'd thank you for showing up in this condition — you'd frighten all the patients away! People come here to get better, not catch the bubonic plague."

"Gee thanks!" said Hollie. "Now, I feel like a giant germ!"

"No worries!" chuckled Niamh. "All part of the Greendale Medical Centre experience. Now, go on, back to bed with ya and I'll talk to you soon."

Hanging up the phone, Hollie heaved a sigh of relief. At least that was over.

## Jack

Try as he might, Jack couldn't forget Rachel's performance in the car yesterday. He had lain awake since early morning contemplating his future. The chance meeting with Jeremy the day before had stirred a thought process that he couldn't seem to shake off. He didn't want to give this woman up

101

— it was as simple as that.

There had been something about the way that Jeremy had looked at her yesterday. His eyes had been filled with longing, but it was more than that, it was more than longing - it was regret that Jack had seen. Jeremy Whitticase, pompous ass that he was, clearly regretted losing Rachel.

And now, Jack was on the horns of a dilemma. He knew he couldn't carry on having an affair with her - that just wouldn't work. Sooner or later, they would be discovered and the fall out from that would be incredible. He couldn't do that to Liz and the kids. But neither could he face ending things with Rachel. At first, he had convinced himself that it was just sex. Now he knew that wasn't the case. She made him laugh; she excited him; she challenged him; she thrilled him in a way he never could have imagined. He felt more youthful with her than he had felt in years, more alive. In short, he was in love with her.

He had sworn never to let this happen, least of all with his wife's best friend. Christ, what a bollocks he was. It may never have been his intention for things to develop this way, but they had. Now, he had to decide what to do about it. They had never even discussed the possibility of a future together. It had simply never been on the agenda. But, yesterday had changed things. For him, anyway. And, although he couldn't be certain, he was pretty sure that what they had was important to her too.

## Annette

The marble floor tiles felt refreshingly cool to the soles of Annette's feet as she plodded sleepily across them, making her way to the bathroom. The air-conditioning was on a timer and had gone off during the night, leaving the hotel suite feeling hot and stuffy. It sounded very loud in the early morning silence when she flicked it back on. She doubted very much that it was loud enough to disturb the girls, but would more than likely wake Maureen, who was a very light sleeper. She put extra water into the kettle, as Maureen was bound to want a cup of tea as soon as she was up.

She was surprised when there was no sign of her mother-in-law by the time the kettle was boiled. Making her a cup of tea, she went and tapped gently on Maureen's door. No reply. Turning the handle softly, she silently eased the door open. The bed was empty. Momentarily perplexed, she had a vague recollection of Maureen mentioning something that she was planning on doing in the morning when they were sitting at the terrace bar the previous night.

The girls, as usual, had headed down to the town with Jody and Debs, leaving Maureen and Annette to watch the very mediocre singer, whom the hotel had booked for the night's entertainment. What he lacked in talent, he made up for in enthusiasm and despite a woeful performance, he was strangely enjoyable. Spotting them sitting alone, Jody's mum, Ruth had kindly invited them to join their table and they had ended up having a right laugh.

Ruth and her husband Simon had been like a comedy double act, with a barrage of one-liners flying between them. Annette struggled to recall even one of the razor sharp comments, but couldn't, despite having spent the entire evening cracking up. There had just been too many of them, her aching sides bearing testament to that fact. The other couple, Ruth's sister, Ellen and her husband, Pete, were a lot quieter, but equally friendly and by the time it came to walk down to meet the girls, Annette felt as if she'd known them all for years. She gratefully accepted Ruth's offer to walk down with her, leaving Maureen chatting away nineteen to the dozen with a group of retired people sitting at the next table.

A warm feeling had enveloped her as she'd walked companionably with Ruth, trading snippets of information about their respective lives. It struck her that, despite a very shaky start, she was actually enjoying this holiday far more than she would have thought possible. She knew that this unlikely outcome would amuse Paddy who still managed to sound uneasy for not only abandoning her, but also, abandoning her with his mother. She made a mental note to call him in the morning and put his mind at rest.

When she and Ruth had returned with the girls, Maureen had bid them all good night, saying she had plans for the morning and needed to get to bed. For the life of her, Annette couldn't remember what they were. Shrugging her shoulders, she went to get her mug of coffee and her book, and then headed out on to the balcony to catch the early morning sun whilst she drank it.

Although it was still early, not yet nine o'clock, there was a tremendous amount of noise coming from the pool area. Whoever it was, they were certainly having a good time, she mused, judging by the peals of laughter that carried on the wind. Intrigued, she laid her book down on the table and went to the other side of the balcony where she would have full view of the pool.

The sight that greeted her eyes caused her to spontaneously combust with laughter. Maureen and two of her cohorts from the senior group she had been sitting with the night before, were partaking in a water aerobics class. Displaying an inordinate lack of coordination, they desperately attempted to follow the direction of the eager young male instructor who was studiously avoiding looking at them, concentrating his efforts on the more able bodied members of his class to the front of the pool.

The three pensioners, occupying the back row, showed no signs whatsoever of being part of the same class as the other participants. Every time the synchronised movements of the first three rows moved to the right, they moved to the left; when everyone else was immersed in water, Maureen and her friends stood bolt upright with their arms akimbo, causing them to collapse in a heap of giggles. It was as outrageous a spectacle as any of the scenes from the slapstick American movies that the girls so liked to watch, with a feel good factor second to none.

Not wanting the girls to miss this fabulous moment, she hurried inside to call them. Almost knocking her over, they crashed through the doorway seconds later as she went in search of her mobile phone to call Paddy.

### *Rachel*

Unable to believe her ears, Rachel asked Jack to repeat what he had just said.

Shifting uncomfortably in his seat, he said. "Ah, c'mon Rach. Don't look so shocked. You must have thought about it yourself at some stage."

Of course she had thought about it, but it had never occurred to her that he had. Choosing her words carefully, she said. "This was only meant to be a bit of fun, Jack."

"Christ!" he exclaimed, "Do you think I don't know that! But it's turned into something more. I don't want to lose you, Rachel. We both know that this can't continue as it is. It's piss or get off the pot time."

"And, what about Liz?" she asked disparagingly.

"What about Liz!" he retorted, guilty anger welling up in him. "Sure, she'll be hurt. But, marriages…., marriages break up all the time. It's the way it goes these days. Better I leave her now while she's young enough to start again, than live a lie."

"Oh! So, you're doing her a favour now, are you?"

"You know that's not what I mean. But the fact is, things have run their course with Liz. It's over."

"Forgive my cynicism, Jack, but it's not all that long ago since you told me that you love her."

"Of course I fucking love her. She's been a part of my life for twenty fucking years. She's the mother of my children. Yes, I love her, but I'm not in love with her — I'm in love with you. I love Liz like I love my sister, she's a good person, a great mother, but that's not enough for me. I thought it would be. I thought I could live out my days with Liz and the kids on one hand and that the odd fling here and there would keep me satisfied."

"Jesus! You're some prick! Is it all about you?"

"Now, Rachel, come on. You're one to talk about self-serving. Maybe that's why we work so well together. We're both selfish."

She went to argue with that statement, then thought better of it. "I don't understand though, Jack. Where did this all come from? You've maintained all along that you were quite happy to keep this casual — a bit of fun, nothing more."

"Yeah, well, I hadn't counted on falling for you like this. I saw the way that pillock, Jeremy, looked at you yesterday. Clearly, he regrets losing you. It just got me thinking. I've had loads of regrets in my life. I've always chosen the safe route. You know — nice cushy job in the Civil Service, permanent and pensionable; four bed semi-detached home; nuclear family — one of each; wife who is the perfect homemaker. It's all very safe. But Christ, it's also all so boring."

"I think the sun has got to you Jack. You're talking like a mad man."

"Rachel, I've never felt more sane in my life. I want to be with you — it's as simple as that. Now, if you don't want to be with me, that's a different story. But, if you do, then, let me worry about sorting my end of things out."

Looking a bit confused, she nodded silently. Her thoughts were racing around in circles. She hadn't expected this conversation — not now, and she knew that she couldn't allow herself be pushed into making a decision without giving the matter due consideration. She had spent her entire adult life carefully avoiding commitment to any one man. But, here she was now, pushing forty — was it finally time to settle down? And, if so, was Jack O'Brien the man to do it with?

The more she tried to think about it, the more melted her head became, until the first stirrings of a headache brought her to her senses. "Whoa! Jack. You can't honestly expect me to answer this here and now. You spring this on me without any warning. I have to think about this — long and hard. You're going to have to leave it with me for a bit. I'll get back to you on it as soon as I've thought it through."

Not entirely happy with her response, but accepting the fact that there was little he could do about it, Jack nodded. "Okay Rach. But, make it sooner rather than later. There's a lot riding on this."

"I know," she said, with the faint traces of a smile. "I'm not doing this to torture you. I just need to think it through clearly. I'll get back to you soon — I promise."

CHAPTER EIGHT

# Monday PM 19th April

*Donal*

Donal was pissed off. But, he knew that he had to keep his emotions in check. The entire morning had been nothing more than a waste of time. He had arrived at the impressive headquarters of The Transglobal Travel Corporation about fifteen minutes ahead of schedule, only to be told by an incredibly snobby sounding, receptionist that Mr. Arthur Carter, Transglobal's Chief Executive, was away from the office for a couple of days and wasn't expected back until Wednesday afternoon.

"That can't be right," said Donal, attempting to keep his voice level and a friendly smile fixed on his face, despite the sinking feeling in his stomach. "Just bear with me," he said, "I have an email here somewhere from Mr. Carter, confirming our appointment."

A slight shrug of her shoulders accompanied a look of contemptuous indifference towards Donal and his plight, as he fumbled through his jacket pockets in search of the email. The switchboard lit up and in a voice completely at odds with her grumpy looking face, she tapped a couple of keys and sang into the mouthpiece.

"Good morning — The Transglobal Travel Corporation. This is Tina speaking — how can I help you this morning?"

To Donal's relief, he had retrieved the email by the time she had put the call through. Sliding the piece of paper towards her, he made a quick mental note to accept her apology graciously, allowing them the opportunity to start again. After all, if he was going to be doing a lot of business with the company, he didn't want to start off making enemies, even if it was with one of the more junior members of staff.

She skimmed over the email, gave another superior shrug of her shoulders, then, pointing with a red taloned index finger at a line of the text, she said in a patronising voice. "As I said, Mr. Carter is away until Wednesday. If you read this email carefully, you will see that your appointment is with Mr. Carter's office, not with Mr. Carter himself. Now, if you would like to take a seat over there, I'll contact Mr. Wilson - Mr. Carter's assistant, and see if he is available to see you."

With a mixture of annoyance and humiliation, Donal shuffled over to the seating area, dragging the large plastic case that contained a collapsible prototype of his spray booth with him. Refusing to let a jumped up little wagon like Tina rattle him, and possibly scupper his chances of pulling off a professional presentation, he once again employed his mindfulness techniques to calm himself, in readiness for his meeting. It was obviously disappointing not to be meeting with the head honcho, but perhaps it had been naive of him to assume that that was whom the initial meeting was with. After all, Transglobal was exactly as the name suggested — a multi national corporation and he had done very well to secure a meeting in the first place.

After only a couple of minutes, the elevator doors pinged and a young woman came out. Smiling at him, she extended her hand and introduced herself as Mr. Wilson's secretary, offering to bring him on up to the meeting room. She seemed a lot friendlier than Tina, even laughing good-humouredly at his attempts to wheel the large plastic case into the lift, the confined space leaving little room to manoeuvre, but made no attempt to help him. She then pressed the button to take them to the fourth floor. Having taken him into the meeting room, she established that he would like a few minutes on his own to set up, offered him a choice of tea or coffee; then, went in search of her boss.

Donal set about preparing his presentation, continually telling himself that perhaps this wasn't going to be a waste of time, but his hopes were once more dashed when Mr. Wilson finally made his appearance some twenty minutes later. Far from being the high-ranking executive that Donal had been anticipating, Mr. Wilson looked like he was on day release from school. A gangly, acne covered youth, in an ill-fitting suit, he sat disinterestedly through Donal's presentation, neither making comments, nor asking questions. Then, when Donal concluded, he nodded silently, gathered up his unused pen and paper, and headed straight for the door.

A bemused Donal, followed him with his eyes, and he was half way out the door, before he spoke for the first time.

"Very interesting, Mr. Kavanagh," he said, "very interesting. I'm quite certain Mr. Carter would like to meet with you personally. How long are you in London for?"

"Well, I was only planning on being here for the day, but…"

Young Mr. Wilson interrupted him, "I really think Mr. Carter needs to see this. It is definitely the kind of innovative product that he would be interested in. Would Wednesday afternoon suit? Say, about three o'clock?"

Totally non-plussed by the whole experience, Donal nodded his consent to the Wednesday afternoon meeting, keeping his irritation at the way he had been treated hidden. Finding himself alone in the meeting room again, he packed up his kit and wondered if Transglobal staff members were this rude to all their guests. By the time he had hauled the case back to the lift single-handedly, he was questioning the wisdom of agreeing to another meeting.

### Annette

The girls had arranged the night before to go to the water park with Jody and Debs, and were eagerly packing up their beach bags.

"Sure you don't wanna come, Mum?" teased Megan, knowing how much her mother hated water slides.

"Eh, no thanks," laughed Annette. "Thank God you pair found someone to go with or I'd have been bullied into taking you. But promise you'll be careful. No showing off in front of your new friends."

"As if!" said Hannah in a scornful manner. "We're not babies you know, Mum. We're all really good swimmers and in any case, there are loads of life guards about."

"Yeah, I know. It's just sometimes messing about can get out of hand and that's how accidents happen."

More sensitive to her mother's worries, Megan gave her a hug. "Don't worry Mum, we'll behave — honest."

"Ok. Well, just make sure you all come back in one piece. I don't want any broken bones, or missing teeth or …."

"Yeah! Yeah, Mum. Whatever!" laughed Hannah. "Look we've got to go. We said we'd meet them at one o'clock at the pool and it's nearly that now. Byeeee!"

And, they were gone. Feeling a bit hungry, Annette went in search of Maureen to see if she fancied some lunch before she headed off with Hollie to the airport to ensure they could all travel back together when the damn ash cloud finally disappeared.

She had little difficulty locating her as she rounded the corner into the pool bar area and heard the roars of laughter coming from the 'pensioner's club' in the corner. Maureen had certainly found her feet with her new pals and the noise from them could compete with any gang of teenagers anywhere. Several of the group appeared to be a little hard of hearing, which accounted for the level of noise they produced. Annette smiled when she saw camp Denis, the waiter; melodramatically clamp his hands over his ears every time that he passed their table.

"Ooohh! She's such a bad influence," he said, throwing his eyes in Maureen's direction. "I reckon she's the ring leader!"

Laughing, Annette shrugged her shoulders in a 'what can I say' gesture and headed over to her mother-in-law. "Hey, Maureen. You ready for a bit of lunch?"

"Oh, definitely," came the reply as Maureen grappled around under her seat for her handbag. "Excuse me everyone, but all that aqua aerobics this morning has left me starving. The man was a monster — he worked us within an inch our lives," she added, theatrically with a sardonic grin on her face.

Her new friends giggled appreciatively at her wit. "You are a card, Maureen," said one of them. "I think the poor man was trying to pretend that we weren't there. And, I certainly bet that he's hoping that we won't be back tomorrow."

"Well, he's in for a bit of a disappointment then, isn't he ladies?" said Maureen, with a twinkle in her eye.

"You betcha!" chirped Maisie, a rotund seventy-something woman with a tight silver perm. "We'll show 'em a thing or two in the morning — won't we Maureen?"

Another peal of laughter reverberated as Annette cupped her hand beneath Maureen's elbow and escorted her off to another table.

"What are you like, Maureen?" she laughed, sitting down and pulling over the menu. "Paddy's going to think his sweet, quiet mother has been abducted by aliens and this 'life and soul of the party' replica has replaced her. Seriously though, it's great to see you having such a good time. You really should try and join a couple of social groups when we go back to Dublin. You'd have a ball."

"That's exactly what Maisie and Lilly were saying to me earlier. They are both widows and they reckon they'd be lost without their over-sixty's clubs. Lilly's husband sounds like he was a lot like Tom. You know, set in his ways and all that. She had never even been out of England before he died. Now, she goes on a trip every three or four months."

"That sounds great," enthused Annette. "You really should look into it. All your lot are well settled now and it's time you had a bit of 'me time'. I never even thought about it before, but you'd have great craic. Actually, I didn't really think you'd be into it, but seeing you here — it strikes me that you are having the time of your life."

"I suppose I am," she grimaced guiltily. "Is that terrible — so soon after Tom has passed away and all?"

"Not at all," soothed Annette. "I'm quite sure that even if this wasn't Tom's cup of tea, that he'd be more than happy to see you enjoying yourself."

"Maybe," said Maureen, not looking altogether convinced.

## Hollie

Holding her breath and offering up a silent prayer to the powers that be, Hollie slipped her cash card into the ATM, selecting the English menu. Optimistically, she tried to withdraw fifty Euro, but as she had known it would, the screen told her that there were insufficient funds in her account. She repeated the process with ever decreasing amounts until the hateful machine reluctantly relinquished twenty.

"Fuck!" she said aloud, then turned to ensure she hadn't been overheard, snatching the money and card she headed back to the hotel. What was she going to do now? There was still no sign of the ash cloud shifting and she could be stuck here for days yet. Twenty quid wasn't going to get her very far. There was no option; she was going to have to call Donal to see if he could lend her some money. She really hadn't wanted to do this, especially with him away in London at his 'make or break' meeting.

She knew that he would be okay with it, she just hated asking. It seemed that she was always getting him to bail her out of some predicament or other. He never made a big deal out of it, but she knew that her lack of self-sufficiency worried him. At least he couldn't hold her responsible for the ash cloud, but running out of money two thirds of the way through the month…again.

Bracing herself for the inevitable lecture about managing her finances, she keyed in his name to her phone, breathing in deeply as she did so.

"Hey Hols," he answered, sounding a little subdued. "How are things?"

"Yeah, yeah — not bad," she said, and then taking her courage in her hands, she launched straight into the purpose for the call. "Actually, Donal — and don't give out to me, please. But, I could really do with borrowing some money. Just 'til the end of the month. It's just I'm still stuck in Majorca and I'm all out of cash. I'm sorry to ask, but I don't really know what else to do."

Amused by her breathless outburst, he said, "Calm it, Hols, will ya? I know you're stuck in Majorca. Half the world is stuck somewhere. But, cut to the chase — how much and when?"

Instant relief washed over her as she realised he was once again coming to her rescue. "I dunno, a hundred; hundred and fifty? It all depends on how long I'll be here. And eh… nowish?"

He laughed. "I should have known! Now, the only problem is that I'm in London and it looks like I'll be here until Wednesday or Thursday. I can lodge some money into your account when I get back — but, is that too late?"

"I'm really sorry, Donal, but yeah. I literally have twenty quid left on me." She knew that she sounded anxious, but there was no way she could last out a couple of days without money.

"Okay, well let's think about this. There has to be a way. Ah, Western Union. That should do it. I'll check it out this end and give you a call back later. As far as I know it's pretty straightforward. I pay money in to a Western Union agent here and you can collect it your end. It's pretty much instantaneous, so I should be able to get something to you later today. How's that sound?"

"Ah, Donal — you're a life saver! Thanks a million. And tell me — how did the big meeting go?"

"Oh, don't even go there," he groaned. He filled her in on the morning's events and his disappointment was palpable. "In fact, I don't even know yet if I'm going to hang around for Wednesday's meeting or not."

"Don't be daft!" she exclaimed. "You've got to go to that. That's the way these big corporations operate. They use the minions to weed out the chaff from the seed. The way I see it — you've just been promoted to 'seed' and the main man thinks your idea warrants a meeting. This is not a bad thing, Donal. I honestly think you would be mad to quit now. Hang on — see what the meeting brings. It could be really good."

"Ever the optimist," he laughed at his younger sister's words, the lift in his voice telling her that she had succeeded in raising his spirits. Pleased with herself, she rang off.

Just as she was slipping her phone back into her bag, she spotted Annette and Maureen walking through the hotel lobby and called out to them.

"Oh hi!" said Annette. "I was coming to find you. I thought we might head out to the airport about five o'clock — if that suits you?"

"Yeah, that would be grand."

"I just thought it might be a bit cooler by that time."

113

"No, that's perfect. I've a couple of things to do first, so, I'll see you here about five."

She was relieved at this arrangement, as it should allow her pick up some money beforehand so she could pay her share of the taxi.

## Denise

In an attempt to keep herself occupied and her mind off what was happening to her body, Denise decided to take a trip down Oxford Street. She had been to London several times and the buzz of the main shopping street had always excited her. Taking the underground to Oxford Circus, she emerged, blinking at the strong spring sunlight and tried to get her bearings.

It was still only eleven thirty, but already the street was alive with eager shoppers. Loud music blared from the various shop fronts as she ambled aimlessly down the road. People hurtled in and out, carelessly cutting across the pavement in front of her, almost knocking her off her feet. Stepping nearer to the curb in order to avoid them, she found herself inhaling the noxious fumes from the many red buses and large black taxis impatiently making their way through the city centre and the smell made her stomach heave, rudely reminding her of her soon-to-be-over unwanted pregnancy.

Realising that another half hour would see the crowds swell with the start of lunch hour for the many office workers in the surrounding streets, she wondered if she might abandon the notion of shopping and simply head back to the hotel. A series of collisions from reckless young mothers, using their baby buggies as missiles to make their way through the crowds, confirmed her discomfort and she headed back to the underground.

The currents of air in the tube station were heavy and warm, carrying their own unique odour that once again had her feeling nauseous. She rejoiced in her decision to return to the hotel and hoped fervently that she would get a seat on the tube as she thought that swaying around, trying to keep her balance whilst holding on to the overhead bobbles that hung from the roof of the carriage, combined with the musty, overbearing smell would surely make her throw up.

To her relief, the carriage was half empty and she settled into an end seat, with her head resting heavily in her hand, concentrating on swallowing down the bile that persistently rose to her mouth. Her stomach had begun cramping and the short ten-minute journey to the station nearest to her hotel, seemed endless. All she wanted was her bed and some sleep. Her mobile phone started to vibrate in her pocket, thankful for the distraction; she pulled it out and looked at it.

Seeing the name 'Donal' on the screen, she had to momentarily think who on earth that was. Then, she remembered — her saviour from the day before. His meeting must be over she guessed, opening the message to see how it had gone.

Mtg bit of a washout. Stuck here 4 2 more days. Hope ur day going better. Donal.

She was sorry to hear that. He had been so excited about it. But, clearly all must not be lost if he had to stay in London for a couple of more days. Taking heart in that thought, she texted him back.

Still any hope?

Some. Tell you later over bite to eat?

Unsure how she would be feeling later, she didn't want to commit, but equally, she didn't feel up to a prolonged texting session or a conversation, so it seemed simpler just to reply.

Maybe. Can't talk at mo. Txt u l8r.

## Rachel

Rachel lay back on her sun lounger, ostensibly engrossed in the paperback book that was perched on her flat stomach. However, if anyone had been watching her they would have seen that she hadn't turned a page for over half an hour. Her mind was swimming with her earlier conversation with Jack. What he was suggesting was pretty huge. She wasn't entirely convinced that it was his brain and not his dick that was doing the thinking.

But, what if he really meant it? She had always deemed herself to be a pretty good judge of men and where her various dalliances with them were taking her. But this, this had blindsided her. She hadn't seen this coming. Normally when she read the danger signs that things were getting too serious, she did a moonlight flit. Could it be that she was losing her touch? Or was there something more to Jack O'Brien that had distracted her?

She knew that she liked him. And in fairness, she had normally tired of a man by this stage. It must be nearly eighteen months that they'd been together. That, for her, was a record. But, did she love him? Did she even know what it was to love somebody? Yes, he made her laugh; yes, he made her feel good and yes, there were even times when she found herself looking forward to seeing him to share some snippet of news or other that she knew would amuse him. Was that love? Maybe it was.

An endless barrage of questions circled round and round in her head. She would be forty before the end of this year, perhaps it was time to settle down, and maybe, just maybe, Jack was the one to do that with. In his favour, he had already had a family — something she had never wanted, so kids would never be a thorny issue for them. Also, he was financially secure, not wealthy by any means, but secure, and with a couple of properties, he would still be left more than comfortable, notwithstanding any divorce settlement. Yes, perhaps he was a better long-term prospect than she'd realised.

Of course, there was Liz to consider. She allowed herself a moment of guilt about her, but knew that in the overall scheme of things, she wouldn't waste too many thoughts on her. Liz was nice enough; she'd had a good laugh with her over the months. Rachel had never valued female friendships all that much. If the truth be told, women bored her — especially the 'nice' ones like Liz. They had no drive, no ambition. Christ, women like Liz didn't even have a career — gave it all up to be the perfect wife and mother and then, when they had achieved their boring little goal, sat back, conceited, assuming it would all be there forever.

She had nothing on her conscience about 'stealing' Liz's husband, because she knew that such a thing wasn't possible. If Liz had wanted her marriage to work, then she should have invested time and energy into ensuring that it did. Instead, she grew complacent, thinking only of herself and the kids, edging her husband out of the picture until it reached the point where he sought validation for himself elsewhere. A string of sordid little affairs until she, Rachel, came along and won his affections. No, she wasn't the cause of the marriage breakdown, a catalyst maybe, but not the cause - Liz only had herself to blame for that.

If Rachel decided that a future with Jack was what she wanted, then, she would happily sacrifice her friendship with Liz. And, right here, right now, she felt herself warming to the notion.

## Jack

Feeling quietly confident, Jack stretched and announced that he was going for a swim, inviting Rachel to join him, even though he knew that she wouldn't. He could tell by her face that she was still mulling over all the options entailed in committing to a future with him. His earlier suggestion had taken her completely by surprise, but the fact that she hadn't dismissed it out of hand, meant that she was giving it due consideration and he was optimistic about the outcome.

He was determined to keep his cool, not pester her for a decision, knowing that any sign of weakness on his part at this stage would blow the whole thing. Walking to the edge of the pool, he dived into the water, crisply breaking its surface and remained underwater virtually the entire length of the pool. He had the pool to himself and taking advantage of this fact, he swam several lengths without stopping. Finally, he pulled himself out by hoisting his upper body up by his arms, turned and sat with his feet dangling in the water, basking in the sun as it quickly dried his muscled torso.

It was from that vantage point that he saw her looking at him. All pretence at reading had been abandoned and she gazed intently in his direction. Seeing him notice her, she smiled and that was the point he knew for certain that his confidence had not been misplaced.

## Liz

Engrossed in her morning's activities, Liz was surprised to learn that it was almost half past one when she checked the time on her phone. Where had the morning gone? Still, she was more than satisfied with the fruits of her morning's labour. Peter had forwarded her a 'social networking for dummies' guide, which she found invaluable. In a few short hours she had achieved a

117

far greater knowledge of this incredible forum than she could have dreamed possible. No longer intimidated at the prospect of using these tools to further her practice, she now understood how simple and effective they were and that it truly was only a matter of familiarising herself with them. She now knew that it wasn't rocket science and continuous usage would have her adept in no time.

Packing up her desk for the day, she switched roles back to 'mum'. She had several errands to attend to before she picked the kids up from school, so she busied herself with giving the kitchen a quick once over before heading out to do some grocery shopping. It was going to take some getting used to switching roles in this manner, but if this morning was anything to go by, she figured that she was going to enjoy it.

Accustomed to doing her shopping early in the morning, she gave a sigh of exasperation on seeing just how busy the supermarket car park was, necessitating a couple of circuits before she found a parking place. Unable to park near her usual entrance, she glanced about to see where the nearest trolley bay was. Relieved to see that it was only a couple of rows over, she was pulling her bag strap up on to her shoulder when something caught her eye, causing her to swing back around in the direction of the trolley bay.

There, parked right next to it, was the distinctive, red, Maserati Gran Cabrio belonging to Jimmy Kinsella, one of the golfing buddies of Jack's that he was away in Portugal with. Liz couldn't help but smile. Wait until she told Jack that Pauline had taken out the Maserati while Jimmy was away — that would really crack him up. Pauline had been hilarious when Jimmy arrived home with that car, absolutely losing her head, calling him every kind of a dickhead under the sun. She had point blank refused to even go for a spin in it, telling him in no uncertain terms that, if this was how he dealt with his mid-life crisis, then, she wanted no part of it. Now, with Jimmy away, she was swanning around Dublin in it — how funny was that?

Liz loved Pauline. She was a total no-nonsense merchant — said it like it was, no matter what the fall out. Her directness often landed her in trouble, but in Liz's eyes, she was the most honest person she knew. That's what made this episode so amusing, Liz would have to swear Jack to secrecy - perhaps on reflection, she would wait until he got home to tell him, not wanting to rat out Pauline to Jimmy. It was unrealistic to expect Jack to keep that to himself under the circumstances. No, she would say nothing. Well, and the thought that was forming in her mind made her laugh aloud, she might just give Pauline a call herself later — just to slag her. That's exactly what she'd do — this was far too good an opportunity to miss.

CHAPTER NINE

# Monday Evening 19th April

*Annette*

The entrance into the airport was like a giant car park when Annette and Hollie arrived in their taxi. Opting to make the rest of the way on foot, Annette paid off the taxi driver, and brushing away Hollie's attempt to contribute to the fare, they climbed out of the car.

"No, Annette, please," protested Hollie, thrusting fifteen Euro into Annette's reluctant hand. "My brother sent me some money this afternoon. It's bad enough that I'm dragging you away like this, without you footing the bill."

Annette acquiesced, seeing that it was causing Hollie more stress to decline. The interior of the airport terminal was not as crowded as the entrance way had led them to fear it would be. There was something very eerie about seeing the large departure boards displaying all flights as cancelled — like something from a Sci-Fi movie following an alien invasion of earth. With far greater ease than they had anticipated, they made their way through the concourse and up to the Ryan Air desk, where they joined a lengthy, yet moving, queue.

The staff behind the desk looked weary. Annette's heart went out to them. The ash cloud was not their fault, but they looked as if they had been on the receiving end of some serious abuse through the course of its disruption. After about half an hour of queuing, a pretty girl with long straight blonde hair and a tired smile waved them forward and looked infinitely relieved to be greeted civilly by both Annette and Hollie.

In her best maternal manner, Annette took charge and Hollie was more than happy to let her do so, feeling embarrassed and awkward as Annette openly detailed the reasons behind their request to secure Hollie a place on the same return flight as her. Taken aback by the nature of the request, the young stewardess glanced surreptitiously in Hollie's direction, noticing her downcast eyes and uneasy demeanour and instantly reassured Annette that she would personally do all that she could to guarantee her a place on Annette's flight.

"However," she said, "I have no way of knowing when that is likely to be at this stage. But, if you would like to give me a contact number, I will call you when we are in a better position to give some concrete information."

Deeply touched by the young girl's thoughtfulness, Annette wrote her mobile number on a piece of paper and handed it to her. "Thanks," she said. "We really do appreciate this. Now, the other thing is, we need to alert airport security, as there is every chance that this Eoin character could also try to board the plane. I know that the Spanish police are looking for him, and not just because of Hollie — there has been a subsequent attack in the town and although Hollie has spoken to the police, it might be a good idea for her to speak to somebody here, at the airport."

"Absolutely," agreed the girl. "Incidentally, my name is Jenny. Jenny Jones." She extended her hand to both women, then, checking the time on her watch, she turned to her colleague on the next desk. "Hey, Anne, I'm going to take my break now, be back in fifteen minutes — okay?"

The dour faced Anne, whom Annette thanked the lord they had managed to avoid, looked as if Jenny taking a break was anything but okay. But, Jenny ignored her and climbed out from behind her desk. Then, in a conspiratorial voice, she said. "Look, my boyfriend works here with Airport Security — we'll go and find him and I can introduce you. He'll take all the details."

Gratefully, they followed her across the great hallway to a doorway marked 'Staff Only'. She asked them to wait there a moment and disappeared through it, re-emerging a couple of minutes later with a tall uniformed Spanish man, whom she introduced as Juan.

"I'll leave you in his capable hands," said Jenny, smiling affectionately up at Juan. "And, I promise I will call as soon as I have any word about the flight."

Thanking her profusely, they bade her farewell, then followed Juan into a small private office, where, without preamble, he sat down and took all the relevant information regarding Eoin. Annette could see the toll that this unexpected interview was taking on Hollie and she was relieved when Juan kept it short and to the point, winding it to a conclusion as soon as he had all the details necessary to alert his colleagues. Assuring them of the utmost vigilance in the search for Eoin, he escorted them back to the main airport concourse.

Once back outside the terminal building, Annette slipped her arm around Hollie's shoulders. "You okay?" she asked, gently. "You look a bit shaky."

Staunchly, Hollie held back the tears that glistened in her eyes, nodding mutely.

"You sure?"

Again, she nodded. This time, finding her voice. "Yeah, I'm okay. It's just that it feels like I have to keep reliving this thing over and over. As soon as I manage to distance myself from it at all, something else comes up and I'm back to square one."

"I know, sweetie," said Annette, drawing her closer into a hug. "But, you have to be strong. What you've been through is a big, big deal. You can't expect to be over it in a couple of days or anything like it. This is going to take time, Hollie."

"I know," she whimpered. "It's just talking about it like that, knowing that he's still lurking about the place, it scares me."

"Of course it does. It would scare anyone. But sooner or later, Hollie — they'll catch him. I know they will. And then, when he's safely behind bars for what he did, then, you will start to feel safe again."

## Hollie

Once she found herself back in her hotel room, Hollie could no longer contain her tears. They now openly spilled from her eyes and her body wracked with big heaving sobs. She had somehow managed to keep herself together in front of Annette, conscious that she had infringed enough already on this kind woman's holiday. Not that Annette had given any indication that Hollie and her problems had been any burden whatsoever, but Hollie knew they had.

She was immensely grateful for all the support she had received from Annette, grateful for having met such a warm, kind soul and knew with certainty that they would stay in touch after the holiday, but right now she needed to be alone. Sinking down on to the bed, she buried her face in the pillow in an attempt to muffle the feral like sounds emanating from her mouth. It wasn't self-pity that had her in this state, it was something much stronger — it was self-disgust.

Despite Annette's assurances over the last couple of days that Hollie was a victim, she felt otherwise. She had brought this whole thing on herself. When was she going to learn? When was she going to grow up? It was so easy, as she had habitually done in the past, to blame her lousy childhood on every stupid move she made. But, she knew that wasn't true. Donal had shared that childhood and he wasn't a mess like her. He didn't use his childhood as an excuse; he used it as an inspiration to make his own life different. As sure as if he was sitting there with her, she could hear him say, 'You can't change the past Hols, but you can make the future different.'

Christ, how she wished that he were here. He would calm her, soothe her in the way he always had done when they were children. Make her feel safe, secure, strong. He always had that ability to make everything okay and she knew that she was lucky to have him, but right here, right now — she missed him. Her grief once more engulfed her and turning on to her side, she drew herself up into the foetal position, and the tears, silent now, streamed down her face unchecked, soaking the pillow beneath her.

She lay there for a long time, until finally exhaustion overcame her and she drifted off to sleep. A restless, troubled sleep, which was suddenly broken by the clattering of the elevator, causing her to shoot upright on the bed. It was then that she heard it, and the sound of it filled her with fear and panic — Eoin's voice, chatting and laughing as it made its way down the corridor towards her room.

Petrified, she edged her bum into the corner of the bed, pulling her knees up tight to her chest as she started to tremble uncontrollably. What had him back here? Who was he with? Beads of sweat formed on her brow. Unable to move, she sat like a wild animal caught in a trap waiting for the hunter to arrive and finish her off. She was terrified, more terrified than she had ever been in her life. Her heart pounded like a drum in her chest, so loudly that she was convinced the beast in the corridor could hear it from there and she waited, paralysed, to meet her fate.

But, the footsteps and the voices passed and it wasn't until then that she realised that it hadn't been Eoin at all, just the demons in her head tormenting her, punishing her for her own stupidity. In a state of heightened anxiety, she nearly jumped out of her skin when her mobile phone rang, sounding inordinately loud in the quiet room. Picking it up cautiously, as if it were likely to explode in her hand, she struggled for breath like an asthmatic in the throes of an attack whilst she tried to focus her swollen eyes on the display screen. A desperate relief swept through her when the name finally became clear to her, and forgetting her earlier determination to shelter him from the truth, she pressed the answer button and in the utterance of one single word she conveyed the full extent of the nightmare that had befallen her on this godforsaken island.

"Donal," she said simply, and the secret was out.

### Donal

With a sigh of contentment, Donal sat up on a stool at the hotel bar and reached across for the nice cold pint of Budweiser that the bar man passed to him. Having come to terms with the disappointment of the morning's meeting, he had now resigned himself to wait and see what Wednesday afternoon would bring. Perhaps, it too, would be a wash out, but he had weighed the situation up philosophically and Hollie had been right, they wouldn't want the head man to see him if they weren't interested in his product.

Thinking of his hapless sister brought a wry smile to his face. What was she like? Always getting herself into some scrape or other. When they both got back to Dublin, he was going to sit her down and give her a serious talking to. It really was time that she got her shit together. It wasn't giving her the money that worried him; it was the fact that she never seemed to have a plan. She just seemed to drift chaotically from one disaster to another. He knew that he was all she had and as such, it was his responsibility to give her a much-needed nudge in the right direction. He would give her a quick call when he had finished his pint — just to make sure that she had got the money okay. She had texted him to thank him, saying she was on her way to pick it up, but he had heard nothing from her since.

He had had no difficulty finding a Western Union agent, the distinctive yellow and black stickers had been on display in a whole plethora of establishments and the process itself couldn't have been simpler. With that task out of the way, he had given Kay a quick call to check on Susan, telling her that he would be staying on in London for another couple of days. There had been no significant change in Susan's condition, she still refused to speak to him and he guiltily felt relieved to be away from it all, even if only for a few short days.

His afternoon had been spent in quiet solitude, ambling around Covent Garden and its surrounds, taking in the colourful market stalls and street performers. Adopting the role of a carefree tourist, he had treated himself to a pint, sitting on the balcony of the Punch & Judy pub in the heart of it all, where he had passed a pleasant hour or so looking down on the frenetic Londoners as they carried out their daily business.

It had been a long time since he had indulged in such simple down time, the benefits of it striking him as he returned to his hotel in the late afternoon, calm and relaxed. He was pleasantly surprised to receive a text from Denise, confirming that she would be free to meet for dinner, happily going along with her suggestion of an Italian restaurant near her hotel. He had assumed from the tone of her earlier text that she would decline, but perhaps she had just been preoccupied with whatever business she had to attend to. In any case, he was very much looking forward to seeing her again.

Finishing off the last of his beer, he headed off in search of a taxi, pulling out his mobile to call Hollie as he did so. The second she answered the phone; he knew that there was something dreadfully wrong.

The conversation lasted the entire taxi journey and it was an ashen-faced Donal, who walked into the restaurant, rattled beyond belief by his sister's terrible ordeal.

## Denise

Not wanting a late night, Denise had arrived at Nico's Trattoria promptly at seven thirty. She had taken a seat by the window where she kept a watchful eye out for Donal's arrival. The cramps and nausea that she had experienced earlier in the day had thankfully passed and a couple of hour's sleep in the afternoon had her feeling much better. Nevertheless, she was unsure how she would be feeling later and wanted to be back at her hotel by ten o'clock.

She was only there a matter of minutes, when she saw him step from a taxi directly outside the restaurant. He looked dreadful. The meeting must have gone far worse than he had let on and she instantly felt sorry for him. Smiling brightly in his direction when he came through the door, she instinctively knew that there was more to his grey pallor than an unsuccessful meeting. Concern registered on her face as she waved her hand to attract his attention.

Despite looking straight at her, he didn't even appear to see her, seeming oblivious to his environs, he looked like he was on the verge of collapse. Hastily, she got up and made her way over to him.

"Donal?" she asked, her voice full of question. "Are you alright? Has something happened?"

Merely nodding in return, he attempted a weak smile, before finding his voice. "I think I need to sit down."

"Sure. Sure," she said, guiding him to their table, frantically signalling to the waiter to bring a glass of water. "Here, sit down. Relax. Take a sip of water and tell me what on earth has happened."

"It's Hollie," he managed after a couple of sips. "My sister — she's been raped."

"Oh sweet Jesus," she said, sinking to her seat. "When? Where?"

"Well, remember I told you that she's in Majorca? Stuck there because of this stupid ash cloud." She nodded, not wanting to interrupt him. "She told me that she went there with some friend from work. Turns out she was lying. She went there with some guy she knows nothing about, and he spiked her drink, battered her, raped her and then, disappeared. Leaving her stranded and alone in some fucking hotel room, like she was a piece of meat."

Denise's eyes filled with tears as she listened to his impassioned outburst. Not sure what to say, she reached across the table and took his hand. "Oh my God, Donal. I'm so sorry."

"I know, thanks," he said absentmindedly. "She just sounded so fragile. She's there on her own, scared and lonely and that bastard is roaming the streets, without a care in the world. It isn't right. I wish I could get my hands on him — just for five minutes..."

He dropped his head into his hands, rubbing the sockets of his eyes with the balls of his palms, then, shook his head slowly from side to side. "I've warned her so many times," he said, angry now. "Why does she have to keep doing these stupid things? Why can't she grow up? Oh God! That sounds terrible, it sounds like I'm blaming her... and, I'm not, honestly. It's just she won't look after herself and I can't be there to mind her all the time. She's a big girl now — she has to stand on her own two feet and stop putting herself in these situations that endanger her."

Helplessly, she sat there, allowing him to get it all out of his system. Touched by the deep love he had for his sister, she wished that she had somebody who cared about her like that. She understood his anger, but knew better than anyone how easy it is to be taken in by a little bit of charm. In many ways his sister's experience mirrored her relationship with John, just a more condensed version. She too had succumbed to a stranger's charms, been battered, abused and raped by him before being abandoned. Except, in her case, she had allowed him do it again and again, seeing clearly now for the first time, that that was exactly what he had done.

"Hey," she said in a gentle voice, prompting him to look her in the eyes. "Don't be hard on Hollie. She's the victim here. Okay, she didn't know this guy very well before she went away with him and yes, that was foolish, but, she has been wronged and she's going to need all the support she can get from you. Obviously, you are very upset by all of this, but save your anger for the bastard that did it. Hollie needs your love and I can tell that you have a lot of that to give her. You're a nice guy, Donal — she's lucky to have a brother like you."

The terrible news had quelled both their appetites, leaving them with little or no interest in the menus that the waiter handed to them. Seeing that Donal was too cut up to even think about it, yet knowing that they both had to eat, she took charge, ordering a large mixed pizza between them. This, they ate, in a perfunctory manner, with little further conversation, before heading back to their respective hotels, Denise promising to contact him in the morning to check how he was doing.

## Liz

With the kids upstairs in their rooms doing their homework and a bolognaise sauce simmering on the hob, Liz picked up the phone to call Pauline. The background noise of the Kinsella household sounded every bit as chaotic and familiar as her own, when an exasperated sounding Pauline answered the phone, letting loose a colourful aside to the kids as she did so.

"Hey, Pauline, it's Liz," she said. "Is this a bad time?"

"When bloody isn't a bad time in this house?" answered Pauline. "Honestly, they are all driving me nuts. If they aren't fighting, they're in my way making toast and what not when I'm trying to do the dinner. I swear, I'm going to murder them."

"I know the feeling," laughed Liz. "I thought I'd grab a minute to call you while they're doing their homework."

"Homework! Don't even get me started on homework! Did you guys hear that — Josh and Jane are actually doing their homework?"

A chorus of 'so' and 'whatever's were audible down the line, causing Liz to laugh again. Then, relative quiet, when Pauline stepped out to the back garden in order to attempt to have a conversation.

"So? What's up?" she asked, closing the back door behind her.

"Well, Mrs Kinsella — you've been spotted," chuckled Liz, good-humouredly.

"Now, you're going to have to enlighten me, Liz."

"Ah, come on now, Pauline. While the cat's away and all that," she said, enjoying the fact that Pauline still had no clue what on earth she was on about.

"Nope! Still don't know what you're on about Liz. And what cat? We don't even have a cat."

"Jimmy — ya eejit! But, your secret is safe with me. If you don't mind being spotted in the Maserati while your poor husband is stranded over in Portugal... Well, what can I say?"

Fully expecting one of Pauline's infamous guffaws to assail her ears, she held the receiver a couple of inches from her ear, but... there was nothing. Checking to see that she hadn't hit the mute button by accident, something she was constantly doing, she said, "Hey, you still there?"

An awkward silence followed, before Pauline, speaking tentatively said, "Jimmy isn't in Portugal, Liz. He was due to fly out last Thursday, but the airport closed 'cos of the ash cloud and he wasn't able to go."

"Don't be daft," said Liz. "He and Peter are over there with Jack. Sure, I've been talking to him every day." A gnawing doubt was forming in Liz's head, she felt her stomach sicken and her eyes sting with hot tears. "You're kidding me, right? Jimmy is in Portugal — isn't he?"

"Look, Liz — I wouldn't do that to you — you know I wouldn't. Jimmy is here. Like I said, he was meant to go last week, but couldn't. If Jack's in Portugal, he's not with Jimmy, or Peter for that matter. He and Helen were round here yesterday. Oh, God, Liz — I'm really sorry."

"Oh Christ!" said Liz, dropping the phone onto the table as if it were a hot poker. She could hear Pauline's voice still coming through the mouthpiece.

"Liz? Liz — are you there? Are you okay? Liz? Liz?"

But, try as she might, she couldn't pick the phone back up.

## Jack

Waiting for Rachel to finish in the shower, Jack stepped out on to the balcony to ring home before they went out to eat. It struck him as somewhat ironic that now, he was having to be discreet about calling Liz. He guessed that was going to be the way of the future. Not that Rachel had said anything, he just felt more comfortable doing it out of earshot now that they were planning a future of their own together.

Josh answered the phone and in character with the eighteen-year-old lad that he was, his attempts at conversation were monosyllabic. Grunting 'yes' or 'no', in answer to specific questions and uncommunicatively divulging that his mother had gone to bed with a headache. Relieved at not having to talk to Liz this evening, Jack asked him to wish her better and tell her that he would call her in the morning.

## *Rachel*

An acutely decisive person, Rachel rarely ruminated over decisions once they had been made. Experience had taught her that once judgement had been employed, and a decision had been reached after weighing up all possible options, then, the conclusion was correct. Her decision to plan a future with Jack was no exception. She knew with certainty that she had made the right choice for her and because of this she sang happily to herself in the bathroom, as she got ready for their celebratory dinner.

Looking at herself appreciatively in the mirror, she knew that she looked good. Jack O'Brien was going to be overwhelmed by her tonight. With her back to the mirror, she turned her head over her shoulder to get the backwards view of the incredibly sexy underwear that she had treated herself to earlier in one of the designer shops along the main shopping strip. Even she could see that she looked amazing — Jack was going to cream himself when he saw her in these, but they were the dessert.

The main course hung on the back of the door in the form of a very short, very revealing, clingy black jersey dress that had had her name all over it when she spotted it in the boutique window earlier. She had applied her makeup with meticulous attention, leaving her eyes looking sultry and seductive, just as she had aimed. Her long blonde hair swung silkily about her face, expertly straightened, framing her face perfectly. Applying a final coat of lip-gloss, she sashayed into the bedroom, casually throwing a glance in Jack's direction to see his reaction.

Immediately, she knew that she had achieved precisely the effect she had anticipated when his jaw dropped open as he looked at her.

"Jesus, Rachel — you look stunning," he grinned, pulling her to him.

She felt him grow hard against her and knew he was every bit as confident about their decision as she was.

"Thanks, babe," she said huskily. "Now, come on, before you get any ideas. We have some celebrating to do."

Reluctantly, he did as she bid him and followed her out of the room, eagerly looking forward to when they would return. Objective achieved, she hid a sardonic grin, sparing a scathing thought for Liz, as they headed towards the elevator. "He's all mine now," she thought nastily.

CHAPTER TEN

# Tuesday AM 20th April

*Rachel*

Wearing nothing more than a salacious smile, Rachel woke early on Tuesday morning. The expensive lingerie that she had purchased the day before lay discarded on the floor, barely inside the doorway of the room. Idly, she wondered if there were security cameras on the corridor or in the lifts, if so, she and Jack had given the unwitting night porter a show to remember.

Beside her, Jack slept. A deep untroubled sleep, borne from the physical and mental fatigue the previous day had produced. The day had been a big one for them both, but in fairness to him, she knew that emotionally it had to have been far more draining for him than for her. She knew from the conversation they had had over dinner that he was right up for this, ready for the many challenges that would face him before they could set up home together and begin life as a 'proper' couple.

Obviously, one of his main concerns was for the kids. He didn't want to jeopardise his relationship with them. To this end, they had decided that he and Liz would separate; he would take an apartment on his own, allowing the kids some time to come to terms with that first. Then, they would introduce the kids to the idea of him and Rachel having a relationship. The kids knew her and liked her already, so that shouldn't be too much of a problem — so long as any mention of an affair while he was still with Liz was kept out of the equation. He really had worked it all out and if everything went according to plan, then they would be playing happy families before the end of the year.

The plan suited her fine, especially as there was no question of the kids living with them. She liked Josh and Jane well enough, but she had no intention of signing up in the parenting department. Having them stay over every second weekend or so was tolerable, she might even grow to like it, although she suspected that enduring it was more likely to be the case. Still, once they were packed off back to their mother's come Sunday evening - she would cope.

Unable to go back to sleep and with the morning looking a little cloudy, she decided to leave him asleep and take a trip into nearby Palma to do some shopping. Leaving him a note to say that she would be back around lunchtime, she headed off.

## Jack

Jack was surprised to discover that it was almost eleven thirty when he woke to find himself alone in the hotel room. Assuming Rachel was in the bathroom, he called out to her. No answer. Dragging himself lazily from the bed, he went and pushed open the bathroom door, but it was empty. Sleepily, he scratched his tousled head, then spotted the note she'd left for him on top of the TV. Grateful that she hadn't dragged him along with her, he grabbed his mobile and went out to the balcony, flopping down heavily into the sun lounger.

His head was thumping and he knew that he had over indulged in wine the night before. Still, he thought, a bit of breakfast and a quick swim should wash away the cobwebs. With a sense of compunction, he dialled Liz's number, but it went to voicemail. Knowing that he was behaving in a cowardly fashion, he left her a message telling her that he was off out to play golf and would give her a shout that evening when he got back to the hotel. It was imperative that he keep some semblance of normality until he got back home and spoke to her face to face — he owed her that much at least.

The upcoming weeks and months were going to be difficult, but if the plans he and Rachel had made the night before were anything to go by, it would all be worth it in the end. He was relieved that he had found a way to handle the kids and Rachel's easy acceptance of his proposal in that regard had him feeling optimistic that despite Liz's initial hurt, and he knew she would be hurt at first, things could all work out.

For him now, this was the only way forward. Rachel had become like an addiction. The more he had of her, the more he wanted. He couldn't wait for the day when they would set up home together and now that they had managed to weave the kids into their plans, he was a very happy man indeed.

### Annette

Reluctant to let a cloudy morning spoil their day, Annette suggested to the girls that they would take a bus into Palma, the nearest big town and do some shopping. The girls jumped at the idea, even washing up the breakfast dishes without having to be asked in a bid to get moving. Maureen said that she would prefer to give it a miss, if Annette didn't mind and that she would be fine at the hotel with her new circle of friends.

"Hey, Mum, why don't you see if Hollie would like to come?" asked Hannah, wiping off the table. "She never came down for dinner last night and maybe she could do with a bit of company."

"That's very thoughtful of you, Hannah," said Annette, smiling fondly at her younger daughter. "I'll go and give her a knock now, see if she wants to."

"Tell her to get a move on if she's coming," said Megan, poking her head out of the bathroom door. "We'll be leaving her in thirty minutes — max!"

"Why, yes, Miss Bossy Boots," laughed Annette.

Hollie, looking tired and drawn when she opened the door to Annette but, eagerly accepted the invitation. "Oh, I'd love to," she said. "Just give me a few minutes to get ready. I know I look a mess. I didn't sleep so well last night, but a quick shower and I'll be grand."

The bus driver seemed to be in an even bigger hurry than the girls to get to Palma, leaving Annette with white knuckles from gripping the bar of the seat in front of her, to keep her balance. A combination of the heat and his driving left her feeling nauseous as they got off the bus, in the centre of town.

"I've got to sit down. Get a cold drink or something," said a green faced,

Annette.

Megan and Hannah looked less than impressed, wanting to get stuck straight in to exploring the shops. In a diplomatic move, Hollie suggested, "Why don't the girls have a little look around? We'll go and get a drink and they can meet us back here in half an hour or so. What d'ya think?"

"Oh yeah, Mum, can we?" begged Megan.

"I don't see why not," said Annette, too sick to really care. "But half an hour, now. No longer. We'll be at that café over there, see," she said pointing in the direction of a small, eye catching café with seating outside. "The one under that big clock."

"Yeah, fine, Mum. See you then."

Taking a seat outside, Annette smiled at Hollie. "Thanks, Hollie. I don't think I could have coped with them moaning at me to hurry up and honestly, I think I'd be sick if I started going in and out of shops right now."

"No worries," laughed Hollie. "I'm always happy to sit and have a cappuccino. Trust me, it's no hardship."

When the waitress brought out their drinks, Annette sipped slowly on the ice-cold glass of Coke, gradually feeling herself return to normal. Eventually, the sickness passed and she took in her surroundings. The café was situated on the apex of two shopping streets, giving clear views down each of them. Suddenly she spluttered, half choking, half coughing as she tried to swallow her drink quickly in order to call out to a familiar figure walking out of one of the shops nearest to her.

"Rachel?" she called, uncertain if it was definitely her. But, sure enough, there in front of her, larger than life was Liz's friend, Rachel Wallace.

"Hey, Rachel," she said. "This is a surprise. Liz never said you'd be here at the same time as us."

"Oh, a bit of a last minute change of plan," said Rachel. "I was originally going to the Canaries, but this came up at the right price. In fact, I probably never even told Liz, it all happened so quickly."

"Well, eh, it's good to see you," said Annette, regretting her impulsive response in calling out her name. She had never really felt that comfortable around Rachel, finding her a bit over-confident and over-bearing for her liking. "So, where abouts are you staying? We're over in Palma Nova — are you anywhere near there?"

"No, no. I'm in a small town about twenty kilometres or so beyond Palma Nova."

"Oh that's a pity," lied Annette, instantly relieved that this would only have to be a brief encounter. "Oh my God, where are my manners?" she asked, swinging around to introduce Hollie, but her seat was empty. "Oh, she's gone," she said, "Must have popped to the loo. Anyway, Rachel, great seeing you. I'll let Liz know that I bumped into you. Enjoy the rest of your holiday."

"Will do — and you," smirked Rachel, before heading towards the taxi rank, weighed down with shopping bags.

## Hollie

Furtively, Hollie stuck her head out the door of the café, scanning the streets with her eyes before venturing out.

"There you are," said a flustered looking Annette. "I just went to introduce you to someone and you were gone."

"Is she gone?" hissed Hollie, nervously looking around.

"Who?" asked Annette.

"That woman. The one you were talking to."

"You mean Rachel?" asked Annette, genuinely confused now.

"Yes, Dr. Wallace. Has she gone?"

"Well, yes. But, how do you know Rachel? And why don't you want to see her?"

"Oh my God! This trip just gets worse and worse," cried Rachel, sinking into her seat and dropping her head into her hands.

"Hollie — you've got to tell me what's going on. Are you okay?"

"No. Not really. That's Dr. Wallace. She works in the same clinic as me — Greendale Medical Centre," she added, as if that made it all clear. Then, seeing Annette's perplexed expression, she explained. "You know I told you how my coming away was a real spur of the moment decision?"

Annette nodded, waiting.

"Well, I did something that I truly have never done before. I phoned in sick. Now, she's here. If she sees me and tells them in the clinic, that's it. I'll be sacked. Oh Christ! What have I done?"

"Oh dear," said Annette lamely, not sure what else to say.

## Denise

The cramping started again at about seven in the morning. More intense this time, Denise got up and walked around the hotel room. Waves of nausea washed over her, causing her to retch, she felt dreadful. Hot and clammy. Opening an ice-cold bottle of water from the mini bar, she gulped it down. She paced unsteadily up and down the room until eventually the pains started to abate. Lifting up the loose T-shirt that she wore, she looked at her stomach in the mirror. She could clearly see her abdominal muscles contract with each spasmodic pain that clenched her. Finally, they subsided altogether and she crawled back into bed, hoping she would fall back to sleep.

But, the Central London hotel had started to come alive for the day and the unfamiliar sounds kept her awake. Giving up hope of drifting off, she got up and made herself a cup of coffee. As she sat up in the bed drinking it, her thoughts turned to Donal and the dreadful news of his sister's rape. He seemed to be such a genuinely nice bloke and she wished that there was something she could do to help. But what could she do? She felt sorry for his sister too. How awful it must be to have such a horrible thing happen when you're so far from home and on her own.

With all the money she now had, it was unbelievable to think that she could still do nothing to help. There must surely be something. But what? She couldn't even offer to fly him out to her with the ash cloud, but there had to be something. The germ of an idea started to grow in her head. She discounted it at first, but the more she thought about it, the more she liked it. She would help him catch whoever had done this to his sister. She would employ a private investigator. Together, they would hunt down the bastard who had raped Hollie. They would see him put away behind bars.

She knew that in theory she should do the same to John — although that was never going to happen. Not that she would have any objection to seeing him put away for all the heinous things he had done to her, but because in

137

order to do so, she would have to admit publicly to the degradation and abuse he had put her through ever since she had met him and she didn't feel able for all of that.

### Donal

"Is everything alright with your breakfast, sir?" asked the waiter, as Donal pushed the untouched plate, with his now cold full English breakfast on it, away from him.

"Oh yeah, sure, everything is fine with it. Just not much of an appetite this morning — that's all."

"A bit of a late one last night was it hey?" he asked, chuckling to himself at his own joke, whilst clearing the plate away.

"Something like that," muttered Donal to his retreating back. Numbed by Hollie's revelations, Donal was in no mood for small talk and seeing the grinning waiter pick up a coffee pot and head back towards him, he quickly rose from the table and hurried out of the dining room.

Deciding that some fresh air might help calm him down, he left the hotel and headed in the direction of a small park that he had noticed from the window of his room. He stopped at a newsagent on the corner and did something that he vowed several years ago, never to do again — he bought a packet of cigarettes and a lighter. Thankfully, the park was deserted at this early hour, save for a lone man walking a Golden Retriever. Donal sat down on a bench, following the man's course with his eyes. The man looked so at peace as if he hadn't a care in the world and Donal envied him that.

With a sense of familiarity that he found alarming, he opened the packet of cigarettes and put one in his mouth, lit it and drew the smoke down deep into his lungs. The nicotine coursed through his blood, leaving him feeling light-headed after the third or fourth pull, but he enjoyed the sensation and abstractedly wondered why he had ever quit. He felt very alone, and not only because he now had the park to himself, 'Golden Retriever' man having completed his walk, but because he had no one to turn to. His wife wouldn't even speak to him; his mother-in-law who had been his mentor over the years was understandably consumed with her daughter's problems and he couldn't possibly heap this latest turn of events on to her as well, which left him firmly on his own.

Denise had been great last night, so easy to talk to and non-judgemental, but in fairness, she was a virtual stranger who clearly had problems of her own to contend with. He was quite certain that despite her kindness of the previous night — out of sight was out of mind, where he was concerned. By nature, he was a positive person and the self-pity that consumed him was foreign to him, but he couldn't seem to pull himself out of it.

He lit another cigarette, his third in less than an hour and in over four years, and sucked deeply on it, exhaling huge plumes of smoke around his head. His phone, which he'd switched to silent, vibrated in his pocket, but he ignored it, not wanting to deal with whatever problem it heralded at that present moment in time. If it was important, they would leave a message and he would get back to them in his own time. A bleep several seconds later signalled that the caller had indeed left a message and fishing it out of his pocket, he checked to see what it was.

It was Denise, sounding breathless and excited. "Donal, it's me, Denise. I've something important that I'd like to discuss with you. Any chance you would be around at lunchtime? Give me a call back when you get this. It's really important."

## Liz

For the first time ever, Liz simply couldn't face getting up and getting the kids out to school that morning. She had barely slept a wink all night and her head was thumping with a ferocity that left her vision blurred. Dragging herself from her bed shortly before seven o'clock, she went and knocked on their doors, telling them that they would need to leave a bit earlier and catch the bus.

Josh groaned grumpily, clearly not impressed with this idea, whereas Jane sprang worriedly from her bed, following her mother into her bedroom.

"What is it, Mum? Are you okay?" she asked, concern palpable in her voice.

"Yes, sweetie, I'm fine. Just a migraine, I think. A few hour's sleep and I'll be right as rain."

"Can I get you anything? A cup of tea or a slice of toast or something?"

"Do you know, a cup of tea would be lovely, sweetheart. And, if you would bring me up the box of Migraleve — that'd be great. They're in the cupboard over the oven. Thanks, love."

She heaved a sigh of relief when she heard them pull the front door behind them. The tablets had started to work and the woodpecker style hammering in her head had begun to subside. With the house to herself, she got up; pulling on the big fluffy scarlet robe that Jane had bought her for her birthday, getting comfort from its warmth and softness.

Her mind had been in turmoil since that fateful phone call with Pauline. Devastated by Jack's deceit, she knew that she had to get to the truth of the matter before coming to any decisions. Perhaps, although she doubted it, there was some plausible explanation for his lies, but she didn't want to confront him until she knew what it was that she was confronting him with. Could he really be cheating on her? Was it possible that he was away on holiday with another woman? Her heart told her not to be daft; but her mind told her that it was very likely the case.

She wasn't stupid. Jack was a lady's man — always had been. Far more comfortable in the company of females, than with other men. She had always felt deep, deep down that there was every chance that at some point he would play away. Long ago she had vowed never to probe too deeply into his activities; assuming that if the worst came to the worst she would one day discover that he had snogged someone or maybe even had an unmeaningful one night stand — a drunken fumble with an unknown and unmemorable woman who would pose no threat to her.

Annette had never understood her thinking, telling her that she was selling herself short and that if Paddy behaved in that way, she would have his bags packed and on the doorstep, no questions asked. But Annette was different to her, more confident. Annette had seen a bit of the world, lived a little, before she got married, unlike Liz who had fallen pregnant within months of meeting Jack and ploughed headlong into marriage, seeing nothing but a rosy future when she did so.

But, a holiday was very different to a drunken fumble. A holiday signified an affair, something substantial and meaningful. That was a completely different kettle of fish and she knew, with certainty that she couldn't cope with that. Sitting at the kitchen table in the depths of despair, she wondered what on earth to do next. Her mobile rang and picking it up, she saw Jack's name on the screen and unable to speak to him just yet, she cast it aside, letting it ring out.

CHAPTER ELEVEN

# Tuesday PM 20th April

*Annette*

Nobody objected when Annette announced that she really couldn't face taking the bus back to the hotel, and that they were taking a taxi instead. Conscious that Hollie might be concerned about the cost of this, she adamantly insisted that it was her treat as it had been her suggestion.

In a couple of short hours, the girls had managed to accumulate several bags apiece, filled with brightly coloured tops, swimwear and jewellery. Despite plenty of temptation, Hollie had resisted buying anything, but still seemed to have enjoyed traipsing in and out of all the shops, 'oohing' and 'aahing' at the girl's selections with an enthusiasm that endeared her to them.

She was like the bridge that crossed the mother/daughter divide, diplomatically keeping the peace at the first sign of inter-generational friction. Annette was very glad that she had come along, enjoying the younger woman's company. She knew poor Hollie was going through a rotten time, displaying a false bravado on occasion, yet vulnerable underneath, but what impressed Annette the most, was the basic niceness of the girl.

How crazy was it that she knew Rachel Wallace? Worked with her. Curious as to how she was perceived in the workplace, Annette made a mental note to quiz Hollie about that later.

The taxi dropped them right at the door of the hotel and stepping out of it, Annette turned to the others and said, "Now, that's better. You can keep those horrible buses with their nutcase drivers!" The girls laughed and disappeared up to the room to try on their various purchases.

Annette and Hollie went to find Maureen who was once again holding court in the corner of the pool bar. As soon as she saw her, Maureen stood up, holding an imaginary telephone to her ear and miming the word 'Paddy' at her daughter-in-law. Everything Maureen did had a comical edge to it at the moment for Annette, causing her to giggle as she exaggeratedly signalled back 'okay — I'll give him a bell' using preposterous hand gestures to do so. Instantly getting the joke, Maureen laughed heartily and the bond between them deepened.

## Hollie

While Annette was on the phone to Paddy, Hollie went up to the bar to order them a couple of cappuccinos. As she was digging her purse out of her bag, she noticed that she had two voice messages on her own phone. She dialled the number to retrieve them.

The first was from Donal, just checking how she was and the second was from Maria Alvarez at the hospital, confirming that the police had successfully obtained a DNA sample from the seminal fluid present in the young English worker who had been raped. She was wondering if Hollie might have anything at all that could have Eoin's DNA on it. Even bed linen, she suggested, but the blood stained bed sheets had been changed the day after her attack.

Picking up the coffees, she made her way over to the table where Annette sat, chatting away happily to her husband. Waiting for Annette to finish her call, she berated herself for being so stupid in destroying all the evidence that could have identified Eoin as the culprit in this most recent attack.

"Are you alright?" asked Annette, hanging up the phone and seeing her troubled expression.

"Yeah. Yeah. I'm grand," she answered. "I just had a call from Maria Alvarez. They managed to get some of Eoin's DNA from the other girl that was raped and she wanted to know if I had anything at all that might have traces of his DNA, but I don't."

"Ah bugger," said Annette. "That would have been so sweet to have that before they actually catch the bastard. Still, on the positive side, at least they have some DNA and when they do get him and it matches, then, he'll be sent to prison."

"I suppose you're right," said Hollie, perking herself up "Anyway, enough about me and my disasters. I never asked you — how do you know Dr. Wallace?"

"Rachel? I don't really know her very well," said Annette, glad that Hollie had brought up the subject. "She's a friend of my sister's. I'm not really sure how much I like her to be honest, but Liz seems to be very fond of her."

"I didn't think she'd be your type," said Hollie with a scornful look on her face. "We all think that she's a bit of a bitch in work."

Intrigued, Annette asked, "Really? How come?"

"Well, she's just real stand-offish and snotty. You know, has a real high opinion of herself; kinda looks down her nose at all the admin staff. She tends to keep herself to herself a lot. No one seems to know that much about her. I guess that's probably why there's so much gossip flying about the place about her," sniggered Hollie, recalling some of the caustic remarks Niamh had made about her.

"Such as?"

"Well, nothing concrete," said Hollie, warming to the conversation. "But, Niamh, the other receptionist, is convinced that she is having an affair with a married man."

"On what basis?"

"As I say, nothing concrete. Just little things really. She's very coy about her private life, which is fair enough, but normally people would make some reference to their partner, in some context or other, but never Dr. Wallace. She never mentions him."

"Well, maybe she doesn't have a partner," laughed Annette. "Certainly as far as I'm aware she doesn't."

"Oh she does!" blurted Hollie. "Every week, at least once if not twice, flowers arrive for her at the clinic. There are only so many grateful patients any one doctor can have. Now surely, if you had an attentive partner like that, once in a while you'd comment on him — wouldn't you?"

"Mmmm. Probably," agreed Annette. "But, that doesn't mean he's married."

"Yeah?" said Hollie, raising a questioning eyebrow.

"Not necessarily," laughed Annette, seeing that she was losing this one. Then, digging deep for an alternate explanation, she added. "Maybe Dr. Wallace's partner is a woman?"

Hollie's eyes went out on stalks as she said. "Jesus! I never thought of that — you could be right."

## Rachel

"You will never, ever guess whom I just saw in Palma?" gasped Rachel as she swanned into the hotel room, in a flurry of shopping bags, dropping them unceremoniously onto the floor.

"No point in trying then," smirked Jack, keeping his eyes on the newspaper he was reading on the balcony.

"Huh? Very funny, Jack, but seriously — guess who it was."

Assuming it to be some high profile celebrity, he scrunched his face up as if he was desperately trying to figure out who it might be. "Nope," he said, "Not getting anything. Give me a clue."

"You SO know her," she said.

"Victoria Beckham," he said, still reading the paper, not altogether interested in whether it was her or not.

With a hint of impatience, Rachel swiped the newspaper out of his hands and climbing astride him, she grabbed his face in both of her hands, then, forcing him to look her in the eyes, she repeated, "You know her."

"Aw, c'mon Rach, I dunno who it was. You know I'm not interested in celebrities. I haven't a clue. Tell me."

"Annette!" she said, waiting for a reaction.

Still looking lost, he raised a questioning eyebrow, "Annette? Annette who? Am I supposed to know her?"

"Annette Forbes ya eejit! Your sister-in-law!"

His face fell, "You're kidding me! Right?"

"No. Seriously. Outside a coffee shop, in the centre of town. I was walking out of a shop and I heard someone calling my name. I turned around and there she was — Annette. I couldn't believe it."

"What did she say? What did you say? Jesus! What does this mean now?"

He was panicked and she knew it, but she had had time to think about it and had decided that she wasn't going to let this little hitch become a problem.

"Hey, it's no big deal," she said, trying to placate him. "It was only me that she saw. It isn't like she bumped into the both of us. I simply told her that I had had a last minute change of plan when a cheap deal came my way and she believed me. Why wouldn't she? There was no mention of you. As far as she's concerned Liz has told her that you are in Portugal. Stop worrying. There's still no reason for Liz to know that you are here."

"I hope you're right, Rach," he said, not looking so sure. "Otherwise this could ruin everything."

"Jack — you are leaving Liz. Your marriage is over. In the overall scheme of things — so frigging what if she finds out a week earlier? But, she's not going to — so, relax."

"It's not just Liz though — is it, Rachel? If Liz finds out about us at this stage, she's bound to tell the kids and then, that'll fuck up all our plans."

"Kids are adaptable," she said petulantly, then, realising her mistake, she added. "They're not going to find out, Jack. Trust me. I played it really cool. Annette has no reason to be suspicious and neither do Liz and the kids."

"I really fucking hope so Rach. I couldn't handle this situation if I was faced with the prospect of losing my kids."

"You won't, baby — you won't," she said, kissing his face and stroking the side of his head in a soothing gesture. "Keep our heads and this will all work out just the way we planned it. I promise you."

She remained astride him, rocking him gently back and forth until she finally felt him begin to relax.

## Liz

Liz was still sitting at the kitchen table gazing into space, when a ring on the doorbell startled her back to reality. Walking into the hall, she could make out Pauline's form through the milky glass of the front door. She hesitated for a moment, not sure if she felt up to talking to her. Maybe she could pretend that she was out, of course, her car was parked in the driveway, but she could have easily gone for a walk — couldn't she? The bell sounded again, and this time she could see Pauline press her forehead to the glass, cupping her hand around her eyes as she did so to deflect any reflection and peer down the hallway straight at her. The bright scarlet of her robe made it all too easy to spot, ruling out the possibility of sidling unnoticed up the stairs. Taking in a deep breath, she went and opened the door.

"I've been trying to call you all morning," said Pauline, looking worried. "I didn't like to come over unannounced, but when I couldn't get hold of you, I thought I better."

"Oh, yeah, sorry," said Liz, lifelessly. "Jack tried me earlier and I don't want to talk to him right now, so I switched my phone to silent and unplugged the house phone. Come, in." She pulled the door wide open, then turned and shuffled into the kitchen, leaving Pauline to follow her.

Putting the kettle on, she caught sight of the time and was astounded to see that it was almost lunchtime. Suddenly conscious of the fact that she was still wearing a robe at this hour of the day, she apologised, "Sorry, can't seem to get it together this morning."

Concern was etched on Pauline's face, "Don't worry about that. Are you okay?"

Liz shrugged. "I suppose so," she said. "Or as okay as I can be having discovered that my husband is lying through his teeth to me."

"I'm so sorry, Liz," said Pauline, the sincerity of her words was evident as she spoke. "I don't know what to say to you. I nearly died when you called last night. The cheek of him to use Jimmy and Peter as cover. Jimmy had no idea; he was as shocked as I was. Have you spoken to Jack at all?"

"No. I don't want to. Not until I know for sure what's going on. But, then again, he's probably the only one who can tell me that."

"Look, Liz, if Jack is having an affair, there's bound to be some evidence of it here. Have you done any digging around?"

"You mean like going through his pockets, his drawers, stuff like that?" she asked horrified at the notion of invading his privacy in that way. "No! I haven't — I can't do something like that — Jack would go mad if he thought I was rummaging through his things."

Gently, Pauline reached out and took a hold of Liz's hand. "Maybe he would go mad, Liz, but as I see it, Jack has told you a major lie and I know for a fact that if Jimmy had done the same to me, then, his right to privacy is overruled by my right to know the truth. If I were you, love, I'd do some digging."

"Do you think?" asked Liz, in a childlike way. "You don't think that's a terrible thing to do?"

"No, Liz. I don't. I think lying to you and taking himself off on a holiday, and using his best friends as cover is a terrible thing to do. Now, if you like, I'll stay here with you or if you would prefer to be on your own, I'll go, but I would only be a phone call away if you needed me."

"Will you stay?" whispered Liz, barely audibly, her sad eyes filling up with tears as she spoke.

"Of course I will," said Pauline, filling up with tears herself at her friend's misery. She hugged Liz warmly, then said. "Come on, let's get this over and done with."

With a heavy heart, Liz led the way up the stairs to her bedroom, then, pointing towards Jack's wardrobe, she sank heavily on to the bed, leaving Pauline to pull open the doors. Thirty minutes later, Pauline had gone through all of Jack's pockets, his drawers and his bedside locker, but the search had yielded nothing.

"Does he have a laptop?" asked Pauline, looking around for one.

"Yes. It should be there on the top shelf of his wardrobe."

Not very tall, Pauline couldn't see on to the shelf and patted her hand around blindly before finding the laptop and removing it. She powered it up, but it asked for a password.

"Any idea what it would be?" She asked.

"MUFCJOB1," answered Liz automatically. "You know Jack and his Man United obsession."

Keying in the code successfully, Pauline waited for the homepage to appear. "Which email provider is he with?"

"Hotmail."

Opening up the hotmail account, there were only two users on the list: jackobrien57@hotmail.com and gr8ass992@hotmail.com. Liz gasped, recognising the name that she had assumed belonged to one of Josh's mates and wordlessly pointed at it, urging Pauline to access it. It took a couple of attempts to crack the access code, but predictably enough it was a combination of numbers from Jack's date of birth.

The in-box contained over a hundred emails. All from the one address — foxy1@hotmail.com. Liz felt her heart drop. The two women sat staring at the screen for several minutes, before taking a deep breath, Pauline opened the latest message.

Hey lover boy, can't wait to soak up those rays. Counting the hours 'til we get away. Can you believe it — seven whole days on our own? Start imagining what I'm going to do to you and I promise I'll exceed your dreams! XXX

Liz's mouth filled with bile as she read the message, and feeling her stomach heave, she dived into the en-suite bathroom, just making it to the toilet before retching violently into the bowl.

## Jack

Whilst remaining outwardly cool, Jack experienced the odd twinge of panic over the course of the afternoon as they lay in silence by the pool. Conscious of the occasional glance from Rachel, he doggedly refused to let his anxieties be apparent to her. There were going to be many difficult situations over the coming months and he knew that he had to learn to deal with them, not allowing them to drive a wedge between himself and Rachel.

Sure, it was unfortunate that she had bumped into Annette, but when he thought about it rationally, Rachel had been right, there was no reason at all that such an encounter should cast suspicion on him. He was being ridiculous. Thinking that a walk on the beach might clear his head, he sat up, looking around for his T-shirt.

"Where are you off to?" asked Rachel, lazily raising her head when he cast a shadow over her.

"I fancy a bit of a walk — wanna come?"

"Do you think that's a good idea?" she asked, teasing him.

"Huh?"

"Well, we could be spotted. You'd never know, Annette could be lurking behind the rocks, hoping to get a glimpse of me so she can report back to Liz."

"Very funny," he said, curling his lip in a derisive manner.

"Ah, come on, Jack. Stop worrying. I can feel your tension."

"That's not tension, babe — that's desire," he said, dropping to his hunkers and nuzzling his head into her neck. "You've got me like a wound up spring, lying there in that skimpy bikini, oiling yourself up and down, putting bad thoughts into my head."

She laughed, relieved that he wasn't making a big issue out of Annette. Then, grabbing a hold of her sarong, she said. "Go on then, I'll take a walk with you."

## Donal

Donal was completely astounded by Denise's offer. Not sure that he had fully understood it, he asked her to run it by him again. Listening intently to her as she did so, he waited until she had finished before speaking.

"So, you're telling me that you want to hire a private investigator to find the man that raped Hollie?"

Grinning at his incredulity, she nodded. "Yep. That's exactly what I'm saying."

"But, Denise, there are so many issues here that I'm not sure where to begin."

Clearly amused by his reaction, she raised an eyebrow, waiting for him to start.

"Firstly," he said. "You hardly even know me and you've never even met Hollie."

She nodded, saying nothing.

"Secondly, have you any idea what a private investigator costs? I don't, but I'm guessing that it's not cheap."

"The money doesn't matter," she said dismissively. "I can afford it."

"Yes, but, Denise…" he said again, unsure what to say.

Cutting across him, she said, "Look, I know this probably sounds really strange to you. But, I've thought about it, long and hard, and truly, Donal, this is something I would very much like to do."

"But why?" he asked, confused.

"Let's just say that I have my reasons. I don't really want to talk about them right now, but believe me it would give me great pleasure to see this bastard brought to justice."

Not wanting to push her for her reasons, he sat back in his seat in the busy coffee shop that he had gone to meet her in, and mulled the whole thing over in his head.

Finally, he said, "I dunno, Denise. It's a very kind offer — more than kind, it's exceptional, but I don't think I can accept it. It's too much, but thank you — thank you very much for offering."

"Hey, don't be so quick to dismiss it. At least think about it properly and maybe we could meet again tonight for dinner and you could give me your decision then?"

Reluctantly, he nodded. "Okay. We'll do that."


## Denise

It was obvious that her offer had taken Donal by surprise, but she was quietly confident that she would be able to persuade him to accept it. His deep love for his sister would win out once he had time to consider the matter properly. She knew he must think her very strange for involving herself in this way, and she was glad that he hadn't tried to extract her reasons for wanting to do this. Maybe in time she would tell him about John, but she wasn't ready for that just yet.

They had parted company when they left the coffee shop, arranging to go for something to eat in a steak house that the barman in Donal's hotel had recommended to him the evening before. He was heading to the West End to have a look at the infamous Carnaby Street area, he had invited her along with him, but fearful of a repeat of her shopping experience in Oxford Street, she declined, opting to return to the hotel for a restful afternoon. She was feeling much better than she had first thing that morning, but the bouts of cramping and nausea seemed to land upon her without much warning and to that end she thought it safer to go back to the hotel.

Once back in her hotel room, she lay on the bed, planning to have a nap, but sleep eluded her as her mind was filled with thoughts of private investigators and how she would go about finding one. She had no experience of private investigators and in fact, didn't even know anyone who had, so, she would have to begin a cold search to find one. Assuming that, as with all other professions, there would be good and bad ones out there, she knew that she would have to be discerning in her selection.

With no hope of sleeping, she decided now was as good a time as any to get started, and pulling her new laptop from her case, she set it up at the desk, got the note pad and pen that the hotel had provided, and started work. She began by googling 'private investigators Dublin' and was astonished when her search produced over seven hundred thousand results. Limiting herself to the first ten pages, she skimmed through the brief blurbs, compiling an initial list of P.I.s, that she felt warranted further exploration.

In less than an hour, she had thirty names on the list and exiting out of the search field, she started accessing the individual websites. Those websites that looked professional, she added to a fresh list, limiting this to ten potential candidates. Satisfied with her new short list, she returned to Google and did a more extensive search on each of the ten names on her list. On the basis of this, she scratched two names off, as they had both received scathing reviews from irate clients who claimed that not only had they not produced results, but also that they were nothing but scam artists, extracting money and delivering nothing. The other eight had no negative reports, but two of them had no reviews at all, so, she settled on six names whose clients had posted very positive recommendations.

She would present the list to Donal tonight, and then he would see just how serious she was about this.

CHAPTER TWELVE

# Tuesday Evening 20th April

*Rachel*

Mixing up a long, cold gin and tonic for herself while Jack showered, Rachel took her drink out to the balcony and pulling a seat around to face out to sea, she sat and watched the magnificent sunset over the ocean. The deep red and orange glow heralded another glorious day to come. And, with no sign still of the airport re-opening, she relished the prospect of another couple of day's holiday.

She felt very relaxed, sitting there with the warm evening breeze blowing into her face, sipping her drink. Idly, she wondered if Liz had any doubts whatsoever about Jack's whereabouts or the company he was in. She doubted it. Liz reminded her of her mother — gullible and naïve and she felt a contemptuous disdain for them both. With conviction, she knew that she would never be like either of them. Now that she had made a commitment to Jack, she had total confidence in the fact that he would never, ever be unfaithful to her. She simply wouldn't let that happen.

What foolish women like Liz and her mother didn't realise was that sustaining a relationship, a long term relationship, took an enormous amount of effort. In their pitiful existence it was all plain sailing — meet a man, marry him, grow old gracefully together — bullshit! For a start, who grew old gracefully? No. Rachel knew that there was a lot more to it than that.

You had to keep things exciting — especially in the bedroom and that simply wasn't possible if you let your looks and your body go the way they had.

No wonder her father had left, she thought scornfully, conjuring up an image of her plump, unkempt looking mother — Christ, the woman never even went to the hairdressers, her straggly hair always had grey roots of at least an inch in length and her face was permanently devoid of make-up. She remembered many occasions when she had been acutely embarrassed by her mother's appearance, wishing whole-heartedly that she hadn't bothered inviting her, but unable to avoid doing so. For instance, her graduation from medical school, she shuddered as she recalled the state of her that day. Luckily, she had been booked on the early train back to Waterford and hadn't been able to stay too long.

By comparison, Liz was a lot better, but even so, she seemed to have no compunction about wearing clothes that emphasised the spare tyre around her midriff, instead of having it removed surgically, if necessary, as Rachel would have done. Frequently, she had called to the house to find Liz loafing about in some appalling tracksuit or other, with her hair pulled up in an unsightly ponytail and not a screed of make-up on. How did she expect to keep a man like that? Surely, she must have known how unattractive that was. How non-sexual. Sending out the message that 'I'm not interested in sex' — virtually giving him the green light to seek it elsewhere.

Well, he had and now, he had found it. Rachel would never let herself go like that. She would use whatever means necessary to keep herself in peak condition and ensure that Jack never stopped fancying her.

She remembered, although only ten years old at the time, the night her father left home. Her mother had been gutted — she had never seen it coming, whereas Rachel recalled, even at that young age, looking at her handsome, youthful father and her overweight, frumpy mother and understanding exactly why he was going. She had never seen her father again after that night.

Her mother's experiences had taught her many valuable life lessons, not least of which were that looks are everything and that her body was her greatest tool. As she burgeoned into a sexual being, she carried this knowledge with her, using it to her advantage, seeking out the older men, playing them, and then discarding them, much in the way her father had once abandoned her.

## Liz

When Liz finally finished vomiting, she rose unsteadily and grabbed a hold of the towel rail, not trusting herself to stay standing. She caught sight of herself in the mirror, barely recognising the blotchy faced, red-eyed woman that stared back at her. Scrutinising her reflection, she searched for any traces of the Liz O'Brien who had occupied that reflection for the past forty-two years, but saw no sign of her. That Liz was gone. Jack had seen to that. Her entire previous existence had been invalidated by his treacherous deceit.

Instead, she saw a shell — a chrysalis, from which she knew, in a blinding flash of enlightenment, would emerge one of two creatures. One, a moth, which seemed full of negative symbolism; the other, a butterfly, symbolising colour and hope with the promise of a whole fresh start. She preferred the latter and encouraged by the analogy that her mind had conjured up for her, she felt a well of strength bubble up inside of her.

Odd as it seemed to her, she knew with the utmost certainty, that Jack O'Brien had no place in her future. Some things there were no going back from; Jack had crossed that line and she wanted nothing more to do with him. Breathing evenly now, she washed her face and with the towel still pressed to it, she came back into the bedroom.

She jumped when she saw Pauline still sitting on the side of the bed, having completely forgotten that she was there.

"Oh Jesus!" she exclaimed, "You frightened the life out of me."

"Are you alright?" asked Pauline, scrambling to her feet, anxious to help but not sure what to do.

"I'm fine. Honestly."

"You've had a terrible shock, Liz," she said, feeling helpless. "Do you want to lie down and I'll make us some tea? I can get Jimmy to pick up the kids if you like."

"Oh Christ, the kids," said Liz looking at the clock radio to check the time. "No, you're grand, thanks. I'll grab a quick shower and then I'll collect them myself."

"Are you sure?" asked Pauline, uncertainly. "Will you be okay to drive and that?"

"Of course I will," laughed Liz, disarming Pauline who clearly hadn't expected a reaction like this. Seeing her perplexed face, Liz added. "Look honestly, I'm fine. Yes, I had a shock — a horrible shock, but I'm over it now. I'm grand. If Jimmy picked up the kids, then they'd know that he wasn't away with Jack and I don't want to tell them anything — not yet, anyway."

## Jack

With a quick glance out of the bathroom door, Jack saw that Rachel was sitting out on the balcony and fishing his mobile out of the shorts he had discarded on the floor before getting into the shower, he quickly dialled home. He knew that he had to keep up the pretext of normality in his calls home and felt uncomfortable doing this in front of her.

It was Jane who answered and in his brightest voice, he said, "Hey, Janey Waney, how's it going?"

"Dad!" she said, clearly excited to hear from him. "How are you?"

"I'm great, my lovely, and you?" As usual, his heart soared at the sound of his beloved daughter's voice. "How's school?"

"Ugh! Don't even go there," she groaned. "I've mountains and mountains of homework. That Ms. Walsh is such a cow, Dad. She's given us at least three hours worth of French homework. She doesn't seem to realise that we do loads more subjects than just French. Honestly, I'm going to be up all night if I'm to get this finished."

Laughing at her habitual rant about the injustices of school life, he said, "Ah, well — only another three years and don't forget 'school days are the best days of your life.'"

"Yeah, right! Whoever came up with that load of crap was so obviously finished school at the time."

"Anyway, love, is your mum there? Stick her on will ya?"

"Ah, Dad — you've just missed her. She's gone for a walk with the dog.

You'll probably get her on her mobile, oh, wait a minute, no, you won't — she's left it behind her. I'll get her to give you a call when she gets back."

"No, don't bother," he said, knowing he wouldn't have another opportunity to talk tonight. "There's some dinner on at the golf club and I won't be able to talk. Tell her I called and that I'll give her a shout in the morning. Love ya."

"Love you too, Dad. Talk soon."

Glad to have missed Liz, he sent her a quick text to keep her happy until the morning. Sorry I missed u, talk tmrw, Jack x.

## Denise

The steak house was surprisingly busy when Denise walked in. The interior lighting was very dim, rendering her temporarily blind as the door swung closed behind her. Blinking to get her bearings, she heard Donal before she saw him. He was sitting at the bar, waiting for her with a pint in his hand and promptly jumped off his stool, pulling back the one beside him, allowing her room to get in.

He offered to buy her a drink and remembering the advice from the clinic to avoid alcohol, she asked if he would just get her a Coke.

"Ah, c'mon," he grinned. "Have something stronger."

"Not tonight, thanks, Donal," she said emphatically, brooking no argument.

"Fair enough," he said, turning to the bar man and ordering her a Coke. "Not much sign of the recession here," he laughed, nodding at all the full tables surrounding them.

"Do you think we'll get a table?"

"Ah, yeah. I put my name down with yer man over there with all the menus and he said he would have something for us in about forty minutes or so. Is that okay?"

"Yeah, that's fine," she said, reaching in to the bar for her drink. "How was your afternoon?"

"Good, yeah. Went down and had a look around Carnaby Street. Some seriously expensive shops with some completely off the wall clothes."

"I know," she laughed. "I was there a couple of years ago. Worth seeing though — isn't it?"

"Absolutely," he agreed. "Even managed to pick myself up a nice shirt." He sat bolt upright on the stool as he said this, sweeping his hand in a downward gesture, showing her his purchase.

"Mmmm, not bad," she said, feeling very much at home with this man whom she had only met two days ago. "So," she said, getting straight down to business. "Have you given any more thought to what we were discussing?"

His face turned serious before he answered. "Yes, I have Denise. And, as I said earlier, it really is a very generous offer, but I can't accept it. Now, I hope there'll be no hard feelings, it just wouldn't be right."

Not allowing herself to be put off that easily, she asked. "What's not right about it?"

"All the things I said to you earlier. And the money — I don't think you realise this could run into serious money — thousands even."

"I told you not to worry about the money. That doesn't matter. Besides," she shrugged. "I want to do this."

"So you said. But, why? I really don't see what's in this for you."

"You're going to have to trust me on that one. Let's just say that I have some old scores of my own that I would like to settle and right at the moment I can't face doing that, but seeing some bastard who has abused another woman brought to justice would be very therapeutic for me. Is that not reason enough?"

Once again, he saw that sadness in her eyes that he had noticed when he first met her, and somehow he knew that this was something she was doing for herself as much as for him or Hollie. Reluctantly, he nodded, "I suppose so. If you're sure?"

"Absolutely!" she grinned back at him, then reached into her handbag and produced the list she had compiled. "Let's get cracking then."

## Donal

When Donal got back to the hotel, it was still early and with his mind still far too alert to sleep, he went to the bar and bought himself a pint. Sitting down at a quiet table in the corner, he allowed himself to contemplate what a bizarre evening it had turned out to be.

Firstly, he was still reeling from the fact that he had agreed to let Denise hire a private investigator. Was he off his head? He barely knew the woman. Although, there was something about her, that made him feel as if he had known her forever. But then, over dinner, he had opened up and told her all about Susan. About her drinking; about them not being able to have a baby; and about the precarious state of their marriage. He found her to be a terrific listener who sat there, taking it all in, in a totally non-judgemental manner. He hadn't meant to be disloyal to his wife, but it was such a relief to share this incredible burden with someone who was out of the loop.

He wondered what the story behind her sad eyes was and with a genuine rush of affection, he hoped that maybe one day she would trust him enough to let him know. Whilst on Sunday night it was pure curiosity that had him wondering about her, now it was out of friendship and a hope that perhaps he could help in some way.

What an extraordinary few days this was turning out to be. It seemed like a lifetime ago that he had discovered Susan drunk on the hall floor last Friday, but it had only been a few days. So much had happened since then, it was hard to take it all in. He thought then of poor Hollie, stranded in Majorca and took solace from the fact that she too had met someone kind who was helping her through her nightmare. He would have to call her and tell her about what Denise was doing — he hoped that she would be happy about it. Too late to call her now, he would have plenty of time in the morning. His big meeting wasn't until three o'clock.

### Hollie

"Oh, God! That can't be right," said Hollie, rubbing her eyes as if they had failed her. Then, blinking, she once again looked at the time on her mobile. She had seen it right the first time — it was almost twenty past seven. Dog tired, she had come up to the room for a nap and had slept far longer than she had planned. She had arranged to meet Annette and the others in the lobby at eight o'clock and still needed to shower and wash her hair.

Springing sprightly from the bed, she went and turned on the shower, stopping to brush her teeth whilst the water ran warm. No time to waste, she quickly shampooed and conditioned her hair, washed her body, shaved her underarms and was all done and dusted in under ten minutes.

With great speed, she rummaged through her suitcase and pulled out a pair of jeans and a relatively uncrumpled top to wear, then reaching under the bed she felt around for the pair of dolly shoes that she had kicked beneath it, before falling into bed earlier. Unable to reach them, she swore under her breath, and lowered herself flat on to the ground, giving her another couple of inches reach. She found one, then tossed it out on to the middle of the floor and went back in for the second one. Grabbing hold of an unidentified spiky object, she pulled her arm out to see what she had got. On seeing what it was, her heart skipped a beat.

It was a small black hairbrush. But, not just any hairbrush — it was Eoin's hairbrush with several stray strands of his hair still in it. Dropping it, like it was a hot coal, she got to her feet and stared disbelieving at it. If that was Eoin's brush, and she knew that it was, she remembered seeing him put it into the black leather toilet bag he had with him, and it contained samples of his hair — then, they could check his DNA.

"Eur-fucking-eka!" she shouted, doing a little victory dance around the bedroom. Then, seeing her missing shoe poking out from the other end of the bed, she hurriedly got ready and went to find Annette to share the news.

### Annette

The moment Annette saw Hollie step out of the lift; she knew that for once, the kid had been given a break. Ploughing her way through the busy hotel lobby, she came to a halt, grinning profusely at Annette.

"Guess what?" she purred, like the cat who got the cream.

"Go on!"

"I've just found Eoin's hairbrush under my bed with…. Wait for it! Several of his hairs still in it."

"Oh! That's fantastic Hollie," Annette beamed, giving the younger woman a massive hug. "You must contact Maria, she's going to be thrilled."

"I know. I was going to take it over to the hospital to her in the morning. What do you think?"

"That sounds perfect. Well done you! Right, at last, we have a cause to celebrate."

Rounding up the entire posse, Annette linked Hollie and Maureen by the arm, and headed off purposefully towards the town. Her two daughters hanging back wanting a bit of distance between them and their insane mother.

CHAPTER THIRTEEN

# Wednesday AM 21st April

*Hollie*

With the first sense of real optimism that she had experienced in days, Hollie got up early, grabbed a quick breakfast and headed off to the hospital. Taking a bus, she arrived there in a little under an hour, walked in through the now familiar doors of the A & E department and instantly spotted Maria behind the desk.

The busy nurse looked up and her face broke into a welcoming smile when she recognised Hollie approaching the desk.

"Hollie! Good to see you — how are you?"

"I'm okay," she answered, excitedly. "Wait until you see what I have for you." She opened her handbag and pulled out the hairbrush, which she had carefully wrapped in toilet paper to protect it.

Immediately guessing what it was, Maria's mouth dropped open in amazement. "Eoin's?"

Hollie nodded, passing the bundle over to her. Maria looked at it. "And these are his hairs?"

Again, Hollie nodded and Maria gave a thumbs up gesture. "This is fantastic. The police should easily be able to get a DNA match from this. I will phone them straight away and they can get to work. It will take them about twenty-four hours to get a result, but fingers crossed, they will have a match by this time tomorrow."

"That's assuming it was him," said Hollie, exercising a little bit of caution.

"I am pretty certain that it is the same guy. The English girl — she described him and to me he sounded exactly like the man you were with. Anyway, if nothing else, at least we will know if it is the same man. I certainly hope it is, the thoughts of having more than one such evil man on our beautiful island is very distressing for me."

"I guess it would be," said Hollie, not having looked at it that way before. "Anyway, will you call me as soon as the police come back to you?"

"Of course, I will. Don't worry, the minute I get a call, so will you."

## *Jack*

Jack timed his call home perfectly, knowing full well that Liz would be rushing to get out the door to bring the kids to school. She answered on the second ring, sounding harassed, as he knew she would and despite everything, he smiled at the familiarity of the scene.

"Eh, yes, hello," she said and he could picture her, grabbing a hold of lunches with one hand, phone perched on her shoulder, tearing around the kitchen in a frantic fashion.

"Oh, Liz, love, it's me," he said casually. "Sorry, didn't realise what time it was, you're probably rushing around like a headless chicken as usual."

"You can sing that," she said, then shouted up the stairs to the kids, "Josh! Jane! In the car now! Sorry, Jack, I really can't stop now. Everything okay with you?"

"Yeah, fine, not a bother," he said. "Just wanted to check in, I've missed you the last couple of times I called and thought I'd catch you before I head out for a round of golf. Everything okay with you and the kids?"

"Peachy! Jack, just peachy!" she said in that sarcastic tone she always used when she was under pressure. "Look, I've really got to go now, enjoy your golf."

He didn't know if the edge to her voice was perceived or imagined and dismissing it as his own guilty conscience, he sat back and signalled to the breakfast waiter that he was ready to order. Job done, he thought smugly, hoping that that one brief phone call would carry him through until the following day. A text should suffice later, avoiding the necessity for another conversation that left him feeling like a hypocrite.

## Liz

Liz was absolutely seething as she put the phone down. The audacity of the man, to phone and sound so blasé. But then again, she had no idea just how long his affair had been going on for. For all she knew, he had been practising this duplicity for months, even years, and perhaps by now it was second nature to him. She hoped against hope that the kids, who were already in the car, and had been for the duration of the telephone conversation, hadn't heard her call out to them or they would think she was losing her marbles.

Sheepishly, she peered out the front door, and was relieved to see them chatting away to each other, completely oblivious to her actions. Totally rattled by the call, she forced herself to take in several deep breaths, exhaling slowly in a bid to lower her heart rate, which had been sent pounding from the adrenalin produced whilst talking to Jack. She needed to remain calm in front of the kids, not wanting them to get any hint of what was going on until she had formulated a clear plan of action for herself. Sufficiently calm, she hurried out to the car.

She was back home from the school run half an hour later and closing the front door behind her, she leant her back against it and slowly slid down to the floor. The effort of keeping up the façade of normality in front of the kids had exhausted her. It was only when she thought of them that a deep sadness overwhelmed her, causing hot, stinging tears to slide forlornly down her face. How would they react to the news that their parents were splitting up? She somehow figured that Josh, by far the least emotional of the pair, would be alright with it. But Jane, the quintessential 'Daddy's Girl' would be devastated.

There was little that Liz could do to spare them the inevitable hurt that they would experience from the break-up. It pained her to think of them suffering in any way, but for the first time since either of them were born, she knew that she couldn't put their needs before her own. She needed out of this marriage.

Picking herself up off the floor, she went into the kitchen and filled the kettle. Waiting for it to boil, she went in search of a pen and paper, and having found them, left them on the kitchen table while she made herself a coffee, before sitting down to work out a plan of action.

Firstly, she needed to see if there was any news regarding the ash cloud. To this end, she turned on the small TV set in the kitchen and switched the channel to Sky News. She heaved a sigh of relief when she discovered that there was no chance of the airports re-opening today, allowing her at least another twenty-four hours before Jack's return. This gave her a bit of time to build a picture of what she was dealing with.

The second thing on her list was to try and establish exactly whom Jack was having the affair with. Automatically, she had assumed that it had to be someone from work, but the more she thought about it, she saw that that wasn't necessarily the case. It could well be a member of that flash gym he had joined last year — although that concept seemed a tad clichéd. In any case, she wanted to know who the bitch was.

Next, she wanted to know who knew about it. It mattered to her knowing just how many people Jack had made a fool out of her in front of. And that's exactly what she felt like — a fool. She had trusted him; loved him; made a home for them and their children; going along with his wishes for her to remain at home to raise the kids and in return he had made a fool of her.

She was glad that Pauline and Jimmy hadn't known, and Pauline had seemed pretty adamant that neither did Peter or Helen. That was good. The six of them socialised together occasionally and she couldn't bear the thought of sitting in their company and being the only one ignorant of Jack's infidelity.

Lastly, she wanted to figure out how she was going to approach the subject with Jack. The only thing she knew for certain was that any such approach would not contain any grey areas — as far as she was concerned their marriage was over and she wanted to convey this message, eliminating any prospect of them working through this, because she simply wasn't prepared to do that.

## Denise

The first person that Denise saw when she walked through the doors of the clinic on Wednesday morning was Nurse Williams, hurrying through reception.

"Good morning, Denise," she called out, stopping at the desk to gather up an armful of files, "Ah, here's your one," she said, then in an aside to the receptionist, she added, "I'll take Denise up, Jackie. She's one of mine."

Then, grinning at Denise, she swept back her free arm, indicating for Denise to pass on by and pressed the button to call the lift. Once inside the lift car, Denise felt her nervousness abate as Nurse Williams chatted away easily to her, making small talk about the weather and the ash cloud phenomenon that saw all Europe's airports still at a standstill.

"I suppose that must affect you," she said and then, the penny dropped. "Oh, so that explains why you came by ferry — I couldn't figure that out the other day. Thought maybe you were afraid of flying or something."

"Not at all," said Denise. "Trust me, it beats the hell out of the ferry and train, although I was lucky enough to get a lift from another passenger on Sunday."

"That was lucky, Sunday trains can be a total nightmare. Will you get a lift back?"

"I dunno. Not sure exactly when he's going back — maybe. But, I believe the trains aren't too bad during the week."

"Anyway," said Nurse Williams as the lift stopped and they stepped out on to the second floor. "How've you been feeling?"

"So, so," said Denise, holding out her hand, palm down and rocking it from side to side to illustrate her words. "Some cramping and nausea, but nothing too bad."

"Well, I did warn you that that was likely to happen and the good thing is, it means the drugs are working. Now, I'm going to pop you into this room here, there's a hospital robe there on the bed, if you want to undress, slip into that and get into the bed, I'll be back into you in a few minutes and we'll get you sorted out."

"Okay," said Denise meekly, pushing open the door of room 209. "How long do you reckon I'll be here for?"

"As I told you the other day, we'll see how it goes, but more than likely until about three-thirty, four o'clock. Did you bring a book or anything?"

"Yeah. I've got one in here," she said, tapping the side of her bag. "I came prepared."

"Good girl, that's what we like to see. There should be a remote for the TV there on the locker as well. We'll keep you entertained. Right, be back in two minutes."

Denise undressed, folded up her clothes neatly, placing them into the small single wardrobe and was sitting up in the bed when Nurse Williams returned. This was the part Denise had dreaded the most as the Misoprostol had to be inserted into her vagina, but aware of her discomfort, Nurse Williams continued talking to her throughout the procedure reducing the embarrassment factor significantly.

"Right. We're all done. Now, can I get you a cup of tea or coffee?"

"A coffee would be lovely," said Denise, fixing the duvet back over her legs and restoring her dignity in the process.

When she brought her back the coffee, Nurse Williams sat down on the side of the bed. "What happens next," she began to explain, "is that the neck of the womb will start to relax, the tablets you've just had will cause you to have some contractions and over the course of the next few hours, your body will expel the pregnancy sac and then, the whole thing will be over. The contractions can be quite painful, generally a bit like a really heavy period, but there is pain relief available, so, don't hesitate to ask if you need something. Ok?"

"Yeah, grand," said Denise, glad to be on the homeward stretch.

### Annette

"There really are worse things than this," thought Annette smugly to herself, as she applied the final bits of sun lotion, before stretching out on the sun lounger and reaching for her book. The girls were still in bed and Maureen had strolled into the town with a couple of her buddies, leaving Annette alone to sunbathe in peace.

Sparing a thought for poor Paddy back home in rainy Dublin, she decided to give him a call. This would have been Paddy's idea of heaven, and she did feel bad for him that he had missed out on it completely. As soon as she heard his voice, still sounding sleepy, she realised how much she missed him. He was such an even-tempered individual, so laid back and calm, and despite all their years together, he always managed to sound really pleased to hear from her, even now, when she had so clearly woken him up. Suddenly, remembering the time difference, she glanced at her watch and saw that it still wasn't quite seven thirty at home.

Giggling, she said, "Oh, sorry, love. Did I wake you?"

"Not at all," he said and she could picture him rubbing his head into the pillows as he did every morning when he first awoke. "I always sound this sexy when I'm just back from my run."

"Yeah right!" she laughed. As the manager of a health club, one of his pet hates was seeing joggers out running on the road, making him the unlikeliest of candidates for doing so himself. "And I suppose you're just about to have your organic Muesli, with low fat; low carb; low sodium, mega healthy trimmings — yeah?"

"Did you wire this place for CCTV before you left? That's uncanny — how did you know?" he quipped back, sounding far more awake now. "Anyway, what are you doing up so early?"

"Maureen was up at cockcrow to go into town with her new 'gang' and I decided to take advantage of the fact that the girls are still comatose and I snuck down to the pool for a little 'me' time."

"Ahhh, but you're missing me," he teased.

"I am actually," she said, smiling. "It's such a pity you didn't make it, Paddy. You'd love it here. We'll definitely have to come back. So, what are you up to?"

"Dunno yet. I'm going to pop into work for a couple of hours, but I'm thinking of slipping away early and maybe playing a round of golf. I'll see what the weather is like, it looks a bit cloudy at the minute, but hopefully it'll brighten up later — that's the forecast anyway. I might give Jack a shout — see if he fancies a game."

"Jack? But, he's in Portugal isn't he?"

"Aw, shit, yeah! I forgot. Sure, he's stranded same as you guys. I can always just go up to the club house, see who's around — there's bound to be someone available."

"I must actually give Liz a shout later — see how she's bearing up with Jack still away."

Paddy laughed at that. He was quite fond of his wife's brother-in-law, but felt he gave poor Liz a bit of a dog's life with his uber-macho attitude, asserting himself as the undisputed head of the house whilst Liz went along compliantly with his assertions. "I'm sure she is coping just fine," he said. "Probably doesn't know herself — free rein of the TV. Unless…."

"Unless what?"

"Unless Jack took the remote control with him!" he teased.

Annette laughed. "Wouldn't entirely surprise me," she said. They regularly joked about Jack's ways and Annette was constantly warning Paddy not to get any ideas. "Anyway, I'll probably give her a call later. Right, great craic and all as it is chatting to you, this pool is looking very inviting!"

"Oh, go on! Rub it in! You always were a heartless woman Mrs. Forbes!"

She was still smiling at their good-humoured exchange, as she lowered herself into the pool, vowing to swim ten lengths before treating herself to a large cappuccino. "Yep, definitely — worse things than this," she reminded herself.


## Rachel

Pulling herself gracefully out of the water, Rachel perched on the side of the pool, where she knew that she would be in full view of the group of young English lads sitting at the pool bar downing pints of lager, despite it only being early morning still. Without even looking in their direction, she could tell that they were nudging one another, making lewd comments about what they would like to do to her and she loved it.

Even though she had no interest in younger men, and certainly not of the lager swilling variety, she always found their attentions titillating, es-pecially when she knew full well that Jack was studiously trying to ignore the whole scene. Lying on his sun lounger, pretending to read his paper, she could both see and sense his hostility towards these young bucks and their reaction to her.

With the length of the pool separating her from her admirers, she acted as if she was oblivious to their presence. Climbing to her feet, she grabbed the towel she had left nearby and slowly began to dab off the beads of moisture that glistened on her mahogany skin. A chorus of wolf whistles broke out as she did this. Then, as if noticing them for the first time, she casually flicked her long blonde hair over her shoulder and in a practised gesture; she threw them a dirty look and strode over to where Jack was.

"Bloody lager louts!" she said in mock contempt, as if affronted by their behaviour. "Honestly, a woman can't even have a quiet swim in peace."

Clearly relieved to have her back with him, Jack said, "Guess that's the price you've got to pay for being gorgeous, babe!"

"Oh, thanks, sweetie," she said, dropping a kiss on the top of his head, before stretching out on the next sun lounger. She lifted her book so he couldn't see her face, hiding a self-satisfied smile and thinking 'and don't you forget it, pal!'

### *Donal*

The combination of an exhausting few days; the drinks of the night before and the knowledge that the morning was his own, caused Donal to sleep deeply, not even stirring until almost nine thirty. Hoping that he hadn't missed breakfast, he jumped straight out of the bed and pulled on the clothes that he had carelessly strewn on the floor, before rushing down to the dining room.

Just in the nick of time, he caught the waiter who had served him the previous morning and resisting the urge to smack him in the mouth when he asked if 'sir was going to eat his breakfast this morning?', he ordered up a full English breakfast with toast and coffee.

He was more than surprised to find that the first thing he thought of when he had finished eating was a cigarette. Years of abstinence counted for nothing, because now his longing for a smoke was as great as it had ever been when he had a twenty a day habit. The realisation amazed him and he instantly regretted binning the pack he had bought, reluctant to admit to Denise, or anyone for that matter, that he had smoked. Succumbing to his urges, with the true smoker's mentality that he could always quit again when he got back to Dublin, he left the hotel and went to buy some more.

Once again, he went to the park, where he was mildly disappointed not to see 'Golden Retriever' man, breaking the 'Ground Hog Day' experience as he sat down on the same bench and lit a cigarette. He tried calling Kay's house to see how Susan was doing, but there was no reply and he wasn't altogether upset about that. Next, he called Hollie, who sounded much more upbeat than she had when they had last spoken.

"Hey, Hols — how are ya doing?"

"Oh, Donal — much better! You'll never guess what happened."

"Go on," he urged, not sure where this was going.

"I found Eoin's hairbrush under my bed."

Not getting the significance of her find, he asked, "And?"

"And nothing. That's it. I found his hairbrush and it has samples of his hair on it, so, now, the police are running a DNA test and hopefully they will be able to identify him as the person who raped that English girl I told you about."

The penny finally dropping, Donal grinned. "That's great, Hollie. Hopefully, they'll get the bastard now." Then, more to himself than to her, he added, "Maybe we won't need Denise after all."

"Hey?" she asked, sounding confused. "Who's Denise and what's she got to do with Eoin?"

"Oh, nothing. Nothing. Sorry. Denise is the woman that I told you I gave a lift to London to. Well, last night, she offered to pay for a Private Investigator to track this Eoin guy down."

"She did what?" spluttered Hollie.

"I know. I know. It all sounds very bizarre. But, it was a genuine offer, Hols. She just really wanted to help."

"But why? I don't get it."

"I'm not entirely sure that I do either. She told me that she had personal reasons, so, I dunno, maybe something similar happened to her before and this is her opportunity to do for someone else what she should have done for herself."

"Sounds a little crazy to me," said Hollie. "Anyway, if this DNA matches up and the police get him, that'll be the end of that."

Donal lit up another cigarette, instantly regretting it when Hollie said, "Hey! Are you smoking?"

"I'm just having one," he answered in a slightly petulant tone. "Don't go making a big deal out of it."

"I won't, but I'm not so sure that your wife won't when I tell her," teased Hollie. "I'm going to give her a call as soon as we've finished!"

"Don't you dare!" laughed Donal, knowing full well that there was no chance that she would ever betray any confidence he shared with her. All through their lives they had been each other's greatest confidante and in many ways they would need each other now more than ever. Wishing him luck for his big meeting, she rang off, extracting a promise from him to let her know how it went.

CHAPTER FOURTEEN

# Wednesday PM 21st April

*Liz*

With a strength and determination that she hitherto hadn't realised she possessed, Liz set about gathering whatever information she could about Jack's affair. The obvious place to start was with his laptop. Going upstairs, she once again removed it from the wardrobe and powered it up. With none of the reservations about invading his privacy that had held her back the previous day, she sat down on the bed and opened up his email account.

Going back to the first page of his 'in-box', she established that the account had been in operation since the beginning of the year, giving a life span of at least four months to the affair. "Lying, cheating, bastard!" she muttered to herself as she opened up the first message, wondering if it would hold any clue as to the sender's identity. But, it didn't, simply asking the question 'Hey Babe, you still okay for tonight? See you in the usual place, 8.30ish, xx'. So, they'd obviously been seeing each other long enough to have a 'usual place', she thought bitterly, still none the wiser as to who this mystery bitch was.

Most of the emails were short and to the point, generally just confirming arrangements to meet or on a couple of occasions, 'the bitch' had to cancel due to work commitments. But overall, they offered no insight into who she might be. Liz actually found the whole process quite tedious, meticulously opening up and reading each one, garnering no real useful information as she did so, other than the fact that her husband was a deceitful bollocks, capable of covering his tracks very well. She would have to check some of the dates against the calendar in the kitchen to see what lies he had fed her in order to keep his dates with his mistress.

The first week in March showed a marked increase in the volume of emails, with the content of these being somewhat longer than the previous ones. Casting her mind back to see if there was anything significant about that time, she remembered that that was the week Jack had been off work with the flu. He had been a right misery guts for the entire week, holing up in the bedroom with the laptop permanently fired up. She had even felt sorry for him, assuming that it was work related and chastising him for not telling them to piss off, that he was sick and to deal with things themselves.

Now, she knew differently. It wasn't a preoccupation with work that kept him surgically attached to his laptop but being confined to the house and unable to meet her or call her, his laptop had been their primary source of communication. Once again, she felt like a fool. Angrily, she opened up a longer than usual email, wherein 'the bitch', clearly no 'Florence Nightingale', offered him little sympathy for his condition. 'I doubt very much that you NEED to see a doctor, it sounds to me like nothing more than the flu, although I do know of some cases of 'Man Flu' that have had some pretty dire consequences! Hope it's not that particular strain you have! Wuss!'

When she thought about how she personally had pandered to him for that entire week, how the kids had walked on eggshells around him, whilst his bad humour had pervaded the house, yet somehow he had managed to keep up this level of jocularity with this silly tart, Liz was furious. She slammed down the lid of the laptop, vowing that the next time the lousy bastard was sick; he certainly wouldn't be her problem.

### Denise

Hard as she tried, Denise couldn't get into the book that she had brought with her. It wasn't as if she was in pain or anything, in fact she had felt far worse on Monday than she did today. Taking Nurse Williams's advice, she had requested pain relief at the first signs of discomfort and despite being able to feel the occasional contracting of her stomach muscles, she felt no pain. As yet, she had still not passed the pregnancy sac, but instinct told her that that time was getting nearer.

Her busy mind was what prevented her from concentrating on the words in front of her and finally, she gave up, casting the book to one side and succumbing to her thoughts. They were all about Donal. It was difficult not to think about him when he had poured his heart out to her the night before about him and his wife's desperation for a baby while she was lying here getting rid of one. She wondered how he would have reacted if he had known the purpose of her visit to London.

She couldn't help but feel that he was very misguided if he thought that having a baby was going to solve his and Susan's problems. Although she hadn't met her, she had formed an opinion of Susan that wasn't altogether favourable. Donal was such a nice man and from what he had told her, Susan sounded to be a very self-absorbed individual and it seemed to Denise that she was always going to be dissatisfied with her lot. Bringing a baby into that equation would be ludicrous in her opinion.

She felt really sorry for him, he had so much on his plate with trying to get his business off the ground and now this thing with Hollie, and his wife, whom she felt should surely be supporting him, wasn't even taking his phone calls. He didn't deserve all this. She hoped with all her heart that today's meeting went well for him, at least, that would give him a much-needed boost to contend with the other issues in his life.

It struck her as ironic that a chance meeting on a ferry brought together two such polar opposite situations. On the one hand, there was her — escaping a damaging relationship, all the money in the world and an unwanted pregnancy and, on the other hand, he was trying to preserve a relationship that appeared to be damaging to him, struggling financially and desperately wanting a baby. Life could be very cruel, she thought, sending him off a text wishing him luck with his meeting.

### Annette

Annette had passed a thoroughly enjoyable day, primarily on her own, which had suited her just fine. When the girls had finally surfaced just before lunchtime, they came down and asked permission to go into Palma with Jody and Debs. Deeming it safe enough with the four of them going together, Annette agreed that they could go and issued them with a long list of instructions that caused the girls to throw their eyes up to heaven.

"I mean it, girls," she said in an authoritative manner. "Stick together, all of you have your phones on at all times and back here by seven o'clock — no later!"

Meekly, they agreed, causing Annette to smile as they retreated from the pool area sedately, and then, she heard them charge off excitedly in search of their friends. Maureen made an appearance shortly after their departure and they shared a very enjoyable lunch together in the pool bar, before Maureen retired to her room for an afternoon nap.

Annette woke with a start when her mobile started ringing and pulling it out from beneath her towel; she struggled to see who it was that was calling her. Dizzy from sitting up so quickly, and with the sun's rays shining on the screen, she couldn't make out the caller's name before it rang off. Assuming it was one of the girls and fearful that something dreadful had befallen them, she shifted around on the sun lounger, causing a shadow to fall over her phone, enabling her to identify the caller.

Instantly relieved to see that it was only her sister, she gathered up her belongings and headed back up to the suite before calling her back. Liz would only be calling for a chat and the day's sunbathing had left her feeling hot and sticky - a shower and a cup of tea would leave her feeling better prepared for a catch up. Twenty minutes later, mug in hand, she settled herself into a seat on the balcony and dialled Liz's number. The moment that Liz answered the phone, she knew that something was very wrong.

"Liz? What is it? What's wrong?" she asked, hearing the catch in her sister's voice.

"Just give me a sec," said Liz, "I need to go out to the garden. The kids are upstairs and I don't want them to hear me."

Annette could hear the sound of the back door being opened, then closed and waited patiently for Liz to come back on the line.

"It's Jack," she said, sounding tearful.

"Oh my God! What's happened to him? Has he had an accident?"

"No, no accident," spat Liz, contemptuously. "He's having an affair."

"What do you mean — he's having an affair? Isn't he away in Portugal with the lads golfing? Are you sure you're not just jumping to conclusions?"

"I'm not jumping to conclusions," she snapped back, hysterically. "Yes, he's still away, but wherever he is, he's not with the lads — they're both here in Dublin."

"Jesus!" exclaimed Annette, trying to come to grips with what she was hearing. "So, where is he?"

"That's just it. I don't know. But wherever he is, he's with some silly tart that he's been seeing for months."

"But, how on earth do you know this?" asked Annette.

Liz filled her in on all that had happened since Monday, starting with seeing Jimmy's car and phoning up Pauline to slag her. Rapt, Annette listened, not interrupting until Liz brought her up to date with the contents of the emails she had read. The evidence was pretty indisputable. Annette was at a loss for something comforting to say, her sister's anguish was heartrending and she wished more than anything that she could be there with her.

Within seconds, Annette's pragmatic side kicked in, her mind computing and analysing the information it had received. Putting herself in Liz's position, unimaginable as that might be, she knew that it would somehow be important to establish exactly where Jack was.

If he was devious enough to have set up a secret email account, then, the chances were that he wouldn't have booked the flights off his computer, although it was still worth checking out. She told Liz to check his regular email account for any correspondence from either an airline or travel company. That would be particularly sweet, as any booking would probably include the names of both passengers. However, she didn't hold out much hope for Liz making such an easy discovery.

With a flash of inspiration, she suggested that Liz should go through the history of the Internet sites that Jack had visited in the preceding few weeks. Perhaps there was a chance that even if he didn't make the booking, he could well have gone in to see what the hotel or resort they were visiting was like. Dispatching Liz to check out both these avenues of investigation, she asked her to phone back as soon as she had finished.

Less than ten minutes later, Liz was back on the phone, sounding breathless. "You'll never guess where the fucker is?"

"You found the booking?" asked Annette, incredulous. "Who's the other passenger?"

"No. You were right. No booking. But, I did as you said and on several different occasions, he has visited a site for a fucking five star hotel, if you don't mind, in…, and you're really not going to believe this?"

"Where?" said Annette, gasping with impatience.

"Ma-fucking-jorca!"

"Majorca! You're kidding me," exclaimed Annette, as a thought crossed her mind, too awful to contemplate. Rachel! Resisting the temptation to mention that she had bumped into her the other day, she decided to keep that information to herself, not wanting to put an even more painful scenario to her beloved sister without a shred of evidence. Instead, she took down the name of the hotel and said that she would see whereabouts on the island it was and if it was anywhere accessible from where she herself was, then, she might pay it a visit.

### Hollie

Doing a double take as she walked through reception, Hollie was surprised to see Annette engrossed on the Internet at the public computer in the corner. She went over to greet her, making her jump when she laid her hand on her shoulder and said.

"Hey, what ya up to?"

Annette swung around nervously, dropping down the screen as if she didn't want anyone to see what she was doing. "Oh! It's you," she said, clasping her hand to her chest, relieved that it was Hollie standing there.

"I'm sorry. I didn't mean to frighten you." Hollie thought that Annette looked a bit rattled, and although she didn't want to pry, she was reluctant to just walk off. "Is everything okay Annette?"

Glancing furtively over Hollie's shoulders to ensure that they were alone, Annette restored the screen to the web page she had been looking at, inviting Hollie to have a look.

"Mmmm, very nice," said Hollie, looking at the images of an opulent hotel with its own private beach. "You're not thinking of moving, are you?" she asked, horrified at the prospect of being left here alone.

"No, but I am thinking of paying a visit."

"Huh?" asked Hollie, confused. "I'm not sure I follow you."

Exiting out of the Internet, Annette stood up and grabbing Hollie by the arm, she pulled her out on to the terrace. "That hotel is about twenty kilometres from Palma Nova," she said, nodding her head in a knowing gesture.

Utterly clueless as to what she meant, Hollie said, "I'm sorry Annette, but I really don't know what you are talking about."

Annette gave a peculiar half laugh, then, as if something dawned on her, she said, "Oh my God! I'm sorry. My head is just swimming with this; you must think I've gone mad." Then, in an effort to explain, she said, "I've been talking to Liz, my sister, and from what she's just told me and what you said the other day, I've put two and two together and come up with a resounding five!"

Hollie stared blankly back at her, beginning to think that perhaps the older woman had stayed out in the sun a bit too long or something. Whatever she was talking about, she really wasn't making any sense at all. "Okay, let's take this from the top — shall we? Why don't you tell me what the conversation with your sister was about and then, maybe, I can figure out what's going on?"

"Well," began Annette. "My sister phoned me earlier and told me that she had discovered that her husband, who's meant to be in Portugal playing golf, is in fact having an affair and has gone away on holiday somewhere with the woman that he is seeing. Now, by chance, two days ago we bumped in to Rachel Wallace in Palma — you told me that everyone in work suspects that she is carrying on with a married man. She tells us that she is staying in a hotel about twenty kilometres from Palma Nova and Liz found details of that hotel I showed you on Jack's computer and, would you believe it, that hotel is about twenty kilometres from Palma Nova — can this all just be a big coincidence? Or, …"

"Or, Dr. Wallace is having an affair with your brother-in-law!" interjected Hollie, barely able to contain her enthusiasm. "You don't really think that's possible — do you?"

"I really don't know what to think," she answered. "Up until a couple of hours ago, I wouldn't have thought that Jack would be that stupid. But, now, it's obvious that he is definitely having an affair. Rachel is here, even though she told Liz that she was going to the Canaries. Maybe, it is all just one big coincidence, but you've got to admit it all smells a bit fishy — doesn't it?"

"What did Liz say about Rachel being here?"

"I didn't actually tell her that we met her. I thought she had enough to contend with at the moment and it would be a bit unfair to upset her unnecessarily if I'm wrong."

"I suppose you're right," agreed Hollie. "So, what are you going to do? Are you seriously thinking of going over there?"

"I think I'm going to have to. For Liz's sake, I need to find out what Jack is up to. I think I'll get a taxi over there in the morning, do a little nosing around and see what I can come up with."

"Do you want me to go with you?"

"Would you?" asked Annette. Then her face clouded over, "But I know you don't want to bump into Rachel and there's every chance that we will, if what I suspect is true."

Hollie pondered on it for a moment, then thinking about all the things Annette had done for her in the past week, she grinned at her. "Who cares? It's a shitty job anyway. If this is true, I don't want to work for the silly cow."

The prospect of seeing the snooty Dr. Wallace caught red-handed, in the arms of her best-friend's husband, by her best friend's sister, was just too sweet an opportunity to miss.

### Jack

Shuffling his sandy feet into his flip-flops, Jack was feeling very relaxed as they packed up their bits and pieces and prepared to leave the beach. With his backpack over his shoulder, he pulled Rachel to him, giving her a warm squeeze and planting a kiss on her mouth.

"What's that for?" she asked, a smile touching her lips.

"Just 'cos you're gorgeous," he said in response, nuzzling his bristly face into her neck.

"Oohh! Get off! You're all scratchy," she said, trying to disentangle herself.

"Says you — all covered in sand," he laughed, reluctantly pulling himself away from her. "Come on you, let's go and get ourselves cleaned up and then, we'll hit the town."

"Oh! That sounds good — I'm starving. This sea air can really give a girl an appetite."

"We know all about your appetites, Dr. Wallace," he said. "And, not all of them are for food!"

Laughing good-humouredly, she accepted his proffered hand and the two of them strolled hand in hand towards the steps back up to the hotel. The pool area was deserted when they reached the top and despite being all grotty from the beach, they decided to grab a quick, thirst-quenching, beer after their arduous climb. They sat up on two bar stools at one end of the bar and tried to catch the attention of the idle bar man, who stood polishing the same glass over and over again, as he stared at the football match being shown on the TV.

"Perdone por favor," called Jack in his finest Spanish, causing Rachel to giggle uncontrollably.

"Smooth, Jack! Really smooth. Spoken like a native!" she teased, still giggling.

"You order the beers then, smart ass," he said, feigning hurt. He watched her slip from the stool, but missed her actually ordering as his phone beeped in his pocket. Fully expecting it to be Liz, he was surprised to see Jimmy's name. Curious as to why Jimmy would be texting him, he opened the message. "Aw fuck! Fuck! Fuck!" he roared, unable to believe the words before him. Dunno what de story is mate, but Liz knows ur not away with me & Pete. Thought u'd wanna no.

The bar man and Rachel threw a horrified look in his direction as his expletives drowned out her order. Calmly, she repeated it, apologising for Jack's outburst as she did so, then taking the two glasses in her hands, she came back to join him.

"What the hell was all that about?" she asked through gritted teeth, embarrassed by his bad manners. "This is a five star hotel, for Chrissake!"

"I know — I'm sorry. Just got a bit of a shock," he said, passing her the phone for her to read the message herself. He stared at her face whilst she read it, waiting to see how she was going to react. But, there was no discernible reaction. She read it, then placed the phone back on the bar, keeping her features static as she did so, saying nothing. Conscious that he was holding his breath, he waited for her to break the silence, but still, she said nothing. Unable to out wait her, he asked. "So? What now?"

Finally, she moved her body around to face him and shrugged, not looking particularly bothered by the text. "So? She knows you're not away with them. Probably even suspects that you're having an affair. But, tell me Jack, what exactly can we do about it now — from here? Nothing, Jack. Absolutely, bloody, nothing. She's going to know a hell of a lot more next week, so, take my advice, Jack and save your energies for that."

Not liking her words, but hearing the wisdom in them, Jack said nothing. He pursed up his closed mouth, and nodding, he silently signalled his agreement to what she had said, then reached for his pint and downed it in one.

### Rachel

Rachel wasn't entirely disappointed by the fact that Liz now knew something. At least this way, Jack wouldn't be dragging his heels about telling her when he got back to Dublin. She was curious however, to know how much Liz knew and was even considering phoning her to see what she could establish, but when she had put that idea to Jack, he had dismissed it out of hand.

"No way, Rach," he said. "I've no idea how Liz found out that I wasn't away with Jimmy and Peter. Therefore, I've no clue how much she knows. Supposing she has somehow got wind of the two of us, then, you phoning at this point would be like rubbing salt in the wound and I don't want to be cruel to her."

"I know, but the odds are on that I'm not in the picture at all and at least, I would be able to tell you what to expect. I'd only be doing it for you, Babe."

The more he resisted the idea, the better she liked it and now wished that she had kept her mouth shut, not said anything to him at all and just made the call. She could always have reported back to him afterwards, but now that opportunity was missed as to do so would undoubtedly cause a row.

She wondered if Liz had said anything to the kids yet — she doubted it. She probably wouldn't want them to find out. Probably thought that a spot of marriage counselling and a weekend in Killarney would save her marriage. Probably had labelled Jack as 'going through some mid-life crisis' the way so many of these pathetic women who had lost their husbands did.

She saw them regularly in the surgery — coming in for something to help them sleep — they poured their hearts out to her, all singing the same tune. None of them had any idea why their husbands were behaving this way — they drove Rachel insane. Sometimes she sat there with a sympathetic look on her face listening to their tales of woe, as they sat there bawling their eyes out, with snot dripping off the end of their noses and they wondered why their husbands were leaving them. And, laughably, would ask her did she think that counselling would help. Of course, she would provide them with names of counsellors; write them a prescription; make sympathetic noises to them, when she felt like screaming 'Go home and look at yourself in the mirror — then, you'll know why your husband is leaving, you silly cow! And, NO! Counselling won't help, so don't kid yourself!' But, of course, she never did.

### Donal

"Taxi!" called Donal as he stepped out of his hotel, on his way to meet Denise for dinner again. The big black cab pulled over and he hopped in, giving the driver the address of the restaurant near her hotel where they had arranged to meet.

His day had been a roller coaster experience and he was glad that she was up for meeting for dinner when he phoned her. She had sounded a bit tired, and he promised that he wouldn't keep her out too late, but desperate for some company tonight, he would have begged her if necessary, but it hadn't been. Despite her pleading, he had doggedly refused to give her any information about his meeting until they met, laughing at her grumblings, but not capitulating.

He saw her crossing at the lights when he got out of the taxi and waving over to her, he waited at the corner while she crossed. With no preamble, she looked him square in the face and said.

"Well?"

Laughing at her, he shrugged. "Honestly, Denise. I'm not sure. The whole thing was not what I expected at all. Anyway, it's a long story, so let's go in, get a table and then I can give you the full low down."

The restaurant wasn't too busy and they were seated quickly. The menu was quite extensive but, not in the mood for trawling through it, Donal just ordered a steak, medium-rare and Denise followed suit. A bottle of house red completed their order, leaving them free to talk.

"Well, I suppose the first good thing was that Arthur Carter himself showed up. So, that was a promising start. But, it felt like less of a meeting and more of an interview if you know what I mean. He clearly had done his homework on my product, knew it nearly as well as I do, in fact. As soon as he saw the prototype, he just went up to it, popped the capsule in and saw it in action. He seemed very impressed."

"All sounds good so far," said Denise, picking up her wine glass and taking a sip.

"Yeah, like I say, it wasn't that it was bad or anything, just different to what I expected. I suppose I kind of thought that they'd either like the product or not, and, if they did like it that they would give me a big order. But, it wasn't like that."

"So, what did happen?"

"Well, he wasn't much of a talker. He spent most of his time peering at his notes, scribbling down some things, a couple of taps on the calculator — half the time he acted like I wasn't even there. Then, when I thought we would get down to discussing an order, he told me that they liked the product, that they would take it on, look after its manufacturing and that

I would receive twenty per cent of the profits from each unit. I mean, the matter wasn't open for discussion, this was the offer — take it or leave it. That's what I mean about it being more of an interview. I certainly didn't feel that I was participating in a meeting."

"And, what did you say to his offer?"

"I told him that I would have to think about it. You know, twenty per cent of the profit was not what I had in mind. Although I know, I know — twenty per cent of something is better than one hundred per cent of nothing! But, it sounds like this way, I'll be relinquishing everything to do with my own product and I'm not sure that I want to do that. I want to be more involved, more kind of hands on — you know?"

"Yeah, I guess this thing is sort of 'your baby' and you feel squeezed out."

"Absolutely! That's exactly it. I want to have a future with this product, not just some cheque in the post each month. He's given me a full report on the kind of volume of sales they would expect to be making within the next two years, and I guess I'll have to go through all that to see how viable their offer is. But, right here, right now, my gut is telling me to walk away from this deal."

"Following your gut isn't a bad thing."

"I know. I suppose this was my first really big meeting. There are still a lot of potential investors out there, people who might be more prepared to do things my way — maybe, I should check them all out first."

"I think you should. I know you're keen to get this rolling, but maybe jumping in with the first person you talk to isn't the way to go. When do you have to let him know your decision?"

"I told him that I'd need a week to think about it."

"And, was he okay with that?"

"Yeah. He told me he would want my answer by lunchtime next Wednesday. So, that gives me a week, but to be perfectly honest, I think I know my answer already."

185

CHAPTER FIFTEEN

# Thursday AM 22nd April

### *Annette*

Not wanting to wake any of the others, Annette crept to the kitchen and put on the kettle before heading into the bathroom. Her plan was to get back before the girls got up and starting asking awkward questions about what she was up to. She had to keep this from them, they both adored their Aunty Liz and she didn't want them knowing anything about Jack's affair.

She hadn't slept much through the night, thinking non-stop about Liz and what the future held for her. There was little doubt in her mind that if she were Liz, she would have Jack's bags packed and ready to go on his return home — end of story. But, she was unsure if her sister would be capable of such action. Annette had never understood her soft natured sister's lack of self-esteem, nor the way she had allowed her own self-worth to be so blatantly dictated by her husband's approval or otherwise.

Right from the start of her relationship with Jack, when Liz was only a teenager, it had seemed to Annette that her beautiful and, outwardly at least, vibrant sister had permitted this completely average man to dominate her. Even confiding in Annette that she would be prepared to overlook an infidelity in order to preserve her marriage. Annette sincerely hoped that didn't include one of this magnitude, but suspected that it might. Liz deserved so much more than this and if that bastard was carrying on with

Liz's purported best friend, then, she for one, would do her damnedest to make Liz wake up and smell the coffee.

Immersed in her thoughts, she never saw Maureen in the kitchen when she came out of the bathroom and nearly jumped out of her skin when Maureen spoke to her.

"Stick a cup on for me there — will you, love?"

"Jesus, Maureen, you scared the life out of me. What are you doing up so early?"

"Oh, I woke up and I heard you out here and thought I'd see if you were okay. You seemed a bit preoccupied or something last night over dinner and I didn't want to say anything in front of the girls. Then, when I heard you up and about so early, I thought you must have something on your mind."

Touched by her mother-in-law's concern, Annette smiled at her. "Ah, I'm okay, Maureen. Just had a bit of bad news from Liz last night and I've been thinking about her ever since."

"Something you want to talk about or not?"

Maureen once more surprised her with her sensitivity and quickly weighing up the situation, Annette decided it wouldn't do any harm to tell her what had happened, telling her that she would rather talk out of ear shot of the girls and mouthing that she'd make them both a hot drink and bring it out to the balcony.

Sliding the balcony door shut behind her, Annette passed Maureen her mug of tea and sitting down beside her, she told her all about Liz's phone call and the conclusions that she herself had come to regarding Rachel. Maureen listened intently, absorbing all the details and Annette went on to tell her about her and Hollie's plan to go over to the hotel and confront the pair of them.

At that point, Maureen interrupted her, "Do you think that's such a good idea, love?" she asked kindly. "I mean, what do you think it will achieve?"

"It'll achieve the truth," blurted Annette, somewhat irritated by her mother-in-law's reaction, instantly regretting confiding in her. "I can't have that little shit over there, taking the piss out of my sister and just do nothing."

"Ah, Annette, love, don't take offence. I don't mean to upset you. It's just that maybe rushing in there, all guns blazing isn't the best course of action."

"Well, what do you suggest?" she asked petulantly. "Ask them over for a drink? See what kind of a couple they make?"

"No, nothing like that. But, I do think you would want to tread carefully. By all means, go — check it out, but, personally, I wouldn't approach them. Take some photos if you like, gather evidence. At the end of the day, love, I know she's your sister and you are very upset for her, but, it is her marriage and much as you want to, you don't really have the right to interfere. Equip her with the facts if that's what you want to do, but allow her to deal with it in her own way."

"That's just it though, Maureen — she won't. I know Liz. That little worm will go home to her, apologise, beg her forgiveness, swear blind that it's never happened before and promise faithfully that it'll never happen again and she'll swallow it. She'll take him back, make excuses for him, probably even blame herself for neglecting him and then, the bastard will do it again to her. I know he will."

Maureen's face was thoughtful as she listened to Annette rant and rave, letting her vent her spleen, then, seeing her fill up with tears, she reached across and took her hand. "I know this is difficult for you Annette, but the best thing you can do for your sister is be there for her — whatever her decision, but truly, my love, you can't interfere. It won't do any good."

Calming down a little, Annette started to hear what Maureen was saying and knew that the older woman was right. She knew now where Paddy got his wisdom from; because as sure as if he was sitting there, she knew he would have said exactly the same thing to her. Tearfully, she regarded her mother-in-law and asked her what she should do.

"Go, take some photos, bring them home, show them to your sister and do your best to convince her that she's worth more than this, because if she's anything like her older sister, then, nothing is surer."

### Hollie

Just putting the finishing touches to her make-up, Hollie jumped when there was a loud knock on her door. Instinctively panicking in case it was

Eoin, she held her breath, planning her escape route if it was him. Then, to her relief, she heard Annette's voice, calling out.

"Hey Hollie, it's me, Annette."

Pulling open the door, Hollie left Annette to make her own way in as she hurried back to the bathroom, calling to her over her shoulder.

"Nearly ready. Just give me two minutes and I'll be with you."

"No rush, there's been a change of plan," said Annette to her retreating back.

"Oohh! How come?" asked Hollie, popping her head around the bathroom door, mildly disappointed not to be playing detective.

Annette talked her through the conversation with Maureen and how, on reflection, she had decided to limit herself to taking some photos without making her presence known. Despite her enthusiasm to see Dr. Wallace come a cropper, Hollie had to acknowledge the wisdom of Maureen's advice.

"You've got a good 'un in that mother-in-law of yours," she conceded. "I know it's tempting to dive in there, and to be perfectly honest, I was quite looking forward to seeing Rachel's reaction when she was caught out, but in reality, I think Maureen is right. I know that there have been many times over the years when I've wanted to give Susan, my sister-in-law, a mouthful over the dog's life that she gives my brother, but Donal would never forgive me if I interfered. He gets so defensive of her if I make any comment at all and now I've learnt to keep my trap shut where she's concerned."

"It's so bloody difficult though, isn't it? I mean, sometimes when Liz talks to me about Jack, I find that I don't even want to look at him. God alone knows how I'll manage to be in his company if this is all true and she, as I am certain she will, decides to stay with him."

"I know. I can never see Donal leaving his wife, even though I reckon that in the long run, he'd be a lot happier if he did. So, what's the new plan then?"

As they tried to figure out when would be the best time to catch sight of the adulterous pair, Hollie's mobile started to ring. Grabbing a hold of it, she saw a Spanish number flash up and shot Annette a glance.

"I think this'll be Maria Alvarez about the DNA results," she said, her voice a little shaky. She pressed the answer button and hearing Maria's voice at the other end, she nodded to Annette, confirming that it was her. "Really? Oh my God — that's great news!"

It turned out that the DNA obtained from Eoin's hairbrush was a perfect match for that taken from the semen found in the raped English girl's examination. The police now had something to tie the two incidents together and were anxious to track down this monster before he attacked again. To this end, they requested, via Maria, that Hollie would come down to the station as soon as possible to assist in the compiling of a photo-fit picture of Eoin which they hoped to have on the streets that same evening. More than happy to assist, Hollie told Maria that she would be there within the hour.

Fifty minutes later, Hollie, chaperoned by Annette, made her way up the steps of the flat roofed police station in Palma Nova. It was nowhere near as busy as Hollie had feared and within ten minutes of their arrival; they were seated in a small office with only one small letterbox style window, high up on the wall, providing any natural light. In total there were four people sitting around a circular table in the corner, Hollie, Annette, Elena Marquez, the female police officer who had interviewed Hollie in the hospital and her colleague, Andres.

It was Andres's role to produce the photo-fit. To this end, he opened up his laptop and ran a programme that offered Hollie every conceivable head shape, facial feature and hairstyle to enable her to produce an image as close to a photographic representation of Eoin as possible. Initially over-awed at the prospect, Hollie was amazed at how quickly Andres guided her through by dismissing characteristics and quickly narrowed the field for her, leaving them with a fairly recognisable Eoin on the screen within thirty minutes.

"Wow!" she said. "This is incredible. What did you guys do before this technology was available?"

"Don't even ask," smiled Elena. "A lot of sketching and rubbing out. Anyway, Hollie, you are pleased with this image?"

"Uh-huh. I think it's as close as we will get. To me, it looks like Eoin. Has the English girl been in yet?"

"Yes. She was in about an hour ago and she came up with this," said Elena, opening up a file and pulling out a computer print out of the facial image they had produced with her assistance. With the exception of a couple of minor differences, virtually the same face looked out from the sheet of paper that Elena passed to Hollie as was on the screen of the laptop.

Although the DNA test results had identified Eoin as the perpetrator of both attacks, Hollie was still freaked out by this reinforcement of the fact. It somehow made him more of a monster - knowing with certainty that he had done this to someone else as well. She knew this thinking was a bit irrational. She still had trouble seeing herself as a true victim when it had been her own stupidity that had put her in the position of danger in the first place, but this other girl, all she had done was unwittingly accepted a drink from a guy she didn't know and he had done this to her.

Elena thanked her for coming in and assured her that the police would be out in earnest searching for Eoin, using any resources that they had available to ensure he was detained and arrested as soon as possible. With an enormous sense of relief, Hollie and Annette left the station.

## Jack

Jimmy's text had been gnawing at Jack all night long. He needed to know what Liz had found out and how. There was still no news on the airports being reopened and Jack couldn't avoid ringing home indefinitely, but he needed to know what he was facing into when he did. Rachel was still sound asleep beside him, with her hair lying across her face and her arm outstretched over his chest. Not wanting to disturb her, he gently raised her arm and slid out of the bed. She gave a soft groan, then turned her head into the pillow, without waking.

He picked up his crumpled linen trousers from the floor beside the bed and quickly grabbing a T-shirt, he slipped into the bathroom for a pee and got dressed in there. Silently, he took his mobile phone from the bedside locker, pushed his feet into a pair of flip-flops and let himself out of the room. Riding down in the elevator, he thought about what he would say to Jimmy, who was bound to want to know what the fuck was going on.

Deciding that Jimmy would have to wait for all the gory details on his return, he resolved to say as little as possible to him at this stage, just find

191

out what the story was with Liz. He went out on to the terrace where he was relieved to find that he had the place to himself and dialled Jimmy's number. Anticipating the fifth degree from Jimmy, he was more than surprised to find his friend curt and hostile sounding on the phone.

"What do you want Jack?"

Taken aback by the manner in which he answered the phone, Jack got straight to the point. "Hey, Jimmy, got your text and was just wondering what the story is with Liz."

"The story is Jack," he said, his tone angry, "that you have caused untold grief back here. I don't appreciate you using me and Peter as cover for whatever sordid little affair you are involved in and certainly don't appreciate that you deemed it alright to do so without so much as a word to either of us."

"Aw, look, I'm sorry, mate…," Jack began, but Jimmy wasn't interested in what he had to say.

"Sorry, my arse! You mightn't give a flying fuck about your wife and clearly, you don't, but I happen to care big time about mine. Do you have any idea how upset she was at having to tell Liz that you weren't away with me and Peter — how awkward and embarrassing that was for her? Do you?"

"I never thought that Liz would be in touch with her. This whole thing …."

"I don't fucking want to know, mate," said Jimmy, livid now. "You put me and my wife in a very difficult situation, without any regard whatsoever for either of us. Not to mention, poor Liz. And yes, for your information, she does know you're having an affair and I sincerely hope that she fucks you out on your ear, mate. 'Cos if what's happened proves anything to me, Jack, it's that you are a selfish bollocks who thinks only of yourself."

And with that, Jimmy hung up, leaving Jack staring at the dead phone in his hand, wondering what the fuck to do next.

### Rachel

Rachel was just coming to when Jack let himself back into the room, looking dishevelled and agitated.

"G'morning you," she muttered sleepily, and then taking in his bad-humoured countenance, she raised her head onto one elbow and asked. "What is it? What's wrong?"

"I just got a total bollicking from Jimmy," he said, slamming his phone down on the table. "I called him to find out what had happened with Liz, but I never even got a word in. He went mental, telling me that I'm nothing but a bollocks and that he hopes Liz fucks me out on my ear."

"What's it got to do with him?" she asked, sitting upright in the bed and pulling her knees up to her chest.

"Everything, according to Jimmy. He's going mad 'cos I said that I was away with him and Peter and never mentioned anything to either of them. Said that I put him and Pauline in a very difficult situation and that Liz definitely knows that I'm having an affair."

Rachel let out an inadvertent snigger, "Well, bet you're glad you made that phone call then?"

"This isn't funny, Rachel," he said, rounding on her.

Holding up her hand in a placatory gesture, she said, "I know it's not funny, Jack. But in all fairness, what did you expect?"

"I dunno," he answered petulantly. "Some element of friendship, I suppose. Not to be spoken to like an errant school kid."

"Look, Jack. This is what it is going to be like — for a while at least. People have known you and Liz as a couple for years now. They're not going to simply turn around and accept that it's no longer 'Jack and Liz' but 'Jack and Rachel'. That's just the way the world is. What you have to do Jack is ask yourself if you are definitely ready for this. If this is what you want."

"You know this is what I want. I want you. We've already decided all of that. I'm leaving Liz and you and I are going to be together. I just didn't expect all this grief from other people — what's it got to do with them?"

Reluctant to get drawn into yet another full-scale conversation on the subject, Rachel got out of the bed, "I'm going for a shower, Jack. As I said to you last night, there isn't a lot we can do about all this while we're stuck over here. If you want this to happen, then, you've got to remember that you can't make an omelette without breaking eggs. Now, I'm off for that shower — you coming?"

She dropped the sheet she had wrapped around her on the floor, and walking naked past him, she saw him pull his T-shirt over his head and knew, with confidence, that he would break as many eggs as it took.

## Liz

Stepping out of the shower, Liz could hear her mobile ringing in the bedroom, but couldn't be bothered rushing in to get it. Another sleepless night had left her feeling drained and jaded and the shower had managed to revive her a little. Enjoying the brief emotional respite it had given her, she was in no rush to take a phone call that could wipe out its beneficial effects in a nano-second. Let whoever was calling leave a message, it was more than likely Jack and she really wasn't in the mood to speak to him.

She made her way into the bedroom where, after drying herself off with the towel, she leisurely applied moisturiser to her body. Next, she brushed out her shoulder length brown hair, contemplating her reflection as she did so, deciding that she would treat herself to a change — nothing drastic, just maybe a couple of inches off and some high-lights. It would definitely make her look more professional, she told herself, making a mental note to call the hairdresser's when she went downstairs.

In no particular rush, she selected her clothes with more consideration than usual, settling on a pair of high-waisted black jeans with a flattering flare that always made her feel slim. Not that she was especially overweight, but in honesty she knew that she could do with losing a half a stone or so, but these jeans disguised that well and she always felt good in them. She put on a black string top over them, and then picked out one of her favourite tops — a silky black and grey shirt that fitted her curves, giving a touch of casual elegance to her outfit. Completing it with a pair of high, black ankle boots, she was pleased with how she looked.

Carefully, she applied some rarely worn make-up, then after drying her hair thoroughly, she meticulously straightened it. She felt much better now, empowered by her groomed appearance and promised herself that this was how she was going to feel every morning. Her night had been filled with self-doubting thoughts as she had ruminated over and over about her husband's rejection of her, seeing herself as ugly and worthless whilst she allowed these negative thoughts to fill her head. It wasn't until she saw the dawn break that she embraced the knowledge she had gained from her life coaching training and putting herself in the role of one of her future clients, she coached herself as she would one of them.

She was astonished at how much more capable she now felt, a sense of confidence rising up within her and feeling ready to take on the world, she finally picked up her phone and checked who had been looking for her. It was Peter McClafferty and he had left her a voicemail, asking her to give him a call as soon as she could. Shoving her personal situation to one side for the first time in days, she went downstairs to call him. His cheerful, booming voice lifted her spirits even further, when he answered on the second ring.

"Well, good morning, Mrs. Life Coach," he said. "Don't you check your e-mails anymore?"

"Oh, I'm sorry, Peter. I've just had a very busy couple of days and to be honest, I haven't even thought about work."

"Well for some," he teased. "Anyway, to get straight to the point. I know we're scheduled to have a meeting tomorrow, but I've actually managed to get everything sorted and wondered if you might be able to pop in this afternoon? I know it's short notice, but I'm keen to show you where I'm at — I think you're going to be very pleased."

Realising that this distraction was exactly what she needed, she answered without hesitation. "Absolutely. I can't wait to see it. What time suits? I need to be back to collect the kids at three-thirty, so anytime before then."

"Well, it'll probably take about an hour, so, if we say two o'clock."

"Sounds good to me," she said. "I'll see you then."

## Donal

As he put his last few remaining bits and pieces into his small suitcase, Donal did a final check around the room to ensure he wasn't leaving anything behind him. He planned to be on the road before ten o'clock, having told Denise that he would collect her from her hotel at ten thirty. Satisfied that he had everything, he left his stuff by the door and sat down on the bed.

Still only twenty to ten, he had a bit of time and keyed his wife's mobile number into his phone, as with all his previous attempts, the call went straight to voicemail. Sighing heavily, he hung up and tried Kay's landline number instead. She answered quickly, with less tension in her voice than he had anticipated and he hoped that boded well before he headed for home.

"Hi, Kay, it's me," he said. "How's Susan?"

"Oh, hello Donal, love," she said and he could hear the anxiety creep back into her voice. "She's a bit brighter this morning, love, but as I've told you, it's going to be a long road."

"I know that, Kay, but at least if she's on the road, there's hope."

"Of course there's hope, Donal, but I don't want you thinking that the end is in sight. She's a very troubled person. It's certainly not going to be as simple as her stopping drinking. Sure, that's part of it, a big part, but she's suffering badly with depression. All her self-esteem is gone. She feels utterly worthless at the moment, Donal and all of that is going to take a very long time to put right. I suppose that the good thing is that she finally seems to be facing all these demons, but facing them and resolving them can be two very different things."

"I know that, Kay," he said again, not sure what else to say. "I don't suppose she'd talk to me?"

"I don't think so, love. I know this is hard for you, but right now, my first priority has to be to my daughter and I don't think she's ready to talk to you yet. Soon maybe, but not yet."

"Didn't think so," he said despondently. "Anyway, I'm leaving here this morning, so, I'll be back in Dublin this evening sometime, and I'll call over as soon as I'm back."

"Look, Donal, please don't take this the wrong way, but I'm not sure that that's a good idea. We have to take this thing at her pace. I don't want anything upsetting her at this delicate stage in her recovery and you dropping in could easily do that. If she wants to see you, she'll let me know and as soon as she does, love, I promise, I'll call you."

"Well, will you at least ask her if she'll see me tonight?"

"Of course I'll ask her, but all I'm saying is don't get your hopes up. Give her the space and time that she needs, because truly, the way I see it, that's the only hope there is for your marriage. I'm sorry to have to say all of this to you, Donal, honestly, I am."

"I know, Kay, I know," he said sadly. "I'll give you a call tonight when I'm back and see what the story is. Anyway, I've got to go now if I'm to make the ferry. Bye Kay and tell her I called and that I love her."

Not waiting for her response, he hung up the phone.


## Denise

Denise was already outside the hotel waiting for him when Donal pulled up. Filled with gratitude for the lift, she didn't want to cause him any delays and had checked out thirty minutes previously. Within minutes, he had loaded her luggage into the car and they were on their way. Although warm for the time of year, there was a heavy drizzle and the windows of the car steamed up as they inched their way along in the central London traffic, making their way northwards towards the motorway.

There was a comfortable silence between them, Donal concentrating on following the road signs which would take him to the M1 whilst she, half-heartedly, listened to the morning DJ on Capital Radio. She was glad to be finished in London, harbouring no regrets about what she had accomplished there. For the first time in days, her thoughts turned to the plans she must execute on her return to Dublin.

She wondered if John had resurfaced yet and, if so, what he made of her disappearance. Shivering involuntarily, she hoped that she never had to find out. Refusing to let thoughts of him steal her energy, she switched her mind to planning a whole new life without him. She cleared a patch on the steamy window and looking out on the grey London morning, she felt a frisson of excitement as she anticipated starting afresh in sunny climes. With her termination behind her, she could now focus on moving to Greece and set a provisional date of the end of May to do so.

That gave her approximately six weeks to tie up any loose ends, although there weren't many of them to contend with, and to decide where exactly she would move to. Images from the Mama Mia movie flooded her brain, bringing a smile to her lips as she contemplated such a utopian existence. She thought of the film's protagonist, played magnificently by Meryl Streep, and indulgently rejoiced that she would not have to endure any of the financial hardships that had befallen the character and could simply live the idyllic dream such a location promised. She couldn't wait.

"A penny for them," said Donal, breaking her reverie. "And by the look on your face, they're worth a lot more than that."

"Sorry?" she said, aware that he had spoken, but oblivious to what he had said.

"A penny for your thoughts," he said. "You seem miles away, and if you don't mind my saying so, you look happier than I've seen you look before."

"I suppose I am," she said, pensively. "I'm just thinking about the future. Did I tell you that I'm thinking of moving to Greece?"

"Really?" he asked, sounding surprised. "No. You never said. When are you thinking of going?"

"As soon as possible. Hopefully, by the end of next month. I just have some things to organise first and then, I'll be on my way."

"Why Greece? Do you have family there?"

"No. No one. And to be honest, that's half the attraction. I want a new start; a new life and Greece seems as good a place as any."

She could feel him looking at her, studying her and for the first time she realised how little he knew about her. Most of the conversations that had taken place between them had been him confiding in her, but she had given very little away about herself. She knew that he was curious, a closeness had undoubtedly developed between them over the course of the past few days and for some inexplicable reason, she decided that she wanted him to know her story, or part of it anyway.

"Look, Donal, I know you must think I'm really secretive and I'm sorry about that. I've had a bit of a rough time over the last few years and to cut a long story short, I'm drawing a line under my past now and starting over."

"Brave move," he said, clearly impressed. "What will you do in Greece?"

"I don't know yet. I came into a bit of money recently that has made this whole thing possible," she flinched at the understatement of her financial affairs, reluctant to impart the truth of the matter as she was still coming to terms with her gargantuan win herself, but he didn't seem to notice, so she continued. "And it's not so much bravery as necessity that has me leaving the country. You see, I've been involved in a very abusive relationship for several years now and if he knew about the money, he would never let me go. But, if I stay with him, then, it's only a matter of time until he kills me. I know that probably sounds really melodramatic, but believe me, it's true."

"That would explain your sad eyes," he said gently, smiling at her. "I knew there was a story behind them. Well, I still think you're brave, Denise and I wish you all the best with your move. You're a lovely woman - I really feel like I made a friend this week and hope we stay in touch."

"Of course we'll be in touch," she said adamantly. "Sure, we have to get that bastard that raped Hollie. Any news from her by the way?"

"I haven't spoken to her yet this morning. She's hoping to get the DNA test results today. They should tell her if it's the same guy that raped her as attacked the other girl. She's pretty convinced that it is. I'll give her a call when we get to the ferry port."

"You can bet your life that the police are hoping that it is the same guy. At least that way there is only one such monster on the island and my guess is that they'll want him caught before the tourist season really kicks off."

"That's pretty much what the nurse in the hospital said to Hollie. It would be disastrous for them otherwise. I just hope that the inevitable chaos that will result from the ash cloud debacle won't allow him slip through. I mean it's going to be manic in the airports when they finally reopen and have to start dealing with the backlogs — can you imagine it?"

"I know. Wouldn't you hate to be an airport employee? I'll bet they will come in for some grief over the next couple of weeks. Anyway, as I said the other night, if he does manage to slip their net, we'll get a private investigator on it straight away. Come hell or high water, we'll catch this bastard. Agreed?"

"Absolutely," he smiled at her, finally understanding why it was so important for her to help.

CHAPTER SIXTEEN

# Thursday PM 22nd April

*Liz*

Slowing down to see the street name before turning into the road, Liz pulled over to the curb and double-checked the address of Peter McClafferty's office that she had scribbled on a piece of paper which sat on the passenger seat. Confirming that it was the right road, she struggled to see any house numbers displayed as she inched her way along the quiet, leafy, suburban street. He had told her that there would be a silver Audi A6 in the driveway, but the opulent greenery that pervaded the entire street, made it tricky to even see into the driveways unless you were directly outside the gates, and the distinct lack of numbering made the task all the more difficult.

Finally spotting a glimpse of silver, she decided to get out of the car and pushing back some ivy that hung over the pillars, she found the magic '52' hidden beneath it. Having anticipated greater difficulty in locating his place than she had encountered, she found herself arriving twenty minutes ahead of schedule, and not wanting to interrupt his lunch-hour, she got back into her car to wait until two o'clock. But Peter must have spotted her and just as she started making some notes in her diary, a loud rap on the passenger window caused her to jump out of her skin.

Laughing at her reaction, he gestured an apology as she lowered the passenger window and his instantly recognisable booming voice, filled the car.

"Liz? Sorry about that," he said. "I thought you'd seen me. Come in. Come in."

Gathering up her bag and her diary, she got out of the car, locked it and followed him into the driveway. "I'm a bit early," she said apologetically.

"No worries," he said, every bit as friendly in the flesh as he had been during their many phone conversations. "Nice to meet you at last."

"And you," she said, accepting his proffered hand and shaking it firmly. "This is a really nice street."

"Yeah, we love it here."

"I didn't realise that you worked from home," she said, as he led the way into the house, shooing an oversized German Shepherd out of the way as he did so.

"Hope you're not afraid of dogs," he said, casting her a questioning glance. "He looks big and fierce, but he's a bit of wuzzy really, aren't you Georgie Boy?" He ruffled the big dog's head as he spoke and the dog gazed adoringly up at his lord and master.

"No. No. I love dogs," she said, extending her hand for the wolf like creature to sniff. "He can smell my one off me. I'll have to go through the 'sniffathon' test when I go home and Sheba smells that I've been out fraternising with other dogs. Her nose will be well out of joint!"

Peter laughed, taking her into the kitchen, where he promptly put on the kettle. "Tea or coffee?"

"Oohh! A coffee would be lovely, thanks."

"Fine. I'll make us a pot and we can take it out to the office," he said, nodding his head towards the window, out of which she could see a flat roofed concrete building at the end of the garden. "That's my HQ out there."

"That's great — you get to work from home but still get a bit of distance between your home life and your work. Good idea."

"That's the only way that my wife could cope with me working from home," he said, grinning. "You see, I'm not the tidiest of people and for a while when we moved in here first, I used to work in there — which is now the playroom, but I did Laura's head in, because try as I might, my paper-work spilled into the kitchen on a regular basis. It was her suggestion that we build the office, and I have to admit it was a good one."

"I might look into that, down the road. I suppose I have to get some clients first though," she added wistfully.

"Well your new super-duper website should get that ball rolling," he said. "Come on, we'll go check it out."

Peter hadn't been exaggerating about his untidiness and Liz couldn't see how on earth he made sense of the miscellaneous piles of paper that seemed to be scattered everywhere in his small home office.

"Organised chaos!" he said in response to her shocked face. "The paperwork gets taken care of once a month. Laura straightens the whole place out for me, only for me to do it all again next month. But hey, it works. Everything I need to carry out my business is on the computers; she leaves me to it, then, comes in here at the start of each month and looks after all the dreary administration stuff that I'm so bad at. Leaving me and my creative genius a free rein."

As haphazard as the process sounded, it clearly worked for them, because when Peter showed her the completed web site, she was completely blown away by it. The site was so professionally presented that she knew, with certainty, as he took her through it, that work would come flooding in once it went live. She was speechless at the amazing job that he had done, and sat listening intently to him as he explained how he had loaded her site with search engine optimisation tools that would ensure its presence high in the list of results of any number of searches.

Finally finding her voice, she said. "Wow! Peter, what can I say? I'm absolutely thrilled with it. So, what happens next? When does it go live?"

"Soon as you like," he said, delighted by her reaction. "If you give the go ahead, I'll have it up and running this afternoon."

"Sounds good to me," she said, keen to get the ball rolling as quickly as possible.

With her confidence growing by the minute, she bade farewell to Peter and getting back into her car, she eyeballed herself in the rear view mirror and promised herself that although her marriage might be over, her new life was only just beginning.

## *Donal*

Whilst busy, the ferry port was nowhere near as chaotic as it had been on their outward journey when Donal and Denise drove in. They joined the line and with nearly an hour to spare before boarding, they went off to get something to eat and drink in the terminal building. Shuffling along in the queue in the self-service restaurant, they got themselves some fairly unappetising looking food and secured a table in the middle of the floor, where a constant stream of diners, pushed and pulled their way past, affording them little comfort.

Having eaten what he could of the plate of stodge that passed as lasagne, the best Donal could say was that he was no longer hungry, but Denise couldn't even make that claim finding her pasta dish nigh on inedible.

"I'll get a snack on the boat," she said in response to his asking if she wanted to get something else. "It all looks pretty shit here."

"I know. I was just hungry enough to have eaten a scabby child," he joked, looking disgustedly at the remnants of food on his plate. "In fact, I'm not convinced that that wasn't what I've just eaten."

Denise giggled, pushing back her chair and getting to her feet, she said. "I think I'd rather wait in the car than in this god-awful dump."

"Yeah, me too," he said, eagerly. "Just need to go to the loo first, though. Here, do you want the keys?"

"No. I need to go as well. I'll see you back at the car."

He was just finishing a call to Hollie when she let herself into the car. Hanging up, he filled her in on Hollie's news about the DNA test results and her trip to the police station to compile the photo-fit. "Apparently, the police plan to be out in force looking for him tonight, so here's hoping that they catch him."

Tired from the drive from London, Donal spent most of the ferry crossing dozing. Denise shook him gently awake when they announced that they were coming in to Dun Laoghaire harbour. Stiff from the awkward angle he had fallen asleep in; Donal stretched and rolled his neck from side to side. "I tell you what, I'm going to sleep soundly tonight," he said.

"Yeah, me too," she concurred. "It's amazing how tiring travelling can be."

"I never asked you — where do you want me to drop you?" asked Donal, yawning as he spoke.

"Oh, don't worry about me," she said. "I'll hop in a taxi."

"Don't be daft," he said. "I'll give you a lift. That's assuming you're in Dublin — right?"

"Sort of," she said vaguely, suddenly embarrassed at the prospect of him knowing that she was staying in the luxurious Ritz Carlton. "Enniskerry, which is technically, Co. Wicklow."

"Sure that's only ten minutes down the road from Dun Laoghaire — if even. I'll drop you there, no problem."

"Well if you're sure," she said, appearing hesitant. "Thanks, Donal."

But Donal was no longer listening to her as he read a message that had just come through on his phone. His face clouded over darkly whilst he read it. It was from Kay, telling him that Susan didn't want to see or hear from him tonight and would he leave off contacting them until tomorrow.

"Welcome home," he thought bitterly to himself, shoving his phone back into his pocket.

### Denise

Whatever had been in the text message that Donal had received, it certainly managed to deflate his mood, leaving him silent and distracted for the rest of their journey. He hadn't volunteered any information about its contents or who it was from and Denise wasn't going to pry, satisfied that he would have felt at liberty to talk to her if he had wanted to. His preoccupied state of mind provided the perfect distraction for her to be able to get him to drop her off in Enniskerry Village, without any awkward questions as to where exactly she was staying. Pointing vaguely at a cluster of bungalows, she told him that just here was fine and after he helped her get her case from the boot of the car, she remained where he had left her, waving goodbye as he drove off slowly in the direction of the city centre and home, she presumed.

Once his car was gone, she walked over to the village taxi rank, where a lone taxi driver sat waiting for custom. After sitting at the rank for nearly an hour, he was disappointed to learn that she was going such a short distance, but with a sigh of resignation he started up the engine. In response to her enquiry, he told her that business had been slack all evening and he nearly fell out of his standing when she handed him a fifty euro note as he took her case from the boot, telling him to keep the change.

Delighted with herself for being able to make somebody's day in that way, she relinquished her case to the hotel porter and made her way directly to her room. Once there, she realised how hungry she was, not having eaten anything since her woeful lunch in the ferry port. Too tired to be bothered with dressing for dinner, she phoned room service and ordered a tasty sounding chicken dish and a bottle of red wine.

The room service menu delivered on its promise and half an hour after ordering, she was devouring a delicious feast. Freshly showered and wrapped in a thick towelling robe, she luxuriated in the simplicity of enjoying fine wine and food, plumped up by several pillows, watching TV. Finishing the last fork full and feeling thoroughly satiated, she put the food tray to one side and powered up her laptop. It was time to start making plans.

She opened a new Word document and began compiling a list of the things that she would need to bring to Greece with her. Most of the things she intended to bring with her would be new, as she wanted few reminders of her old life here in Dublin. When she had left home the previous week, she had taken nothing with her but a hastily packed suitcase containing the few worldly possessions that held meaning for her, some essential clothing — which already she had pretty much replaced, and some photographs and general memorabilia pertaining to her beloved parents. She needed to carefully go through this eclectic collection and select what she wanted to keep.

Deciding that there was no time like the present, she closed down the lid of her computer and pulled her case out of the wardrobe where she had stored it before going to London. With reckless abandon, she threw all of her old clothes in a pile in the corner, she would ask at reception for a couple of bin bags and have the clothes dropped in to a charity shop in the village — not that they were particularly good, but they could be of use to someone. Next, she thumbed her way through the pile of old photographs, evoking strong memories of her childhood and taking comfort from the loving expressions on her parents' faces as they looked lovingly at their only child in a variety of different settings.

Finally, she removed a large shoe box, filled with assorted bits and pieces which had been thrown in there over the years, providing a veritable treasure chest of items with their greatest value being of the sentimental kind. Her father's old pipe, which instantly conjured up images of cosy nights when she was a child, her mother sitting there doing the crossword and her father puffing away on the sweet aromatic tobacco that took far longer to prepare than to smoke. Her mother's face powder compact, a sleek silver container with a small vanity mirror inside of it that released the smell of her mother as she bent to kiss her good night, switching off the bedside lamp as she would do so.

Also in the box were several old diaries of her dad's that she would peruse from time to time, feeling that she got to know him a little more each time that she did. She smiled to herself when she lifted out a small black velvet pouch that contained her mother's limited jewellery collection. Loosening the drawstring, she tipped its contents onto her lap; sifting through them she came across her prized wristwatch with a face so small that her mother used to need her reading glasses to tell the time. A couple of pairs of earrings, a gold chain and a gate bracelet completed the collection, except for her charm bracelet, which didn't seem to be there.

Panic-stricken at the thought of losing it, she jumped up off the bed and searched around on the floor in case she had dropped it. But, it was nowhere to be seen. It had been by far the most valuable piece her mother had possessed, but more than that, she had always found it synonymous with her, recalling its jangling as the first signal of her mother's impending arrival. Pulling the suitcase up on to the bed, she searched through its side pockets, but to no avail. Then, she remembered what had happened to it.

A couple of years previously, at a point when money had been very tight, she came in from work one evening to find John with the bracelet in his hand. He told her that he had had a friend look at it and his friend had told him that he would easily be able to get a couple of hundred euro for it and that he was going to bring it in to his mate's shop the next day. His eyes searched her face, looking for a hurt reaction, but for once she had had the measure of him, knowing that her pain would be as valuable to him as the money, she hid her emotions behind a nonchalant shrug of her shoulders, telling him that Cathy in work had offered her two fifty for it and that's why she had left it out in the first place — she'd just forgotten to take it with her that morning.

Her gamble paid off and she had managed to retrieve the bracelet, dipping into a small but secret pool of money she had accumulated for emergencies to keep up the façade of having sold it. She had then hidden the bracelet in a roll of attic insulation in the loft where she knew that he would never find it. Now, despite all her plans to the contrary, she was going to have to go back to the house one more time to recover it and the prospect filled her with dread.

## Annette

The sun had already set by the time Annette and Hollie stepped out of a taxi across the street from the hotel where she suspected that Jack was staying. She had planned this deliberately, thinking that the dusk and impending darkness would offer them more cover for their spying mission.

There was a large, busy steak house, with an outside terrace situated directly opposite the hotel's entrance and they opted to eat there as it provided the perfect vantage point to keep watch on the comings and goings at the hotel. And, the mediocrity of the restaurant made it unlikely that any of the guests of the five star establishment under surveillance would be likely to be dining there.

The service was friendly, if a bit slow and the food was surprisingly good, although both of these things were somewhat lost on Annette who spent the entire time stretching and craning her neck at every sign of life from across the street. It wasn't until the waitress brought out the dessert menu that their endeavours bore fruit. It was his laugh she heard before she saw him - his distinctive guffaw ringing out on the balmy night air as if he didn't have a care in the world and the sound incensed her.

She swung her head around and there, under the canopy outside the hotel, stood Jack with his arm draped casually around his companion's shoulder. Even with her face obscured by Jack standing slightly forward of her, Annette could tell immediately that her suspicions were correct and the woman whom Jack's arm encircled was none other than Rachel Wallace.

Feeling like she was going to be sick, Annette pushed back her seat and ran to the toilet. Despite thinking that she was, she realised that she had been totally unprepared for actually seeing Jack with someone else, and Rachel of all people - the double whammy of deceit involved for her beloved sister was almost too much to bear. Her heart ached for Liz and she wondered how on earth she was going to manage telling her what she had discovered here tonight. Suddenly she remembered the camera and the object of the night's exercise and hoping against hope that she wasn't too late, she hurried back to the table.

But, Jack and Rachel had disappeared. She sank despondently into her seat, before catching the wry grin on Hollie's face. Shaking the camera victoriously at her, she said, "It's a wrap!"

"Oh, my God! You got them. Thanks Hollie — I dunno what happened, but I just couldn't stomach watching them. They didn't see you — did they?"

"No way. They were far too busy being 'love's young dream' to notice anything."

Annette flinched at her description, shaking her head incredulously at her brother-in-law's behaviour. "What the hell am I going to say to Liz?"

"Does she know that you were coming here this evening?"

"Not exactly. I mean, I told her that I'd check out if the hotel was any-where near where we're staying and that if it was feasible for me to visit, then I would. But, how can I tell her that not only is her husband staying here, having an affair with a woman, but that the woman in question is her best friend."

"Alleged best friend!" Hollie interrupted. "Nothing friendly about what that bitch is doing."

"I know. She's such a hard-nosed cow. I thought women like her only existed in fiction. I mean, you read about them or see them in a movie and think it's all a bit far fetched — that no one is really like that. Like, how does she call around to Liz's house, sit there with her, chatting away, having a drink or whatever, while all the time she's messing about with her husband. It beggars belief — it really does."

"There've been women like that since time immemorial," sneered Hollie. "It's like they've got something to prove to themselves — you know, how fucking irresistible they are. They're not content with pulling the single men; they want to know that they can have anyone they set their eye on. She probably wouldn't have been interested in Jack if he was single."

"You're probably right. The thrill is in taking him away from his wife and family. She probably envies Liz at heart."

"I doubt that," said Hollie knowledgeably. "Women like her don't want all the trappings of family life. They just want to feel more attractive than their married counterparts and then, eventually, they will settle for some poor sucker who has reached middle-age and the financial security that goes along with it and get their claws into him, securing a very nice future for themselves — thank you very much."

"Oh, you don't think that that's what she's after — do you? A permanent relationship with Jack? My guess is that it was all just a bit of fun for her — you know, dangerous and exciting, but when the shit hits the fan, she'll back off, move away and on to the next schmuck."

"Maybe," said Hollie, looking doubtful. "But, from what I saw they looked pretty serious about one another. I reckon she's got her retirement fund all sewn up."

"Poor Liz," said Annette, wearing a crestfallen expression. "I want her to be the one who fucks him out of the house, not the one left behind to pick up the pieces while he swans off to set up his little 'love nest' with Jane poxy Fonda over there!"

Not entirely sure who Jane Fonda was, but getting the general gist of the point Annette was making, Hollie said. "But you reckon that she wouldn't throw him out. So, although it's going to be really tough for her at the beginning, maybe this would actually be the best thing for her. You know, not having any choice in the matter."

"Do you know what? Maybe you're right."

## *Jack*

Meanwhile, on the other side of the street, back in his luxury hotel, completely oblivious to his sister-in-law's discovery, Jack trepidatiously called home. He wasn't surprised to learn that Liz was not at home and wondered idly if she had purposely disappeared wanting to avoid talking to him as much as he wanted to avoid talking to her.

He was, however, infinitely relieved to find the kids chatting away to him as normal. Clearly, Liz had told them nothing and he was pleased about this fact. In fairness to her, he had doubted that she would say anything to them, so protective was she of her offspring that she had always instinctively tried to shelter them from any unpleasantness. He hoped this would extend to their forthcoming separation, but didn't know if that was simply too much to expect.

He knew that he had re-written history to a degree in his own mind, wanting justification for his affair, compelling himself to believe that their relationship had shifted from that of husband and wife to one more like brother and sister, but wasn't altogether convinced that Liz would see it that way too. He nurtured the hope, in the deep recesses of his mind, that once the initial shock of the separation had abated that he and Liz could sustain a level of friendship conducive to the continued joint parenting of their children, but the likelihood of that remained to be seen.

For the time being, he took solace from the fact that she had kept the news of his affair from the kids and chatted away easily with them, telling them that he should be home in the next couple of days.

## *Rachel*

The evening was warm and Rachel sat out on the balcony sipping a glass of red wine, giving Jack a bit of space to make his phone call. He joined her after only a few minutes, looking a lot less stressed than she had anticipated and, assuming correctly, that he had avoided a showdown with Liz, she poured him some wine, waiting for him to fill her in on the call.

"Well, surprise, surprise! Liz wasn't there," he said, with a mixture of relief tinged with disappointment after gearing himself up to call her. "The kids were fine though and obviously she's told them nothing, which is a good thing, I hope."

"Of course, it's a good thing," she said, looking at him intently. "Jack, I know Liz, she's going to do her utmost to spare the kids' feelings in all of this — that's just the kind of person she is and to be honest babe, for us, that's a good thing."

"Yeah, but that's easy at this stage. What about when we go home? What then?"

"Well, the way I see it is that we stick to the original plan. Yes, Liz has somehow found out that you are having an affair, but there's absolutely no reason to assume that she knows who with. I still don't have to be in the picture. For all she knows, you are away with some young one you met in work, or anywhere for that matter, and if you're clever about it, you could turn that to our advantage."

"And how do you reckon I could do that?" he asked.

"Quite easily. You tell her that this affair meant nothing."

"What the fuck is that going to achieve? You're not suggesting that I patch things up with her and we continue as we were before, because I'm telling you, Rachel, I'm…."

But, she cut across him. "No! I'm not saying that at all. I'm saying that you tell her that this meaningless affair came about because you are basically unhappy in the marriage. That you've been thinking about leaving her for some time now. Tell her that you're not leaving her for someone else; you are leaving her because this marriage isn't what you want. That now that you've had one affair, it will only be easier to have a second and a third and that you don't want to live like that and that you're quite certain she won't want to either."

"That's a load of shit, Rachel. Liz would never go for that."

"Trust me, she will. You have no idea the number of times that I hear that very same story from my patients. Preposterous as it sounds, men feed their wives that line every day of the week."

"And the wives go for it?" he said, looking incredulous. "Not Liz — no way."

"Oh sure, they resist it, initially. Think that they can change things, put things right — you know, a little bit of marriage counselling, help him through his mid-life crisis and all will be well in the world. But, inevitably, they split. I don't even bother giving them advice anymore, just prescribe some sleeping pills, give them the name of counsellor and let them at it. But this with Liz is very different. I could talk to her — she listens to me."

"You!" he exclaimed. "Are you off your trolley. Why on earth would Liz listen to you, when you're the reason I'm leaving."

"But, that's just it. That's what I'm saying to you. Leave me out of the picture for the foreseeable future. Let me coach Liz through this. She'll talk to me about it all, you can be sure she will. And if she has no idea that I'm involved, I can work things to our advantage. You know, tell her that she must encourage the kids to have a proper relationship with you — the ole 'Dad and I don't love each other anymore, but we both love you two' line. I can push her with that."

"Jesus, Rachel! This is getting creepy. I mean, it just seems wrong to have Liz confide her problems in you when unbeknownst to her — you're an integral part of the problem. No, it seems all wrong."

"No more wrong than you screwing me behind her back!" she shot back, annoyed now that he couldn't see what she was trying to do for him. "I'm not mad keen on having to do it either, but if it paves the way for the future — then, why not? I'd be doing it for you, for the kids, for us and even to a degree for Liz herself."

"I just think the whole thing is a bit warped. And what happens when we do officially get together? How's that going to look?"

"We'll cross that bridge when we come to it. What's important right now is to initiate the change. Keep Liz sweet, keep the kids on side and trust me, that can only make things easier down the road. When the dust settles, I can always back off on my involvement with Liz but in the meantime I can have an inside track and work it so you don't end up losing your kids."

"You really think that would work?"

"I'm certain of it," she smiled back at him, knowing that he was coming around to the idea. "You'll thank me for this one day, Mr. O'Brien — mark my words!"

## *Hollie*

When Hollie and Annette arrived back to Palma Nova, they made their way directly to Mulligan's pub where they had arranged to meet Maureen and the girls who had gone down to check out the weekly karaoke night in the popular Irish pub. The taxi deposited them at the end of the main strip and as they walked down through it, Annette grabbed a hold of her, pointing over to where two policemen were questioning a group of tourists, handing out flyers to each of them as they did so.

"Oh wow! Do you think that's Eoin's picture?" asked Hollie, peering over to see if any of them were nodding in recognition, but they were all shrugging their shoulders and shaking their heads as they spoke.

"Only one way to find out," said Annette, marching up to them and taking a flyer to have a look. "Yep, that's him alright," she said, seeing the face she had seen on the screen in the police station earlier looking up at her, before passing it on to Hollie.

The wording on the flyer was minimal, with Eoin's image taking up three-quarters of the sheet, it simply asked in both Spanish and English 'Have you seen this man?' with a brief warning to avoid him and to contact the police on the numbers given. Hollie felt a sense of security envelop her, knowing that a full-scale manhunt was now in progress and hoped with all her might that they would find him soon. Feeling safer than she had in a week, she pushed all thoughts of Eoin from her mind and followed Annette through the doors of Mulligan's.

Annette quickly located the girls who were giggling uncontrollably as she pulled up a seat at their table, "Where's Maureen?" she asked, looking around for her mother-in-law.

Hollie, taking up the rear, smiled conspiratorially at the girls as she too sat down, having seen what Annette had missed in her haste to find the girls and with three faces like grinning baboons staring at her, Annette started to get a bit irked when, with impeccable timing, an altogether woeful sound filled the air causing her to stiffen, before slowly turning her head in the direction of the small stage. There, to her horror, stood Maureen and one of the old guys from their hotel, tunelessly, but very loudly, belting out the Frank and Nancy Sinatra song — 'Something Stupid'.

Clearly inebriated, the two old timers cut a comical scene with their enthusiastic rendition of the classic song whilst the entire audience fell about the place laughing at them. But, it was Annette's reaction that caused Hollie to almost wet herself as she watched the look of sheer disbelief on her new friend's face.

"What kind of a monster have I created?" asked Annette. "Paddy is going to kill me when he hears about this. And you girls! You are so in trouble. You've got your grandmother drunk — again! Honestly, what am I doing to do with you two?"

"Oh, chillax, Mum," laughed Hannah. "Dad would think this is hilarious. I've got some of it on my phone, we can show it to him when we get back."

"He's never going to trust me to bring his mother anywhere again," she said laughing, knowing full well that Paddy would thoroughly enjoy this latest development. "The woman is a liability!"

Struck by how lucky she had been to be able to immerse herself in this lovely family's holiday, Hollie felt a rush of gratitude at not being stranded here alone with only the aftermath of her attack for company and reaching over, she took a hold of Annette's hand, saying. "Look Annette, thanks so much for everything. I'd never have got through this week without you."

"Not at all," said Annette, giving her an affectionate hug in response.

"And your girls," said Hollie. "They're so lovely." Then, with a cheeky grin, she added, "And, I have to include your mad mother-in-law — she's a tonic!"

"You would have to bring HER up!" said Annette with a mock scowl on her face, turning back to see the end of Maureen's performance, causing Hollie to giggle once more.

CHAPTER SEVENTEEN

# Friday AM 23rd April

*Donal*

Despite the exhaustion of the day before and his eager anticipation of a good night's sleep, Donal spent the night tossing and turning, unable to get Kay's text out of his mind. The more he analysed the text, the more annoyed he became. For one thing, he felt she could have afforded him the courtesy of a phone call, not a brief, curt message excluding him from his wife's life in that way. Who did she think she was?

Up until now, he had always enjoyed what he regarded as a good relationship with his mother-in-law, but her handling of the current situation changed things. She made him feel like a spare part and he really wasn't happy about it. He needed to be part of Susan's recovery and he simply wouldn't tolerate being excluded like this any longer. Unpleasant as the prospect was, he knew that he was going to have to confront Kay, asserting his role as Susan's husband and insist on being party to her treatment. For Chrissake, he wanted to see her recover every bit as much as Kay did.

The clock on the bedside locker told him that it was still only six thirty, far too early to call yet, but with sleep completely eluding him, he got up and went downstairs to make some coffee. Sitting alone in the quiet kitchen, he plotted out in his head just what exactly he was going to say to Kay. Ideally, he would like to avoid a row, but if needs must, then he was quite prepared to go that route. He jotted down a couple of points that he wanted to get across, including the fact that he wanted his wife to come back home with him — she had been gone now for almost a week and it was time to get things back on track.

With her return in mind, he busied himself with cleaning the house from top to bottom, giving the garden its first mowing of the year and compiled a comprehensive shopping list for a trip to the supermarket. Perhaps restoring order to the chaos that had descended on their home in recent months would be beneficial to Susan — certainly, it put Donal in a better frame of mind.

The house looked so much better when he returned with the groceries and his mood shifted to one of optimism as he loaded the fridge up with fresh, healthy, nutritional food. A more than competent cook, he decided that he would take over the reins of the kitchen, ensuring that Susan would be well fed as she fought her way back to full health. He would make Kay aware of this intention, knowing that she was always concerned about her daughter's appalling eating habits.

Finally, with all his domestic chores completed, it was time to ring Kay. Equipped with his notes from earlier, he picked up the phone and dialled her number. He stayed standing as he called, having read somewhere that mentally it gave one a greater sense of confidence to stand, and he knew that he was going to need all the confidence he could muster for this particular call.

"Good morning, Kay," he said, keeping his voice even-toned. "It's Donal.

"Hi Donal," she said, but without waiting to see what she was going to say next, Donal jumped straight in.

"Look Kay, I got your text yesterday and as requested, I didn't call. But, I'm back now, Kay and I need to see Susan. I really hope you don't have a problem with that, Kay, but to be perfectly frank, whether you do or not, I have to insist on seeing my wife — today."

Preparing himself for the inevitable argument, he was taken by surprise when she responded in a conciliatory tone, "I know you do, Donal. I've spoken to her and she agrees that the two of you need to talk. I have to head out this afternoon, and you two can have the place to yourselves, say, about three o'clockish?"

"Yeah, three o'clock is fine," he said.

"But, Donal," she said, a note of caution in her voice, "Don't expect too much."

Not entirely sure what she meant by that comment, he rang off. At least that conversation had gone easier than he had anticipated and he allowed himself a glimmer of hope for the afternoon, confident that a face to face with his wife would ensure her return to their home and a fresh start for them both.

### Annette

Troubled by the prospect, but knowing that she had little choice, Annette prepared herself for calling Liz. She had thrashed the whole thing through in her mind over night and had come to the conclusion that whilst she would confirm seeing Jack and the fact that he was with a woman, she would hold off on revealing the woman's identity until she got back home, feeling that poor Liz had enough to contend with on her own for now. For the hundredth time in the past couple of days, she fervently wished that she could be there with her sister at this time of crisis.

She checked the time on her phone and seeing that it had just gone ten o'clock in Majorca, guessed that Liz should be just about back from the school run by now. Taking her purse with her, she went downstairs, bought herself a large cappuccino and taking it outside, she easily found a seat on one of the sun loungers by the pool. A lone mother with two pre-school age children were splashing about in the baby pool, but other than that the area was deserted.

Liz sounded tired when she answered and Annette suspected that she probably wasn't sleeping the best at the moment. "Hey, Liz — it's me," she said gently, "How are you doing?"

"Ah, I'm okay," she said in a deflated manner. "Just doing an awful lot of thinking — that's all."

"I can imagine," said Annette, "you sound like you haven't slept much."

"No, I haven't really. Tends to fuck up your sleeping pattern discovering that your husband is a lying, cheating, bastard. Anyway, did you manage to find out if that hotel is anywhere near you?"

Taking a deep breath, Annette said. "Yes. I did. It's only about twenty minutes away from here in a taxi and myself and Hollie went over there last night to see what we could find out."

"And?"

"Well, sweetie, there's no easy way to tell you this, but yes — Jack's there and," she hesitated, "I'm sorry, Liz, but he is with another woman."

"The fucker!" said Liz and Annette could hear her start to cry. "I knew it though, Annette. I fucking knew it, but even so, it feels pretty shit to have it confirmed."

"I know, Liz — that's 'cos it is pretty shit. Honest to God, I could kill the bastard. You've no idea how much I wanted to go up and smack him one when I saw him."

Through her sniffles, Liz asked, "What'd you say to him?"

"Nothing. He didn't even see me. Maureen advised me not to confront him, saying that whatever happens, it's ultimately your decision and me going in there shooting my mouth of mightn't necessarily be constructive. You don't mind do you? I'm more than happy to go back and tackle the little shit, if that's what you want."

"No. It's probably for the best that you didn't. I don't know what the hell I'm going to do, but the one thing that I know for sure is — we're finished."

"Do you mean that though, Lizzie? Or, do you think…"

But, Liz cut across her, "Believe me, Annette, I mean it. I know you're probably thinking 'good ole soft touch Liz, she'll have him back', but believe me, Annette — I won't. When I say that I don't know what I'm going to do — I mean about the kids. Obviously I want them spared as much pain as possible — they're going to be really hurt, especially poor Janie, and I have to figure out the best way of handling this for them."

Taken aback by her sister's assertion that her marriage was over, Annette hoped with all her might that Liz wouldn't have a change of heart, firmly believing that she had a brighter future with Jack gone out of her life. She herself, had several friends who had eventually got themselves out of toxic marriages and despite struggling in the initial weeks, even months, they had all gone on to flourish on their own — she wanted that for Liz — to see her sister flourish.

## Liz

Glad that she had the house to herself when she had received Annette's phone call, Liz indulged herself with a good cry when she got off the phone. Her sister's call had eliminated the last threads of doubt that she had subconsciously clung to that this whole thing was nothing more than a dreadful mistake. Now, for certain, she knew that Jack was having an affair and the pain this knowledge brought was incredible.

She had often heard people talk about having their hearts broken; read enough novels where the likeable protagonist has been subjected to this emotional devastation, even seen it portrayed in many different films, but what she didn't know was that the pain sustained by heart break was a physical one. Her entire chest ached with the weight of the pain that Jack's betrayal gave her. In the silence of the empty house, she heard herself wail, feral like, as she finally gave vent to her hurt.

It was the finality of it all that hurt the most, the sense of bereavement — yes, she thought, 'bereavement' that was the word, because it was the death of her marriage that she was mourning. Despite Annette's reservations to the contrary, Liz knew with complete certainty that her marriage was now over. She may, in the past, have convinced herself that she could have overcome some minor deviation on Jack's part, but not this — never.

Her heart wrenched anew, when for the first time a thought crossed her mind that she had hitherto never considered — perhaps Jack wanted out as well. Maybe this affair wasn't the casual thing that she had assumed it to be and perhaps Jack was actually in love with the silly tart. In some ways, that might make life easier. Obviously not if either of them had been hoping for a reconciliation, but with that off the cards, then, a mutual desire to end the marriage might enable them to present a more united front with the kids. Consoled somewhat by this thought, she went to get a shower.

## *Hollie*

Hollie's first thought on waking was to wonder if the police had had any success in finding Eoin. She grabbed her mobile and looked to see if there had been any missed calls, but there hadn't. Telling herself that she must be patient, after all they'd only been looking for him for one night now, and it was highly unlikely that they would find him that quickly.

Stretching out in the bed, she became conscious of a dull headache, probably the result of too many beers in the karaoke bar the night before. She smiled at the memory of Maureen's performance and wondered if Annette had phoned Liz yet, and if so, how it had gone. The room was very warm and the stuffy atmosphere was aggravating her and loath though she was to get up just yet, she needed some fresh air. Dragging herself from the bed, she pulled open the shutters and instantly welcomed the warm sea breeze that greeted her.

She stepped out on to the balcony and casting her eyes around, she spotted Annette sitting by herself down by the pool. The look on Annette's face told her all she needed to know — clearly Annette had already spoken to Liz and even from this distance, Hollie could tell that she was tortured as a consequence. Figuring that she was in need of some company, Hollie quickly got dressed and made her way down to her.

"Hey," she said in greeting, as she walked through the perimeter fence of the pool area. "How'd it go with Liz?"

Startled by her presence, Annette hastily brushed away the tears that had pooled in her eyes after speaking to her sister. "Oh, you know," she shrugged. "She's pretty devastated. I just wish I could be there with her. She really needs some support."

"Did you tell her about Rachel?" asked Hollie.

"No. I decided that would be better in the flesh."

Hollie nodded her approval. "I think you're right on that one. Look, Annette, this ash cloud thing has to be running its course. From what I heard coming through reception there, there's talk of the airports re-opening over the course of the weekend. So, it shouldn't be too long before you're there with her."

"I certainly hope so."

"Besides, you have to take comfort from the fact that at least while you're stranded over here, so too are Jack and Rachel. So, of course you'd rather be with her now, but you will be back before the shit really hits the fan and that's when she's going to need you the most."

"I hadn't though of it like that," said Annette, mildly appeased by Hollie's perspective. "And, our friend Jenny Jones at the airport has told us that she'll do her best to get us on one of the first flights out, so, hopefully we should get back before the other pair."

"There now, things are looking up already," smiled Hollie.

## Denise

Troubled deeply at the prospect of having to return to her former home, but knowing that she simply had to retrieve the bracelet, Denise wracked her brains to think when would be the best time to perform the dreaded mission. It would be so much easier if the lazy bastard had a job, she thought to herself, then smiled at the progress she had made in making John a thing of the past — a few short weeks ago, she wouldn't have had the courage to even think of him in such a derogatory manner, lest he read her mind and deliver another brutal beating — such had been the fear she had of him.

"Think! Think!" she said aloud to herself. There had to be some routine or ritual that he adhered to at some point in the week that would give her a window to slip in and out of the house without encountering him. Systematically working her way through the days of the week, she realised how little she knew of his movements as she had always been out working in the coffee shop. Then it dawned on her.

Several of his mates knocked off work early on a Friday. For them, it was payday and with a few quid in their pockets for a change, they would go to the pub, have a few pints and place a few bets on the horses. She had inadvertently stumbled upon this practice some time back when, pissed as a newt, John had arrived home from the pub on a Friday evening and surprised her with a bouquet of flowers, slurredly proclaiming that he had

had a bit of luck on the 'gee-gees', then proceeded to beat the shit out of her when she had looked askance at this uncharacteristic gesture.

Well, that was one beating that had paid dividends, she thought, realising that she had her window. Then horrified, she realised that today was a Friday. Not anticipating having to make the visit so soon, she reluctantly knew that she had no choice, as to leave it hanging over her for another whole week was too awful to contemplate. With a flash of resolve, she decided to do it that afternoon.

### Rachel

With enough sense to know that she must keep her thoughts to herself, Rachel stretched out on the sun-lounger, secretly relishing the prospect of playing 'double-agent' with Liz on her return to Dublin. She knew that Jack would never understand how this game, and that's exactly how she saw it, of intrigue appealed to her. It was essential that she keep up the pretext of doing it for his sake, but in truth the whole thing excited her.

Liz was such an open book to her that she knew for definite that she would have little difficulty drawing confidences from her about her husband's affair. She, for her part, would ensure that no shadow of suspicion ever fell on her as she helped Liz to uncover her husband's lover's identity. In her role as Liz's comforter, she could also engage with the kids, forging a relationship with them that would make them more accepting of her when she eventually emerged as the new woman in their father's life.

Her scheme had endless possibilities, putting her in the driving seat to guide the weak and vulnerable Liz into planning a future for herself that would clear the path for Rachel's own future. It couldn't be simpler, she thought smugly, glancing up towards their room to see if there was any sign of Jack getting up yet, as her plotting and scheming had given her an appetite for breakfast.

### Jack

'Hungry? Cos I'm starving!' read the message on Jack's phone, when it beeped at him from under the pillow, waking him from a very enjoyable sleep in. He had no desire to go and sit by the pool when Rachel had called him a couple of hours earlier and his compromise was to tell her that he would join her for breakfast.

Honouring his end of the bargain, he got out of bed, automatically switching on the TV to see if there was any update on the ash cloud. Incredulous, he switched from channel to channel, but the news was all the same — airports still remained closed. He dreaded to think what the financial fall out from this catastrophic situation was going to be. As if the global recession, with entire countries going bankrupt, wasn't difficult enough to handle — now, this.

In fairness, he had escaped the worst of the recession as a Civil Servant, but still and all, its affects were evident with property prices crashing and the numbers on the unemployment line rising on a daily basis. He had seen several of his friends all but financially ruined with the collapse of the construction industry, and the predictions were that things would only get a lot worse before they got better.

From a purely financial point of view, he could have picked a better time to be looking at hugely increasing his outgoings by leaving his wife and setting up a second home, but still, he consoled himself, at least he had a secure job and Rachel was unlikely to ever be without an income. If push came to shove, Liz would have to consider getting herself a job, not that she was going to like that idea, but if it came to it, then she might have to. At least the kids were older now.

His phone beeped again, and smiling as he read her impatient message, 'I'm going to eat now! U coming?', he grabbed his wallet and went to meet her.

CHAPTER EIGHTEEN

# Friday PM 23rd April

*Annette*

Bored with hanging around the pool again for the day, Megan and Hannah had gone off with Jody and Debs to the apartment complex down the road where they were taking part in a tennis tournament set up by the holiday reps, who were worn out with trying to keep their stranded customers entertained. The tournament proved a massive hit with the hoards of mutinous teenagers, desperate to get a break from their families, offering not only the opportunity to participate, but also to hang out with members of the opposite sex between matches.

No fool, Annette knew well what the main attraction was for the girls, but taking comfort from the fact that the tennis served the dual purpose of keeping them entertained and, to some small degree, supervised, she absolved herself for feeling so relieved to see the back of them. The stress of keeping the unfolding drama of Jack's affair from them had left her feeling tense and exhausted, and she was grateful to be able to shed the pretence of normality, if even for a short while.

Maureen, whom Annette had to admit, truly was the soul of discretion, waited until the girls had disappeared before asking her about her and Hollie's spying mission of the previous night. With the girls constantly present since Annette's return, this was the first opportunity for them to talk alone. Annette told her all about it, how they'd spotted Jack and how the woman he was with had indeed turned out to be Rachel, how she had decided to keep all mention of Rachel out of it for now when she spoke to Liz. She could see the empathy in Maureen's eyes when she told her about the difficult conversation she had had with her sister and how, more than anything, she wanted to be back home with her.

"I bet you do, love," said Maureen. "And, for what it's worth, I think you've absolutely done the right thing in not telling Liz yet about Rachel. What a total bloody bitch!"

Despite herself, Annette laughed hearing Maureen refer to Rachel like that. "Oh, God, Maureen, I've got you swearing now as well as everything else."

Maureen curled her mouth up into a look of disgust, and slowly shaking her head from side to side, she said. "It's her that's got me swearing — the bloody bitch!"

This time, they both laughed. The sound of Annette's phone ringing cut short their laughter as she fumbled through her bag trying to find it. Pulling it out, she answered it, pleasantly surprised by the news the caller delivered.

"That was Jenny — from the airport," she said, dropping the phone back into her bag. "She said that although it's not official yet, it looks very likely that they will open the airport tomorrow morning. She's on duty until seven in the morning and she said that if we'd like to get to the airport, preferably during the course of the night, she will do her best to get us all on the first flight out tomorrow."

"Oh, that is good news, love," said Maureen. "So, all being well, you could be back home for your sister by tomorrow evening."

"Absolutely. I'd best go find Hollie and let her know, I'm sure she's going to be delighted to get out of here. Then, I think I'll go up and pack all the bags, that way, when the girls come back, we can all go, get some dinner, then head straight off to the airport. What do you think?"

"That's fine. I'll come up with you and help."

## Liz
Parking at the furthest point in the school car park, in the hope of avoiding the

225

small talk that she usually engaged in with the other mothers, Liz pretended to be busy texting on her phone as she waited for Jane to come out. Not in the humour for exchanging pleasantries, she kept her head lowered, but out of the corner of her eye, she could see someone approach and felt her heart drop. Hoping whoever it was would be dissuaded from waiting for her, she busily tapped away on her phone, pretending that she didn't see them.

But the persistent figure waited patiently, until without being blatantly rude, Liz was forced to raise her head. To her relief, it was Pauline that awaited her and lowering the driver's window, she smiled wanly at her friend who discreetly raised a questioning eyebrow by way of asking how she was doing. The look of genuine concern on Pauline's face, caused Liz to involuntarily fill up with tears, which with a shrug, she tried to fight back.

"Look, I know Jane is due out in a minute," said Pauline, apologising for the intrusion, "But, I just wanted to see how you were doing?"

"So, so," admitted Liz. "I feel caught in a kind of limbo at the moment, to be honest. He's still away, of course, and I'm finding keeping face in front of the kids a bit tough."

"I can imagine," said Pauline, keeping a watchful eye in case Jane appeared. "I thought you should know that Jimmy spoke to Jack the other night and gave him one hell of a mouthful. Look — here's Jane — I'll go. If you fancy meeting for a coffee, I'll be around all day tomorrow — just give me a text."

With a forced cheeriness, Liz waved her off, before Jane opened the door and with the usual bustle of activity that accompanied her dumping her schoolbag, gym bag and inevitable armful of ancillary items on to the back seat, she got into the car. "Hey, Mum," she said, before unleashing the customary torrent of abuse about one or other of her teachers. "That Ms. Walsh is a complete bitch — do you know what she said to me today?"

"No," smiled Liz, grateful that her daughter hadn't picked up on any of the tension that she felt was palpable in the car. "What'd she say, love?"

"She told me that my essay fell well short of honours standard. Can you believe that, Mum? I slaved over that essay and I actually thought that it was really good."

"I'll take a look at it when we get home," she said, trying to soothe her irate daughter. "See what she means. Did she tell you what she thought was wrong with it?"

"No, that's just it, Mum. She's such a crap teacher. If she had told me what I need to do with it, then, maybe, it would make sense. But, she's too lazy to bother telling me that. So, now all I know is that it's crap. I might as well not have bothered doing it."

"As I say, we'll have a look at it later. That seems unfair if she's not telling you how to put it right. If needs be, we can try to get you some extra help with English."

"Shouldn't have to, if she wasn't so crap," said Jane grumpily, then, tired of talking about school, she asked. "Was that Pauline you were talking to? Any news on when Dad and the others are coming back?"

Liz felt winded by Jane's innocent enquiry, and fought to regain control before answering. "No, love. No word yet."

The short trip home seemed interminable to Liz and the confined space of the car was claustrophobic to her. She was glad that Josh had rugby practice, which enabled her to go straight home. Desperate to remove herself from her daughter's company, she mumbled something about needing to check her e-mails and went straight to her office as they entered the house.

Once in the office, she concentrated on breathing deeply, restoring herself to a calm and functioning state. How on earth was she going to keep herself together for the kids in the coming weeks?

### Hollie

Hollie received the news of the airport's impending re-opening with mixed feelings. Happy to be going home, she had really hoped that there would be some news from the police about Eoin before she did so. But, she had heard nothing. He was still out there and whilst he was, there existed a risk that he could slip the net and return unhindered to Dublin.

The thought scared her as, if he did evade capture, he would undoubtedly be aware that the police were looking for him and therefore he would know that she had quite probably had a hand in assisting them with their hunt for him. At least he didn't know where she lived, but he did however know where she worked — assuming that she still had a job on her return. Yes, returning home brought its own complications, she thought.

Forcing herself to stop thinking so negatively, she gathered up her belongings, throwing them carelessly into the small case she had and went downstairs to check out. To her immense relief, the hotel played it fair, only charging her for single occupancy of the double room she had stayed an additional week in, and giving her an 'extenuating circumstances' discount on top, which brought the total payable to just under three hundred Euro. Keeping her fingers crossed, she put her credit card into the terminal and heaved a sigh of relief as it printed off the payment approval slip.

### Jack

Pouring the remnants from the bottle of a very delectable Chateauneuf du Pape, Jack asked the waiter to bring them another bottle. The food they had just eaten in the hotel restaurant had been, as ever, flawless and the wine, recommended by the waiter, had proved the perfect accompaniment. Rachel, sitting opposite him, looked incredible, and the heady mixture of it all almost allowed him to forget temporarily the mess he was going home to.

That was until a dark thought, one he couldn't believe he hadn't thought of before now, crossed his mind — Annette. What if they encountered her in the airport? That could change everything. This thought, occurring to him mid-swallow, caused him to choke and splutter on his wine. Alarmed by the ferocity of his choking, Rachel quickly poured him a glass of water, and jumping up from her seat, went around and slapped him on the back. Unable to speak still, he waved her away, signalling that he was okay, and slowing sipping the proffered water, he managed to compose himself.

"Sorry about that," he said, looking embarrassed at the attention his choking fit had generated, as the eyes of all the other diners were upon him. "It just completely went down the wrong way."

"I thought you were a goner!" laughed Rachel, who still looked shaken from the fright he had given her.

"God job there's a doctor in the house," he said, returning to a normal colour. "I just had a dreadful thought and my mouth engaged before my brain, which would have undoubtedly advised me to swallow my wine before talking!"

"And this thought?" said Rachel, curious.

"Well, I thought what the fuck happens if we meet Annette in the airport? We could even end up on the same flight — that would be pretty disastrous — wouldn't it?"

Rachel's face fell, giving him a clear indication that this prospect hadn't occurred to her either and accustomed to her cool headed reaction in the face of adversity, something he was quickly coming to rely on, he was deeply disturbed to see her looking rattled. Excusing herself, she went to the ladies, leaving him pondering this latest predicament.

## *Donal*

Donal drove slowly, but deliberately, past Kay's house, wanting to ensure that his mother-in-law had in fact left before he called to the house. He was relieved to see no sign of her car in the driveway, and turning around, he went back to the house. Parking up on the road outside, he took several deep breaths, amazed at how nervous he felt about meeting with his wife. Urging himself to be calm and confident, he got out of the car and strode purposefully up the driveway.

The front door opened before he got there and he took this to be an encouraging sign, that she had clearly been looking out for him. Not sure how he had been expecting to find her, as his conversations with Kay had led him to believe that there was little improvement, he was pleasantly surprised to see her looking far better than he had anticipated.

"Hey, Sue," he said, leaning forward to kiss her on the mouth, but she abruptly turned her head, leaving his lips to barely brush her cheek. Taken aback by this response, he reminded himself to stay cool and without commenting, he merely followed her up the hallway and into the kitchen.

As usual, Kay's kitchen was stiflingly warm and he unzipped his jacket, then removing it, he hung it on the back of one of the breakfast bar stools, before seating himself up on it. Susan looked great, much better than the last time he had seen her, but he knew that wouldn't be difficult. Unlike the last time, she was well groomed, her brown hair had a sheen restored to it and once more fell silkily to her shoulders and she was wearing make-up — something he hadn't seen her do in months.

She hadn't uttered a word to him since opening the door, and he shifted uncomfortably in the stool, whilst she filled the kettle and turned it on, not wanting to be the one to break the silence. Without even asking if he wanted one, she made them both some coffee, looking as if she was rehearsing something in her head as she did so. Still he waited, not wanting to crowd her, until eventually he cracked, saying. "You're looking great, Susan."

Her reaction was as if she had forgotten he was there. She turned suddenly and looked at him, almost like she was registering his presence for the first time. Then thrusting a mug of coffee in his direction, she retreated with her own mug to the other side of the kitchen, where she rested her bum against the kitchen units, and looked him squarely in the eyes. Finally, in a voice that brooked no argument and a determined look on her face, she addressed him.

"Look, Donal," she began and he could tell that what she was about to say was extremely difficult for her. "I want us to separate. Permanently. Basically, I want a divorce, Donal. I'm sorry, I don't want to hurt you and I know that this is probably coming as a shock to you, but my mind's made up."

Stunned, he opened his mouth to say something, anything, but words failed him and he stared gormlessly at her, wanting to believe that he had misheard her. He knew that he hadn't. When she spoke again, her demeanour had softened and her eyes were filled with tears, which she swiftly wiped away with the back of her hand.

"I'm sorry, Donal — truly, I am. But, we're no good together. No good for each other and we haven't been for a very long time now."

Finding his voice, he interjected. "But, you're off the booze now, Sue. We can work on things, get ourselves back on track — adopt a baby if you want — whatever."

He could hear the lack of enthusiasm in his own voice, knew that she could hear it too and capitulating, he shrugged knowingly. "The booze isn't the problem though — is it?"

She shook her head sadly. "No. It certainly hasn't helped and again, I'm sorry for that. But it's a chicken and egg situation. If I stay in this marriage I know that it'll only be a matter of time before I start drinking again and once that happens, then, the marriage will be doomed."

He knew that what she was saying was true. For Chrissake he'd been having those self same thoughts himself only a couple of weeks ago, but he still found it shocking to hear from her.

"I need a fresh start, Donal. I haven't had a drink since that awful Friday and, as of now; I don't intend to drink again. But, this isn't going to be easy for me. I have to focus completely on myself for the foreseeable future and I simply can't do that if I'm with you. Besides, you're on the brink of something great with your business, Donal — I know you are and I don't want to be the thing that holds you back and, if I'm in recovery, there's nothing more certain than that's exactly what will happen. We're no good for each other, Donal — I realise that now, and I think if you're completely honest with yourself — you know it as well."

Somehow, he did. With a sigh of resignation and perhaps a small sense of relief that the decision had been taken away from him, he put his mug on the worktop, crossed the floor to where she stood and placing his hands on either side of her head, he gently tilted it forward, kissing her chastely on the top of her head. "Take care of yourself, Susan," he said, then left accepting that any further discussion was futile.

### *Denise*

Blocking her caller ID on her mobile to prevent her new number being displayed on the house phone, Denise hid herself from view behind a large tree across the road from the home she had shared with John and dialled the number. There was no reply, but unwilling to take that as concrete proof that there was no-one in, she peered across at the house looking for any signs of life, but there were none.

Although still daylight, the sky was darkened with heavy rain clouds and she would have thought it likely that John would need some artificial lighting if he were in. However, there were no lights visible and taking this as a good sign, she crept up the driveway. When she reached the front door, she gave one good long ring on the bell before scarpering back to her hiding place to see if anyone answered the door, but they didn't.

As certain as she could be that the house was unoccupied, she once more crept up to the door, this time fishing her key out of her purse and inserting it into the lock. With great speed, she let herself in and closing the door behind her, she stood with her back to it, listening for any sounds that would indicate John's presence. Silence. Tip-toeing down the hallway, she peered through the crack of the open living room door in case he was asleep on the couch, but the room was empty.

Her heart was pounding and she felt certain that if he were upstairs asleep, the steady thumping it produced was loud enough to waken him. Holding her breath, she stealthily made her way up the stairs and was re-lieved to see the bedroom door wide open, just as she had left it, and no tell-tale snoring emanating from it.

Her main objective was to get in and out as quickly as possible, so, relatively confident that he was not there, she headed straight to the box room where the access hatch for the attic was. Opening it up, she lowered the stepladder affixed to the inside of the door and hurriedly scampered up the steps. It took her less than a couple of minutes to locate the roll of insulation and with a sigh of relief; she withdrew her mother's bracelet from its coils.

Mission accomplished, she came down from the attic, not even stop-ping to close the hatch or replace the ladder. She ran down the stairs as quickly as she could and noticing for the first time, the pile of post on the floor inside the letterbox, she suddenly had the sense that the house had been empty since she had left it a week ago. John still hadn't come back. Now, that was unusual. His remorse usually ran its course far quicker than this.

Reluctant to risk being there for his inevitable homecoming, she resisted the temptation to confirm her suspicions and made her getaway before she put herself in danger. It wasn't until she was out the door and down the street that she realised how much she was trembling.

## Rachel

Rachel knew full well that Jack was under the misapprehension that she was worried about the prospect of encountering Annette in the airport when she had disappeared to the toilet. She was quite happy to have him think that. But, the reality was that she was bitterly disappointed at the thought that her opportunity to play 'double agent' with Liz was in jeopardy. She was looking forward to it too much to let that happen. There simply had to be a way around it, she just had to think and she couldn't do that with him sitting there with a face like a smacked arse on him.

Once alone in the cubicle, her mind computed the options available to them and within a matter of minutes, she came up with the only viable solution. Pleased with herself, she flushed the toilet, washed her hands and fixed her make-up before returning to the table where Jack's angst was palpable.

"Easy peasey!" she said as she lowered herself back into her seat. He raised a questioning eyebrow and she continued. "I'll bet you anything that Annette will be desperate to get on the first flight out of here."

"Yep. That would be her style," he said, not certain where Rachel was going with this.

"Well then, it's obvious. As soon as the airport reopens, I'll go there, keep out of sight, keep an eye on the Dublin flights and watch until I see her get on a flight and then, we'll know that the coast is clear for us to get the next available flight. As I say — simples!"

A big grin broke across Jack's face. He lifted his glass of wine in toast to her and said, "That, Dr. Wallace, is pure genius!"

CHAPTER NINETEEN

# Saturday AM 24th April

*Hollie*

Hollie was a complete bag of nerves when they arrived at the airport. Her eyes darted constantly about the place, anxiously looking for any sign of Eoin. Megan and Hannah, sensing her anxiety, flanked her, doing their utmost to conceal her as much as possible and she was immensely grateful for their help. Despite her initial reservations about leaving before the police had caught Eoin, she now realised how desperate she was to get out of Majorca and just how difficult this journey would have been on her own.

Thanks to Jenny's tip-off, they had managed to get to the airport before news of its re-opening had been officially announced which enabled them to be top of the queue at the Ryanair desk when a smiling Jenny Jones took her seat and waved them forward.

"Hey, folks," she said cheerfully. "Bet you guys are glad to be going home."

"You bet ya!" said Hollie, putting her passport on the counter. "And, thanks a million for the tip-off. I'm guessing it's going to be mad here today."

"Ah, no worries. I've been thinking about you guys ever since your last visit and I was determined to try and get you safely out of here at the first opportunity. Juan is working today as well, so he'll be watching out like a hawk for Eoin. The police brought out a load of photo-fit pictures, so all the lads will be being as vigilant as possible. I even have one here," she said, picking up a picture to show Hollie, "and I'll do my best to spot him here and alert the lads. So, don't worry. Let's get you lot checked in, then you can go through security where you'll be able to heave a sigh of relief."

They completed their check in and, after thanking Jenny again profusely for all her help, they made their way through the, as yet, not too busy security, and into the departure lounge, where Hollie felt herself finally beginning to relax, wishing with all her might that they were securely on the plane with the doors shut.

## Liz

Thoroughly exhausted, but unable to sleep properly, Liz finally drifted off some time after six o'clock in the morning, only to be awoken by her mobile phone ringing less than an hour later. At first, thinking that it was part of her dream, she ignored it, but then realising it was no dream, she groped about beneath the pillow, forcing herself awake. Blinking hard to clear her eyes, she saw that it was Annette calling her and pressed the answer button.

"Hello," she said, her voice laden with sleep.

"Oh Liz, I've woken you up. I'm so sorry," said Annette, "Look, go back to sleep — I'll see you later. Just wanted to let you know that we are finally out of here."

"Really?" asked Liz, relief flooding her. "Oh, thank God. I can't wait to see you. What time are you in? Do you want me to collect you from the airport?"

"Not at all. Paddy's going to pick us up. I'll go back home with him, drop off the girls, grab a quick cuppa with him and then, I'll be straight over to you. Should be with you about three o'clockish."

"I can't wait. Any sign of Jack? I've heard nothing from him, so presumably he's not on the way yet."

"Well, as you can imagine, the airport is absolutely manic here, but so far, there's no sign of him. We're through security now, so personally I think he's unlikely to show, but if he surfaces, I'll text you and let you know. If he is on the flight, do you want me to come straight to you? 'Cos I can, if you like."

"Let's just hope that he isn't. I'm sure he would have let me know if he was. Anyway, we'll worry about that when we know for definite."

"Okay — see you soon."

## Rachel

Stopping to catch sight of her reflection in the mirrored glass of the airport terminal, Rachel was confident that there was little chance of anybody recognising her. Her long blonde hair, which she always wore loose, had been tied back in a ponytail and swept up beneath the baseball cap she wore. She couldn't remember the last time that she had ventured outdoors without wearing make-up and that, in itself, would have warranted a second glance to confirm her identity, but, taking no chances, she had purchased a large, tacky pair of sunglasses that successfully concealed half of her face. Certain that she could pull this off, she slipped unobtrusively into the terminal building amidst a group of hopeful travellers.

Once inside, she quickly scanned the crowd and unable to see Annette or any of her entourage, she boldly made her way to the large departure board and peering up at it, she quickly established that there were to be two flights to Dublin that morning. The first, a Ryanair flight, was scheduled to depart at eight o'clock and the second, with Aer Lingus, wasn't due to leave until eleven thirty. Fervently hoping that Annette was on the earlier flight, as she had no desire to hang around here for the entire morning, she headed over in the direction of the Ryanair check in desk.

Check in had already commenced. There was a lengthy queue of people who were shuffling their way along in the roped off confines of the cattle mart style approach to the desk. The queue wound its way snake-like back and forth before releasing its occupants to the next available ground crew staff member who issued them with boarding passes and sent their luggage off on the conveyor belt. Studiously she ran her eyes along the full length of the queue and back again, but could not see Annette anywhere.

Disappointed, she resigned herself to having to wait for the later flight and went to get herself a cup of coffee. It was just as she was stirring her skinny latte that she caught a glimpse of a familiar face in the security queue. "Eureka!" she exclaimed aloud, when on the next shuffle forward, she got a clear view of Annette's face whilst she removed her jeans belt in preparation for going through the security check. Engrossed in conversation with her mother-in-law and with the two girls trailing behind her, Annette never even saw her and dumping her un-drunk coffee into the bin, she left the airport satisfied that she and Jack had just been given the thumbs up for 'Operation Liz'.

## Jack

In a state of complete agitation, Jack had worn a path in the grass outside the breakfast terrace, where he had been walking back and forth waiting to hear from Rachel. There was so much riding on them keeping all knowledge of their affair from Liz that he simply couldn't relax until he knew that Annette had left the country and that they were safe to get themselves on to a flight.

Deeply appreciative of Rachel's insistence on going all the way to the airport to ensure they wouldn't be discovered, he realised what a valuable asset she was going to be in keeping the kids on side and he loved her for it, discounting her duplicity towards Liz as the necessary evil she had pointed it out to be. A year from now, all this would be history — Liz would have moved on, the kids would have accepted him and Rachel as a couple and he would have Rachel to thank for smoothing the path.

All thumbs, he nearly dropped his phone when it started ringing in his haste to see how she had got on. "Rachel!"

"Ze eagle haas landed!" she said through clenched teeth, causing him to laugh.

"Oh thank fuck for that! You're certain? They've gone on the flight?"

"One hundred percent! Saw them all go through security with my own eyes. Annette, her mother-in-law and the two girls. The girls had some friend or other with them, I recognised her from somewhere, but can't remember exactly who she is. Anyway, that doesn't matter. What matters is that Annette has definitely gone, she didn't see me and now, we can try and get ourselves on a flight tomorrow."

## *Donal*

An overwhelming sense of sadness enveloped Donal the moment he opened his eyes on Saturday morning. Refusing to succumb to it, he got up, showered and went downstairs, determined to get his life on track. He hadn't bothered to take his mobile phone up to bed, but had left it downstairs on charge and going to unplug it now, he saw that he had received a few text messages.

The first was from Susan, apologising for her shock announcement of the previous day, but wishing him the best and despite everything, he knew her wishes to be genuine. It still saddened him. The next message was from Hollie, informing him that the airport had re-opened and that she was on a flight home and should be in Dublin airport around ten-thirty. She told him that she would get a taxi home and give him a call when she got there. A quick glance at the time and he figured he was in good time to collect her, not wanting her to arrive back after her trauma with no-one to meet her.

There were two messages from his network services provider welcoming him home, which he deleted, thinking that he had already received the 'welcome home' of the year from his wife. Lastly, there was a message from Denise, asking him to give her a call if he got a minute.

Now, almost ten o'clock, he knew that he would need to get on the road if he was to be at the airport in time for Hollie, so deciding that he would call Denise back from the car, he grabbed his keys and left the house.

"Hey Denise. How are you?" he said when she answered.

"I'm okay, thanks. Just wanted to thank you for the lift. Had a bit of hectic day yesterday and never got to call you."

"Had one of those days myself," he said, shaking his head. "So, what'd you get up to?"

He listened whilst she told him about visiting the house and recovering her mother's bracelet. Astounded at what he was hearing, his protective side kicked in.

"Are you off your fucking head, Denise? What the hell were you doing going back there. Supposing he'd shown up when you were up in the attic — he could have bloody killed you. I can't believe you were that stupid."

"Well, he didn't show up — did he?" she snapped back at him, clearly annoyed at his reaction. An awkward silence ensued.

"Hey, I'm sorry," he said eventually, "I just don't like thinking of you putting yourself in danger like that. From what you've told me, John sounds like a bit of a nutter and God knows what he's capable of if he knows that you're leaving him. You could have always given me a call and I would have been happy to have gone with you."

Softening at his words, she said, "Thanks, Donal. I appreciate that. Look, last thing I want is to row with you. So, let's just forget about it — shall we? How'd things go with Susan? Has she come back home yet?"

He filled her in on his meeting with his wife, endeavouring to keep the despair from his voice as he told her that his marriage was over. He still hadn't quite got his head around it all yet, in some strange way he felt liberated, but was reluctant to admit this to anyone, even himself, at this early stage. Somehow, he felt that she sensed his relief to have that decision made for him, although she never said as much. Instead, she asked if he would be free that evening so she could buy him dinner to thank him for the lift from London.

He explained that he was on his way to collect Hollie and would need to see what she wanted to do before committing to anything. Promising to give her a shout later on, he rang off.

## Denise

Notwithstanding her initial irritation at Donal telling her off for retrieving her mother's bracelet, Denise was quite touched by the concern her actions had evoked in him. In all the time that she had spent with John, he had never shown her any protectiveness and there was a definite feel good factor to having Donal chastise her for endangering herself. He really was a very sweet man and she couldn't help but think Susan a fool for letting him go.

She fervently hoped that the friendship forged between them would be a long lasting one as, despite the brevity of their acquaintance, she felt as if she had known him for a very long time. It was difficult for her to imagine just how different her stay in London would have been had the unlikely twist of fate that the ash cloud produced, not thrown them together on the ferry. He was a good soul; she could feel that, his compassion and kindness had been evidenced when he had spoken about his sister and his wife and for her to be now on the receiving end of his concern warmed her.

Ironically, his current difficulties had distracted her from dwelling wholly on her own situation, allowing her to more slowly absorb the life-changing possibilities that now awaited her. Without even being aware of it, his gift of friendship had instilled in her a confidence that she had not experienced in years. Had he not been there, her emotionally fragile mind could well have questioned her right to get rid of John's baby or even her decision to keep her lotto win from him, but now, thanks to Donal and his blatant admiration and respect for her as a person, she knew with certainty that the future she was planning for herself was the right one. Unwittingly, he had given her this self-assurance and she would always be grateful to him for that.

### Annette

"Sounds like you've had quite an eventful time of it," laughed Paddy, as he slid a mug of coffee across the kitchen island to his wife.

"You can sing that!" said Annette, shaking her head. "I mean you couldn't have written the script for it. It would have sounded too unbelievable. For starters — the ash cloud! Who could have dreamt in this day and age that the world could be ground to a halt in that manner?"

"Phenomenal," agreed Paddy. "And with my mother in tow," he added sheepishly. "I thought you'd never forgive me."

"Trust me, Maureen was the best part of that holiday."

"That in itself was phenomenal," said Paddy who had been visibly delighted to see the closeness that had developed between his wife and daughters and his mother. This newfound unity had been evident the second that they had walked through the arrivals door in the airport. "And that poor young woman — Hollie. She's certainly been through it."

"I know. And she's so lovely. I was really glad her brother came to meet her — she needed that. We must have them over some night for something to eat and you can meet her properly. It was just too crazy in the airport this morning."

Predictably enough, the airport had been chaotic and with everyone anxious to get home, Paddy and Donal had received a hasty introduction before heading back to the car park. Tired, Maureen had requested to be dropped off at her own house and the girls, chattering away at nineteen to the dozen, had filled Paddy in on much of the week's events, leaving Annette unable to tell him about Jack and Rachel until they finally ran out of steam and disappeared off upstairs.

Astounded by what she told him, he shook his head disparagingly, "What a plonker," he said, "and with Liz's friend! Jesus! How's poor Liz taking all of this?"

"Well, that's just it. She doesn't know that it's Rachel yet. I couldn't bring myself to tell her that over the phone. I'm going to grab a quick shower, get changed and then I'm going to call over to her. She's adamant that it's the end of the line for her and Jack, but you know Liz. We'll have to just wait and see."

Finishing off the last of her coffee, she looked at the clock and seeing that it was almost half past two, she said, "Anyway, best get a move on. I told Liz that I'd be over there around threeish."

CHAPTER TWENTY

# Saturday PM 24th April

*Rachel*

With a sense of accomplishment, Rachel strode out the back door of the hotel to the pool area, peering around trying to locate Jack as she did so. Spotting him sitting at the bar drinking a cold beer, she made her way up to him, grinning broadly and brandishing the paperwork for their flight the following morning.

"Mission accomplished," she said, leaning in and kissing him full on the mouth. "We're on the eleven thirty flight in the morning."

Pulling her to him, Jack looped his arms around her waist and nuzzling his face into her neck, he said. "You are some woman for one woman, Dr. Wallace. Not only are you the sexiest woman on this entire island, but clever too. Seriously though, Rach, thanks a million for sorting that out — it would have been a nightmare bumping into Annette in the airport."

"Whoa! Back up there, tiger," she said, stopping him before he started dwelling on what the next day held in store. Then, taking his hand, she guided it through the folds of the wraparound skirt she was wearing, leaving it to rest on the naked wetness that lay beneath, before saying throatily, "Run that by me again, about me being the sexiest woman on this island."

## *Hollie*

Refreshed after a nap and a long shower, Hollie sat curled up on the sofa wearing one of Susan's old robes sipping an oversized mug of hot chocolate that her brother had made for her, just like when they were kids. Smiling gratefully at him, she lifted her mug in salutation.

"Thanks Donal — you know, for picking me up and that."

With a smile that radiated the depth of affection he felt for her, he said, "And why wouldn't I have picked you up Hols? I'd have gone out to Majorca and collected you if I could have. I'm so sorry that you had to go through all that on your own. You look well though, better than I thought you would. But, how are you — really?"

She looked pensive before she answered, as if she were battling with a whole plethora of emotions. "I dunno," she said honestly. "I feel like a whole mixture of things. I'm angry at myself for being so stupid in the first place, but then, I'm angry at him — however stupid I was, I didn't deserve what he did to me. I hate the thoughts that he is still out there, and that other women are at risk, but I'm also not too sure how well I would cope if I got dragged into a court case and had to face him again. And then, I think that I want to be there — I want to see his face when they put him away for years. I want to look him in the eye and let him know that I'm not afraid of him — otherwise, I might feel that he had somehow won. I don't know if this makes any sense to you?"

Donal nodded, but remained silent, letting her get it all off her chest. "Do you know," she continued. "The part that gets to me the most is that I have no memory of what he did to me. That to me is the biggest violation of all. It's as if he got inside my head and that, more than any other aspect is what I hate him for. I think that if I had been conscious and was able to recall bit by bit what he had done to me, then, somehow I could deal with it better. That probably sounds crazy, but it's how I feel."

"No, I think I can understand that," said Donal, his gentle face eaten up with sympathy for the sister that he had spent his life protecting. "Have you thought about getting yourself some counselling? You'll probably need it."

"Yeah, yeah, I probably will. I'm sure that I'll be able to get some names in work on Monday, but I don't particularly want anyone there knowing what happened. I can always say it's for a friend or something."

They stayed chatting companionably for the rest of the afternoon with Hollie telling him all about how good Annette had been to her and about the bizarre coincidence that resulted in Dr. Wallace having an affair with Annette's brother-in-law. He sat enthralled whilst she talked him through their sleuthing mission where she caught them in the act on camera. Then, he told her about Susan and how she wanted to end their marriage, and knowing how upset he was, she managed to feign regret, whilst secretly delighted to have her manipulative, self-absorbed sister-in-law out of her brother's life and hoped with all her heart that she would remain out of it, affording him the opportunity to meet someone worthy of him — though she kept those thoughts to herself.

He spoke about his trip to London and the disappointing outcome from his meetings with The Transglobal Travel Corporation. She brushed their proposal away dismissively, saying, "No way should you go for that, Donal. You'd be cracked. That's the first company you've seen and you can be damn sure that they know that too. They see what a great product you've come up with and they want in before you realise just how good it is yourself. Plenty more companies are going to be interested and you just have to bide your time. You'll see — another six months and you'll have a string of places outbidding each other for a slice of the action."

Laughing at her confidence in him, he said, "That's pretty much what Denise said too, it's just that I want to get moving with it and I know that the odds were against it all falling into place with the first meeting that I had, but I couldn't help hoping that it would."

A cheeky grin formed on her face as he spoke, "Ah yes! Denise!" she said, her voice laden with innuendo, "Talk me through Denise — I'm dying to hear all about her!"

### Liz

Fate dealt Liz a good hand when a rugby match and a trip to town took both of the kids out of the house, leaving her home alone in advance of Annette's visit. A glance at the time told her that Annette would be arriving any minute now, so in preparation, she went to the kitchen and filled the kettle. No sooner had she switched it on, than the doorbell rang.

Despite feeling strong, the sight of Annette's face with worry etched across it reduced Liz to tears when she pulled open the front door. "Hey, Sis — it's good to have you back," she said, burying her face in Annette's shoulder as they embraced.

They remained locked in their embrace for several minutes, oblivious to anything else other than their deep love for each other, until eventually, Annette broke the silence by asking, "Where are the kids?"

"Oh, they're both out. We have the place to ourselves for a couple of hours. Not sure I could have handled them being here."

Relieved to learn that they were alone, Annette held her sister at arm's length, then, shaking her head sadly, she said, "What a total wanker Jack is!"

Liz nodded her agreement, then said. "Come on, let's get a coffee and I'll fill you in on the week from hell!"

Several minutes later, armed with two strong mugs of coffee and perched on the stools at the island, Liz was the first to speak. "So, what was she like? The bimbo that Jack was with. Please don't tell me that she was twenty or something like that."

As soon as she had asked the question, Liz knew by her sister's face that there was something she hadn't told her yet — something big. "What? What is it? I know you Annette, there's something you're not telling me."

"There's no easy way to tell you this, honey," she began, sucking in a deep breath before continuing, "I couldn't tell you over the phone though — it wouldn't have been fair."

"What is it? Jesus, Annette — spit it out will you?"

"It was Rachel," she said, watching for Liz's reaction, but Liz stared back at her blankly.

"Rachel? Rachel who?"

Realising that the penny hadn't dropped, Annette gulped in more air. "Rachel Wallace — your friend."

All the colour drained from Liz's face as she finally absorbed what she was being told. Then, she shook her head incredulously and a small, almost manic, laugh escaped from her mouth as she said, "Ah, Annette — you must have it wrong. Sure, Rachel is in The Canaries — I spoke to her. Maybe she looks like Rachel — I mean that would fit — Jack makes no secret of how attractive he thinks she is — they're always flirting, but there's nothing to it, just a bit of flirting that's all. No way could it be Rachel, Annette — I'm telling you."

But even as she protested, the look on Annette's face told her that it was true and the tears sprang unbidden to her eyes. Blinking them away furiously, Liz said, "The fucking slag! How could she? How could she do this to me, Annette? I trusted her, she was my friend. Christ, I've told her things, you know — confided in her — told her things about me and Jack, things that I'd never have said if I had any idea that she was like that. I mean, I know she likes her men — and yes, married men, but I thought she cared about me. Never in a million years would I have thought that she would do this to me. Jesus! She's worse than he is!"

Then, giving vent to her grief, she dissolved into tears. Annette shot up from her seat and rushing to her, pulled her into her arms where she rocked her back and forth, soothing her, reassuring her, telling her how wonderful she was. Eventually, her tears subsided and with her big brown eyes, so like Annette's own, she fixed her stare on Annette and proclaimed, "They're out of my life, Annette. Both of them. For good."

### Annette

With all her heart, Annette prayed that the words she was hearing were true. Liz deserved so much better than this. So much more than a lying, cheating husband; so much more than a duplicit, two-faced best friend. As Annette had known she would, she received the news of Rachel's involvement very badly — and, who could blame her? She looked broken; defeated and Annette questioned if she would ever be able to trust anyone again. The only certainty in Annette's mind was that any reconciliation of her marriage would be detrimental to her.

They sat in silence for several minutes, the constant flickering of Liz's eyes indicating that her mind was in overdrive as she computed this latest information. Unsure how to begin to offer comfort in such awful circumstances, Annette waited for Liz to speak and, when she did, Annette couldn't have been more surprised at what she had to say.

With a sardonic grunt of laughter, Liz said, "The funny thing is that before all this happened I thought I had some very big news for everyone when you all got back from holiday. Had even planned a dinner party to break it to you all en masse."

As surely as if she had received a blow to the stomach, Annette felt winded as her first thought was, 'Oh fuck! She's pregnant — she'll never leave him now.' Tentatively, she waited for Liz to expand.

"You see, I've been busy these past few months," she said cryptically, eye-balling Annette, whose fear was written all over her face. Knowing her so well, Liz laughed, more wholesomely this time, "And no, Annette. I'm not pregnant!"

Blushing at her own transparency, Annette relaxed, grinning, "I'm sorry sis, it did cross my mind."

"Well relax! That's not my news. And, to be perfectly blunt — if that was my news, I'd be booked on the first boat to England! Anyway — my news. I've got myself a qualification. I've been studying — don't look so shocked!"

"I'm sorry," blurted Annette, genuinely not expecting this at all. "What in?"

"Well, you are now looking at a fully certified Life Coach."

"Wow! That's amazing — tell me more."

Liz told her all about the course she had done, about setting up her website, about all the help and support she had received from Diana, her mentor, and how, not only was she qualified, but thanks to all the groundwork she had done, she now had several clients booked in for the coming weeks. Annette could not have been more astounded. The Liz that sat in front of her was a more confident and capable Liz than Annette could ever remember seeing before and for the first time since hearing about Jack's affair, she felt a surge of hope about her sister's future.

Tears of pride filled her eyes and allowing them to fall freely, she looked at Liz, shaking her head incredulously, "I am so proud of you, Lizzie. You have no idea. I bet you'll make a fantastic Life Coach. I honestly never expected you to come out with news like this, but I think it's possibly the best news I've ever heard. Now, what are we sitting here for — show me this website, quick!"

## Donal

Spoilt for choice as a consequence of his 'pre-Susan's return' shopping, Donal stood staring into the full fridge, deciding what to cook for dinner. Settling on some Sea Bass with a mixed rocket leaf salad, he popped two baked potatoes in the oven and announced that they would eat about seven thirty.

"Sounds good to me," said Hollie. "Fancy some wine? I could run down to the corner shop and grab us a couple of bottles."

Having disposed of all traces of alcohol from the house before his visit to Susan, Donal welcomed the notion of enjoying a glass of wine without the fear of it resulting in a drunken bender as had happened so often in the past. Realising just how long it had been since he had partaken in such a simple pleasure in his own home, he saw the first sign of change that his new separated status afforded him.

"Yeah, sure, Hols. That'd be nice," he said. "Let me give you some money though."

"No, no — you're grand," she said, grabbing her purse and hurrying off before he could protest.

The Chablis that she bought was the perfect accompaniment for the Sea Bass and despite the traumas that they had both endured in the preceding week, the closeness that existed between them left them both feeling relaxed and secure in each other's company. "It's good to have you here, Hols," said Donal, lifting his glass in salute to her. "We'll get through all this shit."

"You betcha!" she said in response, he knew that she was sounding far more confident than she was feeling and he loved her for her spirit. "And look, joking apart, do please tell me about Denise — I want to hear all about her."

Refusing to be goaded by her earlier teasing, Donal had still not told her anything about his new friend. But, seeing the sincerity in her current request, he smiled cautiously at her before speaking.

"Well, firstly, you've got to believe me that there is nothing more to this than friendship."

Unable to resist interjecting, she said, "Whatever!"

He glowered at her now, saying, "If that's what you're going to be like, then I'm not going to talk to you about her."

"Okay, I'm sorry. It's just that it strikes me as odd that some woman, whom you've only just met, would go so far as offer to hire a private investigator for a crime, not even against you, but against your sister that she hasn't even met, without having some major interest in you. Now, you've gotta agree that that is odd — yeah?"

Hearing it put like that, he had to admit that the whole thing sounded unlikely, but the reality had been, that thrown together in the manner in which they were, he and Denise had shared more confidences than he had with friends he had known for years. And, on that basis, he forgot just how new their acquaintance was. Seeing it from Hollie's point of view, he raised his hands in capitulation.

"Alright! I know how it sounds. But, she's just a really nice person. She's been through some really bad shit — she hasn't even told me all the details, but certainly, it involved a very abusive relationship that she has managed to escape. She came into some money that made it all possible and sees herself in a position to avenge what has happened to her by helping you out. Not entirely logical in many ways, but I kinda know where she's coming from. It seems to me that she's too scared to fight her own demons, but to at least fight someone's demons is therapeutic to her."

A cynical look remained on Hollie's face whilst he spoke, but ignoring it, he continued, "I actually think you'd really like her, Hols. She wanted to buy me dinner tonight to thank me for the lift to and from London, but I phoned her when you went to the shop and told her that I'd have to take a rain check on it for tonight, but that maybe I'd meet up with her tomorrow — she asked if you'd come along — said she'd really like to meet you."

"Oh, I dunno about that, Donal. I'm not feeling real sociable at the moment and she'd probably want to talk about the rape and everything. I don't think I'm up to all that right now — not with someone I've never met before anyway."

Instantly remorseful at his lack of consideration by even suggesting putting her in a social situation that would cause her any discomfort, he hurriedly said, "Hey, no pressure, Hols. I keep forgetting that you haven't even met her. Look, another time — no worries."

## Denise

Unaware of quite how much she had been looking forward to seeing Donal that evening, Denise was surprised by how disappointed she had felt when he phoned to tell her that he couldn't make it. However, she couldn't be-grudge Hollie her time with him after all she'd been through, but, not for the fist time, she felt a pang of envy towards Hollie - that she was lucky to have a brother who was so protective of her.

The thought sent her hurtling down the road of self-pity as she contem-plated how few people on the planet gave her a second thought. She knew the situation was of her own making, or more accurately of John's making. His disapproval of the few friends she had had when she met him had led to her isolating herself from them in the misguided belief that he had wanted her to himself. Looking back now, with the wisdom of hindsight, she realised just how foolish she had been.

Although less than two weeks since she had freed herself from him, already her judgement was less clouded and with crystal clarity she could see how much he had controlled her — her thoughts; her possessions; everything. How had she let that happen? How pathetic had she been? But, not anymore. Now, she felt empowered, she knew that was due in part to the money, which opened all manner of doors for her, but also she knew that meeting Donal had had an impact on her too.

As if hearing him telling her to pull herself together, she forced herself to stop the downward spiral of negativity that was racing around in her mind and deciding that she would go downstairs to the restaurant to eat, she went to get herself ready.

## Jack

It was unavoidable, now that Jack was booked on a flight back, he simply had to call home to let Liz know to expect him the following day. With huge reluctance, he picked up his mobile and went out on to the balcony to make the call.

Offering up a silent prayer that it would be one of the kids who answered, his heart dropped when on the second ring, Liz picked up.

"Hello," she said, in an ice-cold tone that left him in no doubt that what Jimmy had told him was true.

"Hi, just wanted to let you know that I'm booked on a flight back tomorrow. Should be back at the house about mid afternoon."

"Fine."

An awkward silence ensued and unsure what else to say, he said, "Look Liz, I think we're going to need to talk…"

She cut straight across him, saying, "Let's leave it 'til tomorrow, eh Jack?" Then, she put the phone down.

CHAPTER TWENTY-ONE

# Sunday AM 25th April

*Annette*

On waking, Annette's first thoughts were of Liz. She was still utterly amazed at everything Liz had unfolded to her the day before, and once more, she felt the pride welling up inside her as she thought of her. Annette had still been with her when Jack had phoned and her sister had once more astounded her with her dignity and decorum as she had calmly told Jack that they would do their talking on his return.

Assuming, correctly, that Liz would prefer this conversation to take place in private, Annette had suggested that the kids sleep over in her house on the Sunday and that she would drop them off to school on Monday morning. Liz had accepted her offer gratefully and it was agreed that Liz would drop them over in time for Sunday brunch, using the somewhat lame excuse that it was a belated birthday celebration for Megan whose birthday had taken place the weekend before going on holiday.

The kids, who were all too happy to have the usual Sunday night 'bath and early to bed' dispensed with, jumped at the idea, not suspecting anything untoward in this arrangement. Liz had been glad of that, not wanting to speak to them about things until after she had met with Jack.

### Hollie

When Hollie's mobile starting to ring as she was towelling herself off, she figured it could only be Niamh, checking to see if she was finally coming back to work the next day. Still undecided as to how much she was going to divulge to her about her time off work, she snatched up her phone, keen to get the initial conversation out of the way. To her surprise, it wasn't Niamh but a Spanish number that flashed on the screen. Tentatively, she pressed the answer button.

"Hola, Hollie?" the familiar voice asked.

"Maria?" asked Hollie, temporarily thrown to be hearing from her again. Immediately, her hopes were up — the police must have caught Eoin, why else would she be calling?

"Yes. Yes, it's me," she said but the tone of her voice told Hollie that she wasn't going to like what she had to say. "Hollie, I am so sorry to ring you with this news, but I thought you would want to know. Eoin appears to have attacked another girl. I got into work this morning and a young Irish girl had been brought in. She too had no memory of what happened to her, the injuries she sustained were very similar to yours and also, her last memory was meeting up with a charming Irish guy called Sean. The description she gave of him matches the one that both you and the English worker gave to the police and I am convinced that it is the same guy."

"Wha… what about DNA?"

"We've given samples to the police and are waiting to hear back from them."

Hollie felt winded, as if all the air had been sucked out of her. She sank onto the bed but unable to speak, she kept her phone pinned to her ear, shaking her head slowly from side to side, oblivious to anything else that Maria was saying to her.

### Rachel

As Jack drew the car to a halt outside Rachel's apartment, she could see the stress showing on his face. She didn't envy him. There was no escaping the fact that the day ahead of him was going to be a tough one and taking pity on him, she suggested that he come in for a coffee before facing the music. Gratefully, he accepted.

"Hey, we'll get through this," she said by way of consolation as she passed him his coffee several minutes later. "We've got to focus on the future. Just think about when we get back from holidays next year. It'll all be legit by then, we'll just be arriving back to our shared home like any other normal couple."

"I suppose you're right," he said, not looking altogether convinced.

"Of course I'm right, Babe. This awfulness will be a memory by then. Liz will have moved on and so will we. Just think about that. Okay, there's a bit of shit to get through in the meantime, but we'll do it. Now, relax, drink your coffee, get yourself calm, then go see Liz. I'll go to the shop, get some food in, and cook us something nice for later. I presume you'll be staying here tonight?"

"Yeah, I'll have to. I'll organise somewhere else tomorrow. It's only going to be for a couple of months, just 'til the heat dies down, so it doesn't have to be anything fancy. Should be easy enough to pick up a place."

"See! Already you're sounding much more positive. Now, I've been thinking — I'm going to hold off contacting Liz until tomorrow. You know, get a feel for how the land lies first from you, then, give her a call, let her know that I'm back and get working on our grand master plan. Simples!"

*Liz*

Liz stared blankly at the untouched plate of food in front of her; oblivious to the noisy chatter of the kids as they wolfed down the magnificent breakfast that Annette had made for them. They were all seated around Annette's large country style kitchen table, but Liz was in a world of her own.

"You're quiet this morning, Mum," said Jane, "Everything alright?"

Snapping herself back to reality, she smiled at her daughter, "Yes, love — everything is fine. Just not madly hungry. Anyway, there's very little chance of getting a word in with you lot jabbering away nineteen to the dozen."

"Absolutely," said Annette, reaching over and starting to gather up the empty plates from around the table. "So, go on you lot — sling your hooks. Give us a bit of peace before Liz heads home. Paddy, love — do you fancy making a nice pot of that coffee of yours?"

The ensuing commotion as the kids pushed back the heavy wooden chairs on the tiled floor was a welcome distraction for Liz, who offered to load the dishwasher whilst Paddy got the coffee underway. The noise levels dropped dramatically when the youngsters raced from the kitchen, fearful that they would be asked to help. Whilst Annette cleared and wiped down the table, Liz found herself alone for the first time in the working part of the kitchen with Paddy, whom she could sense observing her. Looking up and meeting his eyes, she saw the sympathy within them and felt herself begin to cry.

"Ah, Lizzie — come here," he said, wrapping his arms around her, drawing her close to him. "The guy's a gobshite, love — what can I say? Anyway, how are you doing?"

"Alright," she sniffled, embarrassed by yet another outburst of emotion. "I just seem to keep whingeing all the time. Sorry."

"You've nothing to be sorry for, you daft thing. I'm sure this has all been rotten for you — but, you know what Liz, you'll get through this. I know you will."

"Don't let the bastards grind you down," she quipped, giving Paddy an appreciative peck on the cheek. "Hey, thanks for having the kids tonight. That's going to make things a lot easier."

"We're happy to have them," said Annette, joining them and brushing the crumbs from the table off her hand and into the bin. "Any idea what you're going to say to Jack?"

In truth, Liz had thought of little else since hearing Annette's news the previous day. Knowing Jack as well as she did, she had come to the conclusion that he was very unlikely to bring Rachel into the equation at this stage and for the moment, at least, she was happy enough to go along with that. She had decided that, if at all possible, she was going to spare the kids any mention of an affair — she felt that they would find the situation easier to deal with that way.

Her plan was to tell Jack quite simply that she knew he was having an affair, that as far as she was concerned their marriage was now over and that the only thing that mattered to her was protecting the kids from as much hurt as possible. She would make it abundantly clear to him that her not telling the kids was for their sake — not his.

"But, what about Rachel?" asked Annette. "Are you not going to bring her up even if he doesn't?"

"No. I'm not," she said, in a definitive manner. "I've given this a lot of thought and I reckon that if she knows that I know, then, she'll just slink off into the background and avoid any confrontation. However, if she thinks that I haven't any clue that it's her, then, she'll contact me, providing a shoulder for me to cry on and that way, I can deal with Rachel Wallace in my own time and in my own way."

"You go, girl!" said Paddy, lifting his coffee mug to her, "that bitch won't know what's hit her."

The three of them laughed at his little outburst. Liz found their love and support empowering, as she gathered up her belongings and headed for home and the dissolution of her marriage.

### Jack

Wishing that he was anywhere else in the world than where he was right now, Jack pushed his front door key into the lock and sucking in a big, deep breath, he let himself into his house. Unprepared for the silence that lay within, he momentarily thought that there was no one home and was anguished at the prospect of prolonging the agony that the inevitable conversation with his wife would produce by having to await her return. But then, he heard a noise coming from the kitchen and instinctively he knew that she was there and that she was alone.

He should have known that she wouldn't want the kids there for his return and the thought that they weren't, comforted him in some small way. Taking his courage in his hands, he walked down the hall to the kitchen.

"Hey, Liz," he said, pushing open the door and finding her standing with her back to the worktop and her two arms folded across her chest, hands tucked into her armpits. A rush of guilt swept over him, causing him to question if he could see this through, but when she spoke, he quickly discovered just how limited his options were.

"Hello Jack," she said in a frosty manner. Then, with no preamble, she continued, "Look Jack, let's not beat about the bush. I know for a fact that you've been deceiving me, that you've been having an affair. You've been caught out, Jack. Caught rapid. And the bottom line is, Jack, that I want out of this marriage. It's over and I'm afraid that the subject isn't open for discussion. Now what we have to deal with is damage limitation for the kids. I want this whole thing to be as painless as possible for them — I hope you're in agreement with me on this?"

Mutely, he nodded, completely taken aback by her reaction. He thought that he had devised every conceivable scenario in his head, but this, this was off the radar in terms of how he had expected her to react. He had anticipated shouting; crying; gnashing of teeth but not this clinical, business like approach and he was temporarily thrown off kilter. Rendered speechless, he simply stood in the doorway, staring at this stranger who was occupying his wife's body and waited to see what would happen next.

The surreal experience continued, when reaching for an A4 pad that was on the worktop beside her, she pulled back the cover to reveal some neatly written out notes and ripping out the page she passed them to him.

"I've done up a preliminary schedule of costs regarding the house and the kids. It makes sense all round if I stay on here with the kids and I've factored in school fees; holidays; etc. and come up with what I think is quite a reasonable maintenance figure. Obviously, you will want to look over them, but I think you'll find that I've been fairly thorough."

Taking the proffered sheet, he glanced at it, not seeing any of it but promising to look at it later, he folded it and stuck it into his pocket. She was silent then; awkward- looking and he had the sense that she wanted him to leave. But surely, they had a lot more things to discuss. Helplessly, he looked at her.

"What about the kids?" he asked.

"They're staying in Annette's tonight — I thought it best. Perhaps we could sit down with them tomorrow after school and tell them then. They don't have any idea about this and for what it's worth I've told them nothing about your affair. They don't need to know that — it'll only hurt them more."

"Thanks for that," he said.

"I didn't do it for you, you fool — I did it for them."

Jack winced at her words, but accepted them as his just dessert. They left it that Jack would collect the kids from school and that the four of them would go for something to eat. Then, with nothing much else to say, he went upstairs, packed a couple of suitcases and left.

## Donal

"Hollie — are you deaf or what?" called Donal, from the bottom of the stairs. "Your breakfast is ready — hurry up or it'll be cold."

Still no answer, harrumphing to himself, Donal trudged up the stairs to see what was keeping her. He knocked on her bedroom door, but there was no reply. Cautiously, he opened the door and was shocked to see her sitting on the edge of the bed, her mobile phone hanging limply in her hand and silent tears sliding down her face.

"Jesus, Hols! What is it? What's wrong?" he said, rushing to her side and pulling her gently to him. "What's happened?"

Trance like, she turned to him, looking at him blankly as she held her phone aloft as if that in some way explained things. A terrible thought gripped him and snatching the phone out of her hand, he said, "That bastard didn't phone you — did he?" He started to scramble through her call register for his number, but she shook her head and finally, finding a voice, she said.

"No. It wasn't Eoin. It was Maria."

None the wiser, he shook his head in confusion. "Maria? Maria who?"

"The nurse from the hospital in Majorca. He's done it again, Donal. Eoin has attacked someone else."

Seeing just how distraught she was by this news, he held her to him, rocking her gently as he tried to calm her. He could feel her trembling and struggled frantically to find some words of comfort to offer her.

"Look, Hollie, if Eoin has struck again, then, that is only going to make the police all the more determined to catch him. You've got to believe that.

It's only going to be a matter of time before they get their hands on him."

"But that's just it," she said, tearfully. "He's just too smart for them. You'd think that he'd be keeping his head low and doing his best to get off the island. But, no — not Eoin. It's as if he's giving them the fingers. You know — 'fuck you'. He had to know that they're out looking for him - you couldn't miss it. There are pictures of him everywhere. He's playing games with them now. Trying to show how clever he is. And, all the time, he's putting more and more women through the hell that he put me through. What kind of a beast is this guy? They won't catch him, Donal. I'm telling you that. He's just going to keep on and on until eventually he tires of it all and moved on to somewhere else."

"You can't let yourself think like that, Hols. They are bound to catch him sooner or later."

"But, I'm scared, Donal. What if they don't catch him? What if he makes it back here? What if he tracks me down? He's bound to know that I had some input into the police hunt and then what? What will he do to me if he finds me?"

"Look, Hollie. I'm not going to let anything happen to you. I promise. If the police are getting nowhere, then, we'll take matters into our own hands. We'll talk to Denise. Time and time again she's offered to hire a private investigator, perhaps that's what we've got to do."

Reluctantly, she nodded. "Maybe you're right," she said.

### Denise

Having woken early, Denise had decided to go for a swim in the pool before breakfast. She was delighted to find that the entire pool area was deserted and she relished the solitude, enjoying a lengthy swim and an even longer sauna afterwards. Feeling thoroughly relaxed, she showered and dressed and made her way to the restaurant where she caught the final servings of breakfast. She grabbed a couple of the Sunday papers and settling down at a nice quiet table in the corner, she read them from cover to cover before returning to her room.

With no real plans for the day ahead, she hunted around for her mobile, which she had left to charge, planning on ringing Donal to see what he was up to. Retrieving her phone, she saw that she had a couple of missed calls from him, and without bothering to listen to the messages that he had left, she called him straight back.

"Oh, Denise, thank goodness," he said when he answered. "Did you get my message?"

"No, sorry Donal. I saw that you had called, but didn't listen to them. Everything okay?"

It was evident from his tone that things weren't okay and she listened patiently as he talked her through what had happened that morning with Hollie. Sounding very unsure of himself, he finished up by asking in an awkward manner if her offer of a private investigator still stood. Bemused by his discomfort, she assured him that it did and told him categorically that there was no reason to feel uncomfortable bringing the matter up with her.

He went on to explain that as Hollie was still quite upset by this latest development, he was reluctant to leave her alone tonight and didn't feel that she would be up to going out anywhere, but asked instead, if Denise would like to join them at his house for dinner. She told him that she would be delighted to do that and that she would see them both about seven o'clock.

CHAPTER TWENTY-TWO

# Sunday PM 25th April

*Annette*

Confined to the kitchen because the kids, with a vast selection of DVDs, had commandeered the living room, Annette sat in the kitchen with Paddy, anxiously awaiting a phone call from Liz. Repeatedly, she glanced at the clock worrying about how things were going in her sister's house. The roars of laughter coming from the living room reassured her that she had done the right thing having the kids over for the night. Liz had been right to protect them from as much unpleasantness as possible and she hoped that Jack would play ball, putting their needs before his — for once.

Nervously, she jumped when her mobile finally rang, fumbling around for the answer button. Pressing it, she put her phone to her ear without even looking at the caller's name.

"Liz? How'd it go?" she asked, breathlessly.

"Sorry, Annette — it's not Liz, it's me, Hollie. Is this a bad time?"

"No, not at all, Hollie, love — you're grand. Just expecting a call from Liz. Everything okay?"

Silence followed and Annette thought that she heard Hollie sniffle before she said, "Look, sorry — I'll give you a call later."

"Whoa!" said Annette, instantly feeling guilty that she had sounded in any way unwelcoming. "Hang on, hang on. What is it? What's up?"

A tearful Hollie told her all about the call from Maria and the latest attack, explaining how this latest development had left her feeling fearful that the authorities were never going to catch Eoin. Annette did her best to talk her down, offering her words of comfort and reassurances that the Spanish authorities were clearly treating the matter with the utmost gravity and that sooner or later, Eoin would make a mistake and that mistake would lead to his capture. She told Hollie that she thought it highly unlikely that Eoin would make it off the island, but agreed with Donal that, as a back-up plan, it would do no harm to take Denise up on her offer and employ a Private Investigator on the off chance that he did.

As she had done so many times in Majorca, Annette managed to calm Hollie, and when she was confident that the young woman was alright, she asked her to keep her updated on any further developments and suggested that they might meet up during the week.

## Rachel

Surprised to hear the entry intercom buzzing, Rachel checked the time and seeing that it had been under an hour since Jack had left, assumed that it couldn't possibly be him back yet, unless of course, he had bottled it. She answered the intercom and felt her hackles rise on discovering that it was indeed Jack. Waiting in the doorway for him to reach her floor, she vowed to turn him around and send him packing if he was procrastinating about confronting Liz. It had taken a lot for her to finally commit to spending her life with one man and if that man was stupid enough to think that she would stand for him falling at the first hurdle, he had another think coming. Rachel Wallace had never allowed herself to be any man's fool and she had no intention of allowing it now. With fiery determination, she stood and waited for him.

But, it was a buoyant Jack that came up the stairs, taking them two steps at a time, wearing a broad grin as he did so. Confused, she looked at him with a questioning expression on her face.

"Hey, honey — I'm home!" he quipped in an atrocious attempt at an American accent, then taking in her grim countenance, he laughed. "Don't worry. I've done it. I have left my wife. You are now looking at Dublin's newest most eligible bachelor — any takers?"

"You're kidding me! You've been and seen Liz, told her that you are leaving her and come bouncing back here — all within an hour and acting like you are on coke or something. What on earth happened?"

More sober now, he said, "She wants us to separate. Told me that she knew I was having an affair and that as far as she was concerned that was it. She's not interested in trying to work things out and has decided that it's for the best if we separate. She was completely unemotional about it, and said that her only concern is that we handle the kids properly. She's has even worked out a maintenance proposal." He pulled the folded sheet of paper out of his pocket and waved it at Rachel. "It was all quite surreal and not at all what I had expected."

"Did she ask who you were having the affair with?"

"No. Never asked a thing."

Non-plussed, Rachel turned around and headed back into the apartment, leaving Jack to follow her. This was all very strange. Then it dawned on her that perhaps Jack was trying to protect her, assuming that she might be feeling guilty for her role in this scenario, because in her experience this was not how these pathetic women reacted when they realised that they had been cast aside for a newer model. She would contact Liz herself tomorrow and get the real low-down.

### Denise

Sitting in the back of a taxi on her way over to Donal's house, Denise tried to recall the last time that she had gone to someone's house for dinner, but she couldn't. It was definitely 'pre-John', she knew that much, because he refused to accept any of her friend's dinner invitations, claiming that being on other people's territory gave the host the upper hand and he didn't like that, preferring to stick to the neutral ground of a restaurant or bar. That was in the early days of their relationship, but before long he called a halt to that too, telling her that her friends made him feel uncomfortable. Initially, she had found his insecurity endearing, that was before she realised that it was based on a basic madness that would one day rob her of her freedom.

She forced her thoughts back to the evening ahead, telling herself that she had no reason to feel nervous, but not quite convincing herself of that fact. Reaching the front step of Donal's house, she drew in a deep breath and, clutching the bottle of wine that she had brought with her to her chest, she pressed the bell. To her relief, it was Donal who answered the door and seeing the welcoming expression on his face, she felt herself instantly relax.

Donal escorted her into the kitchen where Hollie sat, perched on a bar stool at the breakfast bar. She had a definite wary look about her and Denise could feel her size her up. It only took a few seconds to figure out that this young woman was equally as protective about her big brother as he was about her. Denise liked that about her and hoped that she would make a favourable impression on her over the course of the evening.

Aware that she was being closely scrutinised, Denise accepted a glass of red wine from Donal and went to sit beside Hollie as he then busied himself with some dinner preparations. Making no effort to instigate a conversation, Hollie sat sipping her wine and Denise shifted about uncomfortably on her stool, wishing that Donal would hurry up and join them. Then, deciding that this was ridiculous, she broke the ice.

"Hey, Hollie," she said, looking the younger woman directly in the eyes. "I really was sorry to hear about what happened to you in Majorca and, as I've said to Donal, I'm more than happy to help in any way that I can. Donal said that you might be interested in my offer to employ a Private Investigator?"

"Yes, well — we'll see," said Hollie, through pursed lips, clearly ill at ease still with that suggestion. "You see, the thing is, Denise — I don't get this. Why would you make such an offer? Can you explain this to me please?"

The hostility that was oozing from her every pore was far greater than Donal had led her to believe and she quickly weighed up the situation in her mind, before speaking again.

"It's quite simple really, Hollie. I'd like to help and I'm in a position to help. That's pretty much it."

"Well, forgive me for being cynical, but you don't even know me. You must have a lot more money than sense, if you go around doling out money to complete strangers. This just doesn't make any sense to me."

Denise listened to her, trying to put herself in Hollie's position and she had to admit that it was pretty fantastical from that perspective. In the height of her own difficulties with John, would Denise not have been more than a little dubious if some gallant stranger had offered to help? Of course, she would and in a moment of clarity she saw herself in Hollie and she decided that perhaps it was time to be completely honest if she genuinely wanted to help this girl.

With a shrug of her shoulders, Denise said, "Okay, Hollie. I'm going to tell you exactly why I would like to help you. However, if you don't mind, I would like Donal to hear what I have to say too."

Hollie nodded her agreement and waited for her brother to join them. Denise came clean about everything. She told them all about her abusive relationship with John. How he controlled her; beat her; raped her (although at the time she hadn't understood that the non-consensual sex had in fact been rape — but, now she saw it for what it had actually been); how he isolated her and basically made her life hell for the years that she had been with him.

Next, she told them about her lottery win and ignoring the incredulous look on their faces, she continued to tell them about her unwanted pregnancy and the real purpose of her trip to London. Aghast at what they were hearing, Hollie and Donal sat staring at her until she finally saw a major shift in Hollie as a softness entered her eyes and she got up and came over to Denise, giving her a warm embrace full of sincerity.

"It's okay, Denise. I understand now," she said warmly. "And, thank you. Thank you so much."

Too emotional to respond, Denise simply hugged her back.

### Donal

Blown away by what Denise had disclosed to them, Donal felt a surge of affection for this poor troubled woman who had so recently come into his life. Despite the brevity of their friendship, he knew her well enough to know that it had taken a lot for her to divulge her secrets in this manner. The fact that she had done so was indicative of the esteem she held him in and what she had told them went a long way to clarifying her interest in Hollie's plight.

When Hollie excused herself to go to the bathroom, leaving them alone in the kitchen, he put his arm around her shoulder, pulling her to him and spoke to her in a gentle voice.

"You went through all that in London without saying anything. You could have told me — you know? I would never have judged you if that's what you were afraid of."

Smiling warmly back at him, she said. "I didn't think you would. It just seemed kind of inappropriate or something, especially after you telling me about you and Susan struggling to have a baby and all."

He reddened at this, realising how awkward that must have made her feel. "I'm so sorry about that," he said. "I'd never have told you if I'd known what you were going through."

"Don't be daft," she reassured him. "How could you have known? Anyway, we're talking about two completely different situations here. You were hoping to bring a baby into a warm and loving environment — create a family. For me, it could never have been like that. I would have been bringing a baby into a war zone. How could I protect a baby from John? I couldn't. And what if the baby turned out to be a monster like his father? I don't think that I could have lived with that. To be honest, I never even allowed myself to think of it as a baby. It was just something that I had to get rid of, to free myself from John. It was the only way."

Her eyes filled with tears as she spoke and not wanting to see her upset like this, he pulled her to him, kissing the top of her head. "Hey, you did the right thing. Now, you've got to stop thinking about the past, you need to focus on the future. You've rid yourself of all that baggage, you have financial security, you're a lovely woman Denise — inside and out and the way I see it, the world is now your oyster."

"Thanks," she sniffled, embarrassed to be the focus of so much attention. "And, Hollie's gorgeous, Donal. She'll get through this — she's a strong kid."

"I know," he said, pride swelling his features. "She just seemed so vulnerable this morning when she got news of that other attack. It's going to mean a lot to her to track down this Eoin character and I hope you know how appreciative we both are for your help. I know she was a bit off with you at first, but now that she understands your motivation, she's as grateful as I am."

"I know she is," said Denise, reaching for her wine glass and raising it in his direction, she added. "Here's to catching the little shit and bringing him to justice!"

"I'll drink to that," said Hollie, making her way back into the kitchen. "Thanks Denise."

## *Liz*

Jack's visit had taken it out of Liz, leaving her feeling emotionally drained and empty inside. Somehow she had managed to hold it all together, and she knew that he had been totally unprepared for her to behave as she had. But now, alone in the house, the silence was deafening and the challenges that lay ahead frightened her. It was all much more real now. Despite knowing in her heart that there was no going back with her marriage, the uncertainty of her future was a daunting prospect.

There was still the hurdle of telling the kids to get over. That wasn't going to be easy. She was glad not to have to deal with that this evening. At least Jack seemed as anxious as her to deliver the news as a united front, minimising the trauma for them. She really was dreading telling them, but it was unavoidable.

In an attempt to prepare herself mentally, she decided to take advantage of the night's solitude and went to run herself a hot bath. Whilst the tub filled, she called Annette to tell her how things had gone with Jack, reassuring her that she was fine on her own and that there was no need for Annette to call around. Reluctantly, Annette took her word for it and promised to come over once she had dropped the kids off at school in the morning.

## *Hollie*

In spite of her initial reservations, Hollie couldn't help but like Denise, growing more and more fond of her as the evening wore on. It was with a great sense of reluctance that she bade farewell to her shortly after eleven o'clock, unwilling to stay up too late, as she was due back in work in the morning. She now completely understood how Donal acted as if he had known Denise for years, she was the most empathetic person that Hollie had ever met. A keen listener with a genuine interest in all that she was told, she sat enthralled whilst Hollie took her through all the details of her attack and the subsequent attacks in Majorca, only interjecting to ask pertinent questions that showed how much she was concentrating on the story.

When Hollie had finished, she sat back with her arms stretched out in front of her on the breakfast bar and her two hands clasped together in a tense gesture. Denise reached over and patted her on the forearm and this one simple act offered Hollie more solace than any other consolation she had received since her attack.

"I'll get cracking on employing a Private Investigator in the morning," said Denise, "I can get a list of everything that he will need from you and we'll meet up over the next couple of days — okay?"

"That sounds great," said Hollie. "And, once again, thanks."

"Enough of the gratitude," said Denise with mock sternness. "From here on in we are playing this project as a team, so go on — off with you and get a good night's sleep."

### Jack

Busily rehearsing what he wanted to say to the kids in his head, Jack never even heard Rachel come into the kitchen where he was supposed to be opening a bottle of wine.

"You growing the grapes?" she asked with a laugh, reaching into the cupboard for two wine glasses."

"Sorry, Babe," he said, pulling himself back to reality. "I was just planning what to say to the kids tomorrow. I just don't want to fuck it up with them — you know?"

"I know, sweetheart," she said, taking the corkscrew from the drawer and removing the unopened wine bottle from his hands. "Just be yourself. Talk from the heart. Explain to them that it's reached a stage where you and Liz aren't happy together and you both need to go your separate ways."

"But, I don't want them to think that I'm abandoning them — 'cos I'd never do that."

"I know that. And, so will they when you explain it all to them. Look, reassure them that you love them and that you'll be seeing plenty of them and they'll be grand. Trust me, I see it all the time in work. It's the dads that disappear out of their kids' lives that cause the problems and you're not going to do that. Just make sure that they know that and then, everything will be grand. Look how much you were fretting about talking to Liz and look how well that went."

"I guess you're right," he said, accepting the glass of wine she held out for him. "It's always difficult pre-planning a conversation."

"Of course it is. It'll come naturally to you when you're in the position. Now, stop worrying, let's enjoy a nice glass of wine and then, off to bed, we've both got an early start in the morning."

"Whatever you say, Dr. Wallace," he said with a grin, pulling her to him and planting a big sloppy kiss on her mouth.

"Uuggh!" she said, making him laugh and lifting his tension.

CHAPTER TWENTY-THREE

# Monday AM 26th April

*Hollie*

Tempted to make a general announcement over the public address system in reception to declare that 'yes thanks,' she was feeling much better and that 'it was indeed a rotten dose', Hollie had to bite her tongue instead and politely respond to the never ending enquiries about her well-being. By mid morning, when she paid a visit to the ladies toilet, she fully expected to see a couple of inches on the end of her nose from the innumerable lies she had told since her return.

It was lying to Niamh that was the hardest, especially as she had been fussing and clucking over her like a regular mother hen all morning, but even though she wanted to tell her the truth and had already decided to do so before coming in, she had not been afforded the opportunity, as the reception area had been buzzing with people from the moment the doors had opened.

She would get a chance to tell her the truth at lunchtime and she fervently hoped that her friend wouldn't be too angry with her for lying. In the meantime she would avoid direct conversation with her as much as possible, which shouldn't be too difficult with the clinic this busy.

## Liz

Looking out her bedroom window, Liz saw Annette's car turn into her driveway shortly before nine o'clock. True to her word, she had come straight over from the school run and, having had enough of her own company for the time being, Liz was delighted to see her arrive.

She had woken early, long before the alarm, which, despite the kid's absence, had gone off at the usual time of seven-thirty. By that time she had already showered, dried her hair, laid out her clothes and completed her make-up — a ritual that empowered her more than she ever could have imagined it would. Boldly, she pulled open the front door, surprising Annette with her polished appearance.

"Hey, look at you," said Annette with her eyes out on stalks. "Jesus! You should leave your husband more often if this is what it does to you. You look amazing."

Self-consciously Liz laughed, "Just a little something from my life-coaching training and trust me — it works. Feeling like you look good makes you feel good. If you get my drift."

"Sounds like there's wisdom in those words," said Annette. "Now, have you got the kettle on yet? 'Cos I'm parched. And, before you ask, the kids were grand this morning. I told them that their Dad would be picking them up and they didn't bat an eyelid — but sure, why would they?"

Liz confessed how much she was dreading the afternoon and the subsequent fallout from telling the kids, but unfortunately there was no way around it. Before they had a chance to get too deep into that conversation, Liz's house phone rang and picking it up, she threw her eyes up to heaven when she saw the caller's number. "Rachel," she mouthed over to Annette before pressing the answer button.

## Rachel

Checking her schedule on arrival at the surgery, Rachel saw that she had back-to-back appointments for the entire morning. Anxious to get the ball rolling with Liz, she decided to give her a call before her first patient came in. Bracing herself against the risk that Liz had any inkling that it was her who was seeing Jack, she keyed in the home number and held her breath.

Liz answered after only a couple of rings and despite sounding a little subdued; Rachel could detect no overt hostility in her voice. Allowing herself to relax into the conversation, Rachel dipped her toe further into the water.

"So, any sign of Jack getting back yet? I can tell you if the chaos in Portugal was anything like Majorca, he'll be doing well to get back this week."

"Majorca?" said Liz. "I thought you were in the Canaries."

"Oh, I thought I told you sweetie. I got a last minute unbeatable bargain for Majorca and jumped at it. In fact, I bumped into your sister over there. What a place! You've got to go there. Great food, great nightlife and the men… Wow! What can I say about them? Darling, they're to die for!"

"You really are incorrigible," said Liz in a somewhat flat tone, which Rachel instantly picked up on.

"Is everything okay with you Liz? I mean are you worried about Jack or something. You don't sound like your usual chirpy self."

"Actually, Rachel, myself and Jack are separating."

"What!" exclaimed Rachel, sounding astonished, even to herself. Quietly congratulating herself on her dramatic reaction, she continued. "What on earth are you talking about?"

"We're finished. What more can I say?"

"But what happened? Why?"

"Well, basically, I discovered that he's having an affair with some silly tart and I decided that I want out. That's it, in a nutshell."

"Oh Liz — I'm shocked. This conversation needs a bottle of wine, will you be there if I call over after work? You can tell me all about it. Poor Liz, this must be dreadful for you — are you alright?"

"I'm fine. But, yes, call over after work — I'll be here. It'll be good to talk to you about it."

They finished off their conversation and Rachel hung up the phone, grinning to herself as she did so. Clearly, Liz had no idea about her involvement and that gave her the power to execute her plan.

*Annette*

Gobsmacked, Annette sat listening to Liz's conversation with Rachel and was left completely in awe of her sister's poise and confidence whilst she spoke. She betrayed no signs of knowing about Rachel's involvement and managed to chat away in a normal fashion. When she finally hung up, Annette shook her head in disbelief.

"Wow! You should have been on the stage. Your talents are wasted. How the hell did you pull that off?"

Liz shrugged her shoulders and with an enigmatic smile on her face, she said, "Revenge. If Rachel Wallace thinks that she is going to swan in here, to my home, and make off with my husband with little or no retribution from me, then, she has another think coming."

"You go girl!" laughed Annette.

"I need to know how far she's prepared to take this false friend bit. That's the part that pisses me off more than anything. To be honest, they're welcome to each other. I mean, I'm not an eejit — I know it takes two to have an affair. I could almost accept her having the affair — it's shit, but hey, shit happens. It's the audacity of her to continue to purport to be my friend that gets me. I'm just curious to know how far she's willing to go with this. Clearly, she has some kind of an agenda with this and I don't know exactly what that is yet. But, I intend to find out and when I do, then, I'll deal with her in my own way. I simply won't allow her play me like a fool in that way."

As she sat and listened to her, Annette could feel herself filling with pride at her sister's stoicism. "You've obviously learnt a lot from that course of yours," she said. "I think you are going to make a phenomenal Life Coach, Liz if the way you are handling this mess is anything to go by."

*Jack*

Jack was having difficulty concentrating on his work. His 'in-tray' was bulging with files that had accumulated during his extended absence, but try as he might, he was unable to work his way through them with any kind of efficiency. Somehow he had managed to sit through an hour and a half long meeting with his boss and three of his colleagues, not contributing anything and barely absorbing the topics under discussion.

Back in his own office now, a knock on the door signalled his boss's presence and attempting to look as if he was in the middle of something, Jack shuffled some papers around, clearing a space on his desk for whatever file his boss wanted to pass him.

"Hey, Gerry, what can I do for you?" he asked in an unnaturally buoyant manner, waving his hand towards the seat in front of him by way of inviting his boss to take a seat.

"Eh, just wanted a quick word, Jack — if you've got a minute?"

"Of course. Come in. Sit down. Now, what's up?"

Gerry closed the door behind him before sitting down, then, getting straight to the point, he asked. "Everything alright, Jack? It's just you seemed a bit preoccupied through that meeting. I know that it's your first morning back and everything, but it's just you strike me as a man with something on his mind."

Taken aback by Gerry's astuteness, Jack quickly weighed up the situation and acknowledging to himself that he would more than likely need to be taking some extra time off over the coming weeks whilst the kids adjusted to the new situation, he decided to come clean and tell Gerry exactly what was going on. Not wanting to give too much away, he left Rachel out of the equation, citing irreconcilable differences as the reason for the break-up.

To him immense relief, Gerry, himself divorced, was extremely sympathetic to Jack's plight and suggested that Jack put in an application for some compassionate leave. Jack said that certainly, at this stage, he didn't feel that that was necessary, but depending on the way the kids took the news, he would hold fire on any such application. He would appreciate however, if he could perhaps extend the barriers on his flexi-time options to work around any unforeseen crises with Josh and Jane, beginning with that afternoon when he and Liz planned on telling them what was happening. With no hesitation, Gerry agreed, leaving Jack feeling as if a weight had been lifted off him.

## Donal

"Hey, Denise — it's Donal. I just wanted to thank you for last night. Hollie was in much better form this morning. Thanks to you, I think she finally believes that one way or another Eoin will get caught. I'll give you a call later and see how you got on with finding a Private Investigator and maybe we can get a meeting set up with him. Cheers."

Disappointed to only have reached her voicemail, Donal hung up after leaving his message and found his thoughts returning again to Denise's revelations of the night before. She had certainly taken them by surprise with what she had told them and he felt really ingratiated towards her for exposing herself in that manner, because he understood that she had only done that in an effort to win Hollie's confidence. She had certainly achieved her objective as Hollie had nothing but good to say about her that morning over breakfast.

With Hollie gone to work, he was alone in the house and reluctantly he turned his attention to his need to make a decision about The Transglobal Travel Corporation's offer. With a little over forty-eight hours left to the expiration of their offer, he had to weigh up all the pros and cons involved. Both Hollie and Denise seemed pretty adamant that he should walk away from it, but that was easy for them to say — their future didn't hang in the balance here, only his. Still, a lot of what they said made sense and if he were to go with his own gut reaction, he knew he would decline graciously and seek backing elsewhere.

He had so much happening in his personal life at the minute that he found it difficult to think straight and despite sitting at his desk for over an hour, the sheet of paper in front of him still only had two words written on it — to the left side of the page was 'pros' and to the right 'cons', but nothing appeared in either listing. Exasperated, he pushed back his chair and deciding that a brisk walk on the beach might clear his head, he abandoned the task temporarily.

## Denise

When Denise saw Donal's name flash up on her phone, she resisted the urge to answer it, not wanting to discuss what was on her mind until she had thought it all through properly, and not trusting herself not to blurt it out.

She had had such a wonderful evening with the pair of them and had experienced nothing short of elation when she realised that, through her revelations, she had won Hollie's trust and was going to be able to help them. But there was more to the night - there was a sense of comfort and belonging that she experienced which told her that these people were going to be a major part of her life in the future and she wanted to help them in any way she could. The thought she had had on waking that morning would certainly do just that, but she needed some independent advice on the matter and she must seek that before saying anything.

A cautionary voice in her head told her that she must learn from her experiences with John and not jump into any future decisions on impulse. It was one thing to help them out by tracking down Eoin, but investing in Donal's business — that was a different thing altogether.

CHAPTER TWENTY-FOUR

# Monday PM 26th April

*Jack*

With a knot in his stomach that felt like his body was playing host to a brick, Jack parked up outside Josh's school. Josh got off twenty minutes before Jane; leaving them enough time to get across to her school, provided Josh didn't delay on his way out. In their school uniforms, the gangs of youths that spilled out the front door of the school all looked the same and Josh was almost on top of him before he recognised him.

"Hey, son," he called out to him, waving so he could spot him amongst the throngs of cars in the schoolyard.

A large grin inadvertently broke across Josh's face, before remembering his street cred, when it was hastily replaced by the compulsory teenage scowl, lest any of his pals noticed how pleased he was to see his father. "Alright, Dad. When'd you get back?"

"Eh, yesterday evening," he said. "We've got to get a move on, we need to collect your sister."

By contrast, Jane nearly ploughed down anyone who had the misfortune to be in her path, as she blazed a trail over to Jack. "Daddy!" she exclaimed, hurling herself into his arms. "Oh! I've missed you so much."

"I've missed you too, love," he said, laughing, trying to extricate himself from her embrace. "Come on, we're going to meet your mum for a bite to eat."

An innately sensitive girl, Jane instantly smelled a rat at this unusual turn of events. "Is everything okay, Dad? You never pick us up."

"Your mum and I want to talk to you about something."

"What?" she asked suspiciously.

"Wait and see," he said in a tone that told her there would be no further discussion on the subject until they were with Liz.

Half an hour later, Jack thought that his heart was going to break when his beautiful daughter glared at him with tear filled eyes and asked, "But, why Dad? Why don't you want to live with me anymore?"

"It's not that, Janey," he said, at a loss as to what to say to make this easier for her. "Of course I want to live with you. And my new place will be yours too. You'll have your own room in it, just like you do at home and you'll be spending loads of time there. It's just that me and your mum have reached a point where we feel that we would be happier living separately — that's all. It's nothing to do with you, love. I'll see every bit as much of you as I do now — I promise."

"Of course it's to do with me," she wailed plaintively. "If you're breaking up my family then, it's everything to do with me."

Struggling for words, Jack felt completely out of his depth, when, to his immense relief, Liz stepped in.

"Hey, Jane — this isn't the end of the world you know, love. Your Dad and I both love you and Josh very much, but to be honest, we've come to a point in our lives where we both want different things. We were awful young when we met, love and people change as they grow older. Maybe we will and maybe we won't, but right now, your Dad and I feel that we will be happier apart. You have loads of friends whose parents are separated but they still have two parents, right?"

"Yeah, but Laura never sees her dad. She's always crying about how much she misses him."

"Well, your Dad is not like that, Jane. Trust me, you can see as much of him as you like. Every day if that's what you want."

"Promise?" she asked tearfully.

"Absolutely," said Jack, throwing Liz a grateful glance. "In fact, I want you and Josh to help me choose an apartment."

"Really?" she asked, perking up a little at that suggestion.

"Definitely. I'm actually going to look at a couple of places after we finish eating, if you want to come along — you're more than welcome."

Somewhat placated by this, she turned to Josh who had sat in silence throughout the entire exchange. "Are you coming, Josh?"

"Whatever," he shrugged in a nonchalant manner, not looking terribly troubled by what he was hearing. Then, in a gesture that made Jack proud, he draped his arm around his little sister, saying. "You know, this won't be all bad, Sis. This way, if Mum is doing our head in, we can always go around and stay with Dad and vice versa. Way I see it — it's a win win situation!"

Despite the tension of their little family meeting, they all managed a laugh at Josh's comment.

## Hollie

Hollie need not have worried so much about telling Niamh. Not only was her discretion guaranteed, but also her sympathy overflowed. After telling her the whole story, Niamh was aghast at the pain and suffering that her friend had endured and with no recriminations, she offered to support her in any way that she could.

By way of lightening the conversation in the small sandwich bar that they went to everyday for their lunch, Hollie told her that she had gleaned some really juicy gossip on her trip. Pleading with her to impart it, Niamh swore to carry whatever she was told to her grave with her and laughing at her earnestness, Hollie eventually put her out of her misery and told her all about Dr. Wallace.

"I knew she was a bitch!" declared Niamh on hearing the news. "No one can be that much of a sour faced wagon to their work colleagues and be a nice person underneath it all. What a slapper! And her best friend's husband too! Wow! What did she say to you?"

"Oh, she never saw me. Too rapt up in her married lover's eyes! Honestly, it was sickening. And poor Annette, she was absolutely dying. I mean imagine it — your sister's husband. She's such a sweet woman and I felt so sorry for her having to come home and tell her sister the full story. I certainly didn't envy her."

"How'd the sister take it?"

"Apparently, she's thrown him out. Fair play to her, I say. Cheating fucker."

The afternoon dragged and by the time five thirty came around, Hollie was feeling exhausted. Declining Niamh's invitation to go for a quick drink after work, she walked to the end of the road with her friend, promising to do it another night when she wasn't feeling so tired. After parting company with Niamh, Hollie strolled up to the bus stop, quickening her pace when on a couple of occasions she had a weird sense of being watched. Chalking it up to paranoia, when a couple of quick glances over her shoulder left her looking down an empty pathway, she still felt relieved when there were several other people waiting at the bus stop. Willing the bus not to be too long in arriving, she felt safer once on board the crowded vehicle.

### Donal

"Right, that's it. I'm collecting you from work until this bastard has been caught," declared Donal when Hollie told him about feeling that she was being watched.

"Oh, don't be ridiculous, Donal," she said, clearly regretting having told him. "I'll be fine. I'm quite certain that it was only my imagination. He's not even in Dublin for Chrissake."

"Yeah, but you don't know that, do you Hollie? Look, indulge me. Let me just pick you up for the next couple of days, at least until Denise's Private Investigator establishes his whereabouts."

Not willing to be drawn into an argument on the subject, Donal told her to take a seat that he was putting up dinner. Whilst they ate, he filled her in on the day's developments with Denise. She had managed to engage a P.I. and had set up a meeting in his office for Wednesday morning, asking Hollie if that would suit her. She told him that she should be able to organise taking an early lunch.

He gave her a list of things that Denise had said the P.I. had requested, including a copy of the photo-fit that the Spanish police had produced,

Hollie didn't think that she'd have any difficulty getting her hands on one of them. Also, because Eoin had attended Greendale Medical Centre, was there any chance that Hollie could get her hands on his patient card. Of course, the information he had provided could have been false, but there was a chance that they could strike lucky. Again, Hollie reckoned that she could pull that off.

### Denise

Having put in what she deemed to be a very productive day, Denise was fit for bed, even though it wasn't yet even ten o'clock. Closing down the lid of her laptop, she tidied up the paperwork that was strewn across the desk and although her mind was made up, she decided to sleep on her decision before committing to it.

She had spoken to Donal earlier, but had managed not to let slip her intentions regarding his business, limiting the conversation to the appointment she had made with the P.I. for Wednesday morning. Once she had sorted all of that out, she had contacted Mr. Horgan in the bank who had kindly put her in touch with a Business Advisor with whom she had talked through her desire to involve herself in Donal's business.

To her delight, James Anderson, the Business Advisor, had been intrigued by the product and agreed unreservedly that it had huge potential. Explaining to him that Donal was still considering the two-bit offer from The Transglobal Travel Corporation, he understood her need to work quickly on this and after making a couple of phone calls to free up his diary for the afternoon, he had spent several hours with her, compiling a business plan. She was thrilled with the outcome, not only would she be able to help Donal with his project, but she would secure herself a stake in a very viable business.

Assuming that she still felt the same in the morning, she planned to meet with Donal and put forward her offer. Hopefully, he would be as excited as she was.

### Annette

"I'm really pleased it went so well," said Annette to Liz on the phone. "I bet you're glad to have that over and done with."

"You're not kidding," said Liz. "They've gone off with Jack to look at some apartments. Rachel just texted me, she's on her way over. This should be interesting."

"I'd like to be a fly on the wall for that. You'll have to tell me everything. Are you around in the morning?"

"Yeah. I'll meet you in Dundrum for a coffee, say about ten thirty?"

"Sounds good to me. See you then, and eh, good luck with 'super bitch'."

Wondering if Rachel had let anything slip in work, Annette decided to give Hollie a quick call. But no, according to Hollie she was the same aloof Dr. Wallace. Enquiring if there had been any further news of Eoin, Annette was pleased to hear that a P.I. had been hired and that the ball had been set in motion.

### Rachel

"You're kidding me! That's how you found out. Oh, Lizzie, sweetie — that must have been so awful for you," said Rachel in her most sympathetic voice when Liz finished telling her about phoning Pauline. "And of all the weeks for it to happen. I mean at least if I'd been here, or even Annette, then you would have had some support. You poor, poor thing."

"Yep. But then again, what's a good way to find out these things?"

"And you had no inkling before? None at all?"

"No, Rachel. I had no idea that my husband was having an affair. It might have been something that I would have brought up if I did."

"Hey! I'm sorry, Lizzie. I only asked. No need to bite my head off," said Rachel, sounding wounded.

"I'm sorry. I'm just feeling a bit frazzled at the minute."

"I know, sweetie. I see women in your position all the time in the clinic. I never thought it would happen to you though. I have to say you are being very brave about it all. So many of the women I see go to pieces altogether, but you seem to be coping really well."

"I'm doing my best."

"And what about poor Janey and Josh? How're they bearing up?"

"Well, they only found out this afternoon. They're out looking at apartments with Jack as we speak, in fact, they'll probably be back soon. I've told them nothing about the affair and I want it kept that way. I think it'll be easier for them to accept things that way, especially Janey."

"Don't worry, I won't say a word. And remember, Liz, if there's anything, and I mean anything, that I can do, you only have to ask."

"Ah, no. You've done enough already by being here," said Liz and Rachel wasn't sure if she imagined a slight edge to her voice as she spoke. Deciding that she was being paranoid, she reached across the table and poured them both another glass of wine.

As she finished pouring the wine, they heard the front door close, signalling the return of the kids.

### Liz

Not sure how much longer she could sit there watching Rachel hypocritically play the surrogate, concerned aunt, Liz let out an exaggerated yawn, hoping that Rachel would get the hint and make tracks home, but no such luck, she seemed to be enjoying herself.

But then again, thought Liz, how often had she sat there at that very table with her and Jack, pretending to be Liz's friend whilst all the time sleeping with her husband. The woman had a brass neck and if Liz wanted shut of her tonight, she was going to have to be more direct.

"Jane, I think it's time for bed, love," she said, standing up and clearing the glasses from the table. "We've all had a long day and we've an early start in the morning."

"Oh, a few more minutes won't kill her," pleaded Rachel, pulling Jane tighter into the crook of her arm where she had been sitting since her return from apartment hunting with her father.

Biting back her temper, Liz acquiesced, "Ok — five minutes, but that's it."

Josh had gone directly to his room when they got back after saying a cursory 'hello' to Rachel and giving his mother an affectionate, if somewhat brusque, hug — his way of telling her that he loved her. But Jane had been thrilled to see Rachel sitting there and after throwing a questioning look at her Mum to check that Rachel knew their news, she had cuddled into her and hung on her every word about how much her Dad loved her and how everything would be alright.

Liz wanted to shout out the truth about Rachel, exposing her for the two-faced wagon that she was, but held back, knowing that that truth would only serve to hurt her daughter more. Whatever happened down the road, Jane was in a vulnerable place right now and had to come to terms with her father's departure before having to deal with anything further.

CHAPTER TWENTY-FIVE

# Tuesday AM 27th April

*Rachel*

Busy squeezing some oranges for breakfast juice, Rachel looked up at Jack and smiled when he came into the kitchen. He still looked half asleep, his tousled hair adding to the just out of bed look, but overall, he looked far more relaxed than he had the previous morning.

"Bet you're glad that yesterday is over," she said, passing him a glass of orange juice.

Accepting it, gratefully, he nodded. "You're not kidding! Although, mind you, it did go a lot smoother than I had hoped. Josh was amazing — I just wanted to kiss him when he turned all big brother and had Janey chilling out in no time. I knew that Jane was going to be the emotional one, but between us all, we managed to convince her that she will still be a major part of my life. To give Liz her due, she was great. I know that she was only doing it for them, not for me, but still and all it was good to have her there."

"I really put Jane's mind at rest last night," said Rachel, a little peeved to have Liz cast as his saving grace. "I told you we had a good chat and I spent the entire time telling her how much you loved her and how, once she got used to the change, she would see that things won't be so bad."

"I know, love and thanks for that. How did Josh seem to you?"

"Oh, you know Josh. He just breezed in, grunted hello, and headed off to his room."

She omitted the part about Josh hugging his mother, only interested in relating incidents that painted herself in a good light.

## Jack

The only productive part of the previous evening's apartment hunting expedition had been the opportunity to spend some time on his own with the kids. None of the three apartments they had looked at were particularly nice and he was back to the drawing board on that score. With the initial shock out of the way, the kids seemed to be taking the news of the separation relatively well. At least, there had been no more tears from Jane, which was something.

Reinforcing his commitment to be as much a part of their lives as when he was living at home, Jack texted both of them on his drive into work, telling them to have a good day and promising to talk to them later. He was beginning to feel optimistic about things and recalling Rachel's analogy of not being able to make an omelette without breaking eggs, he smiled.

## Liz

Anxious in case the kids were upset, now that they'd had a proper chance to think about things over night, Liz got up extra early to ensure that she was the first downstairs. She had only been down there two minutes, when Jane appeared. Her swollen eyelids and red nose confirmed Liz's fears that her daughter had spent a large part of the night crying. Opening her arms to receive her daughter in an embrace, she wrapped her to her, gently rocking her back and forth in an attempt to soothe her.

"I just don't understand why this has happened, Mum," she said with silent tears rolling down her cheeks. "I thought you and Dad were happy."

"I know, lovie," said Liz. "But sometimes these things creep up on us. Your Dad and I have grown apart and I know it hurts right now, pet, but soon, you'll get used to the idea and things will start to get better, I promise."

Jane didn't look at all convinced and as Liz cupped her face in her hands, she felt her tense and the look in her eyes changed from pain to anger.

"I know you said that it's not his fault, but I blame Dad. He's the one who left us."

"Sweetheart, in a separation one person has to leave. It was more practical that it was your Dad. That's all."

"No, I don't accept that Mum. You'd never leave. It's him, and right now, I hate him."

## Hollie

It was almost as if a plague had hit Dublin city, sending all its occupants directly to Greendale Medical Centre. She had never seen the place so busy and she was finding it impossible to grab five minutes to contact Maria Alvarez about the photo-fit for the next day's meeting. Fearful that if she left it much later, Maria would be gone off shift, she asked Niamh to cover for her for a few minutes and grabbing her mobile, she slipped out to the car park to make her call.

Maria was more than happy to oblige, promising that she would e-mail the image to Hollie as soon as possible. Then, in a tentative manner, she broke the news to Hollie that the police suspected that Eoin had somehow managed to get off the island as every lead they had on him, drew a blank and someone fitting his description had boarded a plane in Palma the previous day.

A distraught member of the airport security police had confessed to his supervisor that a man who looked vaguely familiar to him had gone through, but the name on his passport had definitely not been Eoin, and this passenger had a shaven head, not wavy brown hair like in the photo-fit. It wasn't until a colleague had quipped about shaving his own head at lunchtime that the officer had made the connection and by then, it was too late.

Deeply disturbed by this news, Hollie thanked God that she had listened to Donal and taken Denise up on her offer and tomorrow's meeting couldn't come soon enough.

## Denise

A night's sleep, and a good one at that, had done little to change Denise's mind on the subject of investing in Donal's business. She had awoken with absolute certainty that she wanted to go ahead and hoped fervently that he would accept her proposal.

Keen to meet up with him as soon as possible now that her mind was set, she sent him a text asking him to meet with her in a coffee shop in Enniskerry later that morning and went to get a shower. Emerging from the bathroom ten minutes later, she checked her phone to see if he had replied, but he hadn't. Wanting to strike while the iron was hot, she called him.

"Hey," she said when he answered. "Sorry to bother you, but I kinda need to speak to you and was wondering if you'd be around for a coffee?"

"Oh, yeah, sorry — I got your text, but I had an early meeting with my accountant, you know about Transglobal's offer and I'm only just out of it."

"Right. How'd it go?"

"Not great actually. He's pretty much of the same mind as you and Hollie. Thinks I'm jumping in without exploring all the options. I dunno, Denise, I'm just finding this soul destroying. I really want to get cracking with this and even if it's selling myself short, at least it's selling. Do you know what I mean?"

"I do. But, you've got to listen to the advice you're being offered. Anyway, look, let's save it 'til we meet. Could you be in Enniskerry in about an hour?"

"Sure, I guess. What's so urgent anyway? Your man hasn't managed to find Eoin already — has he?"

"No. No," she said, but not wanting to prolong the conversation, she added. "Look, I can't talk right now, so I'll see you later, ok?"

## Donal

The rain was pouring down when Donal drove into Enniskerry Village and unable to find a parking space anywhere near the coffee shop, he parked up a side street and ran down the steep hill, getting soaked in the process. The windows of the café were all steamed up, indicating that it was prime time for all the stay-at-home wives to congregate and trade gossip. Stepping in the front door, he brushed the excess water from his mac, scanning the occupants in search of Denise.

He spotted her sitting at a table in the far corner of the busy café, eagerly watching out for him. Sidestepping buggies and practically breaking his neck over baby seats seemingly strewn haphazardly in the aisles, he made his way to her table, feeling as if he had completed an assault course by the time he reached her.

"Popular spot," he said in greeting. "Who'd have thought Tuesday morning in Enniskerry is the place to be!"

Grinning back at him, she said, "Oh, sit down and stop your moaning. I've ordered you a large cappuccino and one of their 'must have' chocolate brownies — ok?"

"Oh, you so know how to please a man," he said, winking at her, causing her to blush.

"Well, we'll see about that by the end of this meeting."

"Oh! It's a meeting now is it — very formal!"

Unprepared for what she laid on him during the course of the ensuing half hour, he was rendered speechless when at the conclusion of her spiel, she presented him with a professionally worked out business plan, proof that she was indeed completely serious about her proposal. Reading through the bound document, he could see how much work had gone into its production and from where he sat, it was the answer to all his prayers. But, he couldn't let her do this; she had done so much for them already and now this.

Finally, finding his voice, he reached his hand across the table and taking hold of hers, he said, "Look, Denise. What can I say? This is terrific and in different circumstances I'd snap your hand off, but I can't accept this offer."

"I'd like a very good reason why not," she said in a haughty manner.

"You know why not. For me, this is amazing, but I would feel like I was taking advantage of you and I don't want to do that."

Harrumphing at what he said, she shook her head. "No, sorry, Donal — you'll have to come up with better than that. The way I see it is that I have money that I need to invest in something. I've spoken to a business advisor; he likes what I've shown him as much as I do. Now, I'm not interested in the day to day running of the business, I'll leave that to you, well you and him actually — if that's alright with you. But, I see a very lucrative business developing from your idea and I want a piece of the action. Are you saying that my money isn't good enough for you?"

Aghast that she'd even think that, he shot her a look, but the grin on her face told him that she was only winding him up by saying that, causing him to smile. "You know this is all too good to be true," he said.

"And winning almost six million on the lotto isn't?" she asked with a wry smile.

### Annette

"These shrubs would look great," said Maureen, "and, according to the label they are pretty tough, requiring very little maintenance."

"Mmm," agreed Annette, strolling around the garden centre with her mother-in-law. "But, they're a little bit bland. What about these ones? They have a bit more colour and would look more interesting — don't you think?"

"Now, that's why I wanted you to come with me, love," said Maureen, bending down and lifting two of them into her trolley. "I was also thinking of getting some of those hanging baskets — they look great."

"Why the sudden interest in gardening, Maureen? You were never much into it before."

Annette could have sworn that Maureen was blushing, as she turned her back and studiously examined all the hanging baskets on display, before answering. "Oh, you know, it's just that Ron, you remember him from the retirement club on holiday, well, he reckons that it's all very therapeutic if you get into it and I thought I'd give it a bash — that's all. He said he'd help me out with advice and that, if I liked."

"Ooohh, Ron!" teased Annette. "You are a dark horse, Maureen. You come away on a family holiday and come back with a fella — what can I say?"

Taking the slagging in good spirits, Maureen surprised her by giving her a hug. "It's good to see you laugh, love. You looked so sad earlier when you were telling me all about your sister and her poor kids, and of course, poor little Hollie. But, you've got to look after yourself too, you know. Other people's problems can weigh you down and of course you want to be there for your sister and her family right now, and it's hard not to be affected by what happened to Hollie, but just remember to make a little room for Annette."

Warmed by her affection, Annette rejoiced that at least one good thing had emerged from the ash cloud debacle — she and Maureen had discovered each other.

CHAPTER TWENTY-SIX

# Tuesday PM 27th April

*Liz*

Liz was surprised at how angry Jane was still, when she collected her from school. The day had done nothing to lift her mood and she had catapulted herself into the car like a human ball of anger, swearing and muttering to herself as she did so. Without so much as an 'hello' to her Mum, she pulled on her seat belt, then launched straight into a torrent of abuse about her Dad.

"He's just so bloody selfish, Mum," she began. "Clearly all he's thinking about is himself and his own happiness. But that's not fair. He doesn't have the right to make himself happy and make his kids miserable at the same time. He's meant to be the one who protects us, not hurts us. I'm sorry, Mum, it's just that the more I think about it, the angrier I feel towards him. I hate him, Mum, I really do."

"Don't be daft, Janey, you don't hate him. You're angry at him right now and that's understandable. But, remember it took two of us to separate, so by rights, if you're angry at him, then, you should be angry at me too. The only real difference between me and your Dad is that he's the one who has moved out, not me."

Glancing at her surreptitiously to see if her words were having any impact, she saw a pensive frown on her daughter's face, and her heart ached for the pain she was going through. She had always been a real 'Daddy's girl' and from the moment she was born, Jack had adored her, putting her up on a pedestal, treating her like the quintessential princess, and Liz could see now that the higher up he had raised her, the harder the fall. For Josh, although the love was undoubtedly there, it was of a more subtle variety, he would be able to handle the whole thing a lot better than Jane. Jack was going to have to tread carefully with her.

"Yeah, but you'd never have left us, Mum. He has. So to me, that's the difference between you and Dad."

## Hollie

There it was again - that feeling of being watched. As Hollie made her way across the pathway that led to the road from the clinic, she swung her head around in one direction, then, the other, but neither offered her any evidence that someone was there. Despite thinking him neurotic for suggesting it, she was glad now that Donal was collecting her. The fact that there was even the slightest possibility that Eoin was back in Dublin had unnerved her, more than she liked to admit, even to herself.

Almost reaching the main road, she spotted Donal's car pulling up to the kerb. A rustle of movement in the large shrubbery area of the clinic's grounds, caused her to quicken her pace. Out of the corner of one eye, she saw a flash of colour through the greenery and she dove through the gap in the wall, out on to the public pathway, and hurtled towards Donal's car, pulling the door open with brute force before jumping in. Safe now, she peered back at the bushes seeing them spring back together expunging the temporary opening that had spat out two children playing chasing through the undergrowth.

Letting out a gasp of relief, she was suddenly aware of how frightened she had been. Her heart was pounding, a lather of sweat had pumped from her and her hands were so shaky that she could barely open her handbag to get a tissue to mop her brow. This business with Eoin had her completely rattled and she hoped that the P.I. was as good as Denise reckoned so that they would track him down soon, because she didn't know how much more of this she could take.

### Rachel

Tidying up her desk before leaving work, Rachel put in a call to Liz to see if she was available to go out for dinner that night, but Liz declined on the basis that Annette was due over to her. Rachel's immediate reaction to this news was to think what a marvellous opportunity it would be to get the two sisters together - she could take a back seat in the conversation, but subtly drive it, extracting views and opinions that could be an invaluable source of information for her and Jack in the future.

Rachel had enough savvy to know that there was a thin line between playing the concerned friend role and appearing to be a gossip monger, and despite commenting on how lovely it would be to see Annette again, no invitation to join them was forthcoming so, she had to let the opportunity slip and settle for having dinner with Liz the following evening.

### Donal

"Are you serious?" asked Hollie, when Donal told her about Denise's proposal over dinner. "She wants to invest? Tell me that you are at least thinking about it?"

Donal shrugged, "Of course, I'm thinking about it. Apart from your situation with Eoin, I've thought about little else all day." He saw her face cloud over at the mention of Eoin's name. When she had finally calmed herself after getting into his car earlier, they had discussed that subject to the point of exhaustion and had finally agreed to make the rest of their evening an 'Eoin-free' zone and the warning look that she now threw at him, caused him to raise his hands in an apologetic gesture for breaching that agreement. "Sorry. My head's just melted with this."

"But why? It sounds like a great offer."

"It is. The answer to all my prayers. But I kinda feel like I'm taking advantage of her in some way — do you know what I mean?"

"Sorry, Donal — I don't. The way I see it is she's someone with money to invest, you have something worth investing in — so, where's the problem?"

"Jesus! The pair of you are so alike," he said, giving an exasperated laugh. "She made it sound like the simplest decision on the planet as well."

"Eh… that's 'cos it is, dumbo. Now, stop wasting your time worrying about it. You've been given a golden opportunity — take it. Ring Transglobal in the morning, tell them to take their shitty offer and shove it where the sun don't shine and get on the phone now to Denise and ask her is she ready to get cracking."

### Jack

The Letting Agent assured Jack that as it was undoubtedly a 'renter's market', there would be little difficulty in finding him a suitable apartment, but Jack's experience of the previous night left him feeling less confident of his assurances. The enthusiastic young agent dismissed Jack's fears, telling him that by highlighting the points that were lacking in the previous selection, he had now narrowed the field sufficiently to be quietly optimistic that at least one, if not all, of the three apartments he was seeing tonight would fulfil his requirements.

Wanting the kids involved in the process, Jack tried both of their mobiles with the intention of collecting them en route to the viewings, but neither answered. Unwilling though he was to call the house number, he had little choice, but to do so. Liz answered, explaining that Josh was at rugby practice and definitely wouldn't be available, then asking him to hold on a minute, she went in search of Jane. Hushed voices could be heard in the background but it was impossible to discern what was being said, although he got the impression that Liz was having difficulty getting Jane to pick up the phone. Eventually, she did.

"What?" she asked abruptly.

Jack laughed. "Hey, Dad — good to hear from you. How are you doing?" he said, mocking her, but she gave no response. Clearing his throat, he ignored her reaction and got straight to the point. "Look Janey, I have a couple of apartments to look at tonight and I wondered if you could come along and give me some of your expert advice?"

"Can't. I have loads of homework."

"OooKay," he said, dragging out the word as he wondered how to play things. "Well, I guess if I narrow it down, then maybe you and Josh could take a look tomorrow night and we could grab some dinner afterwards. What d'ya think?"

"I think it's going to be a busy week. Maybe Josh can do it, but I don't think I can."

"Hey, Janey," he said, his voice softer, almost pleading. "I want to see you, lovie. Couldn't you even manage an hour or so?"

"If you wanted to see me so bad, then, you shouldn't have moved out — should you?" she said and put the phone down, leaving him staring blankly at the handset in his hand.

### Annette

Arriving into Liz's house in the immediate aftermath of Jack's call, Annette marvelled at how calmly Liz handled her troubled daughter. Whilst sympathising with the pain that Jane was going through, Liz told her that there was little to be achieved by avoiding her father and firmly encouraged her to reconsider going out with him for dinner the following evening. Refusing adamantly at first, Jane finally capitulated when Liz convinced her that there was more to be gained by going than by not. With a face like thunder, she held firm that she wasn't going to speak to him again tonight and stormed off up to her room to text him.

"Round One to Liz," said Annette in a tone full of admiration, "Fair play to you, I'm not sure that I could have carried that off. I think that if I was in your position, I'd be secretly quite glad that they didn't want to see him."

"Trust me, I am. But, in all fairness, it's going to be a lot harder on the kids if there's aggro between them and Jack and I don't want that."

"I know and I meant it when I said fair play to you. How do you think they'll react when Rachel is introduced into the mix?"

"Hopefully Jack will have the cop on to leave that until they've come to terms with the separation first. I don't suppose that he's going to be rushing to tell me or the kids that she's in his life. Do you know that cheeky bitch rang me earlier and did her utmost to wangle an invitation out of me to join us tonight? Can you believe the nerve of her?"

"You're joking! How'd you get out of that one?"

"I just played dumb. Obviously that's what she thinks I am, so it wasn't that difficult. I did agree to go out for dinner with her tomorrow night though — that should be interesting."

"Never!" exclaimed Annette. "Jesus, I don't know how you can manage to do that."

"It's all part of my grand master plan. I'm going to play along with her until the opportunity arises to publicly humiliate her and believe me, when I do that, she's going to wish she had never met me."

## *Denise*

Denise was chuffed to bits when Donal called her to accept her proposal. She had such a good feeling about the whole thing and couldn't be happier to know that whatever happened in the future, her good fortune had enabled her to help someone realise their dream. There was a feel good factor to this that was second to none.

Confirming their meeting with the P.I. for the next morning, she was horrified to hear that there was a very definite risk that Eoin was back in the country and warned Donal to be extra vigilant with Hollie. She asked if Hollie had managed to get the information that the P.I. had requested and was delighted to hear that she had. Telling him that she would see them both in the morning, she rang off.

As she was brushing her teeth that night, she remembered a saying of her father's, 'there's no such thing as coincidence — only fate' and she found the words strangely comforting, having no way of knowing at that point just how pertinent they were.

CHAPTER TWENTY-SEVEN

# Wednesday AM 28th April

*Rachel*

"Here we go again," thought Rachel to herself as her first patient of the day sat blubbering in the chair in front of her. Fixing a concerned look on her face, she wondered if the woman had looked in the mirror over the course of the past few years and, if so, why it should come as a surprise to her that her husband was playing away from home.

Devoid of make-up, and with unwashed straggly hair pulled back into an unsightly ponytail, the woman sat crying piteously into a dampened tissue that had bits of it dropping all over the surgery floor. Repulsed, Rachel passed her over a box of man-size tissues from her desk, indicating that the woman should dispose of her existing one in the bin beside her. Christ, thought Rachel, not trusting herself to speak just yet, lest she give this woman a piece of her mind, she's even wearing a track suit, and one which Rachel very much doubted had ever seen the inside of a gym. Why do women let themselves go like this?

The woman mistook Rachel's silence for compassionate listening and whittled on and on about how she had just discovered through a chance encounter at the hair dressers that her husband was having an affair with the lady golf professional at his golf club. Absentmindedly, Rachel concluded that she must have heard this news before her appointment and done a runner as the inch long roots and tatty ends which she now sported had not received a hair dresser's attention in a very long time.

Realising that the woman had finally fallen silent, Rachel made some perfunctory comments about taking care of herself by eating properly and ensuring that she was getting enough sleep and to that end she wrote her out a prescription for sleeping tablets. She also recommended speaking to a counsellor and jotted down a couple of names and numbers for her to try. Then, seeing her swiftly out of the surgery, she swept up the bits of crumpled tissue from the floor and threw them in the bin.

That was when it occurred to her, that to plant the seed that it was someone in Jack's golf club whom he was seeing could be the perfect diversionary tactic to employ with Liz. All of a sudden, she found herself very much looking forward to her dinner date that evening.

## Liz

Despite having had an early night, Jane was very subdued that morning as Liz hurried them through their usual routine, getting them out and into the car by ten past eight. As was customary, she dropped Josh off first and seeing her daughter's pale and drawn face, she made an impulsive decision, turning off their normal route and heading towards Dundrum Town Centre.

"Where are you going, Mum?" asked Jane, alarmed that she was going to be late for school.

"I thought we might play hookie today, love," she grinned at her perplexed daughter. "How's about you and me spend a girlie day — go to Dundrum, grab some breakfast in that café you love, you know the one with all the windows and the terrace and then maybe do a bit of shopping?"

"Are you serious, Mum?" she asked, her eyes lighting up at the prospect.

"Why not?" shrugged Liz. "I think we deserve it — don't you?"

It proved to be one of Liz's better ideas when, as the morning wore on, she saw Jane relaxing into her old self and the tensions and upset of the preceding couple of days lifted. They avoided all conversation about the separation and simply indulged themselves in some retail therapy. When they got back to the car a couple of hours later, they were both armed with a multitude of shopping bags, which they threw into the boot.

Strapping herself into the passenger seat, Jane said, "Thanks, Mum. That was great."

"Your welcome, my love," smiled Liz. "You just didn't look like you were up to a day in school this morning. One day won't kill you. Anyway, I really enjoyed myself. It's lovely to spend time with you like that."

"Look, I'm sorry that I've been acting like a spoilt brat these past few days. It's just that this whole separation thing came as a big shock to me. I really had no idea that you guys were even thinking of it."

"I know, sweetie. It hasn't been easy on you, but you've got to remember that whatever else happens, both your Dad and I love you very much."

"I know that, Mum and I'm sorry. I just find it hard to imagine home without Dad. I guess that I've been kinda blaming him for everything and maybe that's not fair. Obviously I want both you and him to be happy and if being apart is better for the two of you, then I suppose that I'm just going to have to accept that. But, it stinks, Mum — it really does."

Reaching across and pulling her into her arms, she said, "It'll get better, sweetheart, I promise."

"Yeah, well, it can't get any worse," she said with a half laugh. "Thanks for today, though, Mum — it helped."

Liz felt a momentary panic as she considered how much worse it could be if Jane was to find out about Rachel and vowed to do her best to ensure that she didn't.

### Annette

Worried about her niece, Annette gave Liz a quick call mid-morning to see how things had panned out with Jane overnight. She caught Liz waiting outside the changing rooms in H&M where Liz quickly explained that she had decided to keep Jane out of school and put in a bit of girlie time with her. Annette was delighted to hear that, thinking that it was a wonderful idea.

Not wanting to interrupt their quality time, she asked Liz to be sure to give her a call when she had finished her dinner with Rachel and Liz promised to do just that.

## *Hollie*

Some things in life are completely pre-destined, thought Hollie on arrival at Sam Glynn's office, and Sam being a Private Investigator was one of those things.

He was like the archtypical sleuth - considerably overweight, balding, sweating profusely, despite it not being a particularly warm day, and his office reflected his personality, with half drunk paper cups of takeaway coffee strewn all about the place and every conceivable surface in the room piled high with press-cuttings and photographs. However, as soon as he opened his mouth, there was an endearing quality about him that instantly instilled confidence in all who met him. Hollie took to him straightaway, feeling that if anyone could help them find Eoin, then, this was the man.

Clearing off some rickety looking chairs in order to provide his three visitors with a place to sit down, he suggested that some coffee would get the meeting off to a good start. No one disagreed and taking their order, he rang through to his doubtless long-suffering secretary asking her to pop down stairs and grab four large cappuccinos. Hollie could see that Denise was relieved that she and Donal approved of her choice of P.I. and once the coffees arrived, they quickly got down to business.

"So, Hollie — you managed to get the items that I requested?" asked Sam.

Nodding that she had, she passed a manila envelope across the desk to Sam, saying "I've got a copy of his registration card, with an address, which obviously may not be the correct one, but it's what he gave to us. Also, the Spanish nurse e-mailed me across the photo-fit that was compiled with the police."

Opening the envelope, Sam pulled out the contents, examining them before looking up. "Okay, 47 Sweetmount Gardens, as you say, this may or may not….."

But before he got to go any further, Denise choked violently on her coffee, spluttering drops of liquid through her fingers as she tried to find her voice. "Oh, you must have that wrong," she said, "That's impossible."

All eyes were on her, looking for an explanation. Hesitantly, she stared at them all and with a look of total confusion on her face, she said. "That's my address — or at least it was. That's where John and I lived."

Everyone stared at her and it was as if time was suspended, as one by one they tried to compute what on earth was going on here. Finally, Sam pulled out the photo-fit from the envelope and passed it to Denise. Her entire face drained of blood as staring back at her from the piece of paper that she held in her hand was John's face.

### Denise

Her mind was in overdrive and Denise trembled from head to foot as she absorbed the fact that John and Eoin were in fact the one person. The irony that she had been too afraid to go after John herself, but had ended up helping to track him down on Hollie's behalf didn't escape her and she let out a weird half laugh, half gasp as another thought occurred to her.

"Of course," she said. "Eoin is the Irish for John. I never made that connection."

"And Sean!" exclaimed Hollie, but the others had no clue what she meant. "Maria Alvarez told me that the second attack on the young English worker had been carried out by a guy who called himself Sean. The DNA proved that Eoin and Sean were the same person."

"Well, at least we have a definite address for him," said Sam.

Denise shook her head, "He'll be long gone from there. He's too clever. He knows that Hollie was helping the police in Spain and he'll remember that the Clinic has that address for him on file. I bet he's cleared out the bank accounts — my bank accounts — and gone on the run."

"Right, let's get cracking on this," said Sam, anxious to get going before the trail ran cold. "Can you give me details of any bank accounts that he has access to? I know you're saying that he'll be gone from the house, but still and all, I'd like to pay a visit there. I have plenty of stuff to get started with here and I suggest that we try and re-convene here tomorrow morning, same time and see where we go from there. Okay?"

They all nodded and, stunned still from the morning's revelations, they made their way out of Sam's office and headed to the local Starbucks for a 'post-mortem' discussion.

## Donal

Coming back from the counter with three super-sized mugs of coffee, Donal sat down in the leather armchair opposite the two-seater couch on which Hollie and Denise sat. There was so much to take in that for a while none of them spoke, each lost in thought.

"This is so freaky," said Donal, finally breaking the silence. "If you saw this in a movie, you would say that the plot was too far-fetched. It's the biggest coincidence imaginable."

"There's no such thing as coincidence — only fate," said Denise, more to herself than to the others. "That's what my father used to always say. I was actually remembering that last night. It's as if my Dad is there, guiding me on to make John pay for the hell he has put me through since I met him."

"It's unbe-bloody-lievable," said Hollie, shivering involuntarily. "I mean, what are the odds?"

## Jack

Notwithstanding her good intentions, Jack couldn't help but feel rattled at the notion of Rachel going out for dinner that night with Liz. It felt wrong. But Rachel had been insistent that morning that it was all for the greater good. He didn't like the idea of Liz being set up in this way, but it was hard to argue when Rachel convinced him that it was the best way to secure an on-going relationship with his kids. He couldn't bear to lose them and his altercation with Jane the previous day had upset him beyond belief.

He had been so relieved when Jane had texted him agreeing to go for dinner tonight and he knew, without a doubt, that Liz had had a part to play in this turn of events. Deep down he knew that she was basically a far nicer person than Rachel, but a future with Rachel was so much more exciting than any he had ever envisaged with Liz. That was the path he had chosen and he mustn't allow himself look back over the fence where the grass had never been this green.

There had been little to choose from with the apartments that he had viewed the previous evening. All three of them had been highly suitable and he had made his selection on the basis of proximity to the kids. He hoped they would be happy with his choice and he looked forward to showing it to them when they went for dinner that evening.

CHAPTER TWENTY-EIGHT

# Wednesday PM 28th April

*Hollie*

Back in work for the afternoon, Hollie was having terrible trouble concentrating. The clinic was extremely busy and she had difficulty filling Niamh in on the morning's meeting in Sam's office, having to drip feed her the key points, leaving her with more questions than answers.

When they finally hit a lull, Niamh swung around in her receptionist's chair, eyes as wide as saucers, and said in a whisper, "So let me get this straight — Eoin, the bastard that did that to you, also turns out to be the ex-partner of the woman who is paying for a Private Investigator to track him down?"

Hollie nodded. "Sweet!" exclaimed Niamh. "And what about…"

But, the doors of the clinic swung open and once again, the reception area was filled with patients, rendering it impossible for Niamh to finish her question. The phones too were hopping and, leaving Niamh to deal with all the in-coming patients, Hollie busied herself with the over burdened phone lines. With supreme efficiency, she answered each call, taking details and, where necessary, transferring the caller to the relevant department.

By four o'clock she was exhausted and taking a quick look at the surgery clock, she told Niamh that she would take one last call and then she was going to go on a break.

"Good afternoon, Greendale Medical Centre, Hollie speaking — how can I help you?"

When no one answered her, she thought the caller had cut themselves off and was just about to hang up when she heard a voice that sent a chill up her spine.

"Hollie, you little slag!" hissed the unmistakeable voice of Eoin. "Do you realise that you almost got me arrested in Majorca? Now, listen to me, bitch and listen to me good — if you have any more dealings with the authorities in Spain, then, I'm coming to get you — do you understand?"

Forgetting that he wasn't able to see her, Hollie stood there nodding into the phone, until Eoin hissed at her again, louder this time, "I said — do you understand, bitch?"

"Yes. Yes, I understand," she said, feeling sick to the pit of her stomach and more scared than ever before in her life. "I…. I….I won't say a thing to them — promise."

"Make sure you don't. And I'm warning you, if you make any more trouble for me — any more at all, then, you'll rue the day you met me. Is that clear?"

"Yes. That's clear," she said, but she knew that he had hung up by that stage.

### Rachel

Rachel was filled with enthusiasm when she arrived at the restaurant to meet Liz. A Wednesday evening, the place wasn't too busy so she had a choice of tables. Requesting one in the corner where they would have minimum distraction, she sat down and waited for Liz to arrive.

Adopting what she hoped would be perceived as the appropriate level of concern, she fought her impulse to jump in and suggest the golf club hypothesis, enquiring instead about Liz's and the kids' well being, waiting until they had completed their main course before espousing her theory. With neither of them wanting dessert, the waiter went to fetch them some coffee, leaving the stage set for Rachel's performance.

"So," she began, tentatively. "Do you have any idea who it is that Jack is seeing?"

"None," said Liz, somewhat curtly. "And to be perfectly honest, I have no real desire to know who she is either."

"Ah, c'mon Liz, you must be curious. I know that I would be."

"That's you, Rachel — not me."

Fearful that she had teetered on the brink of insensitivity, Rachel reined in her tone, forcing greater concern into her voice. "I'm sorry, Babes, I didn't mean to make it sound like I was on a gossip hunt. It's just that I can't stop thinking about you both and how horrible this whole thing is. Do you know what occurred to me?"

"Enlighten me," said Liz with a definite edge to her voice.

"Well, all this golf he plays and you know, saying that he was going off on a golfing trip, do you think there's any chance that it could be someone from the club? It would make sense, wouldn't it? I mean all those hours it takes to play a round of golf — well, that would be the perfect cover and if she was a golfer too, then it would make things easy for them. Do you see where I'm coming from?"

Liz's face was thunderous and Rachel was confident that she had managed to hit a nerve, congratulating herself for coming up with this magnificent curve ball. There was no one as gullible as a vulnerable woman, she thought.

"As I said, Rachel. I'm really not that interested in who Jack is seeing. From here on in, it's none of my business."

"You're being so strong about all of this, Liz. But go easy on yourself, Babes. I've seen it all before where women initially put on this show of strength and internalise all their emotions, allowing them to build up inside of them until eventually they explode and the results can be quite catastrophic — I don't want that happening to you. If you need me at all, as a friend or in professional capacity, you know I'll be there for you — you only have to pick up the phone. Ok?"

"Thanks, Rachel," said Liz with a strange smile touching her lips. Rachel's work here was done and she was feeling very pleased with the results.

## Liz

Liz's stomach gave a flip as, inadvertently, Rachel had provided her with a way of exacting her revenge and publicly humiliating her into the bargain.

Wiping the smile from her face, she forced herself to sit there and listen to Rachel's false platitudes as she droned on and on about how much she valued Liz as a friend and how much she would be there for her through all of this. It was all Liz could do not to throw up.

When she could finally take no more of Rachel's crap, she let out a massive yawn, and patting her hand to her mouth, she said. "Oh, I'm sorry, Rachel. I guess you're right, perhaps this thing is taking more out of me than I thought. I really am exhausted. Look, thanks so much for a lovely meal and all the advice, but I think I need to get off home to bed. You don't mind do you?"

"Of course not, Lizzie," she said with a saccharin sweet smile. "As I said, you've got to take care of yourself."

Impatiently, Liz waited whilst Rachel called over the waiter and settled up the bill, desperate now to put as much space as possible between them. Keeping the farewells short and sweet, Liz stepped into a taxi, where her earlier smile returned to her face and she could hardly wait to speak to Annette to see what she thought of her plan.

### Annette

As soon as she heard the bones of Liz's plan for Rachel, Annette roared with laughter down the phone.

"Oh, you've got to do that, Lizzie. That's priceless!" she exclaimed.

"Do you think?" asked Liz, the pleasure in her voice audible.

"Abso-fucking-lutely!" laughed Annette. "It's no more than the bitch deserves. I just wish that I could be a fly on the wall. She is going to go ballistic."

"I know!" chuckled Liz. "And you definitely have some photos of the pair of them? I need to have the proof if I'm to carry this off."

"Liz, trust me. There is no ambiguity about the relationship between them when you see these photos. Do you really think you'll have the nerve to do it?"

"Of course I will. At least then, with them knowing that I know, I can make damn sure that they keep their sordid little affair from the kids. They have enough to deal with at the moment."

"Won't they wonder why Rachel isn't coming around to see you anymore?"

"That's surmountable. I can always say she's busy at work, and what with me starting off my own business, that'll be easy enough to overcome."

"Way to so, Sis! Honestly, I'm so proud of you and you know what, a year down the road and I reckon you are going to be a much happier person than you've been in years. I'll drop over in the morning and bring my camera, we can print off the photos then and finalise your plans."

## Jack

He knew that she was putting on a brave face, but Jack could tell just how hurt Jane was at the demise of her parent's marriage and it ate him up with guilt. It was difficult to see if the situation was having any affect on Josh as he was his usual monosyllabic self, but with her it was obvious. Usually, she chatted away nineteen to the dozen, barely coming up for air, but tonight she seemed to have very little to say.

They had gone to have a look at his new apartment before eating and apart from shrugging her shoulders and telling him that it was grand, he got no further reaction from her about it. As he looked across the table and saw the sadness in her eyes, he wondered if he was making a very big mistake.

Rachel kept assuring him that it would all improve with time, but then, that was easy for her to say — they weren't her kids. He wondered how her evening was going with Liz and hoped that it was going smoother than his own.

## Donal

Donal had assumed that after the morning's revelations, Denise could probably do with some company that evening and had invited her to join them for dinner. The three of them now sat in the kitchen, picking at the Indian takeaway he had ordered, none of them with much of an appetite.

Hollie had filled them in on the phone call from Eoin and it left them all feeling perturbed. In an attempt to strike a positive note, Donal said, "Well, at least we know that he is back in Dublin now. That has to count for something."

The others nodded silently, each lost in their own thoughts. Then, as if thinking aloud, Denise said. "You know, we have the ultimate bait for him.

It's just figuring out how to lay it."

"And what would that be?" asked Donal, suspicious, as he had a fair idea where she was going with this.

"Me."

"Oh, no — you don't!" he said emphatically. "Have you forgotten that this guy almost beat you to death last time you saw him? Have some sense, Denise. Sam is on the case, we'll let him know that Eoin, or John, whatever you want to call him, is back in Dublin and let him take it from there."

Denise started to protest, but Donal refused to listen to any plans she had that put herself or Hollie in danger. "I mean it, Denise — this is not a runner."

### Denise

She could tell it was futile to argue with Donal at the moment, but in her heart she knew that she was the best shot they had at luring John out into the open. Unsure yet as to how to go about it, she decided to keep her mouth shut until she had formulated a plan. Knowing a bit of solitude would work wonders with her thinking process, she cut the evening short by declaring that she was exhausted. Arranging to meet them outside Sam's office in the morning, she got a taxi back to her hotel.

Alone in the hotel room, her head raced with various ideas, but one by one she discounted them as either too risky or too preposterous, neither of which would achieve the objective. She knew that if she was going to try to entrap John, then she would only have one crack at it, so it had better be foolproof and not arouse any suspicions in him. To her advantage, he had no notion that she knew Hollie, so therefore he didn't know that she knew about him being wanted for rape — that had to make things easier.

With nothing spectacular occurring to her, she called it a night just after midnight and fell into a troubled sleep. John seemed to fill her subconscious thoughts, featuring in a succession of dreams, until finally, fearful of sleep and the nightmares that it brought, she got up and went for a walk around the hotel at three o'clock in the morning. The place was eerily quiet, save for the crying of a small baby in one of the rooms and it was then the idea came to her.

Going back to her room, she picked up a pen and paper and wrote down a detailed account of how she felt she would be able to entice John into a situation where his capture was guaranteed. Reading over it, she was satisfied with what she had come up with and managed to sleep the rest of the night soundly.

CHAPTER TWENTY-NINE

# Thursday AM 29th April

*Liz*

Anyone who thinks that revenge isn't sweet must be off their heads, thought Liz on waking, instantly remembering her plans for confronting Rachel. By nature, Liz wasn't a vengeful person, but Rachel's deception had been of such gargantuan proportions that to let her off unscathed would just be wrong. For Liz, it was Rachel's continued 'friendship' that had really got to her.

Since finding out almost a week ago that it was Rachel whom Jack was involved with, Liz had undergone every emotion on the spectrum regarding her 'best friend'. From, in her better moments, feeling that love was an uncontrollable force that may have crept up on Rachel, grabbing her, without the intention of it happening, to seeing her as a manipulative, scheming bitch that set out to steal her husband. Either scenario was bad enough in its own right, but the fact that Rachel had then gone on to use her friendship with Liz to manipulate the situation further, was basically beyond belief.

Her actions were designed to take Liz for a fool — phoning her; calling over to the house; taking her out for dinner, for Chrissake, and all with the intent to smooth Rachel's transition into filling Liz's shoes as both wife and mother. Liz couldn't let her away with that without some form of retribution.

## *Denise*

Vengeance was also foremost in Denise's mind as she slowly came to from a deep sleep. Checking the time on her mobile, she saw that she had overslept and jumped quickly from the bed, heading straight into the shower. She had less than an hour to get to Sam's office, where she wanted to be cool, calm and collected so that she could fend off any resistance to her idea.

With minutes to spare, she hurried down the pavement, calling out to Hollie and Donal who had arrived ahead of her. Seeing the determined look and the wry smile on her face, Donal threw her a cautionary look as they made their way up the stairs, clearly suspecting what she was up to. She winked back at him, giving nothing further away.

The meeting got underway with Hollie telling Sam about the phone call she had received from Eoin. He took notes as she spoke, nodding gravely whilst he did so. He then informed them that he had been to the house and that there was no sign of him there.

It was then that Denise piped up. "John will be too smart to go to the house. He'll know that's the first place that they'll look for him. The only way to contact him is for me to call him — he'll take my call. I've changed my number, but I've kept hold of my old Sim card and I can use that. Look folks, it's quite simple, if we want to smoke John out, then we have to dangle what he wants in front of him. Trust me, he won't be able to resist and then, whoosh, we nab him."

"She's talking about using herself as bait," said Donal, shaking his head vehemently. "I've told her that it's far too dangerous, but she won't listen to me. Tell her, Sam. She can't do it."

But Sam was interested to hear what she had to say before ruling it out and held a quietening hand up towards Donal, nodding at Denise to continue.

"Well, there are two things I know for sure about John. One, he would view me having a baby as a way to ensnare me for life, providing him with a lifelong meal ticket because he would know that I would make sure that the child was provided for and two, John is the greediest bastard that I know — one whiff of me winning the lotto and he would go to the ends of the earth to hunt me down, seeing the money as his gateway out of here."

"That's what makes him so bloody dangerous, Denise — tell her, Sam!"

Again, Sam shushed him, wanting to hear what conclusion Denise was coming to.

"Well, what I've been thinking is that if we lure him to a place where he thinks that he could get his hands on me, then we could get him. He's too clever to simply walk into a trap, but if I played him at his own game, you know inadvertently letting him know where I'm likely to be in a certain time frame, then I reckon he'll be there thinking that he's the one who has outwitted me."

"And how do you propose doing this?" asked Sam, intrigued.

"Well, first things first, I've got to tell him that I'm pregnant, then follow it up with my intention to have an abortion. That'll rile him beyond belief. Then, I have to inform him about my lottery win. Let him know that I've won millions and that I intend to flee the country with the lot. That'll totally sicken him. It's a kind of double whammy if you like — the combination of the money and the baby will send him over the edge — trust me."

"Again, how do you propose to do this?"

"A simple phone call."

The other three looked doubtful, but ready for that reaction, she continued. "You have to understand John thinks that he owns me. I've allowed him to control every aspect of my life for so many years now that he has forgotten that Denise as a real person actually exists. For him to have come back from Majorca and not be able to contact me would be major. But if I phone him and make the call out to be some act of vengeance call, he won't even question that I'm stupid enough to give away my whereabouts, he'll just be smug that he's picked up on it."

### Donal

"I think this is crazy," said Donal, looking to Sam for support, but none was forthcoming. "You cannot seriously be thinking about this?"

Sam leaned back in his over-sized chair and rubbed his chin thoughtfully. "Way I see it is this Eoin, or John, guy is a seriously dangerous individual…"

"Exactly!" jumped in Donal. "That's precisely why it is ludicrous to think that Denise should put herself in danger like that. The further she stays away from that creep the better."

"Yes, I hear you," said Sam with a frown etched across his forehead. "But in all fairness, he has to be a lot more dangerous roaming around free. Don't forget he's already got to Hollie in work, what's to stop him getting to her again — in person this time? Dublin is a small city, it's only a matter of time until someone, somewhere spots Denise — then what? Personally I think the sooner this guy is caught the better. At least this way, we get to control where and when he makes an appearance."

"But what if something goes wrong? We're knowingly delivering Denise into the hands of a maniac — I really don't like this."

"And I really don't like the prospect of bumping into Eoin unexpectedly," said Hollie, her fear palpable. "I'm scared out of my wits as it is. Maybe Denise and Sam have a point, Donal. They can draw him out into the open, in a public place and actually catch the bastard."

Donal glanced from one to the other of them and seeing three pairs of eyes staring back at him, unified in thinking that this was the best way to handle the situation, he succumbed to the pressure of being out-numbered. With a hopeless shrug, he said, "Okay, but I still don't like it."

### Rachel

Rachel was feeling very smug. As far as she was concerned, last night's dinner with Liz couldn't have gone any better. Without a doubt, she had given Liz food for thought - feeding her the notion that it was someone in the golf club had been a stroke of genius.

By the end of the night she had been able to see just how thin Liz's veneer of strength was, and had played up the opportunity to be her support through this beautifully. From the way Liz was talking, she felt it was only a matter of time before she came knocking on her surgery door, seeking her professional help, which suited Rachel just fine.

### Annette

Feeling very uncomfortable, Annette sat at Liz's kitchen table wanting to make completely sure that her sister was ready for this, before showing her the photographs of Jack and Rachel. It had been one thing discussing them on the phone the night before, but it felt entirely different now to be sitting here, knowing that what Liz was about to see would hurt her.

Liz reassured her that she was ready, telling her that whether she saw the photos or not didn't change what had happened and if they provided her with the tools to exact her revenge, then any pain involved would be worth it. Reluctantly, Annette passed her the camera. She saw the flash of pain that registered in her sister's eyes and instantly regretted showing her the photos, but a glint of satisfaction replaced the pain and Liz nodded silently as she perused the images in front of her.

"These are perfect," she said. "Rachel Wallace is about to get her come-uppance."

### Jack

"Thanks, Gerry — appreciate that," said Jack as he left his boss's office, pulling the door closed behind him.

He was due to collect the keys for his new apartment that evening and after speaking with Liz, they had agreed that it was probably best if he moved in on the Friday when he could collect the remainder of his stuff from the house while the kids were in school. Liz had felt that it would be too traumatic for Jane to witness her father packing everything up and she herself had an appointment on Friday morning which would leave him with an empty house. Idly, he wondered what her appointment was, but quickly reminded himself that whatever it was, it was no longer his business.

Gerry had been very accommodating, giving him the Friday off with such short notice. Back in his own office now, he busied himself with drawing up a list of things he wanted to take with him. Mostly clothing and books, the whole process shouldn't take too long. Rachel had suggested that some framed photos of the kids would make his apartment feel more like home to them and he added these to his depressingly short list. There wasn't a lot to show for so many years of his life.

He had mooted the idea the previous evening that the kids might like to come and stay with him on the Saturday night, Josh had shrugged in-differently and Jane hadn't given him an answer. Not wanting to push the subject, he had sent them both a reminder text that morning and when he pulled his mobile out of his jacket pocket to check if there had been any response, he was thrilled to see a simple 'k' from Jane. Things were looking up, he thought.

## Hollie

Donal had dropped Hollie back to work after their meeting with Sam and seeing the worried expression on his face as he drove her there, she reached across and patted his hand.

"Don't look so worried," she said. "Sam isn't going to let anything bad happen. He knows just how dangerous Eoin is and he's going to make sure that Denise is safe. You just have to focus on how relieved we are all going to be when Eoin has been caught."

"I hope you're right, Hols. I just have a really bad feeling about all of this."

CHAPTER THIRTY

# Thursday PM 29th April

*Rachel*

Exhausted, Rachel rolled her chair back from her desk and went to return her patient cards into the index boxes. The day had been incredibly busy with back-to-back appointments and she was keen to get home, open a bottle of wine and put her feet up for the evening. The phone on her desk rang again, and she let out a loud groan, "Oh, just piss off," she muttered under her breath, before snatching it from its cradle.

"Yes," she said in a crabby tone, that she knew would leave young Niamh quaking in her boots.

"Sorry to disturb you, Dr. Wallace, but there's a Liz O'Brien on the phone for you, she's quite insistent that she speaks to you before you leave."

Rachel's mood instantly changed and pressing the flashing button, she said, "Hi, Liz — everything okay?"

"Yeah, look, Rachel, I really could do with coming in to speak with you and I was wondering if you would have a slot in the morning at all?"

"Of course, of course, I would, Liz," she said, hoping that the smug smile that had formed on her face wasn't audible. "What time suits? I can work around it."

"Say, about ten o'clock?"

"That's fine, Liz. Do you want me to call over this evening or anything?"

"No, that's very nice of you, but no, I think I'm going to grab an early night. Thanks a million for seeing me at such short notice — see you in the morning."

"I'll look forward to it," said Rachel, hanging up. Liz's veneer was cracking, but then again, Rachel had always known that it would. From tomorrow she would be putty in her hands, thought Rachel with glee.

## Donal

Angst-ridden, Donal sat at his kitchen table, staring worriedly at Denise. She was very nervous and he knew that her ringing John was a big ask. He still wasn't convinced that this was the way to go, but she seemed determined to do it. His insistence on being with her when she made the call had met with little resistance and he was very glad to at least be able to offer her moral support, especially now, when he saw how shook up she was.

"You still don't have to do this, you know," he said, reaching across the table and grabbing a hold of her hand. "We can come up with another way."

But she shook her head vehemently; then, with a weak smile on her face, she said, "It's the best way, Donal. I know you don't like this, but you've got to trust me. I know John better than anyone — I know how paranoid he is, I know how crafty he is and believe me, I know how dangerous he is. But I also know that I am his Achilles' heel. John won't credit me with being clever enough to set him up, all he'll see is how stupid I am to let it slip where he could get to me. He'll have his eye on the money and he'll reckon that me having his baby will be the surest way to tie me to him."

"But what if something goes wrong, Denise?"

"I know, Donal. But, that's where we've got to trust Sam. And, I do. Sam reckons that he'll have the airport crawling with his men and that the minute John makes an appearance that they'll get him. Personally, I believe him and the thing is that the airport is such a public place that John isn't likely to try anything. The worst case scenario, as I see it, is that he gets away, but I really don't think that's going to happen."

"There are no certainties though, Denise. That's what worries me."

Donal knew that there was no talking her out of it and unsure what else to do, he made them some coffee whilst she inserted her old Sim card into her mobile phone.

### Denise

"Right, here goes nothing!" said Denise, throwing a nervous look at Donal, before keying in John's number to her phone. He answered almost immediately and the sound of his voice had her trembling like a leaf. Donal gave her an encouraging pat on the shoulder, which helped alleviate the fear that John's torrent of abuse instilled in her.

"Where the fuck are you?" he roared down the phone at her. "I've been trying to contact you for days. You better have a fucking good reason for this little disappearing act of yours…."

Bravely she interrupted him. "John, it isn't an act — I've left you — for good."

Laughing heinously down the phone at her, he spat, "You've left me! You've fucking left me! Tell me then, Denise — just how the fuck are you going to survive on your own? You don't even have any access to your own money — that's how fucking pathetic you are. I'm telling you, you come and meet me now and we'll pretend like this whole sorry mess never happened, otherwise, I'm warning you — you'll pay and pay big for all this shit you're putting me through…."

Denise held the phone at arm's length so Donal could hear the ranting and raving that was coming out of him, then with unbelievable poise and calm, she once again interrupted him mid-flow.

"John, I didn't ring for a chat. I rang 'cos there are a couple of things I wanted to make damn sure you knew about before I disappear for good. One, I'm pregnant. But the devil's spawn that I'm carrying will never see the light of day. I'm getting rid of it and the sooner the better. In fact, I've got a doctor's appointment in the morning where she's giving me details of the abortion she's set up for me in a clinic in London. And two, I got a little lucky on the lottery when you were away. Real lucky actually — six fucking million worth of lucky! So you

see, you fucker, you don't control all my money. And after I see
the doctor tomorrow, I'm heading straight for the airport and by
mid-afternoon, I'll be out of here forever. So fuck you dickhead! Have a
nice life!"

To her amazement, she found that speaking to John like that purged
her of so much fear that it was actually quite empowering and, hanging up
the phone, she instantly ripped out the Sim card as if by doing so she was
physically severing all ties between them. Then with a look of total confidence, she looked at Donal.

"That told the little bollocks," she laughed. "Jesus! That felt good. Do
you think he got the message that I'll be in the airport tomorrow afternoon?"

"Loud and clear," beamed Donal back at her. "Well done you. That was
a very brave thing you just did."

"Let's hope it works, that's all. I couldn't labour the point that I'd be in
the airport or he'd have smelled a rat."

"No, you handled it perfectly. I'd say he's on the Internet as we speak
checking flight times to London."

"Let's bloody hope so," said Denise. "Then, we can nail the bastard!"

## Jack

With a sense of satisfaction, Jack locked up the door of his new apartment
and headed back down to the car. Having collected the keys after work, he
had had a sudden flash of inspiration regarding the kids and had driven
straight to a major electrical retailer where he had purchased a state of
the art laptop for Josh and an incredible iPod dock for Jane, which he had
now installed in their respective bedrooms. He knew that these purchases
were over the top indulgent, but felt they would provide a great welcome
present when they came to stay with him on Saturday night, softening the
blow for them.

Rachel had sounded tired when he had spoken to her earlier on the
phone and he had offered to collect a takeaway and a bottle of wine on his
way home from work. With him moving to his own apartment the following
day, this could well be their last night together for a while and a bottle of

321

wine and an early night were suddenly very appealing to him.

### Annette

Annette was feeling a little guilty. She had been so preoccupied with everything that was happening with Liz that she hadn't even bothered to contact poor Hollie over the past couple of days to see if there was any news on Eoin. Seeing that it was just gone five thirty and Hollie should be finished work, she tried her number before any further distractions came her way.

"Hollie!" she said, delighted when her young friend answered. "Look, I'm really sorry that I haven't given you a call before now, but things have been a bit hectic with Liz. But how are you? Any developments with Eoin?"

Annette couldn't believe what she was hearing when Hollie told her everything that had happened. Hollie explained how the plan was to set Eoin up to go to the airport in search of Denise, she still hadn't spoken to Donal yet to see how the phone call had gone, but if everything went to plan, they were hopeful of having Eoin in custody by Friday evening.

"That Denise is one brave lady," said Annette admiringly. "But what a bloody coincidence? It's as if fate brought Donal and Denise together on that trip to London. How spooky is that?"

"I know," said Hollie. "We were all absolutely speechless when it all came out in Sam's office. It was completely surreal. Anyway, look, I've got to go, Donal has just pulled up."

"Okay, but promise you'll give me a call and let me know how it goes tomorrow?"

"I promise. I'll talk to you then, bye."

### Hollie

The second that Hollie stepped into the car, Donal barked at her. "Who was that on the phone?"

Laughing at his overreaction, she said, "Whoa, calm down, Donal. It was Annette. What'd ya think? That it was Eoin? Relax!"

Heaving a sigh of relief, he hugged his younger sister, acknowledging that his nerves were getting the better of him, "I'm sorry," he said. "It's just I had some insight into what kind of a lunatic this guy is earlier when Denise was on the phone to him and I just hate the thoughts of him having any further contact with you."

"I know," she said reassuringly. "But, it wasn't him. How'd Denise get on?"

"She played a blinder. Managed to let him know that she was planning on getting a flight tomorrow afternoon. I reckon he went for it. The guy sounds like a complete nutter though, you wouldn't believe the abuse he was hurling down the phone at her."

"Jesus! It must have been terrifying for her. I remember how I felt when he called the surgery. Did she sound convincing?"

"Absolutely. She made out that it was the ultimate 'fuck you' phone call. I'd be more than surprised if he doesn't show tomorrow. Just hope that Sam and his men are on the ball."

"They will be. That's their job," she said, and then added, "Way to go Denise!"

## Liz

Liz was feeling kind of restless. She had put in a good day with two appointments for her Life Coaching, both of which had gone really well. She'd made dinner, cleaned up, walked the dog but despite feeling tired; she was unable to settle down. She had tried to watch a movie with the kids, but the silly American slapstick humour couldn't hold her attention. In the end, she decided to pop over to Annette's for a cup of tea.

Megan and Hannah were in the throes of a sibling row, with Paddy acting as peacemaker, when she walked into the kitchen and the normality of the scene touched her. Annette was thrilled to see her and whooshing the warring sisters out of the kitchen, she put on the kettle.

"Jesus! They'd do your head in," she said. "And Paddy, with his Kofi Annan approach, makes me want to scream."

"Now, don't you be giving out about poor Paddy," laughed Liz. "I think the poor divil has a lot to put up with."

"Whatever!" said Annette, dramatically throwing her eyes up to heaven. "Anyway, wait 'til you hear the latest on Hollie and Eoin. You won't believe it!"

Liz was flabbergasted by what she heard. "This whole ash-cloud thing has managed to unearth a lot of shit — hasn't it?"

"Mmm. I suppose so. Maybe it's some apocalyptic way of outing the bad people," mused Annette.

"Ah, now that you've started talking shite, it's time for me to go home," laughed Liz, getting up and grabbing her bag and keys. "Anyway, I have some outing of my own in store for the morning, so I need my sleep."

"Oh yeah! Good luck with that. I really wish I could be there to see her face. Ring me, soon as you're out — okay?"

"With pleasure!"

CHAPTER THIRTY-ONE

# Friday AM 30th April

*Liz*

It was almost a quarter to ten when Liz walked into the Greendale Medical Centre on Friday morning, clutching an A4 size white envelope beneath her arm. Looking around the reception area, she spotted a large notice board displaying all the various services the clinic had to offer. Ignoring that for the moment, she walked up to the reception desk and enquired which of the two receptionists on duty was Hollie.

With a friendly smile, Hollie raised her hand. "That'd be me! How can I help you?"

"I was just wondering if I could have a quiet word?" asked Liz cryptically.

Shrugging her shoulders and checking to see if Niamh would be alright on her own for a minute, Hollie lifted the hatch and came around the counter to see how she could be of assistance.

"Hollie, I'm Liz — Annette's sister," said Liz by way of introduction.

"Oh, it's so lovely to meet you at last, Liz," said Hollie, extending her hand. "I've heard so much about you." Then, as if realising the implication of what she had just said, Hollie blushed.

Liz laughed off her embarrassment. "Don't worry, I know you know all about my philandering husband and my delightful best friend. Incidentally, thanks for helping Annette out on her sleuthing mission. Actually, it's the fruits of that mission that I'm here with today," she said, holding up the envelope.

Unsure what exactly she meant, Hollie gave her a quizzical look. "I'm here to see Rachel. I've booked an appointment with her for ten o'clock, but I have something that I want to do first and I was hoping that I might be able to get your cooperation."

"Go on," said Hollie.

"Well I was hoping that you and your colleague might be able to turn a blind eye to what I am about to do," she said, pulling out enlarged copies of the photographs that Hollie had taken in Majorca of Jack and Rachel together and nodding in the direction of the notice board.

Realising what her intention was, Hollie laughed. "Go for it," she said. "Niamh and I will be far to busy to notice anything untoward." Then, rubbing her hands together, she went back behind the reception desk, whispering to Niamh as she went, "This should be an interesting morning!"

Liz busied herself covering the entire notice board with photos of Jack and Rachel, and then produced a big black marker with which she labelled the pictures. She drew a large bubble at the top of the board and with an arrow extending from it to Jack's face, she wrote inside it 'my husband', then, another bubble in the same manner to Rachel's face proclaimed 'my best friend'. When she had completed her task, she went and sat sedately in a seat in the waiting area until Rachel opened the door of her surgery and beckoned to her to come in.

### Rachel

"Come on in, Liz," said Rachel, holding the door open, allowing her to pass through. Then, with her best faux sincere face on, she stepped forward to embrace her, air kissing her cheeks in the process. She could feel Liz stiffen under her touch, but marked it down to the fraught nervousness that had brought her here in the first place. Turning all professional, Rachel pulled out a seat, indicating for Liz to sit down.

"So, how are you doing, sweetie? I'm guessing not too well if you're sitting here with me."

"Ah, you know," shrugged Liz. "I've been better. But what can you expect when your world suddenly falls apart?"

"I know, sweetie — it's been awful for you."

"Yep! When everything you valued turns out to be a lie, that leaves the life you were leading to be nothing more than a sham. And I have to say that stinks."

"I can only imagine," said Rachel.

"Can you?" asked Liz, burrowing her eyes into Rachel in a way that unnerved her.

"Hey, I know that I've never been married, but I have been in love. I've experienced the heart ache when the love finishes."

"But, you've always been the one to leave them, Rachel."

"Doesn't mean it doesn't hurt," she said philosophically.

"And tell me something, Rachel — did you lose your best friend too when those relationships broke up?"

Not certain if she was being asked an innocuous question or a loaded one, Rachel decided to play it safe, saying, "Obviously anyone that you are in love with is your best friend, so yes, I've lost my best friend through break-ups in the past."

"That's not what I meant though, Rachel."

A distinctly uneasy feeling crept over her as taking the bull by the horns, she asked, "What did you mean, Liz?"

"I meant was your best friend fucking the man you were in love with?"

Rachel's mouth dropped open. She had been totally unprepared for this. It was pretty clear that Liz knew about the affair, but before they got a chance to take the conversation further, Hollie burst through the door of the surgery, with a scruffy looking man, holding a knife to her throat.

## Hollie

As soon as Liz disappeared into Rachel's surgery, Hollie excused herself and promising Niamh that she would be back in a couple of minutes, she grabbed her mobile phone and let herself out into the back courtyard to make a quick phone call.

"Annette!" she gasped into the phone as soon as her friend answered.

"You'll never guess who's just come in to see Dr. Wallace?"

Giggling at her melodramatic enthusiasm, Annette said. "Liz. I know. She told me that she was going to be paying her a visit this morning. Sorry I didn't mention it, but she wanted to keep it under wraps. I'm guessing from your tone that you know why."

"Eh, yeah! She came straight up to me, introduced herself, asked for mine and Niamh's cooperation and then proceeded to cover the entire notice board with those photos from Majorca. It was sweet! I've never seen anything like it. As soon as you walk through the doors of the clinic, it's the first thing you see. Can't miss it! Honestly, it's hilarious."

"How did Rachel react?"

"That's the sweetest part — she never even noticed. Niamh and I were pissing ourselves laughing; she just came out to the waiting area and called Liz in. She never saw a thing. There were even several other patients looking at the photos, and then staring over at Dr. Wallace, but she never copped. Honestly, it was priceless. Liz is still in with her, so I've no idea how that's going, but…..Jesus!" Hollie screamed, dropping her mobile to the ground as someone grabbed her forcefully by the hair and yanked her head backwards.

At first, she didn't recognise her assailant, the lush head of hair he had had the last time she had seen him was gone and his head was now covered with little more than stubble. His eyes were cold and menacing, but it wasn't until he spoke that she knew for certain who he was — Eoin. Grinning maliciously at her, he kept a firm grip of her hair, and then in a macabre imitation of a TV game show host, he exaggeratedly waved his free hand in her face. "Surprise, surprise!" he said in a singsong voice.

"But…But, Eoin I haven't done anything," she whimpered. "I haven't spoken to the authorities. I did as you said. Honestly. You've got to believe….."

"Shut up!" he roared, yanking her head back again. "It's not all about you, bitch. I need you to help me. Do you hear?"

Hollie nodded, terrified. Her head hurt where he was pulling her hair and there were tears spilling from her eyes. To her complete horror, he reached his hand behind his back and pulled out a kitchen knife with a long, shining blade and held it to her throat. She could hear herself gasp and where the blade touched her skin, she could feel a tickling sensation and realised that he had already cut her and blood was trickling down her neck. Petrified, she stayed as still as her trembling body would allow, waiting for him to tell her what he wanted.

"How many female doctors are there in this clinic?" he demanded gruffly.

"Just the one," whispered Hollie, fearful of the blade pressing deeper.

"Right, this should be easy then," said Eoin. "I want you to take me into her surgery. Nice and easy. Just take me straight in there. Any messing of any sort and I will slit your throat — got that?"

"Uh-huh," murmured Hollie.

"Good! Let's go then."

He pushed her towards the back door of the clinic, keeping the knife in position as they went. As they passed the reception desk, Niamh was busy on the phone and never noticed them heading for Rachel's surgery. It was only when Hollie threw the door open that she glanced up and saw what was happening, but by then Hollie and Eoin were inside and the door was slammed shut and locked.

Once inside the surgery, Eoin let a roar at Rachel. "What time is that bitch Richardson due in to you this morning?"

Not having the faintest idea what he was talking about, Rachel shook her head. "Who?" she asked.

"Denise! Denise Richardson. You're helping her get rid of my baby, you bitch. Now, what time is she going to be here?"

"I really don't know what…..." began Rachel, but Hollie interrupted.

"It was me," she whimpered and all eyes turned to her. Unsure how to play this, but thinking on her feet, she added. "I made the appointment. But, it's not until just before lunch."

Buying time had to be a good thing, she rationalised. But what now?

"Well you better call her and tell her to get over here now," said Eoin through clenched teeth. "If she's not here within the next half hour, I'm going to start slitting throats — everybody clear?"

The three women nodded mutely. Then Eoin fixed his attention back on Hollie. "You call her, don't let her know that anything is amiss. Just get her here quick! I'll be listening to your every word and I'm warning you, one fuck up and you're dead!"

### Annette

Annette was feeling completely helpless. Her call was still connected to Hollie's mobile, but Hollie had obviously dropped the phone after screaming out 'Jesus' when her assailant struck. At first, Annette couldn't make out the muffled conversation, but she knew enough to know that Hollie was under attack. Then quite distinctly she heard a word that threw her into panic overdrive — 'Eoin'. Jesus! Hollie and Denise's plan had gone all wrong. Eoin was at the clinic and, by the sounds of it, he was armed. Reluctant to cut off the call, she grabbed her house phone and dialled 999.

It seemed to take an eternity to connect the call. Endeavouring to stay calm, she quickly tried to explain her suspicions to the operator, giving the Greendale Medical Centre as the site of the possible siege. She knew the whole thing sounded crazy, and rationality escaped her when the even-toned operator seemed to ask question after question that Annette was unable to answer.

Finally, she cracked, shouting, "For Chrissake do something! My sister and my friend are there — they're in danger — you've got to do something — NOW!"

"I understand, Mrs. Forbes," said the operator in a soothing voice. "But, the fact is that the more information we can have before arrival, the greater the chance of averting a real disaster. Now, you suspect this man is armed — any idea what kind of weapon he has?"

"No, Jesus! I was on the phone. I'm guessing that it was a knife, but I really don't know. Please, I've told you everything I know — just get someone there quickly."

"Ok. I'm going to call the medical centre on the other line here, see if we can get a more up-to-date picture of the situation. There's a squad car on its way to the site as we speak and I'll radio through any additional information to the car. Now, the best thing you can do is sit tight and rest assured that we will do everything possible to get your sister and her friend out of there safely."

Hanging up the phone, Annette clasped the mobile to her ear, but there was nothing. Panicked, she cut off the call and rang Paddy, but the call went to voicemail and she left a hysterical message for him to call her back immediately. Fuck sitting tight and waiting, she thought, she had to get down to the clinic, grabbing her bag and keys off the counter; she went to jump in the car. Then, a thought occurred to her, and ripping her bag open, she pulled out her mobile and called Jack's number.

### Jack

When Jack saw his sister-in-law's name come up on his phone, he figured that he was in for an ear bashing. His initial reaction was to ignore it, but some sixth sense told him he should answer the call.

"Hello, Annette," he said, preparing himself for whatever abuse she was about to throw his way.

"Jack! Oh thank God," she said, sounding traumatised. "Jack, listen — a friend of mine, Hollie is being held hostage at the medical centre where Rachel works. Liz is there too, Jack. You've got to get down there quickly — this is really serious."

"What the fuck are you talking about?" asked Jack, wondering if his mobile had turned into a portal to another dimension.

"Look, Liz knows all about you and Rachel. She went down to the clinic this morning to confront her. But this guy, Eoin, who raped Hollie in Majorca a couple of weeks ago, has shown up there too. He's got a knife and I don't know what he's planning on doing, but I suggest you get your arse over there as quick as you can."

"Oh Christ!" said Jack. "I'm on my way."

### Denise

Denise was in the throes of her final planning meeting with Sam and Donal when her mobile rang. Fishing it out of her pocket, she saw Hollie's work number on the screen, and smiling indulgently, she pressed the answer button.

"Alright, Hollie? Stop worrying, everything is under control," she said, but instantly realised that something was wrong when Hollie spoke.

"Hello, Ms. Richardson," she said in an officious manner, then throwing a cautionary look in Rachel's direction, she continued. "This is Dr. Sam Glynn's surgery here. I'm afraid Dr. Glynn has an urgent appointment at lunchtime today and she needs to leave early. She was wondering if there was any chance you could come in to see her sooner?"

"Are you tripping or what?" laughed Denise, before an icy feeling crept over her and she instantly understood Hollie's cryptic message. John was in the surgery. Her face blanched as she tried to let the other two know what was going on, but they stared blankly back at her, unable to get her meaning.

"Say, in about half an hour?"

"I'm on the way," said Denise, reaching down to grab her bag whilst she spoke.

"That'd be great, Ms. Richardson. Dr. Glynn will look forward to seeing you then."

Denise looked extremely worried as she hung up the phone, on her feet now, she was headed for the door, throwing her explanation to the others from over her shoulder.

"John's at the surgery," she gasped. "Hollie sounds really scared. We've got to get there quick."

"Whoa! Whoa! Whoa!" roared Sam. "Hold on a minute. How do you know he's at the clinic?"

"Hollie just told me that she had to change my appointment with Dr. Sam Glynn — that's her way of letting me know that John is there. Jesus, he picked up on the wrong part of my conversation. We all thought he'd jump at the airport bait, but I told you he was clever, I told him that I had a doctor's appointment first and he's gone straight to the fucking clinic. Christ! Sam, we've got to hurry."

Alarm registered on Donal's face as he shoved back the seat he had been sitting on and went to follow Denise. Again, Sam interjected.

"For fuck sake, folks — hang on! You can't just go rushing in there. This guy's dangerous, we need some back up."

"He's got my fucking sister," said Donal, his face thunderous. "We don't have time to sit here and work out a strategy. We need to get there — now!"

Seeing that there was no chance of getting them to sit down and think things through, Sam jumped to his feet to follow them. "Okay," he said, "We'll take my car though, it's parked straight outside, but Donal — you drive. I need to make some calls."

### Donal

Behind the wheel of Sam's car, Donal hit the road in spots in his haste to get to the medical centre as quickly as possible. Denise sat on the back seat looking absolutely terrified. On the passenger seat beside him, Sam punched in a series of numbers into his phone, cursing under his breath as each number drew a blank.

Finally getting an answer from one of the numbers, he barked into the phone "Brian Moran, please, it's Sam Glynn." Clearly not receiving the response he wanted, he lost his cool. "I don't give a fuck what meeting he is in. Get him on the phone now! This is a life and death situation and I don't have the time to start explaining things to you or anybody else. I need to speak to Brian Moran and I need to speak to him NOW!"

His approach paid dividends and seconds later they heard him say, "Brian — thank God. We have a situation and you're the man for the job." He went on to explain everything to this Brian guy, then finished off the call by saying, "Well, we'll be there in less than five minutes, so, we'll see you there."

Sam seemed to have calmed right down after speaking with Brian and turning to the other two, he explained that Brian and himself had worked together many times over the years. "He's a detective with the special branch and he's the best hostage negotiator in the country. He's agreed to meet us there as soon as, if anyone can talk John down — it's him."

Turning into Greendale Road, Donal could see that there were two squad cars outside the medical centre and his fears for his sister escalated. He ignored the first officer who tried to prevent him from pulling into the car park and drove right past him, causing him to run after the car. Sam was out of the car before it even came to a complete stop, and running to the door of the centre, he explained his role to the officers already there and told them that Brian Moran was on his way.

Less than a minute later, an unmarked car pulled in, and a fit looking, thirty-something year old man jumped out. Scanning the faces gathered in the porch of the centre, he made his way directly over to Sam, "So," he said, skipping the exchange of any pleasantries, "What do we know about this guy?"

CHAPTER THIRTY-TWO

# Friday 30th April

*Annette*

The front entranceway to the medical centre was a complete hub of activity when Annette, having parked her car down the road, walked through the gap in the wall and across the pathway that ran over the grass. Judging by the number of people gathered there, the situation was every bit as grave as she had feared. Running the last few metres, she looked through the crowd to see if there was any one who could tell her what the hell was going on.

She spotted Donal, recognising him from their brief encounter in the airport, deeply immersed in conversation with two men and a woman, one of whom seemed to be in charge of operations. Pushing her way through the crowd, she made her way up to them.

"Donal," she said. "Any news?"

"Well, that crazy fucker, Eoin is in there with my sister. He's taken her into one of the doctor's surgeries, where he is holding her and two other women hostage. How come you're here, how did you hear about it?"

"I was talking to Hollie on the phone when he attacked her," she said and all eyes immediately swung around to her. "One of those two other women happens to be my sister. I didn't know that he'd got her too. I thought it was just Hollie."

Annette was crying now, but ignoring her tears, Brian Moran shot several questions at her, trying to establish the exact state of mind Eoin was in at the offset of this siege. She gave him what little assistance she could, telling him that it was only what she could glean from a dropped mobile that alerted her to the scene, and overall the words and voices were pretty indistinct. Assuring her that she had been a great help, he turned back to focus his attention on Denise again.

A sudden pulsing of the crowd indicated that someone was trying to make their way up to the front. A gap opened and Jack emerged, looking anxious and dishevelled.

"What's the story? Where are Liz and Rachel?" he asked, heading as if to open the door into the centre. One of Brian Moran's men pulled him back. "But my wife and … and…her friend are in there," he pleaded, but the officer held firm, telling him that there was an armed man holding hostages inside and no-one else could enter at this point.

Jack looked distraught and despite her recent anger towards him, Annette's heart went out to him. Making her way up to where he stood, she put an arm around his shoulder and guided him to the edge of the crowd. "Hey Jack," she said when they got there. "How are you doing?"

"Fucking terrible!" he said, the stress raging in his eyes. "This is all my fault. Liz and Rachel wouldn't be in danger like this if it wasn't for me."

Worried sick about her sister, Annette found it difficult to argue with his words. "Yep! You fucked up good here, Jack."

Shaking his head dolefully, he pleaded with Annette. "I'm so sorry. I never meant to hurt Liz, but Rachel…well, Rachel is my soul mate. It's like we're two halves of the one whole. I just never thought that I would feel this way about anybody."

"Soul mate, my arse!" sneered Annette. "And I'll tell you one thing Jack, if my sister dies in there, I will never forgive you. Never."

### Denise

Brian Moran had been pumping Denise for information about John since his arrival. He now felt that he had a fairly accurate description of the type of person John was. His quick temper and volatile reactions were areas of great concern to Brian, but it helped for him to know about them. Denise was given a fairly thorough overview of the whole hostage negotiation process.

Brian told her that, provided communication could be established and sustained, then the longer the siege went on for the less likely it was to end in disaster. He was shortly going to be opening up dialogue with John and he wanted to know if she was prepared to be there, if needed, to use as a negotiating tool, perhaps trading conversation time with her for the release of one or more of the hostages. She doubted very much that mere conversation time with her would appease John in any way, but said that yes, she would be willing to do whatever was required.

A few minutes later, Brian rang through to Rachel's direct line and John answered the phone. "Hey, John," he said. "My name is Brian and I'm here to see if there's anything I can do to help you."

"Yeah! Get that silly bitch, Richardson here as soon as possible."

"You mean Denise? Well, John, she's on her way. Shouldn't be too long now, but what is it exactly that you want to do when she gets here?"

"I want her. And I want a car and I want no one to interfere. I just want to get Denise and go."

"Hey, buddy. I don't think that it's going to happen like that. You're holding three people in there. We've got to try and do some kind of a deal here."

"What kind of deal do you have in mind?" spat John. "The kind of deal where I end up in prison and you go on your merry little way. I don't think so."

Brian continued along this same vein of conversation, loosening up considerably as he did so. Putting his hand over the mouthpiece, he turned to the others and told them that, never mind what he was saying, the fact that John was still talking to him was a really good sign. Scribbling down some notes as he spoke, he passed the pad to Sam, motioning towards Denise, indicating that he wanted Sam to talk to her about what he had written down. He was getting ready to put Denise on the line and wanted to be sure that she knew what he wanted her to say.

Then, just as John's interest in the conversation started to wane, Brian announced that Denise had arrived and that he was going to put her on the line.

"Hi, it's me," she said.

"Hey, Denise, thanks for coming down." Instantly she recognised in his voice that same 'trapped animal' reaction that had always followed one of the many beatings he had given her, where he wanted her to believe that he was on her side and that if only she wouldn't do things to provoke him then he wouldn't have to hurt her, so she must stop provoking him. Clearly he blamed her for him being in this current situation. She also knew that this phase was short-lived and that he was at his most pliable when in it, therefore she jumped straight in with one of the things on Brian's list.

"Look, John. Why don't you let young Hollie come out? She's only young and she's probably really scared. She hasn't done anything. So, please, John — let her go. If you give something, then, they're far more likely to give you something back. Please."

"Okay. But, just Hollie. The other two are staying here until we sort some things out."

Nodding over at her that this was a great result indeed, Brian instructed her to go along with it.

"That's great, John. Thanks." Denise was amazed at how accurately Brian had predicted this exchange, when she had deemed it unthinkable, he certainly knew what he was about and she felt safer for having him there.

*Hollie*

Unable to believe her luck, that Eoin had agreed to release her when talking to Denise, Hollie tentatively got to her feet and glanced hopefully towards the door. Fearful of making any sudden movements that could trigger him to change his mind, she kept her eyes on Eoin as she slowly inched her way towards the surgery door. She was virtually there when he raised an arm crossways in front of her, preventing her from reaching the handle. Instead, he held her at a distance, positioning himself behind the door, and then drawing it open silently, he waved her through the opening. Not needing to be told twice, she bolted through the gap to safety.

Once through the doorway, something jostled her, almost knocking her to the ground, then lunged through the still open slit in the doorway.

It all happened so fast that it wasn't until the door was about to close that she identified this figure who had launched himself into the surgery like a human missile as Jack.

There was a considerable amount of noise emanating from the surgery, indicating that a substantial scuffle was taking place within. A couple of high pitched screams rang out, causing her to propel herself out through the main doors of the clinic, with every possible haste, to where she could see Donal waiting for her. Hurling herself into his outstretched arms, she collapsed in their relative safety, giving vent to the pent up fear inside of her as she sobbed uncontrollably. Gently, he soothed her, telling her that she was safe now, that her ordeal was over.

## Jack

With a plan of action that took him no further than getting through the surgery door, Jack barrelled into the room. Liz and Rachel looked on in horror as Eoin, who had been prepared for some sort of ambush on opening the door, quickly managed to overcome Jack, knocking him to the floor, climbing astride him and holding the knife to the side of his head.

"Not so fucking smart now, are you mate?" said Eoin, baring his teeth maliciously as he glared down at Jack. "Hey ladies, your knight in shining armour is here, but he seems a bit incapacitated!"

The phone on the desk started ringing again and knowing that it would be Brian trying to reopen negotiations, Eoin nodded furiously at Rachel to answer it. "Tell the smarmy little bastard that his trick failed. That I've got his little 'have a go hero' lying here on the broad of his back with a knife to his head. And tell him that if he doesn't send Denise in here now, then this fucker is going to get it!"

Jack tried to protest that he was nothing to do with Brian, but Eoin clamped a hand across his mouth preventing him from speaking. Jack's eyes darted about the room, locking with Liz's and seeing the uncontrolled fear that was present in them, he struggled to be able to talk.

"Got something to say — have you, dickhead?" spat Eoin, increasing the pressure from the knife as he raised his other hand a couple of millimetres from Jack's mouth. "Then, spit it out!"

"I'm not here 'cos of him," he said. "I'm here because that's my wife sitting over there and," nodding in Rachel's direction he added, "that's…., that's…., well, that's a friend of ours over there on the phone. Look, these women have nothing to do with your situation here, let them go. You've got me. I'll be your bargaining tool, just let them out of here."

Caught off guard by Jack's explanation of his presence, Eoin lessened the pressure on the knife and seeing an opportunity, Jack tried to throw him off him, but Eoin's adrenalin kicked straight back in and without any further thought, he raised the knife and brought it crashing down bang in the centre of Jack's skull.

"Jesus Christ!" screamed Liz, shooting up from her seat and rushing to her husband, whose blood was spurting from the top of his head in powerful jets. "For fuck's sake, Rachel — do something!"

At that precise moment, the door of the surgery flew open and four special branch officers burst through it. Quickly and efficiently, they overpowered Eoin, disarming him, then locking his arms behind his back in a set of hand cuffs, they escorted him from the room and out to a waiting paddy wagon, leaving the two women staring down at Jack as his body jerked and spasmed on the floor. Liz dropped to her knees, holding his head in her hands as the blood continued to spurt from the oversized wound on his skull, covering her face and hair so that it looked like it was her that was bleeding.

Again, she screamed, "Do something, Rachel. NOW!"

### Rachel

Rachel remained where she was. Her feet had turned to lead and staring down at Jack and his convulsing body, she knew that there was little hope of him surviving. It was obvious to her from the amount of blood lost that he had sustained a Traumatic Brain Injury and death was practically inevitable. In fact, she thought, death was preferable, because if Jack somehow managed to survive, then, without any doubt, he would be left profoundly brain damaged. Little more than a vegetable.

With a self-preservation instinct that was second to none, Rachel shook her head, then looked Liz straight in the eyes, and said. "I'm sorry. I didn't sign up for this." Then, slowly she got up from her seat and walked towards the main reception area, turning to Liz when she got to the door, she said, "I'll have one of the other doctors have a look at him."

### Liz

Liz stared after her, incredulous that she could leave like that and something told her that she would never again set eyes on Rachel Wallace. Moments later an ashen faced Annette appeared in the surgery, gasping when she saw her sister covered in blood.

"Jesus, you're hurt," she screamed, but Liz shook her head.

"No, it's all Jack's blood. Get a fucking doctor in here quick," she snapped, although she could feel the life draining out of him and somehow she knew that it was too late.

A doctor arrived promptly, and gently removing Liz's hands from Jack's head, he performed a brief examination, but it didn't take him long to confirm what Liz already knew — Jack was dead.

### Donal

Standing outside the clinic with one arm around Denise and the other hugging Hollie to him, Donal watched as an ambulance loaded Jack's body inside to take it to the hospital mortuary. Annette was doing what she could to comfort her distraught sister and Donal's heart ached when he heard Liz's plaintive question to her.

"But, what am I going to tell the kids?"

Impulsively, he jumped in, releasing the two women from beneath his arms and cupping Liz's broken face in his hands, he said. "You'll tell them that their Dad died a hero — saving their Mum's life. What else do they need to know?"

His words were comforting and with nothing more to be achieved by hanging around the clinic, he gently shepherded the four women to his car. The day had turned to tragedy, but they all had little doubt that it could have ended up a whole lot worse.

Printed in Great Britain
by Amazon

70362819R00197